IN FOR A
PENNY

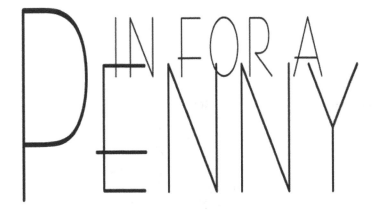

IN FOR A PENNY

A BAY TANNER MYSTERY

KATHRYN R. WALL

BellaRosaBooks

BellaRosaBooks

IN FOR A PENNY

ISBN 1-933523-12-3
2006 Reprint Edition by Bella Rosa Books

Previously Published in the U.S.A. by
Writers Club Press; 2000; ISBN: 0-595-13851-9
Coastal Villages Press; 2001; ISBN: 1-882943-13-9
HJW Publications; 2005; ISBN: 0-9768590-3-3

Printed in the United States of America on acid-free paper.

Cover illustration by Ryan Kennedy
Book design by Bella Rosa Books

BellaRosaBooks and logo are trademarks of Bella Rosa Books

10   9   8   7   6   5   4   3   2

In loving memory of
Doris Cooper Everson
1912—2000
Thanks, Mom.

Acknowledgements

While writing is a solitary occupation, the publication of a book always involves many more people than just the author. I wish to thank the following for their special contributions to making this long-held dream a reality:

Erik Woidtke, Beverly Rocher, Shirley Wall, Theresa Bryant, and Allen Wright—first readers whose insight and enthusiasm proved invaluable.

Fred Bassett and Brewster Robertson for instruction and guidance.

Bill Merrit for allowing me a glimpse of the possibilities.

Barbara J. Everson—reader, editor, and sister-in-law *par excellence.*

The Group—Peg Cronin, Vicky Hunnings, and Linda McCabe—wonderful writers, exceptional women, and treasured friends.

The rest of my friends and family for their encouragement and support.

And most importantly, this book is for my husband, Norman, who always believed.

CHAPTER ONE

The blue and white Gulfstream taxies slowly to the end of the private air-strip, then executes a sharp, 180-degree turn. The pitch of its engines climbs to an ear-splitting whine. I can almost feel her yearning to be off, like one of the Judge's golden retrievers straining at the leash.

A fierce August sun, glinting off the sleek metal skin of the plane, nearly blinds me. I raise a hand to shade my eyes just as the pilot releases the brake, and the graceful jet seems to leap into the air. With a final wave, I turn back toward my car.

The explosion knocks me to my knees. Windows in the tiny service building shatter. Flaming debris rains from a smoking sky. Instinctively I throw my arms up over my head.

White-hot pain sears my left shoulder, and I choke on the sickly-sweet smell of burning flesh. Dust swirls in the aftershock, and pieces of the dying plane clatter off the corrugated metal hangar.

Inside my head a voice is screaming, but no sound comes. A deathly still-ness blankets me . . .

I struggled to free myself from the grip of the relentless images. My lungs gasped for air, and my heart thudded against the wall of my ribs. I could feel my head whipping from side to side in frantic denial, and still I could not escape . . .

Again I lie stunned and helpless under the blazing sun. Again I feel the sharp curve of pebbles beneath my cheek, smell the dank sweat that rolls down my side, as I cower on my face in the dirt and listen to my husband die . . .

The shrill of the telephone jerked me back. Heavy silk drapes, stretched across French doors that gave onto the deck, kept the room in total darkness. I fumbled for my reading glasses and flipped on the lamp. I drew a deep, calming breath and picked up the receiver.

"Hello?" My throat was still thick with the horror of the dream-memory, and it came out more like a croak.

The clock radio on the nightstand glowed 7:35. Not exactly an ungodly hour for someone to be calling, but still early enough to send a little shiver of fear skittering down my back. I cleared my throat and tried again. "Hello?"

My hand reached automatically for a cigarette. It was alight, and the first deep, satisfying cloud of smoke had settled into my lungs before I remembered that today was the day I was going to quit. Again.

"Lydia? Is that you, dear?" The tiny voice was barely audible over the pounding of my heart.

No one—*no one*—ever calls me Lydia. At least not to my face. I was born Lydia Baynard Simpson, but I'm Bay to my friends and to anyone who aspires to join their ranks.

"This is Bay Tanner. Who is this?"

"Oh, yes, of course, dear, how silly of me. It's just that your dear mama, rest her soul, always called you Lydia, and so that's how I always think of you. This is Adelaide Boyce Hammond."

Miss Addie! Lord, I hadn't seen her since my mother's funeral more than fifteen years ago. For all I knew, she could have been dead, too. She and Emmaline Simpson had been Braxton girls, inmates of that stuffy academy that had finished so many of their generation of aristocratic Southern debutantes. Her soft, melodious voice conjured up memories of lazy summer afternoons and tea on the verandah.

Unconsciously, I sat up straighter, pulled the sheet tight across my naked breasts, and stubbed out my cigarette. "Miss Addie," I crooned, "how lovely to hear from you. I hope you're well?"

The years of my mother's relentless campaign to turn her tomboy daughter into a proper lady had not been entirely wasted. I could, when pressed, trade social niceties with the best of them.

"Why, yes, dear, I'm quite well, thank you. I was deeply saddened to hear of your poor husband's untimely passin'. So tragic when the young are taken before their time. I hope my note was of some small comfort to you?"

Note? I didn't remember any condolence message from my mother's old childhood friend.

But then, it had been almost a year ago, and the weeks following Rob's murder had been a blur of physical pain and emotional anguish. I had been allowed out of the hospital only long enough to sit huddled in a wheelchair while dignitaries from Columbia and Washington extolled the virtues of my dead husband. The memorial service had been as much media circus as tribute.

There hadn't been enough pieces of him left to warrant a burial.

Absently I fingered the deepest of the shiny-smooth furrows of scar tissue that criss-crossed my left shoulder.

"Yes, Miss Addie, it certainly was a comfort," I lied, "and very kind of you."

"Not at all, dear. I do so admire the brave manner in which you've conducted yourself since your bereavement. Your poor mama, rest her soul, would have been very proud."

I could see I was going to have to draw it out of her, the reason for her call. Otherwise we might be dancing this courtly minuet of pleasantries until lunch time.

"Thank you. Is there something I can do for you, Miss Addie?"

"Oh, yes . . . well. Oh dear, this is somewhat difficult." I could almost see her tiny octogenarian's hands fluttering, like hummingbirds around a feeder. With a gentle sigh, she got down to business. "I spoke with the Judge yesterday, and he suggested I call you. About a little problem I may have? He was certain you could advise me as to what's best to do."

I should have detected the fine hand of my father in this. Though retired from his law practice, as well as from the bench, Judge Talbot Simpson was still a full-time meddler in my life. "What problem is that, Miss Addie?"

"Oh, just a little investment I made awhile back. Quite safe and certain to be very profitable. The young man assured me. Perhaps you know him, Millicent Anderson's boy, Geoffrey?"

My fingers tightened around the receiver, and I felt a hot flush creeping up my neck. Oh yes, I knew him. Or rather, I *had*. Geoff Anderson had been my hero, my knight, my first, serious love. The fact that I was a gawky adolescent and he a much older

Citadel cadet had made no difference. The only saving grace had been his total ignorance of my deep, but undeclared devotion. We'd lost touch after his graduation. I'd heard somewhere that he'd recently abandoned his Miami law firm in favor of real estate development.

"I remember him," I said with studied understatement. "What exactly is it you and the Judge think I can help with?"

I was fairly certain I already knew the answer, or at least the gist of it.

The Judge had an apoplexy when I transferred out of pre-law and into the business school during my junior year at Carolina. He was so angry he refused to pay my tuition bills. I promptly applied for and received a full academic scholarship to Northwestern and marched defiantly across the Mason-Dixon Line into enemy territory. A masters degree in accounting and another in finance had not been enough to earn me his total forgiveness, but he never had any hesitation about sending his friends around for free advice. I did his tax return every year, too, the ungrateful old buzzard.

My mind wandered back in time to catch the last of Miss Addie's reply. ". . . for lunch today? It would be lovely to see you again, and I'd feel so much easier if we could discuss it in person."

I couldn't think of a graceful way to refuse. I jotted down the directions to her condo and promised to be with her by twelve-thirty.

I plumped up the pillows behind me and lit another cigarette. My second of the day, and my feet hadn't even hit the floor yet.

Damn the Judge and his meddling!

It wasn't that I minded so much advising Adelaide Boyce Hammond about whatever financial problem she imagined she had. There was nothing to keep me from picking up my professional life right where it had left off. Not physically, anyway. The scars would remain, and a slight weakness in my left arm, but I'd learned to camouflage both pretty well. And, even though my mother's trust fund and my own knack for picking stock market dark horses made earning a living optional, I loved my work.

But after Rob was killed, I just had no desire to get back in the race. I had dropped out, scurrying back to the refuge of the beach house to lick my wounds and mourn.

"Baynards are made of sterner stuff." I heard my mother's reproach as clearly as if she towered next to the bed, frowning down on me. I got my height, almost five feet, ten inches from her side of the family, along with leaf-green eyes a lot of people assumed were colored contacts. The auburn tint to my dark brown hair and a tendency to wisecrack my way through uncomfortable situations came courtesy of the Judge.

Nightmares about Rob, and now visions of my dead mother!

This was exactly the reason I didn't want to sip weak iced tea and pick at mushy shrimp salad across the table from Adelaide Boyce Hammond. She was the past, mine and my mother's. I had expended a large chunk of my adult life trying to shove those painful memories to the farthest recesses of my mind. Miss Addie would bring them all back. Not that she'd mean to. She just wouldn't be able to help herself.

I squashed out the cigarette and flipped back the covers. I shrugged into Rob's tattered College of Charleston T-shirt and padded barefoot across the room. Drawing the drapes, I opened the French doors and stepped out onto the deck.

Two ancient live oaks, their twisted limbs dripping Spanish moss, provided dappled shade, but I could already feel the promise of the scorching heat to come. It was low tide. Beyond the dune crowned with sea oats swaying lazily in a light breeze, the ocean retreated from a wide expanse of empty beach. Not quite empty, I realized, as a solitary jogger rounded the headland and trotted into view. Beside his master, a young black lab, not yet grown into the promise of his oversized paws, loped along in the surf.

The mid-July sun glistened off the runner's golden arms and chest.

Rob always looked like that after a few days at the beach: his unruly shock of light brown hair bleached to the color of ripe wheat; his long, rangy body drinking up the sun.

I buried my face in the shoulder of his T-shirt. Though it had been laundered many times in the year since his death, I could still smell that faint, musky man-odor that had been his alone.

At least that's what I told myself.

A car door slammed somewhere below me. Seconds later the

soft voice of Dolores Santiago, my part-time housekeeper, drifted up. Her Spanish endearments, interspersed frequently with *el gato*, told me she was fussing over Mr. Bones, the ragtag tomcat that adopted us not long after I came home from the hospital. The scruffy, battle-scarred tabby had wandered erratically in and out of our lives ever since. Apparently he had decided to grace us with his presence this morning.

I turned my attention back to the beach. The jogger had stooped to pick up a piece of driftwood and fling it out over the water. With a yelp of delight, the black lab bounded in after it.

Something about the sweet joyfulness of the scene caught at my throat.

We had been happy like that, Rob and I. Carefree, unmindful of how fragile it all was. We had taken so much for granted.

And some bastard had shattered it, blown our joy into a million bits of steel and glass . . . and flesh.

"*Señora* Tanner?" A soft tap, and the bedroom door slipped open. "*Señora?*"

"Out here, Dolores."

I wiped my eyes on the sleeve of the sacred T-shirt and turned back into the room.

"Your paper, *Señora.*" She dropped the *Island Packet* onto the linen chest at the foot of my bed. "Breakfast in twenty minutes?"

Dolores always seemed to be smiling, her white teeth a sharp contrast to the olive skin and blue-black hair drawn up into a tight bun at the back of her head.

"Make it thirty, okay? I haven't showered yet."

"You have the tennis at nine, no?"

"I'll make it. And just fruit this morning, please," I added, heading for the bathroom.

"*Si, Señora.*"

Dolores would undoubtedly cook me eggs or French toast or hotcakes and stand over me just like my mother used to do until I cleaned my plate. But I kept trying.

I snatched up the paper on my way by and glanced briefly at the headline: Body Pulled From Chicopee River.

Another drowning, I thought as I peeled off the T-shirt and stepped into the shower. *How can people be so incredibly careless?*

Only a few hours would pass before I realized just how wrong that snap judgment would turn out to be.

Come Labor Day, the permanent residents of Hilton Head Island, South Carolina breathe a collective sigh of relief, thankful to have our golf courses and beaches, restaurants and roadways returned to us once again. Then, from September to May, the island is almost paradise. Except for an occasional brush with a hurricane, the weather is temperate, sunny and mild, with only a few cold days in the dead of winter.

However, on this steamy July afternoon at the peak of tourist season, at least half of the one hundred thousand average daily visitors that clog the main island thoroughfare had conspired to make me late for my appointment. Traffic had come to a complete standstill, and the sun beating down at high noon made me wish I hadn't put the top down on my white LeBaron convertible. I kicked the air conditioning up a notch and reached for the newspaper I'd tossed into the front seat beside me.

I skimmed over the drowning story and flipped to the state news section. Although I had been out of the official loop since Rob's death, I still recognized most of the names associated with affairs in Columbia. I had worked with many of these people as a special consultant on financial fraud cases, building evidence and even testifying on occasion. I had thought I was gaining a reputation of my own, outside of Rob's influence, but requests for my professional services had been non-existent since his death.

I knew I hadn't endeared myself to any of them with my relentless demands for action during those first few months. Someone had viciously murdered three men: Rob, his civilian pilot, and a state trooper assigned for protection. Not only had no one been prosecuted, they weren't even close to making an arrest. While everyone—including me—had their suspicions about who had planted the bomb, there was no evidence and no new leads. The trail had gone cold.

A few weeks ago, when it dawned on them that I would never resign myself to accepting that, they stopped taking my calls.

A blare from the horn of the big van filling my rearview mirror jerked me back to the present. I dropped the paper and eased the gearshift into drive.

Fifteen minutes of crawling brought me to the Sea Pines Circle, that landmark of the island and bane of drivers uninitiated into its mysteries. I had no doubt this was the origin of the backup. Locals often told tongue-in-cheek stories about tourists stuck for days on the inside lane of the traffic roundabout. I exited at the first right and left them to battle it out.

The Cedars, a fairly new retirement community, nestled among the pines and sweetgums at the edge of the marsh along Broad Creek. Planned for the active senior, most of it was devoted to independent housing designed for those who could take care of themselves. Miss Addie was in the "assisted living" area, a three-story building where residents purchased their own apartments but received cleaning, transportation, and meal service as part of their monthly fee.

I gave my name to the officer at the security gate and parked in front of the main building where Miss Addie and I had agreed to meet. A blast of frigid air, in sharp contrast to the stifling heat outside, greeted me as I pulled open the heavy door. I flipped my sunglasses on top of my head and approached the antique reception desk. The woman's smile looked as artificial as her stiff blonde hair. Her beige suit, however, was impeccably cut, and gold bangles clanked on her wrists as she folded her spotted hands primly in front of her. The nameplate to her right read "A. Dixon".

"Good afternoon, and welcome to The Cedars. How may I help you?"

Her perfect diction revealed the hint of an English accent. Her expression held that mixture of arrogance and superiority so common among many expatriate Brits. She glanced disdainfully over my navy blue polo shirt, slightly wrinkled white duck pants, and espadrilles before returning her pinched gaze to my face.

I half expected her to inform me that the servants' entrance was around back.

I brushed a stray lock of hair back off my cheek and stretched myself up to my full height. Two could play this game. "I have a luncheon engagement with Miss Hammond," I replied in my best Southern aristocrat's voice.

"And you are . . . ?"

Lord, this woman was something! You'd think I was trying to

sneak into Buckingham Palace.

"Mrs. Tanner. Mrs. Lydia Baynard Simpson Tanner."

There! Match that mouthful, honey, I thought.

"You're expected, Mrs. Tanner," she replied, consulting a list on the desk. "Please proceed straight down this hallway. The dining room will be on your right. Our Mr. Romero will seat you."

I gave her an icy nod, then marched off, shoulders squared, back ramrod straight. I could have balanced the entire Encyclopedia Britannica on my head without losing a volume. Mama would have been proud. Only the slap of my scuffed espadrilles on the polished Mexican tile detracted from my grand exit.

The entrance to the dining room was flanked by two potted ficus trees, a *maitre d's* stand, and Mr. Romero. He was tall, Latin, and gorgeous. If I'd been twenty years older, I'd have had a run at him myself.

"Madame?"

"Mrs. Tanner for Miss Hammond."

"Of course, right this way."

His smile was a knockout, even if the mouthful of gleaming white teeth weren't his own. I followed him to a table set for two in a small alcove by a window. Pulling out the unoccupied wicker chair he seated me with a flourish.

"Enjoy your lunch, ladies."

Almost every pair of female eyes, including mine and Miss Addie's, tracked his progress back to his station at the door.

"Such a charming man," Miss Addie said, a look of almost girlish adoration on her wrinkled face. I turned away, slightly embarrassed for her. Miss Addie had never married. Some tragedy in her youth my mother had hinted, but never quite got around to explaining. With an effort, my hostess dragged her attention back to the table.

"Well, Lydia, let me look at you. How lovely you are, dear. Quite lovely. Those green Baynard eyes, so like your mama's. How I've missed her these last years."

Miss Addie raised a delicate lace handkerchief and dabbed at the corners of her faded blue eyes, magnified by thick, wire-framed bifocals. She was dressed formally in an aqua print summer dress she probably still called a frock. Her pure white hair had been recently styled and lay in soft curls around her sunken cheeks. She wore no makeup, and her skin had the pasty-white cast of those who have heeded all the warnings to avoid the sun. Miss Addie's aversion would have come long before the fear of melanoma. In the times in which she and my mother were brought up, girls whose skin became darkened by exposure to the sun were thought "common". A single strand of pearls—real ones, I was sure—lay against her bony chest, and pearl clips adorned her ears.

"Thank you, Miss Addie. You look wonderful, too. You haven't changed at all." I glanced down at my hastily chosen sports clothes. "I wish you'd told me y'all were so formal here, though. I would have dressed up a little."

A sweet smile softened her face. "Nonsense. You young people have the right idea. Comfort should be just as important as those stuffy rules we learned at Braxton. But I'm too old to change now, and it's probably just as well."

She laughed lightly and indicated the other occupants of the dining room with a wave of her delicate hand. I had been right this morning in comparing her to a hummingbird. "Just look at some of these old fools. Why, if I had legs like tree trunks, I certainly wouldn't display them for all the world to see."

Her gaze rested on an overweight woman who had risen a few tables away. The short skirt of the obviously expensive tennis ensemble barely covered her ample rearend. And her legs did resemble some of the gnarled live oaks that dotted the property.

Miss Addie caught my eye and winked conspiratorially. In that moment, I remembered why I had always liked her best of all that group that had danced attendance on my mother: Miss Addie had a sense of humor.

Maybe this wouldn't be so bad after all.

If the company turned out to be a pleasant surprise, the meal was even more so. Miss Addie had "taken the liberty" of choosing the menu: a crisp green salad, followed by an exquisite salmon with fresh asparagus in hollandaise sauce. We waved away the offer of an extensive wine list, both of us opting for freshly brewed iced tea in frosty glasses.

The reminiscences proved less uncomfortable than I'd feared. Even Miss Addie's continual use of my hated first name became almost bearable. Though her chatter scratched against long-buried memories of a childhood I had thought safely repressed, I managed to smile and nod as she recalled with fondness the days when my mother had reigned supreme over local society.

Over thin wedges of *real* key lime pie—with *real* meringue—I tried to edge the conversation around to the reason for her call. "Now then," I said firmly as we both laid our heavy linen napkins on the table next to our plates, "tell me about this investment problem of yours."

Miss Addie fidgeted a little, but eventually realized it was time to get down to business. "Well, it has to do with Grayton's Race."

My blank look betrayed my ignorance.

"That old rice plantation on the Chicopee? Oh, surely Emmaline must have talked to you about it, dear? Your mama loved the old place so." Miss Addie's smile melted years off her face. "You should have seen it in its prime. Well, not that we did either, exactly. By the time your mama and I were old enough to attend parties there, it had fallen into some disrepair. But there were paintings of it, as it had been in the last century, a truly imposing greathouse. Wide verandahs, white porticoes, a magnificent avenue of oaks. Quite similar in many ways to your house, Lydia."

"Presqu'isle was my mother's house, not mine," I snapped. My hackles had risen again, and I couldn't really say why. Maybe because the Judge and I were always aware that it was my mother, Emmaline Baynard, who had brought the antebellum mansion into the family. My father and their unplanned, change-of-life little girl had always been interlopers. We might live there, but we'd never really *belong*.

"Of course, dear, I know that. Your mother's people have lived there for almost two hundred years. But, like it or not, you are a Baynard. Some day Presqu'isle and all its responsibilities will be yours."

I didn't want to talk about this. I hated the house. I wanted no part of it after the Judge was gone, and it had passed to me. They could tear the damned thing down and turn it into a parking lot for all I cared.

"You were saying? About Grayton's Race?" I forced a smile.

"Oh, yes. Well. One of the sons was killed in the First War. Another drank himself to death. Then it all fell to some northern cousins, and they sold off parcels willy-nilly, and . . . oh dear."

Miss Addie applied the lace hanky to her eyes once again. "We had such lovely parties there when I was a girl. It's all so sad."

It was beginning to come back to me now from articles in the local paper, scanned and forgotten, and from gossip around the Club. A real estate investment company had been formed to buy up the surrounding land and restore the old plantation house to its former glory. The Race would become the centerpiece of a planned community with antebellum style homes on large lots, with one or two golf courses thrown in for ambiance. Most of the acreage fronted what locals always referred to as "the pristine" Chicopee River. Those who lived along its unpolluted banks, as well as some outside environmental groups, had protested loudly. I didn't blame them. It was just the kind of desecration I hated. We had already lost too many trees to the greedy axes of the developers.

Miss Addie sniffed delicately, reclaiming my attention.

"So Geoffrey Anderson talked you into investing. How much?" I asked bluntly.

Miss Addie hemmed and hawed, fluttered her hands, and refused to look me in the eye.

I finally managed to worm it out of her. She had plunked down two hundred thousand dollars, almost everything she had left of her inheritance after buying her apartment at The Cedars. Without the income generated by that money, invested in CDs and solid mutual funds, she would soon be hard pressed to meet her monthly fees at the swank retirement home.

I struggled to keep control of my temper.

"Why didn't you call me *before* you made this decision, Miss Addie? Unless you can find someone to buy you out, I don't see how I can help you."

"Well, really Lydia, it seemed so safe. Geoffrey promised we'd have our money back, and with a sizable profit, in just a few months. And he *is* Millicent Anderson's boy. After all, one just has to have faith in one's oldest friends, doesn't one?"

I had my doubts about that. Every family, regardless of how far back its lineage could be traced, had its share of scoundrels and ne'er-do-wells.

"So why the sudden concern?" I asked resignedly. I should have listened to my instincts this morning and found some plausible reason to beg off.

"Well, I've talked with several people, friends from the old days, you understand, and they seem to think it might drag on for a long time. There are rumors circulating, something about a piece of land they need to complete the project. Apparently the owners won't sell. I'm told it could endanger the whole project." The faded eyes behind the thick glasses glistened with unshed tears. "I've called and called, but Geoffrey doesn't seem to get my messages. The Judge thought that maybe you could talk to him and find out when we can expect to get our money."

"*Our* money?" I jerked upright in my chair, my hand sending the sterling silver salt shaker rolling across the table. "What do you mean, *our* money?"

Miss Addie absently gathered a few grains of the spilled salt in her arthritic fingers and tossed them over her left shoulder. "Why, mine, Lydia. And the Judge's. It was upon his advice that I relied. Well, his and Geoffrey's."

"My father has money in this scheme?" I could feel my voice rising, and other late diners glanced uneasily in our direction.

"Well, dear, of course he does. Didn't I mention that on the telephone? In honor of your dear mama, of course. You see, we local investors are to have bronze plaques with our names embossed on them. A Gallery of Honor in the main hallway of the Race, an eternal memorial to our help in restoring one of the truly great plantation houses of the old South."

I was nearly hyperventilating with anger. I had to get out of there before I embarrassed myself and this dotty old lady.

Bronze plaques, Gallery of Honor! What a crock! Geoffrey Anderson had really been reaching when he came up with gimmicks like that to entice investors into his project. And what would happen if they never got title to this disputed land? The investment would be worthless; the property, unsaleable to another developer. How could my father have been so gullible, a man with his education and experience? And to have taken Miss Addie down along with him!

I regained my composure long enough to solicit Geoffrey's phone number and mark it in my address book. I thanked Miss Addie for lunch, promised to get back to her soon, and planted a gentle kiss on her paper-thin cheek. I left her staring out the window, a sad smile on her wrinkled face.

Mr. Gorgeous said something as I passed, but I was too upset to respond.

Geoffrey Anderson was going to wish he'd never messed with *my* family and friends. But before I tackled him, my father and I had a few things to discuss. Like, where he had gotten the cash to invest in this harebrained scheme, and exactly when it was that he had taken total leave of his senses.

CHAPTER
TWO

As it turned out, my father beat me to the punch. I arrived home to find the red light on my answering machine blinking furiously. And, fastened to the refrigerator door with a magnet shaped like the Harbour Town lighthouse, was a note from Dolores. While her spoken English is pretty good, she tends to spell things just the way they sound. It took me a few minutes to decipher her meaning:

Juj cald (My father had phoned.)

V are erjent (It was a matter of some importance.)

U cal kwik (He wanted me to return his call as soon as possible.)

I'll just bet he does, I snorted as I poured myself some lemonade and carried it, along with the portable phone, out onto the deck. The incoming tide brought with it a nice onshore breeze. I'd check my messages later. They were probably all from the Judge, anyway. Patience was not his strong suit.

Miss Addie, sensing my shock at her revelation, had undoubtedly called to warn my father of my extreme displeasure. She would never be so gauche as to use an expression like "blew her top", although that would have been a more accurate description of my reaction.

I punched in the number and flopped myself onto the bright cushions of the chaise. I tried to remember when it was that our relationship had changed . . . when it was that I had become the disapproving parent and my father, the bad-tempered child.

After my mother died, the Judge had seemed to come into his own. Presqu'isle, formerly famed for the splendor of its gardens and Emmaline Baynard Simpson's celebrated teas and formal dinners, had become more like a real home for him. The Judge's courthouse cronies, previously persona non grata with their loud voices and smelly cigars, now made the old plantation house one of their regular stops.

Thursday night poker. Saturday morning duck hunting. Sunday afternoon barbecues.

Then, his first stroke, mild, but a warning. Kentucky bourbon and contraband Havana panatelas faded into fond memory. The Judge's reformed lifestyle lasted a little less than six months. His second "cerebral vascular incident" had left him a semi-invalid.

Thank God for Lavinia, I thought. I could never have taken over his care, especially after Rob . . .

It had dawned on me that I had been listening to the phone ring unanswered in my father's house for an unusually long time. I had my finger poised over the redial button when my father snapped, "Yes?" in my ear.

"Judge? It's Bay. Why the hell are you answering the phone? Where's Lavinia?"

"I'm just fine, dear, thank you for inquiring. And you?"

The deep resonance of my father's courtroom baritone thundered down the line. Though partially paralyzed on his left side, his speech had been relatively unaffected. I ignored the sarcasm. Putting your opponent on the defensive was a tactic I had learned at his knee.

"Could you please just answer my question? Where is Lavinia? Are you in your study or did you wheel yourself all the way out in the hall to get the phone?"

"You should never have given up the law, daughter. Your cross-examination technique is classic."

"Thank you, Your Honor."

Why do our conversations always have to go like this? I asked myself. They seemed to start out bad and go downhill from there.

"I got your message," I said into his grumpy silence. "Is something wrong?"

"Of course something's wrong! Why do you think I'm answering the damn phone myself? You need to get over here now, right away. Vinnie's taken off, probably for a few days she said, and it's my night for poker. The boys'll be here at seven-thirty, and they'll expect to be fed. So if you leave now, you'll have time to help me get dressed and then throw something together for us to eat. Better bring some clothes with you, too. If Vinnie doesn't get back . . ."

"Whoa! Slow down and back up."

"Bay, we don't have time for this. If you don't start out soon—"

"Objection!"

That stopped him. Then I heard his low chuckle. "On what grounds?"

"Confusing the witness."

"Sustained. Sorry, honey, but can't you just get here and leave the explanations until later?"

With a shrug I gave in, as we both knew all along I would. "Okay, okay, I'm coming. But at least tell me where Lavinia is. It's not like her just to take off and leave you alone to fend for yourself."

Lavinia Smalls had been the housekeeper at Presqu'isle since shortly after my mother had inherited the house. Long before I was born, the two had established a relationship based on two hundred years of social and racial custom. They addressed each other formally, although Lavinia's title of "Mrs." may have been honorary since no mention of a husband, either past or present, was ever made, at least in my hearing.

As a child I called her Miss Lavinia, dropping the title as I grew up. No one but the Judge, to whom she was devoted, had ever gotten away with "Vinnie".

"Did you read today's paper?" The non sequitur brought me up short.

"I glanced at it. Why?"

"See the story about the drowning in the Chicopee?"

"I saw the headline, but I didn't read any farther. What's that got to do with anything?"

"The victim was Vinnie's nephew. You know, her sister Mavis's boy, Derek? She went to be with her family. I told her it would be okay, that you'd come and stay with me. You will, won't you, Bay, honey?"

He was starting to whine. I much preferred his Mr. Hyde personality—the crusty, sarcastic tough guy—to this needy and helpless Dr. Jekyll side.

"How awful for them. Okay, Judge, I'll be there as soon as I can. And if Lavinia calls, tell her how sorry I am, will you?"

I hung up the phone and sat brooding beneath the shade of

the live oaks. I felt sad for Lavinia, annoyed by my father's erratic personality shifts, and restless in a vague way that had become all too familiar lately.

I knew what part of it was: I was lonely. I had thought I was getting used to being on my own. After Rob's murder, my friends had been more than supportive. They had rallied around me, fending off the media, trying to give me a chance to heal, both inside and out. But after a while, their concern became cloying, smothering. At least that's how I perceived it. I pushed them gently away; and, for the most part, they went. Some with regret, others, with relief.

It was their pity I really couldn't handle. Their careful avoidance of Rob's name. That self-conscious lull in any conversation that strayed too close to him . . . to *us*.

And that was the heart of my problem. I yearned to be part of an *us* again, to feel that shared joy that needed no words, the quick anger more quickly melted in a knowing smile.

I needed love.

I needed Rob.

Enough!

I mentally slapped myself and did the only thing that seemed to work now when I began to sink into pointless grief and self-pity. I got up off my butt and got moving.

I was throwing my overnight bag into the back of the convertible when it struck me that neither my father nor I had mentioned Miss Addie or Grayton's Race.

I had picked the worst possible time of day to leave the island. Rush hour traffic spluttered and crawled, so it was almost five o'clock when I bounced down the rutted avenue of oaks on St. Helena Island and pulled in behind the Beaufort County Sheriff's cruiser parked in Presqu'isle's circular drive.

I was annoyed rather than alarmed. The Judge's circle of acquaintance encompassed all branches of the local criminal justice system, so it was not unusual to find solicitors, attorneys, or even old-timers from the sheriff's department trading war stories with my father over cold drinks on the verandah.

I lifted my bag from the back seat and stood for a moment

contemplating the deceptively pleasant facade of my childhood home. To an outsider it would certainly have seemed impressive. Its central outside stairway rose from two small side staircases, spilling onto a wide front porch supported by six square columns. The upstairs was deck rather than porch, and its openness allowed one to admire the central pediment and dormers off each end of the hipped roof.

The foundation was tall, arched, and made from tabby, that mixture of oyster shells and lime that had been the preferred building material in the Lowcountry for more than two centuries. The white frame structure had a rear aspect nearly as pleasing as the front. Situated on a spit of land jutting out into St. Helena Sound, it had taken its name from its location. Presqu'isle, the French equivalent of peninsula, revealed the Huguenot ancestry of my mother's family.

As I mounted the sixteen steps and crossed the verandah to the carved oak front door, I tried to shake off my deep-seated antipathy to what many considered one of the finest examples of antebellum architecture on the South Carolina-Georgia coast. After all, the house could hardly be blamed for my unhappiness inside its walls.

As I stepped into the cool dimness of the entry hall, I heard voices coming from my father's study at the rear of the house. After his stroke, we had moved his bed down there and turned an old storage closet into a modern, wheelchair-accessible bathroom. A door led onto the back verandah with a ramp installed so that he could wheel himself outside whenever he got restless.

I set my bag down at the foot of the graceful, free-standing staircase and headed for my father's room. I could smell the cigar smoke when I was still five feet from the doorway. Though they had opened the windows in a hurried attempt to conceal the evidence, the slight breeze off the Sound had only blown it right back into the room.

When I charged into the study, the Judge had that hand-in-the-cookie jar look on his face. He still had almost a full head of thick, white hair, and his broad shoulders were only slightly bowed. His left hand lay useless in his lap. With his right, he made a futile effort to fan away the telltale haze.

"Hello, sweetheart," the Judge boomed, "look who's here."

I had spared only a brief glance at his tall, uniformed co-conspirator whose back was turned to me as I entered the room.

"Hello, Bay. Good to see you."

My heart stopped for a couple of beats, the way it always did when I came unexpectedly face-to-face with my brother-in-law. Sergeant Redmond Tanner was a slightly shorter, slightly younger version of his dead brother. But the strong resemblance always stabbed that secret part of me that could still not accept Rob's death.

"Hey, Red. How's it going?"

He had crossed the heart pine floor in three strides and would have engulfed me in a khaki embrace. Instinctively I stepped back, lifting my cheek instead to invite a chaste, brotherly kiss. I regretted the look of hurt that flashed briefly across his rugged face, but I couldn't help myself. He was too much like Rob. It would be too easy to close my eyes and pretend, just for a moment . . .

Red recovered himself quickly. "You look great, Bay." He settled one haunch onto the arm of the dark green sofa. "The beach life must agree with you."

"Thanks, it's good to see you, too. I never would have guessed it was you, though, aiding and abetting."

His laugh was deep and hearty, just like Rob's. "Hey, when did I ever have any influence over the Judge? He wants a cigar, I say, 'Yes, sir' and grab the matches."

"Well, I'd love to stay and chat, but I understand I'm on KP tonight. I'd better get out to the kitchen and see what I can rustle up for the Bay Street Irregulars."

The name, taken from the main avenue of Beaufort on which most of them had their offices, had been given to the Thursday night poker group by one of its former members. Before his death, Henry Constable had been a devoted Sherlock Holmes fan. Time had whittled the original eight down to five.

"Wait, Bay. I think it would be helpful if you stayed. I was just getting around to the real reason I dropped by."

"This sounds ominous." I crossed the room to flop myself onto the wide seat beneath the bowed window that looked out on the Sound, a favorite spot of mine as a little girl.

The Judge activated the controls on his motorized wheelchair and maneuvered himself closer to my perch.

Red stood alone.

If it was trouble, we had already chosen up sides.

"Did you read about the body we fished out of the Chicopee last night?" In characteristic Tanner fashion, Red had begun to pace.

"I guess everyone in the county but me must have seen it," I replied. "The Judge said the victim was Lavinia's nephew, Derek. That's why she's not here. So what's your interest? It was just another drowning, wasn't it?"

"That was a heartless remark, daughter." My father's eyes were pinched in disapproval. "The boy was only nineteen years old. Try to show a little compassion."

I swallowed hard, embarrassed by his rebuke. Maybe he was right. Maybe my protective wall *was* getting a bit too thick.

"Well, actually, it wasn't just a drowning." Red's face had begun to color up, and his eyes refused to meet mine. My husband always looked like that when he was about to tell me something he knew I didn't want to hear. Red picked up the ivory-handled letter opener off the Judge's desk and studied it as if he'd never seen one before.

"Why don't you just spit it out, Red?" His evasiveness was beginning to get on my nerves.

"The coroner says he was dead before he went into the water. Blunt trauma to the back of the skull, delivered with considerable force. It was no accidental drowning."

"Murder." The judge spoke the word with a strange mixture of repugnance and reverence.

Violent death was rare in our quiet corner of the South. I couldn't remember his ever having been involved in a murder trial. I watched the fantasy play out across his face: The Honorable Judge Talbot Simpson—whole and straight again—presiding over a case that would make headlines all across the state.

"Nonsense," I said, both to the idea of murder and to my father's wishful thinking. I didn't know why I felt so strongly about the improbability of it, I just did. "And even if it wasn't an accident, what does that have to do with us? You said something about the 'real' reason you stopped by. Were you planning on getting to that anytime soon?"

The Judge shot me the kind of look I used to get when I was ten and being bratty.

"Lavinia's grandson, Isaiah, had a fight with the victim yesterday afternoon, outside the school. Isaiah apparently took the worst of it. A lot of threats were exchanged, in front of a lot of witnesses. Pretty much the whole damn football team, far as I can tell."

"And?" I swung my legs off the window seat and sat up straighter.

"And, damn it, the Captain sent me to try and find him. Isaiah, that is. He's not at home. His parents claim they haven't heard from him since last night around supper time."

"So you came here, thinking that Lavinia might have stashed her fugitive grandson somewhere at Presqu'isle? Or that she and the Judge had spirited him off?" My voice had turned icy with contempt. "Really, Tanner, it's no wonder you're embarrassed to have to investigate such a screwball theory."

"Knock it off, Bay. It's not that farfetched. The boys had a fistfight. Isaiah said he'd kill Derek if he ever came around practice again. That night, Derek's murdered, and Isaiah disappears. What are we supposed to do, pretend it didn't happen?"

"No, you're supposed to realize that a—what? Sixteen, seventeen-year-old . . . ?" I looked to the Judge, who nodded confirmation of my guess.

"So?" Red interrupted. "You think a kid that age couldn't be involved in violence like this? Where the hell have you been, Bay, living on another planet? Don't you watch the news? Twelve-year-olds are doing hard time for murder these days."

"Maybe in L.A. or Miami or New York. Not in rural Beaufort County," I fired back. "And not someone with the kind of family background Isaiah has. His father grew up here at Presqu'isle. Lavinia whupped him as often as she did me. Thaddeus Smalls wouldn't raise up his son to be a murderer."

"Look," Red sighed, running his big hand through his light brown hair in a gesture I found painfully familiar, "let's all calm down a little. We just want to talk to Isaiah, that's all. If he has a good alibi for the time in question, we eliminate him as a suspect and move on. He might even have some idea of who else might have had a beef with Derek."

He bent and picked up his hat from the side table near the doorway.

"It's S.O.P., nothing more. You ought to know how we operate by now."

My indiscriminate rage at the inability of anyone to bring Rob's murderers to justice had spilled out onto every branch of law enforcement in the state. I knew I had sometimes vented my frustration unfairly on Red simply because he was a cop. I had to keep reminding myself that he, too, wanted justice for his dead brother.

The Judge had been strangely silent during our exchange. His angry voice startled me as much as it did Red.

"You're welcome to have a look around, Redmond," he said stiffly.

Red's face closed down completely. "Not necessary, Judge. I just wanted to talk to Lavinia, see if she had any thoughts on where the boy might be. But thanks for the offer, seein' as how I don't even have a search warrant. Yet."

"She's probably at her sister Mavis's." I spoke softly, hoping he could hear the contrition in my voice as I curled back up on the window seat. "Derek's mother's place. Out by Cherry Point."

"Thanks. I'll try to catch up with her there." Red turned, hesitated, then walked quickly back across to the window seat. He twirled his hat nervously in his hands.

"Can I call you sometime, Bay? Maybe we could have dinner, or something?"

I knew Red had been lonely since his divorce. His schedule didn't leave much time for socializing, one of the big factors in the breakup of his marriage to his high school sweetheart, Sarah. Weekends were reserved for visitation with his two kids, when the rotation allowed him to swing it.

I also knew that dating my dead husband's brother was not a good plan. But I needed to atone for my bad attitude, so I gave him a smile and as non-committal an answer as I could.

"Call me."

"Okay. Thanks."

The Tanner grin lit his face as he nodded to the Judge and strode out of the study. I heard the heavy front door close behind him.

"That wasn't a kindness, Bay, letting him think you might be interested. You aren't, are you? It would be a mistake, daughter, believe me. You can't substitute—"

"Butt out, Your Honor. My love life—or lack of it—is out of your jurisdiction." I bit back the anger that always boiled up whenever my father began dispensing advice, especially about relationships. He and my mother hadn't exactly provided a sterling example of marital bliss. "And speaking of mistakes, I had lunch with Adelaide Boyce Hammond today. Care to explain to me how you got mixed up with this real estate scam? And why you had to drag that poor old lady down with you?"

"It's not a scam. It's a legitimate business investment. But we have more pressing problems right now. Vinnie's going to need our help."

"Why don't we wait until she asks for it? She's a very private person. I don't think she'd appreciate your sticking your nose in before you're invited."

"Don't lecture me about Vinnie." I started to protest, but he cut me off. "And anyway, we don't have time for that now."

As if on cue, the deep-throated *bong* of the antique grandfather clock sounded in the parlor. I glanced at my watch.

6:30.

"Okay. But don't think you're off the hook. We *will* talk about this investment business. Tonight."

As it turned out, we didn't.

By the time I helped my father change into clean clothes and did the same for myself, the front doorbell was chiming. They all arrived together, four men who had known me almost from the day I was born. I braced myself for the inevitable questions about Rob's murder, for the pitying looks I had come to despise. None of that happened. Instead, they all expressed genuine delight at seeing me again and wrapped me in the warmth of their fatherly embraces.

They had their routine down to a science, helping themselves to drinks and setting up the table while I threw together platters of cold meat, cheeses, fresh vegetables, and assorted breads. I set the whole thing out as a buffet on the sideboard in the Judge's study.

They refused to let me sneak off to the novel I had brought along. Before I knew it, I found myself seated in the midst of these contemporaries of the Judge with a pile of red, white, and blue chips in front of me and five cards in my hand.

The death of Derek Johnson provided a hot topic of conversation, as did various minor courthouse scandals and the latest gossip involving local dignitaries. The poker, however, was serious business. No one wanted to go home a loser. So it was past midnight when, twelve dollars richer and stuffed full of Lavinia's homemade blueberry pie, I dragged myself up the stairs and flopped gratefully into my old four-poster. I'd smoked too many cigarettes and eaten way too much, but I had enjoyed every second of it.

It seemed like only a minute later when the phone once again rescued me from the grip of the explosion nightmare only to plunge me headlong into the middle of another.

"Bay? Is that you?" The voice quavered with barely controlled emotion. "It's Lavinia. Please let me speak to the Judge." A shuddering breath, then a spark of anger broke through. "They've arrested my grandson."

CHAPTER
THREE

The sun had barely risen as I replaced the receiver and threw back
the crisp white sheets. I knew the Judge had to be worn out from
last night's excitement, so I had taken the sketchy information
from Lavinia and let my father sleep. I threw on shorts and a T-
shirt, made myself some Earl Grey tea and toast, and got back on
the telephone.

My first call caught Dolores just as she was leaving home. She
didn't sound thrilled about my request but agreed to come. I
asked her to let me know when she got to my place and made a
mental note to be sure my gratitude was reflected in her paycheck.

Next I dialed the sheriff's office in Beaufort. The dispatcher
told me that Sergeant Tanner had just gone off his shift and could
probably be reached at home in about ten minutes.

Sarah and the kids had remained in the Lowcountry cottage
the couple had built shortly after Red's discharge from the
Marines. My brother-in-law's "home" was now a one-bedroom
apartment in a non-descript building that looked as if it were part
of the prison system. His furniture consisted of a card table, three
folding chairs, an air mattress, and a thirty-one-inch rear projec-
tion TV that took up one entire wall of the living room.

The phone rang twelve times before I gave up. Apparently an
answering machine did not rank high on Red's list of life's necessities. Maybe he'd stopped for breakfast. I'd have to try him later.

I was about to pour myself another cup of tea when the muted
whir of the Judge's wheelchair sounded in the hallway, and he
rolled into the room.

The sight of my father brought a catch to my throat. His hair
stood out at odd angles from his head, even though wet comb
tracks testified to his attempts to tame it. He had nicked his face
in several places, and little bits of Kleenex were stuck to the cuts.
His legs, thin and pasty, stuck out of his pajama bottoms. His

bare feet were blue-veined and scaly, the nails thick and yellow.

"What the hell's going on?" he growled, maneuvering himself up to the kitchen table. "What are you doing up so early? Who was that on the phone?"

I covered the only way I knew how. "What the hell are *you* doing up? And who said you could shave yourself? God, look at you! It's a wonder you didn't slit your throat."

I rattled another cup out of the cupboard, filled it with tea, and banged it down in front of him. We sat glaring at each other, neither willing to make the first move. The shrill of the telephone next to my elbow saved us the trouble.

I took notes for about five minutes as Dolores relayed the messages I had neglected to take off the machine yesterday. I gave her detailed directions, along with a list of things I wanted from home. She promised to be with us in about an hour. I hung up, determined to stop acting like Mrs. Attila the Hun with my father.

"Want some breakfast? Dolores is on her way, and she'll probably want to cook for you. But how about some toast or cereal to tide you over? I think I can just about manage that."

My uselessness in the kitchen was a family joke. Rob had done most of the cooking at our home in Charleston, and there are more than three hundred restaurants on Hilton Head.

"Any more of that cinnamon raisin bread?"

The cease-fire was holding.

I plucked the bread from the toaster, spread a thin layer of forbidden butter on each slice, and set it down gently before the Judge. The sparkle was back in his deep-set gray eyes, and his appearance seemed more silly now than pathetic.

That I could deal with.

"You look like Mag Sauers," I said, and he laughed. The legend of the local crazy woman with wild, tangled hair and mismatched clothes and shoes was a favorite of my father's.

"You're not exactly a fashion plate yourself this morning," he retorted around his old familiar grin. "So who called so damned early?"

I had put the bad news off long enough. A part of me wished I could spare him, but I knew he wouldn't thank me for keeping him in the dark.

"Lavinia." His head snapped up, all semblance of laughter

gone from his face. "They've arrested Isaiah. I assume it's to do with Derek Johnson's murder, but Lavinia said they wouldn't tell her anything or let her talk to the boy."

"Damn it, Bay, why didn't you tell me right away? Why didn't you wake me?"

"So you could do what? I've already tried to call Red, but he's between work and home somewhere."

"I could have talked to her, reassured her . . ."

"I did that. Besides, she knows we'll do whatever we can. Both of us."

The Judge glared at me, unconvinced. Then he used his good right hand to edge the notepad and pencil toward him. "They'll need a good attorney. I'll make a list."

"Lavinia wants Mander Brown."

The Judge raised one bushy white eyebrow.

"I know, she probably wants him because he and Thaddeus are friends, and she's known him since he was six," I replied to his unasked question. "He'll be okay if this turns out to be the stupid, knee-jerk reaction by the cops that I think it is."

"But," the Judge interrupted, picking up my train of thought, "if they have any kind of evidence at all, and it gets to trial, Mander has no experience. He's used to pleading out petty larcenies and car heists."

"Lavinia was pretty adamant about getting him."

"You leave Vinnie to me. Besides, Mander's a good man. He'll be the first to admit it if he gets in over his head."

"Think they'll set bail? I thought I'd take care of that. I don't imagine Thaddeus and Colletta will be able to raise the money if it's too high."

"Hard to say in a capital case. Depends on if they charge him as an adult or a juvenile. But we're getting ahead of ourselves here. Let me make a few calls and see what I can find out."

The front doorbell pealed, and I went to let Dolores in. I relieved her of the garment bag she had packed for me and led her into the kitchen. She and the Judge had met on the few occasions when I had been able to persuade him to attend the parties Rob and I used to throw on a fairly regular basis. Dolores always did the cooking for us, sometimes serving as well.

I heard my father's hearty laugh amidst the clatter of pots and dishes. Dolores would take good care of him. I was off the hook.

I tried to shove that unfamilial thought away as I climbed the staircase to my old room to change.

The Judge was just mopping up the last of the syrup on his plate with a forkful of hotcakes when I made my entrance.

"Ah, *Señora*." Dolores's smile of approval lit up her black eyes.

The Judge just whistled.

The lifestyle on Hilton Head is decidedly laid-back, so dress tends to be casual except for very formal occasions. Though I had a closet full of beautiful clothes from my working days in Charleston and Columbia, I had pretty much lived in shorts and T-shirts since I moved permanently to the beach. And my social life since Rob's death had been just about non-existent, too. No sense complaining, though. My choice.

So I knew it would be a shock for my father and Dolores to see me for the first time in months in my ivory linen Armani suit, my unruly hair worked into a smooth coil at the nape of my neck. Cream-colored, slingback pumps pushed my height close to six feet. I had decided against a blouse. The solid gold cartouche Rob had given me for our tenth anniversary hung suspended from its herringbone chain and nestled against the cleavage exposed where the lapels of the jacket crossed. Thick gold hoops dangled from my ears.

I had to admit it felt good to be dressed like a professional again.

" 'Gird up now thy loins like a man' ," the Judge quoted in his best courtroom voice.

I frowned in concentration. Then I had it. "Job," I announced, carried back unwillingly to the rainy days of childhood when my well-read father had first initiated the game.

"Too easy," he said with a grin.

" 'Thrice is he armed that hath his quarrel just'," I fired back.

"Hmmm." The Judge closed his eyes. "Shakespeare, of course. Let me see. *Henry V*?"

"Close. *Henry VI*. I'll give you half a point."

"Your generosity is overwhelming."

"You made the rules."

Dolores had set a fresh cup of tea on a green paisley placemat, so I folded myself carefully into the chair and draped the matching napkin across my lap. My mother would have been appalled to find us eating in the kitchen instead of at the nineteenth-century mahogany table in the heavily paneled dining room.

"So what did you find out? Where are they holding Isaiah?" I reached for the cigarettes I had left lying on the table and lit one. Another day without quitting. Maybe I'd get one of those patches. Or the gum.

"You mean Mustapha Rashid?"

"What? Who the hell is Mustapha Rashid?"

"Isaiah. Seems he's been studying Islam. That's his adopted name. Wanted it put on his record at the sheriff's office." The Judge shook his head. "Kids."

The word held not contempt, but a sad perplexity. This generation was so far removed from his own experience, they might be visitors from another galaxy.

"Have they charged him?"

"Not yet. They're holding him as a material witness. He's scheduled to be questioned this morning. I got hold of Mander. He'll meet you at the jail. Vinnie, too."

I opened my mouth to question his decision to let Lavinia pick her own lawyer, but he cut me off.

"They can only hold him for six hours without either formally charging him or letting him go." The Judge slapped the armrest of his wheelchair with his good right hand. "Damn! I could be so much more effective if I were there myself."

"So what's stopping you?" I asked and was rewarded with a formidable scowl.

Although the van we had bought him was equipped with a lift and handicapped controls, the Judge refused to use it except for occasional outings with Lavinia at the wheel. Even then he forbade her to stop anywhere, the two of them riding aimlessly around, savoring the sights and smells of his beloved Lowcountry. No one but close friends and family was allowed to see the great man brought low, one useless hand immobile in his lap, a slight droop dragging down the left side of his still striking face.

As I expected, he ignored my challenge.

"I'll keep trying to reach Redmond. He'll be our best bet for inside information."

"If he's not still ticked off at us about yesterday." I was not proud of my performance. The thought of it brought a fresh rush of color to my cheeks.

"Redmond's not one to hold a grudge; you should know that. Besides, one look at you in that getup, and he'll probably spill every secret he's known for the last twenty years."

I stubbed out my cigarette, rose, and lightly brushed his shoulder with my hand as I passed. He looked up, startled. We were not a *touching* family.

"I'll call you if anything comes up I can't handle."

"That'll be the day."

I stuffed my notebook in my handbag, hoping I'd have a chance to return the calls from yesterday. Bitsy Elliott, my best friend since childhood, had phoned three times, once during the day and twice last night. Dolores said she sounded as if she'd been crying.

Probably had another fight with Cal, I thought as I carefully negotiated my way down the sixteen front steps. I'd forgotten how precarious they could be in highheels.

She never should have married the moron, even if he did get her pregnant their senior year at Clemson. Better to raise an illegitimate baby than be stuck with a redneck jock for the rest of your life. My low opinion of Cal Elliott had been formed early, and he'd done nothing in the intervening years to elevate it.

As I settled myself into the convertible, I felt an exhilaration I hadn't known since before Rob's death. Those had been heady days as we schemed against the bad guys, then waited breathlessly to see if they'd step into the trap. As a special investigator for the State Attorney General's office, Rob had engineered dozens of sting operations against organized drug traffickers, and I had been his faithful sidekick and co-conspirator.

Of course, it wasn't the same without him. Nothing would ever be the same again. But today, with a mission to fulfill and right on my side, for the first time in almost a year I felt as if I might just survive without him.

CHAPTER
FOUR

Coming upon the city of Beaufort from the crest of the bridge that connects it to the outer islands is one of the most beautiful sights on the Southeast coast.

To the left, Waterfront Park stretches like a tiny jewel along the shore of the Beaufort River. Today its wide esplanade, dotted with wooden benches, was alive with tourists, their bright resort clothes adding splotches of color to the cool green of the live oaks. To the right, the stately mansions of the antebellum Sea Island planters stood in restored splendor. Built high off the ground with wide porches along both floors, they all faced the water, capturing whatever breezes might waft their way.

Before the War of Northern Aggression, wealthy cotton planters had moved their entire households every spring to these summer retreats in an often futile attempt to escape the killing fevers that could strike so suddenly in the low-lying marshes of their island plantations.

I had spent many happy childhood hours wandering the narrow lanes of this area, marveling at the graceful beauty of arches and columns, verandahs and rosy brick. Thankful that the triumphant Union Army had spared them from the torch, my neighbors had lovingly cared for these monuments to a lost way of life, preserving them for future generations to marvel at from the seats of horse-drawn sightseeing carriages.

I crossed over Bay Street with its art galleries, bookstores, and antique shops and fought rush hour traffic up Carteret to where it turned into Boundary at the graceful curve of the river. Passing the high brick wall that protected the hallowed ground of the National Cemetery, I felt a familiar tug. The Judge had early on taught me a reverence for those who had sacrificed their lives in the service of their country. We had spent many brilliant summer afternoons strolling solemnly among the rows of pristine white markers, pausing to read an inscription here and there, and to speculate on the man and the life he might have led had he not given it for the good of others.

I didn't play that game anymore. The speculation would strike too close to home.

The massive complex of the new Government Center loomed up ahead of me. I took a left on Ribaut and a right on Duke Street and turned into the parking lot across from the Law Enforcement Building which housed the Sheriff's Office. Behind it, and to the left, the walls of the detention center were crowned with coils of barbed wire.

I had just pushed the door of the convertible open when I spotted the group walking slowly along the tree-lined sidewalk between the two buildings. Thaddeus wore his postal worker's uniform. Colletta was also dressed for work, the mustard yellow dress with the SAV-MOR logo embroidered on the pocket stretched tightly across her heavy bosom. Her once pretty face was lost in folds of fat. Her legs beneath the too-short skirt were chunky and solid.

I swung myself out of the car and went to meet them.

They made a handsome trio, these three generations of Smalls. Isaiah stood nearly as tall as his father, just over six feet. He had the body of an athlete: wide shoulders and trim hips beneath a narrow waist, long muscular legs. Sometime in the months since I had last seen him, he'd shaved his head. Some sort of football ritual, I imagined. As I got closer, I marveled at the beautiful shape of his naked skull. He looked like those carvings of ancient African tribal chiefs you see on National Geographic specials on PBS.

The sun glinted off his deep mahogany skin highlighting a swollen right eye and a couple of cuts on his high cheekbones. He wore his battle scars proudly. Altogether an attractive young man. Or he would have been but for the dark scowl that distorted his face as Lavinia waved a long, menacing finger under his nose.

". . . a perfectly good Christian name," I heard her say as they stopped to meet me under the sparse shade of a newly-planted pear tree. "It's an honorable name, full of the history of our people. I won't allow you to abandon it as if it were something to be ashamed of. Do I make myself clear?"

Lavinia Smalls spoke in the same quiet, yet forceful voice I remembered from my childhood. She never shouted. She simply fixed you with those piercing black eyes and dared you to ignore her. It was like being a rabbit, frozen in fear, caught in the stony stare of a crouching fox.

Her grandson mumbled something unintelligible and stepped back, dropping his eyes.

"I didn't hear you, Isaiah. And look at me when you're speaking to me, please."

"Yes, ma'am. You've made your feelings perfectly clear."

"Good. Now, there'll be no more of this 'Mustapha' business. I'll expect to see you on Sunday morning. And in a suit and tie. Understood?"

"Yes, ma'am."

"Good. Hello, Bay." Lavinia turned her attention at last to me. "Thank you for coming."

"Yes, thanks a lot, Bay. We appreciate it."

Thaddeus extended a big brown hand that swallowed up my thin, white one. He could have been an athlete, like his son, but his interests had always lain elsewhere. I remembered his spending a lot of time in the Judge's library, his nose planted firmly in a book. He should have gone to college. I know my father had offered to help with the cost. But Thaddeus had settled for a civil service job and marriage to a woman who, while pretty enough in the fresh bloom of her youth, had very little interest in anything more literary than the *National Enquirer*.

"You're welcome, Thad. You know, if the Judge were able, he'd have been here himself."

"I know that. Always been real good to our family, the Judge has. And Miz Simpson, too," he added quickly. My mother would have been furious to be considered merely an afterthought to her socially inferior husband.

"Thad, I got to get to work." Colletta Smalls plucked at her husband's sleeve. Her only greeting to me had been a shy bob of her head.

"So what's the story? Have they released him?"

Isaiah had retreated to the low curb of the semi-circular drive. He sat hunched over, elbows on knees, staring at the ground.

"For the time being. But it's not over. Don't any of you fool yourselves into thinking that it is." Lavinia's frankness was another remembered trait. I had never asked for her opinion unless I was prepared to hear the bald truth as she saw it.

Thaddeus Smalls winced at his mother's harsh words. He wanted desperately to believe their lives could now get back to normal.

"We've got to get the boy over to the school, Mama. And ourselves back to work. What time should we be at Aunt Mavis's?"

"I think it's best to just leave that be for tonight. Under the circumstances. I'll let you know about the funeral. They haven't released Derek . . . Derek's . . . body yet."

The full force of her pain resonated in that one word—*body*. A nephew dead and a grandson suspected. I moved closer to her, filled with an unfamiliar need to offer protection to the woman who had always protected me.

Isaiah leaped to his feet.

"I didn't do it! I didn't kill Derek, Granmama, I swear to God I didn't! I couldn't! You know I couldn't!"

His muscled shoulders shook, and tears spilled over the bruises on his smooth brown cheeks. He looked like what we had all forgotten he really was: a scared boy in a man's body.

Lavinia took his anguished face in her wrinkled hands and gently wiped away his tears. The gesture brought a vivid flashback of skinned knees and other, more subtle pain soothed away by those same tender fingers.

"Of course you didn't, my sweet baby. We all know that."

The uncharacteristic softness of her voice held us all spellbound. Then the old, autocratic Lavinia re-emerged, and we were back on familiar ground.

"Go on, then, all of you. Be about your business. I'll call you later."

"Okay, Mama." Thaddeus brushed his mother's cheek in a hasty kiss, nodded to me, and led his family toward the parking lot. His awkward attempt to put a comforting arm around his son's shoulder was shrugged off impatiently. Apparently the little boy had retreated behind the bravado of the teenager.

"Buy you a coffee?" I asked as Lavinia removed a ring of keys from her navy blue handbag. I wanted details, and I didn't think standing in the shadow of the detention center was a good place to discuss murder and its aftermath. Although sleek and modern, the place still gave me the creeps.

"I really should check on the Judge."

"He's fine. Dolores is with him."

I recognized the tightening of Lavinia's jaw. The news did not reassure her.

"I hope she doesn't try to feed him any of that spicy, Mexican food. His stomach won't tolerate it. He has very particular tastes. We discuss the next week's menu every Saturday, before I do the shopping. Maybe I should call and—"

"They'll be fine, Lavinia. At least for a couple of days," I added, knowing how proprietary she was about the Judge. "And Dolores is Guatemalan, not Mexican."

Lavinia snorted, unconvinced.

We all have our prejudices, I thought.

We crossed the road together, the older woman matching me stride for stride. We were almost the same height. I was never quite sure just how old she really was, but simple math told me she had to be well into her sixties. She was trim and straight, her tight, gray curls clipped close to her head. Her coffee-colored skin had once led my mother to speculate that Lavinia's father must have been white, since both her younger half-sisters, Mavis and Chloe, were a deep, rich brown.

"The Fig Tree?" she asked as we approached my convertible. The little cafe on the waterfront had been a favorite haunt of the Judge's before his stroke.

"Fine. Meet you there."

A remarkable woman, I thought as I turned the key in the ignition. Like Thaddeus, I, too, wanted to believe this was the end of their troubles. But Lavinia was convinced that it wasn't, and I wanted to know why.

We just managed to beat the local lunch crowd, swelled as usual today by the ever-present mob of tourists. Lavinia had commandeered the last table on the outside deck overlooking the park and the sparkling Beaufort River. I ordered iced tea on my way through the cool, dark bar area and joined her under the welcome shade of the striped awning. Lavinia sipped sweet, black coffee.

In the harsh glare of the noonday sun reflecting off the placid blue water, she looked old.

"Tell me," I said brusquely. She would no more welcome sugar-coating in my questions than I would expect any in her answers.

With a swift glance around to be certain she couldn't be overheard, Lavinia gave me what details she had. According to Isaiah, after his confrontation with Derek he had left football practice and driven home in his beat-up Chevy Nova. He had showered, changed, and packed up his camping gear. He left a hastily scribbled note saying he was going fishing with some friends and would be home by the weekend.

It wasn't until late the next afternoon, when a Beaufort County Sheriff's deputy approached her in the SAV-MOR, that Colletta became aware that her son was in trouble. It was also the first she or her husband had heard of the fight or of its possible connection to Derek's death.

The Smalls had begun calling everyone they could think of that Isaiah might have gone off with. They hit paydirt with CJ Elliott.

Bitsy's son! Was that why she had been trying so frantically to reach me last night?

CJ had told his mother a similar story. Practice had been suspended for the rest of the week while the coaches attended meetings. CJ, the star quarterback, and Isaiah, his favorite wide receiver, had been friends since a love for sports and an uncanny knack for anticipating each other's moves had made them a tandem to be reckoned with in area high school football. They hoped to attend college together, both counting on athletic scholarships to help their families with the expense.

A sheriff's deputy had spotted Isaiah's Chevy in the early hours of the morning. A few hundred yards away he had come upon the boys, wrapped in sleeping bags alongside the river, less than a mile from where Derek's body had washed up.

"So they alibied each other," I said as Lavinia accepted a refill from a harried waitress, then emptied three blue packets into the steaming cup. The thought of all that sweetness set my teeth on edge. "That's good, isn't it?"

"Or were in it together. That's what those detectives seemed to be implying. They questioned them separately, but both boys stuck to their stories. Denied knowing anything about it, said they were just fishing and didn't see or hear anything. Mr. Elliott's lawyer had his son out of there inside of an hour. It took Mander Brown a little longer, but they eventually had to let Isaiah go, too."

The restaurant was emptying out now, only a few businessmen in dress shirts and loosened ties still lingering over their lunches.

"So why are you being so pessimistic? The police obviously don't have anything concrete, or they wouldn't have let them walk."

"Mander said they have to tread carefully because they're only sixteen and still legally juveniles. But they told both boys to stay close to home and to be available in case they had more questions."

"That sounds pretty standard to me."

"Listen, Bay, I've lived a long time in this town. And all my life in the South. Maybe things have changed on the surface, but underneath . . . Well, let's just say I won't rest easy until whoever really killed my nephew is locked up for good."

"Do they have any other suspects?" I asked as Lavinia fumbled again for her keys.

"Not that anyone's tellin' *me* about. I thought maybe the Judge . . ."

She let the sentence hang expectantly between us. For the first time that I could remember, I saw fear in her fearsome black eyes.

"He'll have been on the phone all morning, calling in markers. If there's any inside information to be had, he'll get it."

Lavinia rose and smoothed out the creases in the skirt of her best navy blue suit.

"You'll be at Mavis's?" I asked, realizing what an awkward position she was in. One member of her family was suspected of killing another. I wondered how Mavis, the dead boy's mother, was dealing with it.

"Yes, I expect I will. For a couple of days, anyway. She's not handling it too well," Lavinia said, answering my unspoken question.

From what I remembered of Mavis Johnson, that probably meant hitting the bottle pretty hard.

"You take care now, hear?" I said.

"You, too. And thanks for coming down." She paused awkwardly. "It was kind of you."

Being obligated to anyone did not sit well with Lavinia Smalls. That brief expression of gratitude cost her some effort. I watched her walk away toward the esplanade, her proud carriage mirroring her inner strength. I had been fortunate to have her as a role model in my growing up.

So, I said to myself as I lit a cigarette and leaned back in my chair, *here I am, all dressed up and no place to go.*

Of course I was glad that my services as bail bondsman had not been required. Yet there was a part of me that was a little disappointed. I had come prepared to do battle in a just cause, only to find that the enemy had surrendered without a shot having been fired. I could feel the old, familiar lethargy seeping back into my bones.

I'd leave Dolores with the Judge and get on back to the beach. Everything was under control here. CJ Elliott and Isaiah Smalls had competent counsel and caring families. Besides, it was ridiculous to think that either one of them had been in any way involved in the murder of Derek Johnson.

I smiled at the waitress who filled up my iced tea glass and waved away her offer of a menu.

Maybe the coroner had jumped the gun. Who was to say for certain it even *was* a murder? Maybe Derek had been drunk. He was, after all, Mavis's son. Maybe he'd stumbled into the river and hit his head on a rock. Maybe . . .

The hand that fell heavily on my left shoulder made me wince. The mangled skin there was still tender.

"Now, just give me a peek at those gorgeous green eyes, and I'll know for sure this is who I think it is," a voice boomed behind me. I recognized the wheezing drawl immediately.

I gave a fleeting thought to pressing the lighted end of my cigarette into the pudgy fingers splayed across my injured shoulder. When their owner lumbered around to face me, my worst fears were confirmed.

"I knew it! I said to the boys, I said 'That there's ol' Tally Simpson's gal, settin' there with that nigra woman.' And, sure enough, here you are!"

"Unfortunately." I tried to put as much of my distaste for the man into that one word as I could. I knew, however, from long experience, that he was impervious to insult.

"Mind if I join you?" He didn't wait for permission, but pulled out the chair Lavinia had just vacated and flopped his considerable bulk down across the table from me. "My, my. Just look at you. Your mama was a looker, but she couldn't hold a candle to you, sugar, no siree. Not on her best day."

He raised a fat, stubby finger, and a waitress materialized out of nowhere. "Another gin, honey, and bring the lady whatever she's drinkin'."

He beamed at me, his porky little eyes dancing. His thin, delicate lips were almost lost in quivering jowls that hung in loose folds nearly to his neck. As a teenager I had called him the Pig Man. My father had reproved me while suppressing a smile.

Hadley Bolles. Sometime politician, real estate broker, attorney. Rumor had it that if there was a deal going down anywhere in the county, Hadley was sure to have a hand in it. He proudly referred to himself as a "facilitator".

His beltless tan trousers strained across a vast expanse of ample belly, and wide sweat rings stained his rumpled white shirt. His trademark red bowtie hung slightly askew, like a bright poppy wilted in the heat. His patterned suspenders and exaggerated Southern drawl were straight out of Tennessee Williams.

The Judge tolerated him. I loathed the ground he waddled on.

"Is there a point to this, Hadley, or are you just table crawling?" I lit another cigarette and exhaled the smoke directly into his face. "If you're running for something, I'm voting for your opponent, whoever it is."

His laugh, in contrast to his voice, was high-pitched and feminine, almost a giggle. "You not only got your mama's face, darlin', you got her mouth, too. That woman could flat out cut a man to ribbons when she put her mind to it."

"Why, thank you. I do my best to carry on the old family traditions."

"In the case of your mama, I wouldn't try too hard, sugar. She had a few other habits it wouldn't do for a sweet young thing like you to pick up on."

Bastard!

"Don't let me keep you, Hadley," I sneered. "I'm sure you have some land to despoil or a commissioner to bribe."

Just for a moment Hadley Bolles let his mask of honeyed amiability slip, and the chilling combination of hatred and lust that glowed in the depths of his piggy little eyes sent a current of fear racing up my back. Then it was gone, so fast and so completely I might almost have imagined it.

I hastily crushed out my cigarette, ripped a ten from my wallet, and flung it on the table as I pushed back my chair.

Hadley rose with me, shaking his head as one might over the antics of a naughty child. Then his attention was caught by something over my shoulder.

"Catch up with you boys later," he called, gesturing toward the dim recesses of the bar.

I turned in time to see the retreating back of a medium-sized man in a wrinkled white suit making his way toward the front entrance of the Fig Tree. I had a brief impression of long, oily black hair and an obscenely large diamond sparkling against the olive skin of a hand raised in acknowledgment.

Then the doorway was filled with the broad shoulders of one of the most devastatingly handsome men I had ever seen. He was tall, probably six-foot-three at least, and he wore his khaki summer suit and pale blue, button-down collar shirt with casual elegance. His hair, combed smoothly from a high part, was mostly silver with just a few strands of its original dark brown still showing through. He reached a sun-browned hand up to shade his blue eyes from the glare off the river, and I realized with a start who he was.

My heart turned sixth-grade flip-flops, even though he was out of uniform.

He recognized me at the same moment.

If it had been night time, the sparks that flew between us would have been visible to the naked eye.

Hadley Bolles stood ignored, his head swiveling back and forth between the two of us. "Well, now, what have we here?" I heard him murmur as Geoffrey Anderson crossed the short space between us and took both my hands in his.

CHAPTER
FIVE

"Bay? Is that really you? My God, you went and got gorgeous on me!"

"You didn't turn out so bad yourself," I laughed, stepping back from the intensity in his eyes.

Geoff's answering smile brought back memories of hazy Charleston afternoons, heat rising in waves from the parade ground of the Citadel, as the cadets marched in precise formation. My father, a proud alumnus, had been delighted to introduce his daughter to the storied rituals of the military academy, while at the same time regretting that she could never follow in his footsteps. Now that women had been reluctantly admitted to the once all-male bastion, the Judge was torn between bemoaning the loss of a sacred tradition and wishing it had happened in time for me.

"So y'all know each other already, do you? I don't even get the pleasure of playin' matchmaker?" Hadley insinuated himself between us, and his snide voice dripped with innuendo. "The dashing Lawyer Anderson and the delicious Widow Tanner. Y'all better be careful. It's a small town. Tongues will wag."

"Nice to see you, Hadley. You take care now." Geoff, towering over the fat little weasel, made him seem more ludicrous now than menacing.

Hadley Bolles, totally unaccustomed to being summarily dismissed, covered his anger well. With a knowing leer and a grunt of effort, he turned and waddled off toward the river. Within only a few steps, he had gathered a small group of sycophants around him. His absurd, lilting laugh floated back to us on a welcome breeze as he patted the shoulder of a hopeful favor-seeker.

"I used to call him the Pig Man when I was a kid," I said, breaking what was becoming an awkward silence.

Geoff laughed as he pulled out my chair, then folded himself into the one across the table. "You always were a mouthy little thing, as I recall. It was one of your more endearing qualities."

"I don't know how you figure that. I seem to remember being totally tongue-tied whenever you were around."

"Tongue-tied? You? Not the skinny little tomboy I'm thinking of. I'm talking about the one who always had a bandage stuck on an elbow or a knee, and who followed me around asking a zillion questions whenever I brought my mother over to visit."

I couldn't control the blush that spread across my cheeks. I had been certain the boy-man I'd idolized hadn't even known I existed.

Geoff smiled sweetly and covered my hand with his own. "I'm embarrassing you, aren't I?"

"Just a little."

"Sorry. I'm just so damn glad to see you. I don't even want to think about how many years it's been."

"It has to be twenty-five, or close to it. You went on to law school right out of the Citadel, didn't you? Someplace up north?"

"Yale. Had to follow in my daddy's footsteps, didn't I? That's how it's done around here." A note of bitterness had crept into his voice, and I wondered what he would rather have done with his life. "Hadley called you the Widow Tanner," he went on. "That wasn't your husband in that plane bombing last year, was it?"

I hated talking about Rob's death, especially all the gruesome details that seemed to fascinate people despite their pretended horror. But somehow I found it easy telling Geoff everything, from witnessing the explosion, to my disfiguring injuries, to my gnawing frustration that no one had yet been made to pay. As I talked, his hand tightened around mine, his thumb gently stroking the deep ridge left by my wedding band. He didn't speak, didn't interrupt, just stared intently into my eyes as if trying to absorb the pain into himself. When at last I fell silent, Geoff handed me a clean linen handkerchief, and I wiped away the few tears that, despite all my efforts, had managed to slip down my cheeks.

He never let go of my hand.

And I, who had been virtually untouchable for almost a year, felt comforted by the contact.

"I'm so terribly sorry, Bay. My God, it's a miracle you survived." He paused, giving me a chance to get myself under control. "Did you love him very much?"

I should have been offended, but somehow I wasn't. "Yes, I did. We never had any children, so we were all each other had."

"He sounds like a special kind of man."

"He was. You would have liked each other."

"Probably. But then I might have resented him when I realized what a beauty my little tomboy had turned into, and that he'd stolen her right out from under my nose."

I welcomed the lightening of our somber mood, and suddenly realized that I was ravenously hungry. We ordered a pound of local shrimp, boiled in the shell, with crusty sourdough rolls still warm from the oven.

We peeled shrimp, dipped them in spicy hot sauce, and talked. Or rather, Geoff talked this time while I attacked the food, pausing only long enough to ask an occasional question. I learned of his two marriages, both ending in divorce, his two sons, both living now with his ex-wives, and his disillusionment with life in south Florida. Estranged from his parents over his decision to set up practice in Miami with two fellow Yale graduates, he had come home when his father's failing health had become too great a burden for his mother to carry alone.

"We eventually had to put him in a home. Alzheimer's or senile dementia, they're not sure which. Either way, he's basically lost his mind." Geoff shook his head sadly. "God, if I ever get like that, I hope someone shoots me. It's not fair when the child has to become the caretaker of a parent. But then, I guess you know something about that, huh? The Judge's strokes, and all."

It was my turn to offer comfort. It seemed so natural, my hand in his.

It wasn't until people began to drift onto the deck and the noise level in the bar rose a few decibels that I thought to look at my watch.

Ten past five! This was the after-work crowd beginning to gather.

"Geoff, I can't believe the time. I have to get home. I mean, back to the Judge's. I'm staying there for a few days. Because of Lavinia's nephew . . . and her grandson's being arrested . . . Well, not exactly arrested, but . . . Oh, I don't have time to tell you the whole story now. The Judge will throttle me for not reporting in."

I was frantically stuffing cigarettes and lighter into my bag and groping for car keys when Geoff reached across the table and gently touched the corner of my mouth. The gesture, so strangely intimate, stopped me in my tracks.

"Shrimp sauce," he said, wiping his fingers on a napkin.

"Oh, God," I groaned, grabbing my own crumpled, messy ball of paper and dragging it across my face.

Geoff's grin was infectious, and in a second we were both laughing uncontrollably.

"You can tell me all about it tonight over dinner," he gasped, catching his breath. "I'll pick you up around nine."

"I don't know, Geoff. I mean, I'd love to, but the Judge . . ."

"Will be glad to see you out enjoying yourself. I'll come a little early, and he and I can swap Citadel stories over a glass of that Kentucky bourbon he's famous for." His smile faded, replaced by an appealing earnestness I couldn't resist. "Say yes, Bay. Please?"

"Yes," I answered, for once acting on impulse instead of weighing the pros and cons of my decision. "Yes. Nine o'clock."

Geoff gave my hand a squeeze as I reluctantly disengaged my fingers and ran lightly down the steps toward the river. I turned once, sure I would find his eyes still on me. He raised his hand, and I could feel the warmth of his gaze follow me all the way down the walkway to my car.

Lydia Baynard Simpson Tanner, what the hell do you think you're doing? I asked myself as I gunned the LeBaron onto the bridge and headed for Presqu'isle. Barely five minutes had passed since I'd accepted a *date*, and already my feet were beginning to ice over.

I had misjudged my father's reaction to my being late. He wasn't upset. He was in a towering rage. He treated me to the kind of tongue-lashing I used to get from my mother when I had committed some social gaffe and embarrassed her in front of her friends. Funny, but I remembered the Judge's taking refuge in his study whenever she launched into one of her tirades. He must have been paying closer attention than I realized.

I let him rail at me as Dolores carried a tray of iced tea and lemonade into his room, left it on the antique cherry coffee table, and scurried off.

I was selfish, ungrateful, inconsiderate. I had no idea what it was like to be stuck in a wheelchair, cut off from the action, always having to rely on others to be your legs, your eyes. I poured my accuser a tall glass of lemonade, added ice, and crossed to the sideboard that served as the drinks cupboard to splash in a generous tot of bourbon before placing it in front of him. A weird combination, but his drink of choice.

I was only half-listening to his enumeration of my shortcomings as a daughter, not to mention my utter uselessness as his surrogate. I was vacillating between trying to decide what to wear and trying to figure out how to get out of going at all; between calculating whether or not I had time to drive back to Hilton Head to raid my little-used closet, or calling Geoff to plead a sudden recurrence of malaria.

My father was winding down. I knew he was getting desperate when he started bringing up things I'd done to aggravate him when I was twelve. Besides, the fact that I refused to defend myself was taking a lot of the sport out of it for him. I knew I had been thoughtless in not calling to let him know about Isaiah's release. But it certainly didn't warrant this kind of virulent attack. I knew it was mostly his frustration talking, probably not all that much to do with me. And he was entitled. Up to a point.

I went to his dresser—a tall, beautifully carved cherry highboy—and opened the third drawer from the top. My fingers closed around a slim, wooden case hidden beneath a neatly folded pile of pajamas and handkerchiefs. Turning, I flipped it open, offering my father one of his treasured Cuban cigars.

"Better get in touch with Eddie, or whoever's acting as your procurement officer these days," I said, flicking the crystal desk lighter into flame. "Your supply is running low."

The Judge clipped the end from the panatela, sniffed the rich aroma of the tobacco leaf wrapper, and allowed me to hold the lighter as he rolled the cigar in the flame until it was glowing brightly. He refused to give me the satisfaction of asking how I knew where he kept his stash. I lit a cigarette, and we sipped and smoked in companionable silence.

My father offered me no apology for his tirade; but then, I didn't expect one. My own had been made in the form of bourbon and tobacco.

"Vinnie okay?" he finally asked. He avoided my eyes by studying the cloud of blue smoke that rose above his head.

"She seemed to be," I answered in the same calm tone of voice. "She's feeling better about it now that Isaiah's out of jail, but she tossed around some pretty broad hints that he could still get railroaded. The South being what it is, and all."

"That's a load of crap, and she knows it. It's just the stress talking."

"Well, what would really help is another viable suspect."

"Of which there are none, according to Redmond." The Judge tapped ash from his cigar into a cutglass bowl, an heirloom wedding gift from some Baynard cousin or other. I could hear my mother spinning in her grave. "He called this afternoon, looking for you. Said he might stop by later."

His disapproval was evident in his voice, as well as in the lowering of his bushy white eyebrows.

"I ran into Geoff Anderson in town today," I said by way of changing the subject. "We're having dinner tonight, so I'd better get changed."

That got his attention. He took a long swig of bourbon-flavored lemonade. "Business or pleasure?" he asked.

"And what's that supposed to mean?" I snapped, bristling at the smug, know-it-all smile that had replaced the fatherly frown.

"It means, is this a *date* or did you set it up so you could pump the poor boy for information about the Race?"

It wasn't that I had *entirely* forgotten my mission on behalf of Miss Addie. It was just that an afternoon spent in a mutual baring of souls with the alleged perpetrator had softened my suspicion somewhat. I couldn't imagine those intense blue eyes hiding the heart of a con man.

"I'm sure the subject will come up," I said loftily as I gathered my things and headed for the hallway. "I need to let Dolores know I won't be home for dinner."

My father's laugh followed me out of the room. "Hope those two boys don't both show up at the same time. I'm too damned old to be breakin' up fistfights in the parlor."

If there had been a door handy, I would have slammed it.

CHAPTER
SIX

By eleven-thirty, Geoff and I sat alone in the deserted dining room of the popular local seafood restaurant overlooking the Broad River. Judging from the noise level, the bar, however, was still doing a brisk business. I could hear the Braves' play-by-play announcer railing against a questionable call in favor of the Dodgers. Sliding doors stood open wide toward the water, and the soft, heavy stillness of the humid night air was punctuated by alternate cheers and groans from the Atlanta faithful.

We had dined leisurely on sea scallops and scampi, both broiled to perfection in white wine and garlic butter over angel hair pasta. I declined dessert, settling for hot tea and a cigarette.

"Your brother-in-law didn't seem particularly thrilled to meet me," Geoff remarked around a mouthful of hot apple tart dripping with melting vanilla ice cream and caramel. "I hope I didn't step on anyone's toes."

Temptation got the better of resolve—a recurring theme in my life lately—and I swiped a spoonful of warm apples.

"*Mmm*. That's heavenly."

Geoff moved the bowl closer to me, and we polished it off in a few more bites.

"Red just worries about me, that's all," I said. "He's big on family responsibility."

"Trust me, his interest is not brotherly."

I turned away from him toward the open doors. I watched as a late night fisherman chugged toward home, the lights of his small boat dancing on the black plane of the water.

"I've made you angry," he said softly. "I'm sorry."

"It's okay. I guess I'm just touchy about Red. He's been through a lot lately—the divorce and then Rob's dying. He's been a good friend to me."

What really gnawed at me was that Geoff was probably right. I had been trying to forget the look of longing I had seen on Red's face yesterday, the schoolboy awkwardness as he asked if he could call me. The fact that I didn't *want* him to feel that way about me wouldn't change anything. And blaming Geoff for pointing it out wouldn't either.

I turned back to find him regarding me anxiously, his eyes full of unasked questions. His face was already becoming familiar to me: the way the light played on his silver hair, the slight bump on his otherwise patrician nose. I hadn't felt this way about anyone since Rob and I had locked eyes across a banquet table at a noisy Chamber of Commerce dinner in Charleston almost fourteen years ago. Corny as it sounds, I had not really looked at another man in all that time.

Geoff had already stirred up feelings I didn't want to examine too closely. I had no interest in any kind of romantic involvement—with him or anyone else. What Rob and I had was a once-in-a-lifetime thing. Trying to duplicate it would only lead to disappointment and more pain.

Keep telling yourself that, Tanner, I admonished myself as Geoff signed the credit card receipt and reached for my hand.

"How about a walk by the water?"

We strolled out onto the boardwalk, our arms occasionally brushing as we left the lights of the restaurant behind. A sharp, dank odor, peculiar to the Lowcountry marshland, rose from the reeds and grasses along the bank as we moved farther away from the docks.

"God, I missed that smell." Geoff paused to stand gazing out across the placid water as he sniffed the air. "I'm going to build my house right on the river, so I can sit out on the porch and feel as if I'm on a boat, right out in the middle of it."

"Which river?" I asked. No sense letting a perfectly good opening like that slip by. Besides, it would be nice to get my amateur sleuthing out of the way, to discharge my responsibility to Miss Addie. That would leave us free for . . . well, for whatever was coming next.

Geoff turned from his contemplation of the water and reclaimed my hand. He tucked it protectively into the crook of my arm, and we resumed our aimless walk along the shore.

"The Chicopee, of course. Can you think of a more beautiful

spot? Actually, it's the old Grayton plantation. We're going to re-store the main house, develop the rest. I staked out my lot the first time I walked the property. Lots of live oaks, some pines, and a gradual slope down to the river. I'm going to build on the rise."

Even in the dim light of a quarter moon I could see the enthu-siasm in his eyes, sense it in his voice. We came to a wooden bench set alongside the path by the local Audubon Society and settled onto it, our attention fixed on the small chirps and rustles of the nighttime residents of the marsh.

"Wait 'til you see it, Bay," Geoff went on. "It's going to be the finest development this county has ever seen." His arm along the back of the bench moved to encircle my shoulder. His touch warmed me, as if he had absorbed the heat from this afternoon's sun and was radiating it back to me now in the cooling night air.

"Who's 'we'?" I asked, settling comfortably into his casual em-brace.

"Well, we have several investors, aside from the original part-ners. Mostly local folks, or so I'm told. I don't really get into that part of it, except for a couple of presentations I made early on. You know how it goes," he said, easing me closer while his hand absently stroked my bare arm. "My family's well known in the area. Makes people feel more secure when there's a local connec-tion."

It was a jarring note in an otherwise straightforward narrative. I sat up, putting a little distance between us. Geoff sensed the withdrawal was more than physical.

"What?" he asked, concern tingeing his voice.

"I don't know, you make it sound as if you let them believe something that wasn't quite true. Like you were some kind of front man or something. How exactly *are* you involved?"

"There's no mystery here, Bay, nothing sinister, if that's what you're implying. I found the property; I put the deal together. I got some of my contacts in Miami interested, set up the corpora-tion. It's a good, sound investment. Plus we're restoring a part of our heritage that might otherwise be left to fall into total ruin." Geoff laid a finger against my cheek and gently turned my head until I faced him. "You sound concerned. Is this more than just idle curiosity?"

I stood abruptly, fumbling in the pocket of my slacks for a cigarette. It was all perfectly plausible, the kind of deal that went down every day in any rapidly growing resort area like ours. There was just something about Geoff's recitation, smooth and polished, as if he'd said it all before, in exactly the same words.

I waited for him to mention my father's involvement, the investment I knew he could ill afford. He didn't.

"I heard you had a roadblock," I said, looking out over the water. "A property owner who won't sell."

Geoff was instantly alert. "Where'd you hear that?"

"Around," I hedged. "Is it true?"

"I'm getting a little confused here. What exactly is it you're accusing me of? Grayton's Race is just what it appears to be—a legitimate investment with solid backers and more than adequate funding. What more can I say?"

"So there's no truth to the rumors? About the possibility of the whole thing going sour?"

Why the hell doesn't he say something about the Judge? Surely he knows?

"Jesus, you're not going to let this go, are you?"

"Why don't you just answer the question?" I asked as I turned slowly to face him.

I flinched at the deep sadness I saw in his eyes.

"I guess I was wrong, but I thought there was something happening here, Bay. Something good between us."

I looked back toward the river, away from the need I saw etched so clearly on his troubled face

"Am I wrong then? Did I misread you so completely?" His voice, full of pain and soft as a caress, floated over me like a gentle breeze.

Deep inside me, unbidden and unwanted, something stirred. Viciously, I pushed it back down and whirled to face him.

"Look, Geoff, I asked a simple question about your business venture, and I don't understand why you refuse to answer it." Anger—at myself, at him, at the whole damn situation—made me stumble over my next words. "And yes, I thought something was happening between us, too, though God knows I'm not ready for it. Maybe I'll never be ready. Maybe I don't even want . . ."

I could feel tears pooling behind my eyes.

You will not cry, I ordered myself. *You. Will. Not. Cry.*

I drew a deep breath, and exhaled the anger and tears along with it.

"But I'll tell you this, Geoff," I said softly. "If you can't be honest with me about something as trivial as this, then whatever is beginning will end, right here."

For a long moment we stared into each other's eyes. Then a great white heron rose majestically from the marsh, the beating of its wings sending ripples of sound across the black, humid night. We turned in unison to watch its graceful glide as it caught a warm updraft and floated away, toward the sea.

"Fair enough." Geoff's voice echoed in the empty darkness. He held out his hand to me, palm up, a gesture that seemed part supplication, part surrender. "But you're shivering, darling. Here, come sit down and let me warm you up. And we'll talk."

His smile, so sweet and open, the casual endearment, touched that place within me I had thought dead on the tarmac of a country airstrip. For a moment, I wavered. Then, seemingly without conscious thought, I crossed the space between us and laid my hand in his.

My body had made the decision for me. I settled into the warmth of his arms.

We sat like that for a long while, my head resting on Geoff's shoulder. I could feel his warm breath ruffling my hair, feel the pulse in his throat beating steadily against my cheek. A watershed had been crossed tonight, and it seemed only right to be still and savor it.

Geoff moved first, sighing as he set me upright and removed his arm from around my shoulder. "Okay," he said, the boyish grin I remembered from my childhood back on his face. "Now that we've got *that* settled, it's time for me to keep my end of the bargain."

I ran a hand through my rumpled hair and dug the crinkled pack of cigarettes out of my pocket.

"Here, give me those."

Puzzled, I handed them and my lighter over to Geoff. He fumbled around inexpertly, but finally got one going. With a flourish he presented the lighted cigarette to me, filter end first.

"Saw that in an old Cary Grant movie once," he said, his eyes bright with mischief. "I've always wanted to try it."

It was a silly, theatrical gesture. I loved it.

Geoff launched into his explanation with no preliminaries, as if anxious to get it over with. "We did have some trouble with getting title to a piece of land, a vital piece, actually. It had the planned right-of-way for the utilities right smack in the middle of it. We want the Race to be reminiscent of the antebellum South, but I don't think our homeowners want to go back to kerosene lamps and wood stoves."

"Couldn't you go around it, bring the lines in somewhere else?"

"Sure, we could have, but it would have meant redesigning the whole layout, possibly shortening the golf course, or moving the plantation house. Any way you cut it, it would have cost a fortune and set us back months while we waited for new reviews and approvals."

I could see now why rumors of such a holdup would be bad for business. More investors than Miss Addie might have gotten cold feet, wanted out, a domino effect that might have sent the whole project tumbling into collapse.

"Why wouldn't they sell?" I asked, surprised that the planning had gotten to this advanced stage without something as crucial as this having been resolved.

"Initially, it wasn't that they wouldn't. They couldn't." Geoff paused, then dropped the two words that struck fear into the heart of every real estate developer in the Lowcountry. "Heirs property."

When the Union naval forces emerged victorious from the Battle of Port Royal in early November, 1861, the white population of Beaufort, Hilton Head, St. Helena, and the surrounding area fled inland, abandoning their plantations—and their slaves— to the triumphant invaders. The government in Washington, D.C. promptly confiscated this immensely rich farmland (for back taxes, they said, although the rightful owners were never given an opportunity to pay up). Much of it was sold at auction for an average ninety-three cents an acre. Many freed blacks, aided by abolitionist groups in the north, became landowners.

Over the next century, many of these parcels were divided, subdivided, willed in fractional shares to children, grandchildren, their children, and so on until no one individual had clear title to any specific plot.

The Judge had explained it all to me when he had been in-volved in trying to probate a will for one of his black clients many years ago, at a time when he was certain I was going to follow him into the law.

"Couldn't you clear it at sheriff's sale?" I asked. Geoff nodded approvingly, as if I had passed a test.

The practice was for whichever member of the family was paying the property taxes to let them lapse. Then, when the land was certified for auction by the county treasurer, it would be declared "heirs" property. Other potential bidders would back off, leaving the family representative to buy it for the back taxes and secure title. Problem solved. At least I was pretty sure that was how the process went.

I gave a Geoff a quick synopsis, and again he beamed his ap-proval.

"Want a job? You've just summarized in thirty seconds what it took a team of attorneys three weeks and a forty-page brief to explain."

"Don't be so hard on your profession," I quipped. "I never knew a lawyer yet who could do things the easy way."

"*Former* profession," Geoff laughed and helped me to my feet. "We'd better head back, don't you think? I'd hate to find the Judge waiting for us with a shotgun resting across his knees."

"So what happened with your heirs property?" I asked as we strolled along the boardwalk, holding hands like a pair of teen-agers.

"We didn't have to go to sheriff's sale because this was a fairly neat one. Only five parties, and three of them were local. We had tracked them all down, and they'd signed off, all except one, but he was committed. Just had to get him in to do the actual sign-ing."

We reached the parking lot, and Geoff paused to open the passenger door of his black Jaguar XJS. I slid into the leather bucket seat as he moved behind the wheel.

"Want the top down, or will you be cold?"

"It's definitely a top-down night. If my teeth start to chatter, we can always turn on the heater."

Geoff resumed as soon as we were underway. "Anyway, we

think one of the sleazier members of my former profession latched onto the guy and convinced him to hold out. We assume they wanted to up the price, although what we had agreed on with the others was more than generous. I figure it was the lawyer who leaked it, hoping to put pressure on us to raise the ante. No doubt he had cut himself in for a healthy percentage of whatever the new price turned out to be."

"Sounds like one of Hadley's stunts," I remarked, recalling the thinly veiled animosity I had sensed when the two men had confronted each other earlier in the day.

"Give the little lady a prize."

The wind whipped my hair as the sleek convertible sped along the deserted highway. I loved this feeling of freedom, of being disconnected somehow from the rest of the world, with only a thin slice of moon and a zillion winking stars to light our way.

"But don't quote me on that," Geoff added as he reached over to caress my arm where it lay against the console between us. "I don't have any real proof, and it would be just like the bastard to sue me for slander."

"So what happened?" We were almost at Presqu'isle, and I wanted to hear the end of the story so I could report in to Miss Addie and set her mind at ease.

"Well, it's a good news-bad news kind of thing. The guy . . . died a few days ago. His share passes to his mother who has already signed. So . . . we're back in business."

Geoff took the turn into the driveway too fast and braked to a skidding halt in front of the long stairway, gravel from under the Jag's tires spewing out onto the lawn. Before he could get out, I opened my own door and paused, one foot on the dew-damp grass.

"Call me?" I felt awkward, like the infatuated adolescent I had been the last time Geoff and I had spent so much time together.

"Every hour on the hour, if you think the Judge won't mind the racket."

I laughed, a carefree sound that surprised even me. I was remembering what it was like to be happy. "Don't get out. It's late. I can find my way home from here."

"No goodnight kiss, huh?"

"Not on the first date. I'm not that kind of girl."

Geoff lifted my hand from where it rested on the console and gently pressed his lips against my palm.

"We'll have to work on that. Goodnight, Bay. Sleep well."

"You, too."

I stopped halfway up the steps and watched until the black Jaguar was swallowed up by the night.

The grandfather clock in the parlor struck three as I locked the front door behind me and walked dreamily toward the staircase. The note was taped to the carved newel post at the end of the polished oak banister, just at eye level for someone in a wheelchair. A quotation: *"Be wise with speed. A fool at forty is a fool indeed."*

That little gem was followed by an original admonition, "Don't sleep late. We need to talk."

My first reaction was to rip the damned thing into little pieces and scatter them all over the heart pine floor where my father would be sure to roll over them first thing in the morning. Instead, I grabbed a pen from the hall table and added my own quotation, an appropriate line from the French fablist, La Rochefoucauld: "Old people like to give good advice, as solace for no longer being able to provide bad examples." And my own postscript: "Mind your own business!"

I stayed awake just long enough to peel off my clothes and crawl beneath the cool sheets. For the first time in months, I couldn't remember my dreams.

CHAPTER
SEVEN

I slept through breakfast but managed to be showered and dressed in time for lunch. I slid into a chair at the kitchen table just as Dolores began ladling steamy fish chowder into earthenware bowls. Although it smelled wonderful, it was not my idea of what to put in an empty stomach. I settled for a buttered sweet-potato roll, one of Dolores's specialties, and a glass of iced tea.

The sky outside the mullioned window over the sink had turned gray and lowering. Black clouds hovered on the horizon. I could hear the slap of the Sound against the pilings of the dock at the back of the property as the wind kicked up.

"Looks like a storm brewing," I said to Dolores who had gone to stand in the doorway out to the hall. "Maybe it'll cool things off a little."

"Your father, he is very angry," she said, glancing anxiously toward the Judge's study.

"At whom?" I asked, helping myself to another warm roll from the napkin-lined basket, and slathering it with butter.

"He talks all morning on the telephone. He shouts. I hear him, even in the kitchen." Dolores frowned at me over her shoulder. "He says words I do not know. Not nice words, I think."

I laughed, imagining Dolores thumbing through the battered English-Spanish dictionary she carried in her car, searching for the translation of some of my father's more colorful expletives.

"You're probably right. And, trust me, you're better off not knowing."

I rubbed my bare arms against the air-conditioned chill of the old house. My mother had spent a fortune on updating the wiring, plumbing, and heating after she inherited Presqu'isle, humidity control being vital to the well-being of her precious antiques and paintings. I much preferred the feel of soft breezes through open doors and windows, but I hadn't been around to vote.

"Want me to go get him?" I asked. "Before everything gets cold?"

"No, no, *Señora*. He has a visitor. He says, 'Do not disturb'."

I didn't like the pinched look of anxiety on Dolores's normally open face.

"Has he been bullying you? No, don't defend him. He has, I can tell. The ungrateful old coot!" I pushed my chair back and jumped to my feet. "Just because Lavinia is willing to put up with his foul moods is no reason . . ."

Dolores ducked back into the kitchen shaking her head vigorously. "No, *Señora*, is fine. Is no *problema. El Juez* . . ."

Voices drifting up from the back of the house accompanied the soft squeak of motorized wheels on wood floor. I heard my father's booming laugh, followed by a high-pitched giggle that froze me in my tracks.

What the hell was *he* doing here?

I bounded out of the kitchen to confront my father, his hand resting on the polished brass knob of the front door as he prepared to usher out his visitor. Hadley Bolles stopped in mid-waddle as I approached.

"Well, Bay, darlin', what a pleasant surprise. I was just tellin' your daddy what a nice little chat we had yesterday, down at the Fig Tree."

"Lunch is ready," I said, reaching for the handles on the back of the Judge's wheelchair. "Don't let us keep you, Hadley."

My father twisted around to glare at me for that blatant breach of manners. "Care to join us, Hadley?" he asked perversely. His fingers stabbed at the buttons on the armrest in an effort to gain control, but my hands on the chair overrode him.

"Well, now . . ."

I was suddenly conscious of my bare feet, faded red shorts, and the white cotton T-shirt I had thrown on without bothering with a bra. I knew my nipples had to be standing straight out through the thin fabric because Hadley's piggy eyes were fastened on my chest.

". . . depends on what's on the menu," he finished with a nasty little chuckle that made my skin crawl.

"I'm up here, Hadley," I snarled, forcing him to drag his gaze away from my breasts.

The Judge noticed, too. "Another time perhaps," he said stiffly as he pulled the door open wider.

Getting bounced twice in two days couldn't have been a novel experience for someone as obnoxious as Hadley Bolles, but he took this rebuff with less grace than he had Geoff's dismissal of the day before.

"Just remember what I said, Tally," he growled, wagging a thick, well-manicured finger in the Judge's face. He didn't even bother to leer at me as he slapped his stained white fedora onto his head and shuffled across the porch. The first fat drops of rain began to fall as he puffed his way down the steps. I closed the door on the sound of thunder echoing across the open water.

"What the hell was he doing in this house?" I turned and headed down the hallway, not waiting for a reply.

"Business," the Judge said to my retreating back. He rolled behind me into the kitchen and positioned himself at the table.

Dolores had returned the cooling chowder to the kettle, and now began dishing it out again.

"I'll have some, too, please." I flipped the napkin onto my lap and grabbed another roll. What the hell, people ate herring for breakfast, didn't they?

Dolores, who had already eaten, got the Judge settled, then scurried off to check in with her husband. She normally didn't do "overnights", but had made an exception for me in light of Lavinia's trouble and the Judge's special needs. She didn't deserve to be browbeaten for her efforts.

We ate in strained silence for a while, my mind chewing on all the things I wanted to say and knew I shouldn't. The hot soup felt good going down, appropriate somehow with a thunderstorm raging outside. When I had calmed down sufficiently to be pretty sure I wasn't going to bite his head off, I spoke matter-of-factly to the Judge.

"You shouldn't badger Dolores, you know. She's very sensitive, and she's also doing us a tremendous favor. I think you've hurt her feelings."

My father was attempting to butter a roll. I flinched as he tried to anchor it under the rim of his bowl while wielding the knife with his good hand, his face creased in concentration.

How he must hate this, I thought, echoing our conversation of the night before. He was right. I really couldn't imagine what it must be like. I picked up the roll and finished it for him.

"Thanks." He looked at me, a sheepish grin on his lined face. "You're right, of course. I'm just used to Vinnie's ignoring me when I get cranky like this. Don't worry about Dolores. I'll make it right with her."

"Good." The rain had stopped while we ate, and a weak sun was beginning to break through the overcast. "What did Hadley want?" I asked conversationally. I lit a cigarette and leaned back into the swatch of checkered sunlight now falling through the window.

"Actually, I called him. He was in his car, on the island, so he stopped by. Look, honey," the Judge said, patting my hand, "I know he's an odious little man. If I weren't a wasted old hulk, I would have pitched him down the steps for the way he looked at you today."

"Don't worry about it. I can handle the Pig Man."

My father chuckled. "Yes, I guess you can. Lord, but you put me in mind of Emmaline, the way you stood there and faced him down."

"So why did you call him?" I asked, ignoring the reference to my mother. My conversation with Geoff last night jumped unbidden into my head. "Something to do with the Race?"

"No," he barked in exasperation. "Because he knows every damned thing that goes on in this town. I thought he might have heard something about Derek Johnson, something we could use to help Isaiah. It's not looking good for the boy."

I got up to fetch the iced tea pitcher from the refrigerator and refill our glasses. "I don't understand. I thought they released him because he had an alibi. He and CJ Elliott were together."

"So they say. After you left with your old flame last night, Redmond stayed for awhile. It seems the detectives aren't entirely satisfied. They're going to talk to young Cal again, see if they can crack his story."

I was reminded with a jolt that I had never called Bitsy. "They're that certain Isaiah is guilty?"

"Means, motive, and opportunity. He appears to have it all."

"Have they found a weapon yet?"

"No, nothing specific. Redmond said it could have been a

heavy tree limb, tossed into the river along with the body. They may never come up with it."

We sat quietly, both of us contemplating the ramifications of the detectives' having settled on Lavinia's grandson as their prime suspect. There were plenty of stories around about cops who never looked too much farther once they'd made up their minds.

"So was Hadley any help? And what was all that finger-pointing and dire warning business about?"

"Oh, nothing, really." The Judge spooned up the last of his chowder, wiped his mouth, and maneuvered his chair back from the table. "You know how he likes to throw his weight around."

We smiled at each other, both of us thinking the same unkind thoughts.

"I think I'll take a little rest now," my father said, avoiding my eyes as he rolled toward the door. "See you later."

I sat for a moment, my chin resting in my hands, elbows on the table. Something was going on here, some undercurrent I couldn't quite get hold of. The Judge hadn't answered any of my questions directly. In fact, he'd been downright evasive.

I rose and began to clear the table, stacking the bowls and glasses in the dishwasher. Something else was nagging at me, some question I should have asked, had intended to ask, but had gotten sidetracked from. I wasn't even sure who it was I had meant to put it to.

Can brains rust? I wondered as I set the soup kettle in the stainless steel sink and filled it with soapy water to soak. My head had certainly gotten little use in the past few months. Maybe that was why I couldn't drag the niggling thought into focus from the back of my mind.

It would remain stuck there, needling me like an unscratched itch, until it was almost too late.

My conversation with Miss Addie was short and to the point. I relayed Geoff's assurances that the project was progressing on time and added my own that everything about Grayton's Race seemed to be legitimate. She was effusive in her gratitude, and I could hear the genuine relief my news had brought her.

The call to Bitsy Elliott was another story.

Elizabeth Quintard, as she had been in the days of our growing up together, was my antithesis in almost every respect. Petite
—hence her nickname—blonde and blue-eyed, Bitsy was everything my mother had wanted me to be. More than just conven-
tionally pretty, Bitsy had that wholesome, cheerleader freshness
that attracted everyone to her. The most common word used to
describe her had been "sweet".

"Elizabeth is a lady," Emmaline Simpson would announce to
me about a hundred times a day. "Elizabeth knows how to be-
have properly."

It always amazed me, thinking back on it, that we had become
friends in the first place. It was a downright miracle that we had
remained so for over thirty years.

"Bay, honey, thank God!" she exclaimed when we made connections that Saturday afternoon. "I thought you had dropped
right off the face of the earth!"

Bitsy tends to talk like that, in exclamation points.

"Sorry, Bits. It's been kind of a hectic couple of days." I filled
her in on my activities, leaving a few large, intentional gaps
around Geoff Anderson. I wasn't ready to *think* about the implications there, let alone talk about them.

"So you know all about the poor Johnson boy? And Isaiah?
Imagine them thinkin' he could have had anything to do with
such a thing! Ridiculous! I was never so frightened in my entire
life as when a deputy showed up at our door in the dead of night
and told us CJ was in jail! Thank God it's all cleared up now."

Poor Bitsy! I didn't want to be the one to tell her the cops
weren't finished with CJ quite yet.

I was also trying to work out the timing. Her messages had all
been left on my answering machine on Thursday; the boys hadn't
been picked up until early Friday morning. So that couldn't have
been the cause of her tearful urgency.

"So, Bits, what's the problem? Dolores relayed your messages,
and she said you sounded pretty upset."

The pause lasted only a few seconds, but I knew my friend
well enough to be certain that whatever she was about to say was
not going to be the truth. At least, not all of it.

"Oh, you know how I get sometimes, Bay, honey." She kept
her voice light, but an undercurrent of something—fear, anger?—

rippled just below the surface. "Big Cal and I had a little set-to. About money, of all things. He threw a fit over somethin' I bought, but you know I just can't say no when the kids really want something. I just overreacted, that's all. I'm fine now."

"Did he hit you?" I hated asking the question, afraid to hear the answer. But it wouldn't have been the first time "Big" Cal Elliott, former Clemson fullback gone to fat, had smacked his five-foot-three wife around. I would have called the cops on him any number of times if Bitsy hadn't gotten hysterical at the mere suggestion of it.

"No! Oh, no, really, Bay, he didn't. Honest! Just yelling. And then he stormed out of the house and didn't come back for two days! I called all over the state and couldn't find him anywhere. I got a little frantic, that's all. I just needed someone to talk to, a shoulder. You know."

I did some more mental arithmetic. "You mean he wasn't home when you got the news about CJ? Where the hell was he? Is he back now?"

"Oh, yes, everything's fine, just fine. Cal met his attorney at the jail and brought CJ home. They're out back now, the two of them, fishin' off the dock."

"And all this over some toy or whatever you bought for one of the kids?" The four Elliott children seemed to grow at such a rate I kept losing track of just how old they were. CJ would be a senior; Mary Alice, called Mally, also in high school, was maybe a couple of years behind. Margaret had to be in junior high; and Brady, the youngest, somewhere around third or fourth grade.

"Yes, can you believe it? Actually, it was a CD player for Margaret. She always seems to get Mally's hand-me-downs, and she wanted a new one, just for herself." Bitsy sighed, and I could almost see her shining, shoulder-length hair flipping back and forth as she shook her head in exasperation. "It was only two hundred dollars!"

Calvin Elliott had inherited a moderately successful used car business from his father and had parlayed it into a string of seven "Big Cal SuperLots" from Greenville to Beaufort. His grinning, pudgy, red-neck countenance beamed down on unsuspecting consumers from billboards all up and down the state.

"He walked out over a couple of hundred bucks?" I asked.

"What a jerk! Did he ever say where he was all that time?"

"Well, not exactly. He said he was just drivin' around. Stopped at a couple of bars and lost track of time."

"For two days?"

"I know it sounds feeble. But he's back now, and CJ's home, so I can't raise too much of a ruckus. And to be fair, things have been a little tight lately, I think. Not that Big Cal ever tells *me* anything, at least not directly. But I've overheard him on the phone a few times, shoutin' at someone about some big investment he made that's run into problems."

I could hear tears creeping into Bitsy's voice. My fingers itched to wrap themselves around her husband's flabby neck.

"If only he'd talk to me, maybe I could take some of the burden off him." She swallowed hard. "But he just tells me to mind my own business, take care of the kids, and leave the rest to him."

"Anything I can do to help?"

"You already have. As usual. But don't worry, sweetie, I'm sure everything will be fine. After all, from what I gather, it was the Judge who recommended this investment to Big Cal, so there really isn't anything to fuss about, is there? Your daddy is one of the smartest men I know."

The bottom fell out of my stomach. It had to be Grayton's Race. There couldn't be two projects with rumors flying and investors panicking, both connected to my father.

What the hell is he up to? I wondered as I reassured Bitsy and hung up the phone. Why was the Judge out touting Geoff's development? First Miss Addie and now Big Cal Elliott. And why hadn't Geoff mentioned anything about all this last night? God knows, I'd given him plenty of opportunity. If everything was as up front as Geoff claimed it was, why all the secrecy?

I needed answers. I marched into the study and stopped short. My father lay stretched out in his recliner, his useless legs draped with a light cotton throw. Soft snores bubbled from his partially open mouth. He looked so damned *vulnerable*.

I closed the door softly behind me and took the stairs two at a time.

Last night I had been lulled by the soft river breeze and my own loneliness . . . by a tender smile and a girlhood fantasy. In the cold light of day, reality was reasserting itself.

Something was wrong. I could smell it, sense it in the unanswered questions, the averted eyes, the smooth plausibility with which every objection was explained away.

It was time for me to get back to work. Maybe I couldn't get into the courthouse on Saturday afternoon, but my computer could. I would head back to Hilton Head and begin accessing files, checking records. The names of the new owners of the Grayton's Race tract seemed like a logical place to start. Maybe I could find out who else my father had enticed into investing—and why. Rob's clearances had probably been canceled on his death, but he had taught me how to hack back in the days when our financial sleuthing had necessitated accessing databases we weren't meant to see. Most of those belonged to the bad guys, but the technique was the same. If I could just remember how . . .

I threw my toothbrush and a few other necessities into my overnight bag and slipped on my well-worn Birkenstock sandals. Dolores had apparently made peace with the Judge. She cheerfully agreed to hold the fort for a couple of days and followed me out onto the porch. As I trotted down the front steps, the phone began to ring.

"Remember, you don't know where I am," I shouted over my shoulder. If it was Geoff, I was glad I'd missed his call. I needed a little distance right now, time to think with my head instead of my glands.

A quiet night in front of the computer screen was what I had planned. It was not exactly what I got.

CHAPTER EIGHT

My house smelled stale after being closed up for the last two days. I wandered through the high-ceilinged rooms, opening windows and French doors. The soft susurration of the ocean, just across the dune, was a soothing presence, like a piece of well-loved music playing in the background.

I kicked off my sandals and walked barefooted up three steps onto the highly-polished oak floor of the expansive kitchen. Dolores said she'd left a Caesar salad with grilled shrimp ready for me in the refrigerator. All I needed to do was dump it in a bowl and add the dressing.

I can handle that. I smiled to myself, remembering Rob's light-hearted teasing about my ineptness in the kitchen. I put everything on a tray and carried it out onto the deck. Although it was still only early evening, I lit some citronella candles to ward off the no-see-ums and sat down at the round, white, wrought iron table.

My nearest neighbors were well hidden behind a cluster of live oaks and pines. The silence was almost complete, broken only occasionally by the bright squawk of a mockingbird perched somewhere over my head. I picked desultorily at my dinner as the sky over the water gradually faded from crystal blue to soft orange.

My head whirled with all the troubling events of the past couple of days: Isaiah and CJ as apparent suspects in a murder investigation, Bitsy's distress at her husband's strange disappearance, my own father's evasiveness about his role in the Grayton's Race development, not to mention all the other inconsistencies in what I had been told about the project.

I pushed the half-finished salad away, lit a cigarette, and propped my bare feet up on the chair next to me. I needed a plan, a roadmap to help me navigate the tangle of conflicting stories. A sharp flash of memory kicked me in the stomach.

Rob. His presence was almost palpable here in the house we had designed and built shortly after our marriage. He used to laugh at me when I called it our beach place. With three bedrooms and as many baths, it was twice the size of the condominium that had been our permanent home in Charleston.

My darling Rob . . . I could almost hear his soft, upstate drawl. *Make a list, honey, three columns: What do we suspect, what do we know, what can we prove?*

He would pace and talk. I would take notes. We'd bounce ideas off each other, knock down the most outrageous ones, and end up, after several hours of brainstorming, with a blueprint for his investigation. Later he would transcribe it all onto the computer. Even though my participation was unofficial, I always shared in his work. We were a team.

So why did you have to go and die? I silently screamed, the enormity of his loss crashing in on me. *You had no right to get blown up and leave me alone like this! No right! I need you!*

"I need you," I whispered to the empty night

I lit another cigarette and exhaled slowly. I concentrated on my breathing, the way they'd taught me in therapy. Gradually, the pain receded to the dark corner where I kept it stored.

"Get on with it," I ordered myself. "You need a plan."

But the moment my thoughts turned again to Grayton's Race, another face drifted into that black place behind my closed eyelids. Geoff, his direct blue gaze filled with tenderness, gently kissing my trembling palm. At thirteen, I had dreamed of his touch, my skinny, flat-chested body yearning for the feel of his hands on my skin.

Geoff had been the object of my first, terrifying sexual fantasies.

Last night had shown me the power he still possessed. I had walked without hesitation into his arms, my body somehow believing that was where I belonged. Geoff had dropped miraculously back into my life at the exact moment my heart seemed ready to receive him.

And the doubts? I asked myself ruthlessly. *The seeming half-truths, the smooth evasions? He could be a fraud. What do you really know about him now?*

No! I was a good judge of character—always had been. Geoff

couldn't have changed that much. I couldn't be so wrong . . .

What do we suspect, what do we know, what can we prove?

Stealthy movement registered on the edge of my half-lidded vision.

I jumped, fear shooting through me like a lightning strike.

Mr. Bones, my on-again, off-again feline companion, sat perched in the chair to my right. His slim, gray paw shot out and speared another shrimp from the soggy remains of my salad. It disappeared in two quick gulps. He looked like a bear swiping salmon out of a rushing stream.

I blew air out of my lungs and ruffled the fur on the back of his head. "Damn it, Bones, you scared the hell out of me. And who invited you to dinner?"

I had named him for his emaciated appearance the first time I found him sunning himself on my deck. I knew Dolores left a dish out for him every night and the tiny skeletons littering the yard testified to his hunting prowess, so it wasn't that he was hungry. Food was available, and instinct told him to take what was offered when the opportunity presented itself.

The soft pink glow of the fading sun bathed the deck in an eerie light. The cat finished his after-dinner grooming, padded across the table, and curled himself onto my lap. His deep, satisfied purring increased as I stroked his back.

Instinct. Rob always said I could spot the holes in a financial deal from half a mile away. While that was, of course, an exaggeration, I *had* developed a nose for ferreting out a scam. Neither Rob nor I had ever considered ourselves brave. We preferred to do our fighting with brains rather than bullets. We had nailed a number of illegal operations in the state, not by swooping down with SWAT teams to interdict drug shipments, but by following the money.

Instinct. That was what had been gnawing at me for the last couple of days. And it was telling me that something just wasn't right about Grayton's Race.

The sun had set over the mainland. The darkness was total, enveloping, except for the feeble flickering of the candles and the glow from the end of my cigarette. Tree frogs squeaked their nightly chorus, and the cat resettled himself across my legs.

Lost in the peace of the soft summer night, I was half-dozing.

The screech of an owl, swooping to its prey, jerked me awake. Mr. Bones leaped to the deck. I heard a rustling in the sharp leaves of the palmettos along the dune, then a frenzied squealing, quickly cut off as the owl glided away, dinner clutched in its fierce talons.

Instinct.

I piled the dirty dishes on the tray, carried them back into the kitchen, and loaded the dishwasher. I filled the tea kettle and set it on the stove. I selected a box of Constant Comment tea bags from the cupboard. None of that mild, soothing, herbal stuff. Tonight I was going to need all the caffeine I could get.

Brains could, in fact, rust I decided as I sat frustrated before the bright rectangle of the seventeen-inch monitor. The desk in the bedroom we had converted into an office was littered with disks and crumpled wads of yellow legal paper.

I couldn't get into the damn courthouse computer! And I couldn't figure out where I was going wrong. It should have been child's play. It had to be something simple, some small command I was forgetting to execute.

In desperation I had opened the floor safe concealed in the far corner of my walk-in closet. Against all the rules, Rob had kept duplicates of his case notes here, on three-and-one-half-inch disks. Government corruption was not unknown in the Great State of South Carolina, and Rob preferred to trust no one but himself. And me.

I had retrieved the boxes of disks that held much of the information we had illegally downloaded during our midnight plundering of supposedly secure databases. I was hoping for some clue, a scribbled note, anything to jog my memory and get me past the roadblock of the flashing "Access Denied" messages that filled my screen.

I had sorted through all these files right after my release from the hospital. My hopes of finding something that would lead me to Rob's murderers had been quickly dashed. The number of cases in which he had been involved and the sheer volume of the data defeated me. And my grief had been too new then, too raw. The memories evoked by these tangible reminders of our life together had been more than I could bear.

I turned back to my list-making which wasn't meeting with any greater success. I had eliminated the "What can we prove" column from my deliberations. I had no interest in prosecuting anyone even if I were able to make a case. All I wanted was to find out enough about the finances and the backers of the Grayton's Race project to reach an informed opinion about its legitimacy.

Guilt was a hard little knot in the center of my chest.

I had probably jumped the gun in reassuring Adelaide Boyce Hammond about the safety of her investment. I had made similar noises to Bitsy Elliott, though with less fervor.

Moonlight and seductive blue eyes were my only excuse.

I didn't intend to open my mouth again until I knew for sure what I was talking about.

I dumped the overflowing ashtray into the wastebasket next to the desk and headed for the kitchen. The clock above the stove read twenty past two. I'd already gone through two pots of tea and was starting on my third. Even if I decided to hang it up now and go to bed, I'd probably never get to sleep. Caffeine hummed through my veins like electric current through a wire.

I was also starving.

I was leaning over, peering hopefully into the open refrigerator, when a sweep of headlights flashed across the ceiling, freezing me in the glare. They were quickly extinguished, followed a few seconds later by the *thud* of a car door slammed with considerable force.

Soft-soled shoes crunched on the carpet of dead pine needles that covered the driveway. I followed their progress up the wooden stairway.

Two sharp, staccato bursts of the doorbell were followed by a pounding on the stout oak door.

Well, if it's a burglar, I thought, *it's a pretty damned inept one.*

I glanced down at the short cotton nightshirt I'd thrown on before I settled down in front of the computer. I was running for the bedroom to grab a robe when the pounding resumed, punctuated this time by an angry voice I had previously heard speak only with warmth and laughter.

"Bay! I know you're in there. Bay! Open the damned door!"

Anger won out over modesty. I flung myself down the three

steps, strode across the white-carpeted great room and flipped on the outside light. When I yanked open the door, I caught him in mid-pound, his fist poised to strike again.

"Will you shut up, for God's sake? You want the neighbors to call the cops?"

I stood with my feet set wide apart, one hand gripping the knob, the other planted firmly against the doorframe. If he wanted in, he was going to have to go through me.

Geoff Anderson lowered his hand and his voice at the same time. "Hi," he said sheepishly.

He wore a white T-shirt with a Salty Dog logo tucked into rumpled khaki shorts, and dark brown deck shoes with no socks. His square jaw was peppered with several hours' growth of beard. He looked like the answer to every single woman's prayer: handsome, boyish, slightly disreputable.

My hand itched to stroke his cheek, to feel the rough stubble beneath my fingers. Or maybe to slap him 'til his teeth rattled. I couldn't decide which.

"What the hell are you doing beating on my door in the middle of the night?" I relaxed my guard dog stance as he shoved both hands into his pockets.

"Can I come in?" He swayed a little, then shook his head as if to clear it.

"You're drunk." I couldn't keep the accusatory tone out of my voice. A familiar hole opened up in the pit of my stomach.

"Am not." He grinned, shaking his head again.

"Geoff, I'm really not in the mood for this. It's late. Why don't you go home and get some sleep." I realized I didn't even know where he lived. "I'll call you a cab."

"How about some coffee? Please?" Geoff's voice was plaintive, pleading. "I'll just stay a few minutes, I promise. I need to talk to you, Bay."

I hesitated, and he looked directly into my eyes. "Please?"

Fool, I berated myself as I stepped back and swung the door fully open.

A snippet of an old Negro spiritual popped unbidden into my head: . . . *and the walls came tumblin' down.*

• • •

I made instant coffee—the only kind I couldn't screw up—and scrambled some eggs for the two of us. While the water was boiling, I ducked into the bedroom to pull on a pair of shorts under the nightshirt. I ran a brush through my hair while I was at it. I thought about makeup, but decided the hell with it. Anyone who came calling after midnight would just have to take me the way I was.

With food and coffee under his belt, Geoff appeared to sober up quickly. I was beginning to wonder if it had all been an act when he seemed to read my mind.

"I only had a couple of beers, you know, and I haven't eaten since lunch. I guess they went right to my head. Sorry."

I waved his apology away. Seated across the kitchen table from each other, we both grew strangely quiet. We sat that way for some time, each of us wrapped in our own thoughts.

For my part, there was a war going on inside. My head demanded confrontation, explanations for all my suspicions. My heart smiled at the quiet joy I felt having him near. I knew I had only to reach out and touch his hand, and I would be in his arms, warm, secure, and safe.

Loved.

I read it in his eyes as they lifted to meet mine. My body yearned toward his, drawn to the desire I saw reflected on his face . . .

I stepped back from the brink. I slumped in my chair and folded my arms across my breasts. I wasn't sure which of us the familiar defensive posture was meant to protect.

Geoff sagged, too, as the sexual tension drained out of him.

"You said you wanted to talk to me," I said quietly, "so talk."

"Why did you run away from me?"

"I didn't 'run away'. I came home. This is where I live, where I belong."

"Where you hide."

I flinched at the accuracy of his shot. I bought time by lighting a cigarette.

"If that's how you see it. I had things to do here, things I couldn't accomplish on St. Helena. So what's the big deal?"

"The big deal is that you told the Dragon Lady not to let me know where you were."

His characterization of sweet-tempered Dolores as a fire-breathing guardian made me smile in spite of myself.

"I needed a little space. Time to think. I was going to call you."

I realized that it was true. I would have sought Geoff out in a day or two if he hadn't beaten me to it.

"That's your trouble, Bay. You think too damn much. What's wrong with just feeling?"

"Geoff, there are things . . ."

"I know, I know. I realized last night after I dropped you off that there was still something bothering you about the project. I don't begin to understand what your problem is, and you don't seem willing to enlighten me."

Geoff took my cigarette from me and stubbed it out in the ashtray. He covered both my hands with his and lightly stroked my fingers.

"Ask me anything you want, Bay, anything. I don't want this hanging over our heads, coming between us. I think I'm falling—"

I stopped him with a finger to his lips. I wasn't ready to hear a declaration of love, not yet. He was right. There were too many questions. But I couldn't bring myself to ask them, not now. Maybe I really didn't want to know the answers. Suddenly, I was overwhelmingly tired.

"You'd better go, Geoff," I said, glancing at the clock as we rose from our chairs. "It's after three. We seem to be making a habit of staying up half the night."

"There's an alternative to staying up, you know." He moved around the table toward me.

"Out!" I pointed sternly at the door, and Geoff backed away, hands held high in mock surrender.

"Okay, okay." He took my hand again as we walked slowly into the hallway. At the door, he turned to face me, that boyish grin back on his face.

"Do you have any hiking boots?" he asked. His fingers smoothed tangled locks of hair back off my cheeks, his touch so gentle I could barely feel it.

"Any what?" I was nearly hypnotized by his soft voice and delicate caress.

"Hiking boots. Or maybe work boots. Something sturdy, anyway, with hightops. There may be snakes."

"Snakes?" I stepped back, batting his arm away. It was much easier to think with his hands no longer on me. "What the hell are you talking about?"

"Tomorrow. I'm picking you up at eleven. We'll have brunch at the Hyatt, then I'm giving you the grand tour of Grayton's Race. I want to show you where I'm building my house."

"But . . ."

Geoff grasped my shoulders and drew me gently to him. In my bare feet, I fit perfectly into the curve of his arm, my head just below his chin.

"I can't go to the Hyatt in work boots," I murmured into his neck.

Geoff's laugh echoed in the enclosed space of the hallway.

Then he drew aside the neck of my nightshirt. I flinched as the cool night air touched my injured shoulder. With a tenderness that made my legs nearly fold up under me, Geoff brushed his lips across the shiny ugliness of the grafted skin.

"Tomorrow," he whispered as he released me and slipped quietly out the door.

CHAPTER
NINE

"How did you get into the plantation last night?" I asked. I was stuffing my hair up under a battered Chicago Cubs baseball cap while Geoff secured the boot over the lowered convertible top of the Jaguar.

Although the fierce midday sun bounced shimmering heat waves off the blacktop of the Hyatt parking lot, yesterday's storm had chased most of the humidity south, at least temporarily, and the wind off the ocean felt fresh and relatively cool.

"Magic," Geoff answered, pointing to the array of multi-colored stickers covering the lower left-hand corner of the Jag's windshield. Access to the wooded enclaves of homes and golf courses, like Port Royal where I lived, could be gained only by residents with permanent passes or by temporary paper ones issued to authorized visitors.

"Where'd you get all those?"

"One of the many perks of being in the real estate business," Geoff replied as we eased out of Palmetto Dunes onto Route 278 and headed west.

It was a glorious day, and I was determined to forget everything and simply enjoy it. Last night I had barely enough energy left to log off the computer and sweep the disks into a file cabinet, although I returned them to the safe first thing in the morning. Except for a brief interruption when I'd thought I'd heard the cat clawing at the French door, I'd slept like the dead.

Conversation was difficult with the wind roaring in our ears, so Geoff and I contented ourselves with exchanging occasional smiles. We crossed over the twin bridges, leaving the island behind. On our right, we passed the glinting metal power line supports that always looked to me like alien giants with huge arms and no heads. Embedded deep in the soft mud of the marsh, they made an ideal nesting spot for ospreys and other birds of prey, the towers a perfect launching pad for them to swoop out over the water, their talons ready to sink into the tender flesh of unsuspecting fish.

"Music?" Geoff mouthed at me as we swept past Moss Creek. Horses grazed in the paddock near the highway.

I nodded.

Geoff slipped in a tape, and the pure, clear tenor of Pavoratti surrounded us.

The man is amazing, I thought as I closed my eyes and let the sun, the wind, and the "Nessen Dorma" wash over me.

Luciano, of course, for that marvelous voice. But I had been thinking mostly of Geoff who, without asking, had unerringly picked my favorite piece of music.

Past Belfair and Rose Hill, we took the off-ramp and turned right toward Beaufort. A few miles farther on, Geoff flipped on his right turn signal and slowly edged toward the berm. The sandy track he pulled onto was barely discernible among the thick stand of loblolly pines and waist-high weeds.

The sharp blast of a horn made me whirl around in my seat. A scruffy, bearded teenager yelled something out the window of a chrome-laden pickup truck as it roared past us. A gun rack hung in the rear window, and the bumper was plastered with slogans. All I could catch was something about ". . . Hunting Grounds" before the boy and his friends disappeared around a bend in the road.

"Idiots," Geoff muttered as he slowed the big Jag to a crawl.

Thirty yards in we bounced to a halt before a rusty metal gate secured to weathered wooden posts by a shiny, new padlock. Geoff killed the engine and cut Luciano off in mid-note.

"This is as far as we ride, unless I trade this baby in for one of those four-wheel-drive monsters," Geoff said as he slid out of the car. "You game for a hike?"

"I didn't dress like this for the Spring Cotillion. Lead on."

I had ferreted out my old hiking boots from the attic that morning. Rob and I had gone through a short-lived rock climbing phase early in our marriage. Packed away in the same box, I found my heavy woolen socks. An oversized T-shirt and faded jeans completed my ensemble.

Geoff was similarly clad. We'd been a big hit among the

starched and suited after-church crowd at the Hyatt brunch.

"Better use this, or you'll get eaten alive."

Geoff tossed a can of insect repellent across the open car. I sprayed it liberally over the exposed skin of my arms, neck and face. It smelled awful, but that was probably good. Where we were going, mosquitoes the size of hummingbirds were not uncommon.

Geoff shrugged a small backpack onto his shoulder, and we set off. We rounded the posts of the gate and headed down the deeply rutted track. It was littered with potholes so large and so numerous we had to walk on either side of the path. Thick woods provided a measure of shade from the merciless afternoon sun, but they also blunted what little breeze ruffled their highest branches. We were soon soaked in sweat.

The silence is never complete where there are trees and plants. Insects buzzed and whirred, for the moment, at least, properly repelled by the smell of the spray. Soft rustlings marked the passage of larger, unseen creatures—squirrels, raccoons, and assorted other rodents. Birdsong filled the quiet spaces with so many varied calls I couldn't begin to identify the singers. Woodpeckers tapped industriously high over our heads as we walked deeper into the woods.

"Want to talk?" Geoff glanced over at me, then quickly away. It was a nervous, edgy gesture.

"Not especially. You?"

"Not if you don't."

We trekked on, our heavy boots making little sound and less impression on the sandy red soil and underbrush. Sweat was trickling between my breasts, pooling around the waistband of my jeans.

"Not much farther," Geoff said as he drew a handkerchief from his pocket and mopped his face. "This was a pretty stupid idea, wasn't it? We should've waited until evening when it was cooler."

"What's the matter, Cadet Anderson? Didn't those parade ground drills at the dear old Citadel prepare you for a little hike in the woods? Gotten soft, have we?"

"I'm fine. I was worried about you."

"Don't bother. All that rehab at the hospital, plus tennis or golf almost every day have done wonders. I don't think I've ever been in better shape."

"I noticed." He grinned, eyeing the sweaty shirt now plastered to my chest.

I reached down and grabbed a pinecone from among the hundreds littering the forest floor and pitched it underhand at him. He caught it in mid-air and flipped it right back. I ducked, and the battle was on.

We trotted down the track flinging missiles at each other and shrieking like a couple of ten-year-olds. Energy spent, we called a truce at last and flopped breathlessly down onto an outcropping of rock. I sipped gratefully from the bottled water Geoff carried in his pack.

We set out again, more sedately this time. Fifteen minutes later I smelled the river. Nothing identifiable, just a slight change in the taste and feel of the air, the cool, clean ripple of a breeze.

The track petered out at the base of a small rise. Geoff took my hand, and we trudged up the gentle incline. I could feel his eyes on my face as we crested the top.

"It's perfect," I breathed, "absolutely perfect." I felt the tension in his hand relax.

Twenty yards ahead and slightly below, the Chicopee River flowed serenely over well-worn stones along its edge. The color of the water changed from sparkling blue to a soft, rippling green as the wind fluttered the branches reflected in its depths. We stood between two ancient live oaks, their screen of Spanish moss making it seem as if we looked through a shifting veil.

Only one or two pines would have to be cut to assure an unobstructed view to the river. The oaks could stay, guardian sentinels at either side of the house.

"Exactly!" Geoff exclaimed when I voiced my observation.

He began moving back and forth, pacing out the dimensions of the house. This room here, that one there. Porches all around and windows everywhere. His enthusiasm was contagious, and soon I was deep into the game. I knocked out imaginary walls, expanded closets, added skylights.

We discussed, argued, compromised, agreed until I could almost see the magnificent Lowcountry house taking shape before my eyes.

The heat finally got to me, and I dropped gratefully onto the sandy ground, my back resting up against the bole of one of the oaks. I lit a cigarette as Geoff unloaded his pack. More water, apples, a couple of candy bars, along with the bug spray were spread out around us.

"How can you stand to see this developed?" I murmured, almost to myself. Geoff's love for this piece of ground, his passion for the home he would build here, was evident in every word and gesture. "This is what Hilton Head must have been like before Charles Fraser got started on Sea Pines."

What had once been an isolated island, rife with deer and woods and accessible only by boat, had become a world-class resort with its attendant hotels, restaurants, visitors, and traffic. I loved living there, but I knew at what price my enjoyment had been purchased.

"Someone's going to do it. Just like Hilton Head. They were lucky it was a man like Fraser, someone who valued the land and the marshes. He set the standard for all the development that followed, helped to keep it in check."

Geoff rose, took a bite out of one of the apples, and looked once more out across the river. "I want to do the same for Grayton. That's one reason I was so excited when they asked me to head up the project. I can make sure it's done right."

"Look," I began, "I'm not exactly a registered tree-hugger. I understand that people have a right to use their land, make a profit, whatever." I grabbed the other apple and joined him. "I guess it just bothers me to think of all this . . ." I flung my arm wide to encompass the quiet beauty that surrounded us. ". . . all of it torn up, bulldozers and graders everywhere. The birds and wildlife chased God knows where."

Geoff slipped an arm around me and smiled ruefully. "You give a damned good impression of a tree-hugger," he said, and I punched his shoulder. "Maybe you should join our young friends down at the barricades."

"What barricades? What friends?"

"Come on, let's go stick our feet in the water."

He pulled me along down the slope to where a dead pine, toppled by wind and time, lay rotting, its barren trunk jutting out over the river. We shed our heavy socks and boots, rolled up our pantslegs, and straddled the tree. My toes just barely skimmed the water.

"Is this by any chance a clumsy attempt to change the subject?"

Geoff, taller than I and farther out on the log, splashed water up at me with his feet, and ignored my question.

"And what was that you said about being selected to head the project? I thought it was all your idea in the first place."

Geoff picked at the rotten bark, tossed a few pieces aimlessly into the current, and watched them float downstream.

"Hey, wanna go skinny dippin'?" He reached for the waistband of his jeans, and I slapped his hand away.

"Knock it off, Geoff."

"What's the matter, you chicken?"

It was the kind of taunt that, thirty years ago, would have set me to ripping off my clothes in a determined effort to prove I was no such thing.

"Nice try."

I finished off the apple and tossed the core sidearm into the woods. It would make a nice lunch for some lucky animal. Geoff did the same.

"Okay, Anderson, give," I said, wiping my sticky hands on my jeans. "What is all this stuff about barricades?"

"The Committee Against the Rape of the Environment. CARE. Ever heard of them?"

"No. Catchy little name, though. Have they been giving you trouble?"

Geoff snorted. "Yeah, you could say that. They've taken to blocking the main entrance to the property, over off the highway. We've cut a driveway and set up a temporary information center in a modular building near the river. These sterling pillars of the community are not happy with our development plans. Let's see, how does their propaganda go? 'We are merely exercising our First Amendment rights to peacefully voice our opposition to the proposed rape of our pristine river and adjacent woodlands.' Or some crap like that."

Geoff shinnied off the log and waded back onto the bank. I followed and flopped down beside him. Little shafts of sunlight filtered through the branches and glinted off the silver of his hair.

"Can't you get a restraining order or something?" I picked up a smooth pebble and tried to skip it across the water. It sank after one bounce. I was sadly out of practice.

"Tried that. No go. They don't actually come onto the property, at least not when anyone's around to catch them at it. They just park their four-wheel-drives all up and down the highway so it's nearly impossible for anyone to see the signs, let alone turn into the drive."

He plucked a long-stemmed weed from the ground beside him and chewed on it absently. "I mean, would you want to run a gauntlet of bearded rednecks like that bunch that nearly ran us off the road today just to look at a piece of property?"

"That was them? They didn't look like environmentalists to me. In fact, I've seen that line of pickups parked along the road. I didn't realize it had anything to do with your project. I thought it was a gun club meeting or a duck shoot or something like that."

"Not exactly your usual Sierra Club material, are they? It's really kind of scary when you think about it. Sort of like a marriage between the NRA and Greenpeace. Very strange bedfellows."

"What do you mean 'scary'? I admit they look a little rough around the edges, but they're just kids, right? Surely they're not dangerous?"

Geoff tossed aside the weed and began pulling on his socks. "Come on, we'd better head back. Looks like we're about to get dumped on."

I followed his gaze to the southeast and saw dark storm clouds piling up against each other out over the ocean. Against the backdrop of the blazing sun overhead, they looked alarmingly black and ominous.

We gathered our things together and stuffed them back into the pack. I collected my cigarette butts and slipped them into the pocket of my jeans for later disposal. I may not be a card-carrying environmentalist, but I'm not a litterbug, either.

We took one last look at the view from the top of Geoff's rise, then trotted back down the track. The air had cooled since we'd set out, and the woods seemed less alive with creature-sound. They, too, must have sensed the coming of the storm.

"You never answered my question," I said into the heavy stillness.

"About what?"

"About whether or not there's been any violence."

"Not technically, I guess."

The breeze had picked up, and more of it was reaching the floor of the woods. I lifted the sweaty strands of hair that had escaped my baseball cap and felt a cool rush against my neck.

"What does that mean?"

Geoff shrugged. "There have been incidents."

We picked up the pace as the sky overhead continued to darken. I began to wonder if we would reach the car in time. Not that I'd melt in the rain, but we'd left the top down on the Jag, and I didn't want to have to bail it out.

We almost made it. I caught a glimpse of the Jag's shining chrome just as the first dime-sized drops began to splatter through the leaves. We sprinted the last few yards. I helped Geoff wrestle the boot off and toss it into the back seat. We were completely drenched by the time we got the top and the windows up.

"Timing is everything," I laughed, tugging off my cap and shaking out my hair.

The glass all around us had immediately fogged up, and Geoff flipped on the defroster. Thunder echoed around us as warm air filled the car.

The smell hit us both at the same time.

Sweet, wet, slightly nauseating.

"God, what is that?"

"Those bastards!" Geoff whirled around, his hands scrabbling over the back floor on both sides. "Where the hell is it?"

With another curse he flipped up the crumpled leather top cover we had thrown into the back seat, and I screamed.

One open, glassy eye seemed to be staring right at me as the dead squirrel lay curled in a pool of its own still-warm blood.

CHAPTER
TEN

"You should have let me call the cops."

Two hours later, wrapped in Geoff's fluffy white robe, I was still fuming. I paced back and forth in front of the wide sliding glass door that looked out over the balcony of the penthouse condo in Harbour Town.

Geoff rescued the empty mug from my flailing hand and went to refill it from the pot of tea steeping on the counter. I gazed unseeing as, below me, a tall-masted motor sailer inched its way slowly out of the snug marina, past the famous lighthouse, and out into Calibogue Sound.

"I told you, there's no point. They can't do a damned thing."

"Can't or won't?" I accepted the cup of steaming tea and resumed my pacing.

After his initial outburst, Geoff had dealt calmly and efficiently with the mess in the backseat of his Jaguar. He retrieved the Sunday paper and a couple of beach towels from the trunk while I stood shivering in the pelting rain. He wrapped the mutilated squirrel in several sheets of newspaper and laid it gently at the foot of a towering pine. With one towel, he mopped up the worst of the blood, then covered the stained seat with the other.

I had to be coaxed back into the car. I can tolerate just about anything except cruelty to animals. I lusted for the blood of whoever had slaughtered an innocent squirrel in order to make his point.

"Well, at least we could have gone down there ourselves and kicked some redneck butt." My left hand had unconsciously curled into a tight fist, and I was banging it against the side of my leg.

"With what? You may have noticed that I don't have a rifle rack strapped to the trunk of the Jag. I think we'd have been pretty much outgunned as well as outmanned."

I snorted, unconvinced, and turned away from the view. "You

said you have some other little souvenirs from the CARE gang?"

"Nothing quite as dramatic as a bloody corpse in the backseat, but the message is pretty much the same."

Geoff patted the sofa beside him, and I settled myself into a corner, my feet drawn up under me. He opened the metal clasp on a legal-sized envelope and slid the contents out onto the coffee table in front of us. There were three Polaroid snapshots and some pieces of brown grocery bag paper folded over several times.

I picked up the first photo. Geoff's beautiful black Jaguar rested on four flat tires.

"What's that sticking out?" I pointed to what looked like sticks, red streamers fluttering on the ends, that protruded from each wheel.

"Surveyor's stakes. You know, what we use to mark out the lot lines? They're wood. It took some effort to drive them into the tires."

The second picture showed the remains of a golf cart that had obviously been dismantled with a sledgehammer. Battered pieces lay scattered across the scrubby grass. In the background, the modular welcome center, as well as the propane storage tank beside it, were covered with red, spray-painted graffiti.

"These guys are a real piece of work. Didn't you call the Sheriff?"

"Sure. But without witnesses, what can the cops do? As they were quick to point out to me."

"Where they'd get your car?"

"On the site. I left it in the drive while I took the golf cart out to my lot. Happened while I was gone, apparently."

"So they were definitely trespassing." I shivered as the implication hit me. "God, Geoff, they had to be following you. Or they have the project staked out."

"Probably both. But remember, a lot of these guys are hunters. They're good at stalking. They could be anywhere in the woods, in camouflage, and I'd never spot them."

I studied the last Polaroid, another shot of the drive. The sun glinted off a shiny carpet stretching for several yards into the property.

"Metal shavings, nails, broken bottles, screws," Geoff answered my puzzled look. "Four inches deep. Took one of my crews almost an entire day to clean it up."

I shook my head in disbelief. These people were playing hardball. While the incidents resembled the sort of actions environmental activists had taken in other parts of the country when endangered habitats were threatened by logging or development, there was a viciousness here that seemed out of character. Nastier. More personal.

Geoff unfolded one of the stiff, brown papers and smoothed the creases as he spread it on the table.

I studied the drawing. It was crude, but effective. The old Grayton plantation house, its dilapidated condition conveyed in a few clever pen strokes, was on fire, realistic flames shooting through its sagging roof. In the foreground, a stick-figure man stood beside an open sports car. Large teardrops fell from his head to the ground. Along the sides and top, thick, red paint had been cleverly drizzled, conveying the impression of dripping blood without obscuring the rest of the drawing.

There was no message, not in words, anyway. The threat seemed clear enough without them.

"Whoever the creep is, he's got talent. You're right, Geoff. This is scary stuff."

"The others are pretty much the same. Variations on a theme. I find them tucked under the windshield wipers of the Jag every few days."

He refolded the paper, replaced everything in the envelope, and tossed it on the table. I picked a cigarette out of the pack, and Geoff lit it for me.

"I can't believe this is the work of legitimate environmentalists," I said. "I know some of them have gone to extremes, like chaining themselves to trees, but this is more like. . . I don't know, like terrorism, I guess."

Geoff propped his bare feet up on the coffee table and leaned back, his hands clasped behind his head. He had changed into clean shorts and T-shirt after his shower. My clothes were still in the dryer.

"What I think," he said, staring up at the high ceiling, "is that there are some local bad-boy elements mixed up in what started out as a legitimate peaceful protest. I know there are people of good conscience who don't want to see any more development in this area. Hell, you're probably one of them."

Geoff glanced over at me, and I nodded. "Guilty as charged."

"But you wouldn't go to these lengths to stop it, would you? No," he answered for me. "People like us write letters to the editor, attend the review board meetings, talk to officials. We don't trash golf carts or threaten to burn down one hundred fifty-year-old historic buildings."

"You're right. So what are you going to do about it?"

"What can I do? I hired a private security force to patrol the property. I put up a chain link fence all across the front, and a ten-foot-high gate across the driveway. But there are any number of ways to get in, if you're really determined. Hell, we walked in today without encountering a soul. Another half hour hike down the river and we would have been at the plantation house."

I shuddered, wondering with a little tremor of fear how far we had been from the site of Derek Johnson's murder. The placid Chicopee had been witnessing some less than peaceful events lately.

Geoff reached to pull me into his arms. I went with only a brief hesitation, my head coming to rest on his shoulder.

"All I can hope for is that, once we break ground and they realize they're not going to stop us, maybe they'll just go away."

"When do think that'll be? Groundbreaking, I mean." The little worms of doubt had begun squirming around in my gut again. I snuggled closer against the solid warmth of his body, trying to shut out the image of Miss Addie's concerned face.

"I can't really say, for sure. A couple of months, maybe. There's still a few glitches to be worked out."

Talk to me, Geoff, I pleaded silently. *Tell me. Don't make me cross-examine you. Offer it openly. Please.*

"Any problem with the investors?" I forced myself to ask softly, when he didn't elaborate. "About the delays or any of this trouble on the site?"

"I've managed to keep those incidents out of the papers, so it's not common knowledge. And no, I haven't heard any complaints." I felt the tension as his hand tightened on my shoulder. "Why?"

I couldn't do it, couldn't spoil the wonder of being cradled again in strong, loving arms. The late afternoon sun, as brilliant as ever after the passing of the storm, streamed through the glass door. I felt like a child—safe, warm, and drowsy.

"Never mind," I whispered.

He relaxed a little then, running his fingers through my hair where it lay curled against his shoulder. My arm lay loosely across his chest. I fought unsuccessfully to stifle a yawn.

"Why don't you take a little nap? You know, it's mostly my fault you're exhausted. I've kept you up until all hours for the past two nights. And this afternoon was a pretty unnerving experience. You're entitled."

"Yeah, you sure know how to show a girl a good time." I tilted my head back so he could see I was teasing. The look on his face took my breath away. I gulped and tried to wriggle out of his embrace. "I'd better check on my clothes."

"Oh, no you don't. You stay right where you are." Geoff eased me gently back into his arms. "I've been dreaming about this moment ever since I first touched your hand, first felt your skin on mine."

"Geoff, I . . ."

I felt the tempo of his breathing change, and the air crackled with that same electricity that had jumped between us on the deck of the restaurant two days ago.

Slowly, tentatively, Geoff lowered his face to mine. He gave me every opportunity to turn away, pull back. I did neither. Our first kiss was everything my teenaged heart had imagined it would be.

His lips brushed my eyes, my cheeks, my neck. He pushed the robe back to caress my shoulders. His fingers gently stroked the puckered skin, traced the scars that criss-crossed my back. Tenderly he made love to my hurt, drawing it into himself, setting me free to give—and to receive.

I helped him peel off his shirt, then ran my hands over the warmth of his chest, felt the swift pounding of his heart, echoing my own.

It was a waltz, a slow, dreamy dance. There was desire, but no urgency. Passion, but no haste. We touched, tasted, explored as the dying sun cast its soft glow across the sofa where we lay.

When Geoff rose and held out his hand to me, I clasped it

without hesitation. As we walked slowly toward the bedroom, he paused to tilt my face up toward his own.

"Are you sure?" he whispered. His eyes searched mine, demanding honesty.

Am I? I asked myself. For a moment I wavered, closing my eyes as Rob's sweet face floated up out of my memory. And then he was gone, never to be forgotten, *never*, but stored away in a special place in my heart that would always belong only to him.

Death receded, and life beckoned.

I opened my eyes and laid my hand tenderly against Geoff's cheek as I reached up to brush his lips with mine. My robe dropped to the floor as I pushed the door closed behind us.

I awoke to whistling and the smell of charcoal. There was no momentary disorientation, no *Where am I?* panic. I knew exactly where I was. And why.

My body glowed, my skin alive to the touch of the cool sheet where it lay across my legs. I stretched luxuriantly and sat up. In the dim light cast by a small lamp on the bedside table, I could just make out Geoff's robe draped over the back of a Queen Anne chair. I grabbed it up and headed for the shower.

When I stepped back into the bedroom, toweling my hair, I found my clothes neatly folded on the foot of the bed. I tossed the wet towel over the shower rod, tightened the belt of the robe, and followed the smell of grilling steaks out into the kitchen.

Geoff, wearing only a pair of navy blue sweatpants, was on the balcony flipping T-bones off the grill onto a platter. The glass-topped dining table was set with colorful earthenware plates on woven rattan placemats. Candles in long-stemmed, crystal holders stood incongruously amid an array of mismatched cutlery.

Geoff slid the door open, set the platter on the table, and pulled me into his arms. His kiss against my forehead was sweet and tender.

"Hungry?" he asked, releasing me.

"Ravenous. Though maybe I should get dressed first," I added as he opened the drapes wider.

"Not a chance. Besides, we're invisible up here."

The marina below was alive with activity. Harbour Town is a

favorite with tourists and islanders alike. Even with the doors closed, the hum of voices and the muted strains of live music drifted up to us.

Geoff reached around me to place a bowl of salad on the table, followed by two brimming wine glasses.

"Gingerale for you," he said before I could ask.

He lit the candles, then turned off the remaining lamps. Suddenly, the marina seemed to leap into life. The boats riding at anchor were outlined by their dock lights against the deep purple of the night sky. People, silhouetted in the spill of light from the windows of the shops that lined the harbor, crowded the broad esplanade, savoring the soft breeze that floated in off the Sound.

"To us, and to our future." Geoff raised his glass and touched it briefly to the rim of my own. The deep, rich red of his Cabernet Sauvignon glistened in the candlelight.

"To tomorrow," I responded, "and to whatever it brings."

I had learned, in the past year, not to look too far ahead.

A brief frown flitted across Geoff's face and was quickly gone. "Eat," he commanded, grabbing the salad and serving me out a generous helping.

I cut into the steak. It was pink and moist.

"Perfect," I announced around a mouthful of salad. "How did you know?"

"You look like a medium-rare kind of girl."

Geoff reached behind his chair to slide the door partway open. Music and laughter from the crowd below accompanied us as we attacked the food.

"Interesting table setting," I remarked as I sat back, full and satisfied.

Geoff retrieved my cigarettes from the coffee table and did his Cary Grant routine again. "Interesting, huh? I prefer to think of it as eclectic. When you've been divorced twice, you tend to end up with the leftovers of the household goods."

"It must be tough being so far away from your kids," I said. "Do you see them often?"

"No, not really. But you know how it is. Teenagers never have time for their parents, even when they live in the same house."

He stood abruptly and began to stack the plates.

"Here, let me do that," I said trying to cover the awkward

silence my tactless question had created. I rounded the table and pushed him back into his chair. "The cook shouldn't have to clean up, too."

He reached up and pulled me playfully onto his lap. The robe fell open, and he ran his hand lightly up the outside of my bare leg.

I appeared to have been forgiven.

"The dishes can wait," he murmured into my hair.

His lips traveled down my throat, across the sharp ridge of my collar bone while his fingers fumbled at the belt of my robe. I lay back in his arms, my body already responding to the new familiarity of his touch.

When the doorbell rang, we nearly toppled onto the floor.

Geoff clutched me tightly as we struggled to regain our balance. He looked so dismayed, I had to bite back a fit of the giggles.

"Maybe they'll go away," he whispered, kissing me lightly on the lips.

The bell pealed again, longer this time, as if someone leaned on the button.

"God damn it," Geoff growled. Reluctantly he set me on my feet and ran a hand through his tousled hair.

I couldn't help myself. The suppressed laughter burst out of me. Geoff held onto his scowl until the absurdity of the situation struck him, too. We hung on each other, gasping for breath, trying unsuccessfully to control ourselves.

The bell stopped, to be followed by a sharp knocking.

"Persistent little bugger." Geoff gulped and wiped his streaming eyes.

"I'll wait in there," I said, wrapping the robe around me and heading for the bedroom as Geoff approached the door.

I had just slipped from the room when I heard a low exchange that quickly escalated into loud voices. One of them sent a flush of embarrassment washing over the entire length of my half-naked body.

"Look, Tanner," I heard Geoff yell, "you can't just barge in here and throw your weight around. I don't give a damn if you are a cop."

"Where is she?" my brother-in-law barked as I turned and bolted into the bathroom.

CHAPTER
ELEVEN

The silence in the white sheriff's cruiser crackled with unspoken anger. Static and an occasional garbled squawk from the radio broke the quiet, but not the tension.

Sergeant Redmond Tanner and I stared straight ahead as the overhanging limbs of the live oaks and pines along Greenwood Drive flashed by. The uniformed guard at the security gate snapped us a brief salute as we passed out of Sea Pines and negotiated the Circle.

"How did you know where to find me?"

I didn't exactly mean it as an accusation, but it came out sounding like one, anyway.

Red shot me a look that was part anger, part exasperation. The scowl puckering his face had not relaxed since the moment I'd emerged, fully dressed, from the bedroom. Red had delivered his news in a tight voice and few words. Then he'd hustled me out the door of Geoff's condo with the same degree of solicitude he might have shown to an escaped felon.

"Red? I asked you . . . Oh, this is ridiculous! You're acting like a damned two-year-old."

I snatched my bag off the floor and rummaged for my cigarettes.

"You can't smoke in the cruiser."

"So arrest me."

I rolled down the window and let the humid night air suck the smoke away in lazy spirals.

"I mean it. It's against regulations."

"Tough. I pay a hell of a lot of taxes in this county, so this is *my* damn car, bought and paid for. And you have a damn nerve lecturing me about regulations. Is it regulation for off-duty cops to hunt down ordinary citizens using county property?"

"I didn't hunt you down. The Judge asked me to find you, and

I did. End of story."

"Did he ask you to embarrass me, threaten my friends, and kidnap me, too? Or was that your own idea?"

I flipped the half-smoked cigarette out the window and wound it back up as we made the turn into Port Royal Plantation.

"And don't start in about littering," I snapped as Red opened his mouth to speak. "This is private property—my private property—and I'll throw out whatever I damn well please!"

Red slowed the cruiser and rolled to a stop at the gate. I leaned over, and Harry, the regular night-duty guard, recognized me.

"Evenin', Miz Tanner," he drawled. "No trouble, I hope?"

"No, everything's fine, Harry. Thanks."

The short, chunky black man waved us through. I used the few minutes it took us to wind our way around the golf course and into my driveway to try to get my temper under control.

Red pulled up alongside my LeBaron, put the cruiser in park, and turned off the ignition. I was reaching for the door latch when he laid a tentative hand on my arm.

"Look, I'm sorry, okay?"

The house and grounds were in total darkness, and I couldn't see his face. If his voice was any indication though, the scowl had been replaced by a look of repentance.

"Maybe I got a little carried away," he said.

"A little?"

Red's laugh dropped the tension level several degrees. "Okay, more than a little. But I worry about you, damn it. I know you don't like it, but I can't seem to help myself."

"I know. And I appreciate it. Really. Most of the time."

"Friends again?" he ventured, holding out his hand.

"Friends."

I took the hand, and he quickly covered mine with his other.

"Be careful, Bay, all right? I'm sure you think you know this guy, but that was a long time ago. People change. Anderson may be a different man from the boy you remember."

His echoing of my own thoughts made me squirm just a little. Reluctantly, he let go of my hand as I drew away. "Thanks for the advice."

"But I should butt out, right?"

I smiled and opened the door. "Thanks for letting me know

about Miss Addie. They didn't give you any hint of what happened to her, did they? How serious it is?"

"Nope, sorry. All I know is what the Judge told me, that some English dame from the home called him and said they needed someone down there right away."

"Okay, thanks. I guess I'll find out soon enough. Tell the Judge I'll be in touch when I have some news."

"Want me to drive you to the hospital?"

"No, thanks. I'll probably need my car. See you later."

I hadn't intended to go into the house first, but I was pretty certain Red would hover until I was out of reach. I snapped on lights and waved to him from the kitchen window as he backed slowly out of the drive.

I poured myself a glass of ice water from the jug in the refrigerator, then punched the PLAY button on the answering machine.

The clipped, British voice of Mrs. Dixon resonated off the kitchen walls, and I reached to turn down the volume. She was probably used to talking to folks who were just a bit hard of hearing.

"Mrs. Tanner, this is Ariadne Dixon of The Cedars. Please call me immediately upon your return. I have some urgent news regarding your friend, Miss Hammond. Thank you."

Next came the Judge and Red, both with basically the same *Where the hell are you?* tone. Mrs. Dixon must have called my father after failing to reach me. He, in turn, had sent Red out to track me down.

How did she know to do that? I wondered, as her voice boomed out again from the machine.

"It is imperative that I speak with you immediately. Please meet me at the hospital the moment you return. Miss Hammond has been admitted."

I switched out the lights, locked the door, and jumped in the car. The hospital was only a couple of miles away. I could be there in ten minutes. Though why *I* was being summoned was still a mystery, one I intended to unravel soon.

Ariadne Dixon, immaculate in a navy blue linen dress that

screamed Saks, was pacing the tiled floor in front of the nurses' station when I stepped off the elevator. The look of relief that lit her face when she spotted me made my heart sink.

"Mrs. Tanner, thank heavens you're here. I've been quite frantic."

She didn't look frantic. Every hair was glued precisely in place, and her makeup was flawless. She took my arm and guided me to an alcove furnished with two chairs upholstered in teal green cotton and a low table spread with tattered magazines. We sat, and Ariadne Dixon crossed her trim ankles and regarded me solemnly.

"What happened?" Now that I was here, she seemed reluctant to speak. "How's Miss Addie?"

"This is not really my responsibility, you know. The director and his assistant are at a conference in Washington. The Council on Aging, I believe. So dedicated, Mr. Fuenes is. And Miss Grace, as well. Quite respected in their fields. We're very fortunate to have such—"

"About Miss Addie?" I interrupted her without a qualm. I had been virtually hijacked for this supposed errand of mercy, and my patience was pretty well shot.

"Of course, Mrs. Tanner. I was merely trying to explain why it is that I am here rather than those more properly in charge."

"I'm sure you've handled everything quite competently. Now, what happened? How badly is she hurt? And why did you call me?"

She didn't answer my questions immediately. It was her story, and she was going to tell it in her own way.

"About eight o'clock, Miss Hammond's call button was activated. Briefly, you understand, as if she might have bumped it accidentally. It happens all the time. The staff were busy with other residents, helping them settle in for the night, running errands. The usual. We call it assisted living because we try to help with whatever tasks the residents find difficult to handle themselves. We're not a nursing home. We don't keep a twenty-four-hour watch on everyone."

"I understand. Go on."

"I simply want to make clear that we were not ignoring Miss Hammond. The call was not repeated, so staff saw no need for urgency. It was a matter of priorities."

"I'm sure they do an excellent job." I could see the specter of a negligence lawsuit lurking behind all this self-absolving explanation.

"We *all* try to do our best for our residents," she said stiffly.

"So it was some time before anyone went to check on Miss Hammond?" I prompted.

"Fifteen or twenty minutes, no more. It was little Maria, one of our newer aides, who found the poor woman, on the floor next to her bed. Maria quickly summoned senior staff who determined that Miss Hammond was unconscious, but, thank God, not . . ."

"Dead," I finished for her.

"Quite. The ambulance was ordered, and I accompanied her here. The examination has revealed a badly bruised hip and a broken wrist. Also, a slight concussion and a cut on her forehead where she apparently hit her head on the bedside table during her fall."

"But she's going to be okay?"

"Of course," Ariadne Dixon nodded.

"But what actually happened? I mean, how did she come to fall in the first place?"

"I really have no idea. Perhaps her doctor can enlighten you."

The irritating woman rose and smoothed out the wrinkles in her linen dress. "Well, then, I shall leave things in your capable hands, Mrs. Tanner. Please keep us informed of Miss Hammond's progress." She turned toward the hallway.

"Hold it!"

My voice echoed off the tiled floor and low ceiling. A nurse, studying charts behind the desk, glared at me over the half-glasses perched on the end of her nose.

Mrs. Dixon paused and raked me with that same disdainful look I had received from her on the day of my first visit to The Cedars. Still in jeans, wrinkled T-shirt and hiking boots, I had once again failed to measure up to her exacting standards.

"What do you mean, you leave everything in my hands?" I lowered my voice and tried to force some of the belligerence out of it. "I don't understand."

"As next of kin, I assumed you would be taking charge of Miss

Hammond's care."

"Next of kin? We're not even related. She was . . . is an old friend of my mother's, that's all."

"How odd. Just yesterday she altered her file, naming you and your father, Judge Simpson, as next of kin to be notified in case of emergency. She even consulted with her attorney about it."

Mrs. Dixon fumbled with her handbag, adjusting the strap more comfortably over her shoulder. For some reason she didn't want to look me in the face.

"I was reluctant to handle such a serious matter myself, it being more properly the place of Mr. Fuenes or Miss Grace to do so. But Miss Hammond was quite insistent that it be done immediately."

"Look, Mrs. Dixon—"

"I'm afraid I may have overstepped my authority." She appeared to be talking more to herself than to me. Then she sighed, the great weight of the bureaucracy of The Cedars apparently too great a burden for her fragile shoulders to bear. "But, what's done is done. You are named as next of kin, so naturally I assumed . . ."

This made no sense. Surely Miss Addie had family. I remembered sisters and a brother somewhere. Pictures of nieces and nephews. . .

"Who was on her file before? I mean before she changed it?" I asked.

Ariadne Dixon drew herself up to her full five feet, four inches and raised her chin a fraction. "I really couldn't say. That information is confidential. Good evening, Mrs. Tanner."

The little heels of her navy blue Ferragamo pumps clicked loudly in the charged stillness that permeates hospital corridors in the dead of night. I watched her disappear into the elevator without a backward glance.

I shoved my hands into my pockets and resisted the urge to bolt down the steps, intercept the elevator, and shake her until she got it through her head that I was not being saddled with this responsibility. Instead, I flopped myself down onto the soft cushions of the chair and slumped, my long legs stretched out in front of me.

Now what?

I glanced up to see the disapproving nurse eyeing me once

again. Her expression had softened, now that I had quieted down. She beckoned to me with a crooked finger.

A sheaf of papers was stacked neatly in front of her, and she held a pen in one hand. She was a big woman, blonde and blue-eyed, forty-ish. Her white uniform stretched tightly across impressive breasts and hips. She looked like the kind of nurse who could be both sympathetic to her patients and hell on wheels with anyone who failed to follow procedure.

Reluctantly, I hauled myself up out of the chair. Little clumps of dirt from my mud-caked boots littered the floor around me. I ignored them and approached the desk.

"Sorry, but I couldn't help overhearing," the nurse, whose name tag read *Judy McKay*, said pointedly. "You're the next of kin of Adelaide Hammond?"

"No, actually I'm not. We're not related at all. I think there's been some mistake here."

Nurse McKay consulted some papers attached to a brown clipboard. "You're Lydia Tanner, right?"

"Yes, but—"

"Here's the power of attorney, signed and notarized. There's also one for a Talbot Simpson."

"My father."

"Well, apparently Mrs. Hammond trusted you to look after her. I'll need you to sign some forms."

"It's *Miss* Hammond, and I'm not at all sure about this."

"Medicare is primary, plus she's also got supplemental coverage, so you won't be held personally liable for any payments." The disapproval was back on her face and heavy in her voice.

"It's not that. It's just . . . Look, is her doctor around? Maybe I should talk to him before I sign anything."

Bad move. I had questioned her authority.

"Dr. Winter has left for the night," Nurse McKay snapped. "And he has nothing to do with the paperwork. Perhaps I should contact your father, as the other power of attorney. Maybe he'll be a little more cooperative."

I was batting a thousand tonight. I had managed to alienate just about everyone I had come in contact with.

I surrendered, picked up the pen, and held it poised over the stack. With a grunt of satisfaction, Nurse McKay pointed and flipped while I scratched my name. Our business concluded, we were pals again.

"Miss Hammond is sedated and resting comfortably," she replied to my request to see Miss Addie. "Come back tomorrow, around ten. You can talk to her doctor then, too. Don't worry," she added, patting my hand in motherly fashion, "we'll take good care of her."

It was after one o'clock when I emerged through the double doors of the hospital lobby and into the sweet night air. The next thing to hit my lungs was the smoke from the cigarette I needed so badly my hands actually shook as I lit it.

I leaned against the warm stone of the building and stared up at an unbelievably clear sky. A thin sliver of new moon lay cradled in the branches of a swaying pine. Tree frogs chorused around me, and the swift beat of an owl's wings ruffled the air overhead.

What the hell is going on here? I asked myself. *Why am I constantly being dragged into everybody else's problems? Why can't they all just leave me alone?*

I crushed out my cigarette in the sand-filled receptacle and plodded wearily across the deserted parking lot to my car. My shoulder ached, and I rubbed it absently as I swung out into the drive. An ambulance, its lights dark and siren quiet, rolled past me and up to the emergency room entrance. The paramedics seemed to be in no great hurry. I tried not to think about what that probably meant for whoever was inside.

Through a haze of weariness that penetrated down to my bones, I headed toward home. My only thoughts were of a hot shower and bed. Despite my nap at Geoff's, I felt as if I could sleep for a week.

Geoff!

My face flushed in embarrassment as I relived the scene in his penthouse living room. My brother-in-law had done everything short of accusing Geoff of rape. It hadn't taken a rocket scientist to figure out what we'd been up to when Red came pounding on the door. And Sergeant Redmond Tanner, his instincts honed by years of being lied to by experts, had surely read the guilt written all over my face.

And why the hell should I feel guilty? I demanded, getting angry all over again as Harry waved me through the security gate, and I turned toward home. It was none of Red's business who I slept with. In fact, it was nobody's damn business except mine.

I had forgotten to leave any lights on, and the house looked dark and forbidding. Strange that it should seem so tonight, I thought. I had never been afraid of being alone, at least not in the sense of being the only one in the house, not even after Rob's murder.

Far out toward the beach, I saw the faint glow of a flashlight, bobbing up and down as if someone carried it while they ran. Or maybe it was in a boat, riding the soft swells of the ocean.

Probably a crabber, or late-night fishermen taking advantage of the tide.

I trudged slowly up the steps, my climbing boots feeling as if they weighed forty pounds apiece.

The hell with a shower, I told myself as I dropped my keys on the hall table and headed straight for the bedroom. I'd already had two today, three if you counted getting drenched in the rain.

I thought briefly about calling Geoff and the Judge, both of whom would no doubt be fretting to hear from me.

Tomorrow is another day, Scarlett whispered in my ear.

I left my clothes in a heap on the floor and dropped naked onto the king-sized sheets. I didn't even bother to close the drapes. The breeze off the ocean was deliciously cool.

Had I been less exhausted, I would probably have been more alert to the signs, subtle though they were. Whether it would have made any difference to the eventual outcome of things, I'll never know for sure.

I try not to think about it. But it's hard.

CHAPTER TWELVE

Adelaide Boyce Hammond lay propped up by several pillows, her rose-colored bed jacket a sharp contrast against the snowy hospital linen. Her chalky face looked naked without her thick bifocals.

"Lydia, is that you, dear? How thoughtful of you to come."

Miss Addie's left wrist, encased in plaster, lay immobile against the light cotton blanket tucked in at her waist. Her right hand fumbled for her glasses, just out of reach on the table beside the bed.

"Here, let me." I crossed into the room and fitted the wire-rimmed spectacles onto her face.

It was a semi-private room, but the other bed was unoccupied. The privacy curtains had been pulled back from around Miss Addie's space, and the full force of the morning sun streamed through a tall, wide window.

Though I loathed hospital rooms, this one was better than most. An attempt had been made to bring some civilized touches to its stark utility, with overstuffed chairs flanking the window and soft Monet prints grouped on two of the walls. But the IV stand with its tubes snaking down and the constant beeping of the monitors left no doubt that this was still a far cry from home.

I leaned over and planted a kiss on her forehead, drew up the straight-backed visitor's chair, and sat down next to the bed.

"How are you feeling?" I heard myself asking.

How I had hated that question, repeated endlessly by every solicitous friend and co-worker who had dutifully trooped up to visit me when I had been the one trapped in the grid of tubes and electrodes. Yet here I was, asking this poor old woman that same inane question, in the same soft, lugubrious voice that had driven me crazy a few months before.

Miss Addie, however, was a better woman than I. She patted

my hand where it lay next to hers on the bed. "Don't you worry about me, dear. We Hammonds are pretty tough old birds. It's in the genes, you know."

"Can I get you anything? Books, magazines, a newspaper?"

"No dear, but thank you all the same. Apparently someone from The Cedars brought me some of my things last night." Miss Addie fingered the bed jacket with her good hand. then her face clouded over.

"What is it? Are you in pain? I'll get a nurse." I was on my feet, headed for the door, when her voice, surprisingly loud and commanding, stopped me.

"No!" Then, "No, thank you," she said more calmly. "Please, sit back down here, Lydia."

I went meekly back to my chair, puzzled by the change in her demeanor. For some moments, she was silent. Her face pinched in concentration, she seemed to be struggling with some question in her mind. Then she nodded, a decision apparently reached.

"Lydia, something very strange is going on. I really don't want to involve you, but I believe I have no choice."

"What is it? You know I'll help in any way I can."

"You already have, dear, just by being here. I feel much safer already."

"I don't understand. Why wouldn't you feel safe?"

"Lydia, do you think I'm senile? I mean, do I seem to have control of my faculties?"

Loaded question, I thought as the old woman's eyes searched my face. I'd spent only a couple of hours in her presence in the last fifteen years. Who was I to make such a judgment? She had been a little vague at lunch the other day, unsure about her investment in Grayton's Race and confused about the details. And she seemed to dwell a lot on the past. But did that make her senile? At eighty-plus, she had a lot of past to remember.

Then I recalled her twinkling eyes and the wry humor she had displayed, and I shook my head. "No, I don't think you're senile. Maybe a little forgetful . . ."

She smiled at this and nodded.

". . . but from what I've observed in the brief time we've spent together, you seem as in control as anyone your age has a right to expect."

"Good. Because what I'm about to tell you will sound crazy, and I wanted to be certain you were inclined to believe me before I begin."

"Let me ask you something first. Why did you have the Judge and me listed as your next of kin? Surely you still have family, don't you?"

"Of course, but they're all so far away. My younger sister, Edwina, is in Natchez and in poor health. The oldest, Daphne, is in a home outside Atlanta. Clarissa passed away twenty years ago. And their children are scattered all over the country. I only hear from them at Christmas."

"Don't you have a brother?"

"You mean Win."

Edwin Hollister Hammond II had been "Win" since the day he was born, or so I'd been told. I remembered him now. A tall, imposing man, approaching middle age, or so it seemed to me, the first time I was aware of him as a visitor at Presqu'isle. A cheek-pincher who reeked of rum as I recalled, which was why I tended to avoid him.

"Of course. Win. Where is he?"

"I have no idea. Daddy disinherited him, you know. Win never quite believed he'd actually do it, you see, no matter how many times Daddy threatened, so he hung around, waiting for Daddy to die. After the will was read and he found out he really *had* received nothing, he just disappeared. Walked right out the door of the study and vanished. I heard once he'd gone to South America, but no one really knows for certain."

Miss Addie smiled, a sad, sweet expression that made me swallow hard. "I've always missed Win. He was the baby of the family, you know, and my sisters and Mama spoiled him terribly. Oh, I know what everyone said. That he was a scoundrel, always involved in some shady scheme or other. But he was so dashing, a real charmer. The girls were wild for him. Why, I remember—"

The interruption came in the shape of a formidable black woman whose starched white uniform was dazzling against her ebony skin. She had shoulders like a linebacker. The inevitable question was out of her mouth before she even reached the bed.

"And how are we feelin' this mornin'?"

Miss Addie and I exchanged a knowing look.

The nurse continued her interrogation without waiting for a reply. She inquired about headaches, dizziness, pain, while she fussed with the IV, straightened the bedclothes, and made note of temperature, blood pressure, and pulse.

She had asked me to leave when she first began her examination, but Miss Addie had insisted that I stay. The nurse, who had apparently forgotten her name badge, had grudgingly agreed. Finished prodding at last, she placed a cup with two tiny white pills on the wheeled tray table, swung it across the bed, and poured water from a carafe.

Miss Addie pushed the table away.

"Y'all need to take 'em now, Miz Hammond. They'se for the pain, and they'll make you sleepy. And then we'll have to aks your daughter here to leave, so's you can get some rest."

"I'm not—" I began, but was cut off.

"I'll jes wait 'til ya swallow 'em down."

The nurse stood, arms folded across a surprisingly flat chest, her stance somehow menacing. Miss Addie finally gave in.

"Tha's a good girl," Nurse No-Name crooned as she took the glass from Miss Addie's hand and set it on the bedside table.

I itched to slap her. She made the old woman sound like a puppy being praised for peeing on the newspaper instead of on the rug.

"I'll just sit with her until she falls asleep." I didn't phrase it as a question, and Florence Nightingale got the message. She lumbered out without another word.

I promised myself I would find Dr. Winter as soon as possible and see about getting Miss Addie out of here. I knew from my own experience that she'd recover more quickly in her own surroundings. I would hire a private duty nurse to look after her.

"Lydia, dear, you must listen now. I need to tell you about these incidents."

"Incidents?"

"Yes. Over the past few days, someone has been in my rooms. Not the cleaning people, you understand. I know them, and they're quite trustworthy. No, it's someone else, someone going through my things."

"Are you sure?"

"Yes, I'm afraid I am. First it was my desk—papers and so on.

Then some of my little geegaws, figurines and such. Not quite where they should be on the tables, you see. Even my lingerie has been disarranged. Whoever it is, they're very neat and careful. But you see, I'm quite a meticulous person myself. That's how I know."

Miss Addie's eyes were beginning to glaze over as the painkiller took effect. "Mama always insisted on orderliness, everything in its place."

"But why? Do you keep money in your rooms? Jewelry?"

"A little. But nothing is ever taken. Just . . . disturbed."

She stifled a yawn and slid a little farther down in the bed.

"We'll talk about this another time, all right?" I asked. I could see she was struggling to stay awake. "You just rest now. I'll come back tomorrow."

"No. Please. I want to tell you." Miss Addie's voice was slurred. It reminded me somehow of my mother's. "My fall was not an accident."

"What are you saying?"

"I came back early. Forgot my sweater. Someone was there."

"In your apartment? Who?"

"Didn't see. Pushed me."

Her eyes were closed now, but her face was still scrunched up with the effort to hold on to consciousness.

"Someone did this deliberately? But why? I don't understand."

Miss Addie was fast asleep. Her head rolled gently to one side, pushing her glasses askew. I stood and eased them off her face. I removed one of the pillows from behind her back and eased the blanket up over her arms.

A wave of tenderness for this vulnerable old lady swept over me. I smoothed a stray lock of white hair off her forehead, and her eyes popped open, startling me. For a brief moment they were clear and aware, her gaze locked on mine as if trying to send a message directly into my brain.

"It was those awful gardenias," she whispered, her lips barely moving.

Or at least that's what I thought she'd said. But that made no more sense than anything else she'd told me that morning.

I had meant it when I'd reassured her that she was not senile. Yet she claimed someone had been rifling her rooms, going through her things. That this someone had pushed her when she surprised him or her in the act, causing her injuries.

It was much more likely that she had suffered a spell, perhaps even a mild stroke, lost her balance, and fallen, striking her head on the nightstand. That made more sense than a deliberate attack by an unseen prowler.

And yet, fantastic as her story seemed, she'd given me no good reason not to believe her.

The last few days, I thought, watching the gentle rise and fall of her thin chest. *Since she had talked to me about her fears for her investment? Surely this couldn't have anything to do with Grayton's Race, could it?*

My decision came swiftly and easily.

With a quick look over my shoulder at the closed door, I eased out the drawer of the bedside table. A spare box of tissues, some straws, and a well-thumbed Bible were all I found. Crossing to the wardrobe, I opened the double doors. A soft pink dress in a muted print hung neatly from one of the wooden hangers. On the floor, a pair of low-heeled beige shoes rested precisely side by side. The top shelf yielded a surprisingly delicate lacy white slip, bra, and panties folded in a neat pile. Underneath them, I found the object of my search: a trim, beige leather handbag.

I stepped back into the bathroom and closed the door partway. I didn't want to get into a lengthy explanation of why I was digging through Miss Addie's purse should some officious aide come bustling into the room.

There is no such thing as privacy in a hospital.

Her wallet contained forty-six dollars and change, a gold Visa card, a bank ID card, and a driver's license that had expired four years ago. The rest of the bag held a white handkerchief, her resident's pass to The Cedars, an expensive-looking gold fountain pen, and her keys.

I pocketed the key ring and the pass and returned the bag to the wardrobe shelf. I stole a quick look at Miss Addie, who seemed to be sleeping peacefully.

I'll check it out, I promised her silently. If nothing else, I could reassure her that her fears were groundless.

I picked up my bag and slipped quietly out the door.

I had missed Dr. Winter. He had completed his rounds and returned to his office in nearby Bluffton by the time I checked in again at the nurses' station. The woman on duty gave me his number, and I left mine with her, along with a request for him to call me after he'd examined Miss Addie again later in the day.

The full force of the midday heat struck me like a blow when I emerged from the hospital and headed for my car. I lowered the windows, then the top, and cranked up the air conditioning. I thought stopping for a sandwich before I headed down to The Cedars, but this might be a good time to snoop while everyone was busy eating. I could stop for a sandwich now or head on down to The Cedars. This might be a good time to snoop, while everyone was busy eating.

Traffic was heavy, the usual tourist influx swelled by the locals on their lunch breaks. Half an hour and a few frayed nerves later, I turned in at the gate of The Cedars, flashed Miss Addie's pass at the guard, and followed the signs through the piney woods to the building marked Marsh Edge. I'd gotten her condo number from her bank ID. I maneuvered into the designated space and sat, the motor running, my nerve slipping away.

What do you think you're doing here, Tanner? This isn't one of your detective novels, you know.

I lit a cigarette and ran a hand through my tangled hair.

The annoying voice in my head was right, of course. If there really was anything to Adelaide Boyce Hammond's story, I should call Red—turn it all over to the cops. That would be the logical thing to do.

However, logic—and orderly thinking—had not been governing my life lately. I had been running off in all directions, first getting myself involved in Derek Johnson's death and Isaiah Smalls' arrest, then jumping into the Grayton's Race controversy. I had flung accusations, attempted illegal computer hacking, and slept with the chief suspect. Now here I was, ready to leap into . . . what? I couldn't explain what I was looking for, not even to myself.

Not exactly the kind of behavior an obsessive-compulsive bean-counter was expected to display. Chaos had always been my enemy. Even as a child I had reveled in neat columns and rows of numbers, their unwavering perfection susceptible to no capricious whim or subjective interpretation.

Two plus two will always equal four.

Truth—constant, predictable, immutable—in a simple equation. Therein lay happiness, safety—and control.

Or so my personal philosophy had always gone.

So what's it gonna be? I asked myself as I crushed out the cigarette.

Two white-haired ladies, trim in tailored slacks and low-heeled shoes, cast suspicious glances in my direction as they strolled past.

Time to fish or cut bait, little girl, the Judge's voice boomed inside my head.

I rummaged in my bag for Miss Addie's keys, turned off the car, and marched purposefully toward the building.

"In for a penny, in for a pound," I mumbled under my breath as I pushed open the door and headed for the elevator.

Empty, the apartment would have been open and spacious. It was a corner unit with tall windows flanking a real brick fireplace. Ten-foot ceilings rested upon carved oak crown moldings. A formal dining room stood opposite a bright, cheery kitchen with a breakfast nook nestled in the curve of a bay window.

Unfortunately—or so it seemed to me—almost every square inch of space was occupied with what must have been the entire contents of the old Hammond estate. Spindly-legged tables were crammed in between massive chests and armoires; overstuffed chairs fought for space with a delicate Empire sofa. One entire wall of the dining area was taken up by a nineteenth-century mahogany sideboard stuffed with several different patterns of china. It looked as if there were at least three complete services for twelve or more.

I edged my way through the maze of furniture along a well-worn path that offered the only unobstructed route across the plush cream carpeting. I paused in the doorway of the master suite and turned back to survey what had to be a fortune in genuine antiques.

Hand-crocheted antimacassars adorned the back of every chair; Queen Anne tables were littered with expensive bric-a-brac: Lalique, Dresden, and Hummel, along with carved jade Chinoiserie, and several squat little figures that looked to my untrained eye like pre-Columbian art.

The walls, a soft ivory, were plastered with paintings of all sizes and periods, most of them oils in heavy gilt frames. I was no expert, but some of my mother's obsession must have seeped unnoticed into my brain. I was sure one was a Holbein, and another looked remarkably like Sargent.

"This stuff belongs in a museum," I told the refrigerated air that circulated gently through unseen vents. Already the place had that dead, flat smell that pervades closed-up, unused rooms.

I turned my attention back to Miss Addie's bedroom. A beautiful cherry rice bed dominated the center of the room, its graceful tapered posts polished to a deep, rich glow. The tops of the matching bureau and nightstand held the same, priceless litter as had the tables in the living room. An inlaid teakwood jewelry case rested on a cutlace runner across the top of the dresser. I lifted the lid and did a cursory examination of its contents. The pearls were there—the ones she had worn at our lunch date—along with a square cut blue topaz ring that I immediately coveted. The rest looked to be costume stuff, nothing remotely worth bashing a little old lady over the head for.

Two heavy crystal perfume bottles caught my eye, and I reached to remove the stoppers, bringing each to my nose. Essence of violets in one. The second was empty, but a faint fragrance lingered . . . I struggled with the memory . . .

The soft brush of her sable wrap as she leaned over my bed . . . the Judge in the background, tall and elegant in his white coat and black tie, checking his watch.

'Now you be a good girl for Miss Lavinia, hear?'

A touch of cheek on cheek. Dazzle of light off the huge diamond as her strong, elegant fingers disengaged my scrawny arms from around her neck.

'Don't mess mama's hair, Lydia. And don't start snivelin'. I swear, you are the most exasperatin' child!'

The click of the light switch. My father's soft, 'Night, darlin'. Sleep tight.'

Then darkness—and more tears. At four, I wasn't sure why she didn't love me. I only knew for certain that she didn't . . .

Sticky fingers pulled the scratchy, sun-dried sheet up over my head releasing the echo of a scent I would forever associate with loneliness and rejection and my mother . . . Mint and bourbon and . . .

"Chanel Number Five," I said aloud, choking a little on the

lump in my throat.

I returned the stopper to the bottle and resumed my snooping.

I checked out the bathroom, all pearl-pink tile and fluffy towels. I even pushed back the shower curtain.

I returned to the bedroom and opened the drawers of the bureau, giving each a cursory glance. I couldn't bring myself to rifle through them as Miss Addie's unseen attacker had supposedly done.

What the hell do you think you're accomplishing here? I asked myself and couldn't come up with a reasonable answer.

I glanced toward the bed and spied the call button recessed into the wall, just at the height where Miss Addie might accidentally have pushed it in trying to break her fall. I knelt in front of the nightstand and ran my fingers lightly over the carpet. It was still slightly damp, stiff and discolored in a couple of spots where the effort to wash out the blood had not been entirely successful.

Remembering the thin bandage on Miss Addie's forehead, I guessed that the cut had been small and had probably bled only a little.

But someone had been in here since last night, that much was evident. And now that I thought about it, there had been footprints impressed into the thick carpet, along with the tracks left by the wheels of a vacuum cleaner.

And? What's your point? I flopped down on the floor, leaned against the fluffy down comforter, and crossed my legs, Indian-style.

Housekeeping had been in and done what they got paid for—housekeeping. Nothing sinister in that. In fact, that was probably the logical explanation for everything. Things got moved around when they were being cleaned. And what if something *were* missing? How the hell could *I* tell? It appeared to me that someone could cart off a good-sized truckload of Hammond antiques and still not make a dent in the collection. There were no obvious blank spaces on the tables, no telltale circles of clear wood surrounded by a thin layer of dust that might have pointed to a missing object.

So if nothing was stolen, what was the point of the attack? Miss Addie had mentioned papers, so I unfolded myself from the floor and crossed to a delicate rosewood writing desk tucked into the far corner of the room. Its tiny drawers could hardly hold much. They appeared to be more for decoration than utility. I pulled out the matching chair and sat down.

A few receipts, a savings passbook showing a little over twelve thousand dollars, and a box of heavy, embossed stationery were all they yielded up. A black, lacquered Chinese box embellished with bright red poppies held odd buttons, bits of colored thread, a cloth tape measure, and several business cards. I leafed through them. Local businesses—a dry cleaner, hairdresser, and so on. Nothing of interest.

What could this shadowy someone have been looking for?

I rested my chin in my hands and gazed out the window across the marsh. A pair of snowy egrets, their white wings brilliant against the soft blue of the sky, glided gracefully in to land on the trunk of a dead tree lying exposed in the mud at low tide. Behind the marsh, Broad Creek ran sluggishly into Calibogue Sound. One span of the new cross-island highway bridge was just visible between the sweet gums, pines, and palmettos.

A not-too subtle reminder of what some folks thought of as progress and others as desecration. We would always be at odds here, I thought, the preservationists and the developers.

Which led me to Geoff, a subject I had been trying to avoid thinking about all day.

He had called early that morning, full of questions about last night, his concern for Miss Addie's condition sounding genuine enough. He was off to Miami, an urgent meeting with his backers. They were sending a plane for him. He wished I could go with him, but he understood my need to stay close to home in case Miss Addie needed me. He should be back tonight, but would call if he got delayed.

He missed me.

He loved me.

There. It was out.

I knew what he wanted to hear from me, and I sidestepped as best I could. In the cold light of day, the niggling doubts were creeping back. Red had been right. What did I really know about Geoff—except that he was handsome, a tender and skillful lover, and apparently crazy about me?

As Neddie Halloran, my old college roommate, would have

said, three out of three ain't bad.

So what was my problem?

A low growl rumbled in my stomach, reminding me it was way past time for lunch. Even Holmes and Watson had to eat. Unfortunately, I had no Mrs. Hudson to carry in a tray laden with tea and goodies and the best Victorian silver.

Well, this has been a fool's errand, I chided myself as I rose and retrieved my bag from the bed where I had tossed it. As I flung its strap across my shoulder, a picture popped into my head.

Beige shoes, beige purse.

I generally lugged this same, oversized canvas tote with me no matter what I was wearing. Rob used to joke that I could live out of its contents for months, even if I were marooned on a deserted island. But someone of Miss Addie's generation and upbringing would always have a bag to match her shoes. Braxton rules.

I approached the doors of the walk-in closet and flung them wide. She didn't have many clothes, but what she had was of top quality. Shoes were neatly hung on racks along one wall, and above them, a shelf with several handbags in colors ranging from black to navy blue to brown to white. I lifted down the latter, a medium-sized straw with two handles. It was festooned with bright flowers and shells. I recognized it as the bag that had sat next to her chair in the dining room the day we had lunch.

I could tell from the heft of it as I lifted it from the shelf that this was where I would find all the flotsam and jetsam that had been missing from the neat little beige number in the hospital wardrobe. I carried it back into the bedroom and dumped the contents onto the white comforter.

A couple of hankies, one clean, one not. A package of tissues, comb, compact, loose change. The address book it had not occurred to me to miss from the desk, as well as a checkbook with the last few checks not deducted from the balance. I did a quick calculation and figured she had something more than fifteen hundred dollars in her account.

There were several envelopes among the jumble, all opened, most advertisements and credit card offers. I removed the enclosure from the one with The Cedars as the return address. It was an invoice for her fees for the month of August, due on the first, now just a few days away. The sum was staggering. No wonder she had been so upset about the delays in Grayton's Race. At this rate, Miss Addie's savings would be gone by Christmas.

The last item was a sheet of plain white paper, folded over several times into a small rectangle. I had just opened it out and realized it was a photocopy of a handwritten letter, when I heard the click of a key in the front door lock.

Hastily I scooped up the address book and checkbook and dropped them into my own capacious bag. The rest I stuffed back into the straw purse, crossed swiftly to the closet, and replaced it on the shelf. I was heading for the hall when I realized I still had the photocopy in my hand. I quickly refolded it and stuffed it into the pocket of my slacks just as Mrs. Dixon stepped into the room.

We nearly collided in the doorway.

"Mrs. Tanner!" she cried, her hand flying to her chest. "My God, you nearly frightened me half out of my wits!"

"What is it, Ari?" a voice boomed from the living room. "Who's here?"

I recognized the Spanish lilt of the dashing Mr. Romero even before he joined Mrs. Dixon in the doorway. I had no choice but to retreat. They were blocking my only avenue of escape.

"Mr. Romero, how nice to see you again. I just popped in to pick up a few things for Miss Hammond. One always feels so much more at home if one has one's own things at hand, don't you find?"

God, I was prattling like an idiot! What was the matter with me? Why should I feel so intimidated by two resthome employees?

"Quite." Ariadne Dixon's face hardened into its habitual sneer of disapproval. "However, I personally sent over what I thought Miss Hammond would require in the way of necessities last night. Did I miss something?"

It was probably only my lurid imagination that read a *double-entendre* into the question.

I smiled sweetly and moved toward the door. Neither of them budged.

"If you'll excuse me now, I really should be getting back to the hospital."

"And did you get what you came for?" Mrs. Dixon asked archly as she reluctantly moved aside, allowing me to pass.

"Yes, thanks so much," I bubbled.

I clutched my tote bag tightly against my side and nearly sprinted for the front door.

"Visitors are required to register at the reception desk." Romero's voice was low and accusatory. "I did not see your name."

Okay, buster, that's enough. I wheeled to face them.

"Oh, but I'm not a visitor. I'm the next of kin. Isn't that right, Ari?" I dangled Miss Addie's keys in front of her nose.

She bristled at my use of her pet name. Maybe it was reserved for friends—or lovers?

"And, besides which," I went on, the arrogance bred of my Southern aristocratic ancestors dripping from every word, "I fail to see why my comings and goings should be of concern to a *maitre d'* and a part-time receptionist."

Ari looked as if she'd like to rip me to shreds with her well-manicured nails. Mr. Macho Romero betrayed his anger only by a tightening of his fists at his sides. The supercilious smile never left his face.

I was appalled that I had ever found him attractive.

I wrenched open the door and stepped aside, a pointed invitation for them to precede me. With a quick glance at each other, they filed out, pausing in the hallway while I locked the door behind me. I waited them out, determined that they would not re-enter the apartment the minute my back was turned.

"Was there something else?"

Again they consulted each other with their eyes. It was Mrs. Dixon who spoke.

"We merely came to be certain that everything was in order. In Miss Hammond's absence, we felt it our duty to safeguard her possessions."

"How very commendable of you. However," I sneered back, "that will no longer be necessary. I live very close by, so I'll be dropping in from time to time to check on things myself. Until such time as Miss Hammond can return."

"As you wish." Ariadne Dixon stepped into the elevator alongside her accomplice, and the three of us rode down in strained silence.

We parted at the outside door, and the two of them moved off toward the main building. They stopped a short way down the sidewalk and stood watching me, their heads together in earnest conversation.

My hands shook a little as I leaned against my car and lit a cigarette. This time it wasn't from nicotine deprivation. There was something scary about those two. I had no trouble picturing either one of them pushing Miss Addie down, then slithering away, leaving her to be found by someone else.

And the other thing that made my knees wobbly was that trip down in the elevator. In the enclosed space, I had become aware of a smell, sweet and flowery. Whether it was his aftershave or her perfume, I couldn't tell. Neither could I identify it for certain as gardenia. But it could have been.

The paper I had thrust hurriedly into my pocket crackled against my leg as I slid behind the wheel. All I had been able to see before Dixon and Romero had come barging in was the start of the inside address, written in a formal, spidery script that had to be Miss Addie's.

Mr. J. Lawton Merriweather, Attorney.

I knew Law Merriweather. In fact, I had scolded him for recklessly drawing to an inside straight last Thursday night in the Judge's study. I had taken that pot with a full house—aces over eights, as I recalled.

I couldn't read the letter with my two antagonists glaring at me from just a few feet away, but I would examine it the minute I got home.

I hoped it was only a coincidence that Law Merriweather shared office space with Hadley Bolles.

CHAPTER
THIRTEEN

I stopped long enough to grab a cold sub sandwich to carry back to the house with me. The confrontation at The Cedars had decided me—I was calling Red as soon as I got in the door.

I didn't know exactly what was going on, but that little scene had convinced me that Miss Addie's fears had to be taken seriously. I wanted Red there to hear her story first-hand as soon as she woke up.

There was a strange car parked in the drive as I pulled in. I didn't know anyone with a red Mustang convertible, so far as I could remember. Then I spotted the dealer tag and realized who it had to be, just as Bitsy Elliott trotted down the steps to intercept me.

"Bay! Thank God! I thought I was goin' to have to sit here on your stairway for *days* waitin' for y'all to get home!"

"How'd you get into the plantation?"

It wasn't the friendliest of greetings, but I was getting a little irritated at people dropping in on me with no warning. What was the point of having a security gate if the whole world could just wander in unannounced?

"Well, when I couldn't reach you, I called your daddy, and he told me about Miss Hammond. How is the old dear? Lord, I haven't seen her in dog's years. I'll have to call Mama and let her know. I'm sure she'll want to send some flowers and a note. I remember Miss Hammond was especially kind to us when Daddy passed."

One good thing about a conversation with Bitsy was that you didn't have to contribute if you didn't want to.

"So anyway, I called the hospital, and they told me that Miss Hammond was doin' as well as could be expected and that you had already left."

The running monologue continued as I unlocked the door and

headed for the kitchen. If I didn't eat soon, I was going to be sick.

Bitsy helped herself to iced tea and poured one for me while I unwrapped the sandwich.

"So then I thought, who do I know in Port Royal? Besides you, of course. And Jane Anne Bingham's name just popped right into my head. And she very kindly called me in a pass and here I am!"

I was wolfing down the sub, nodding at Bitsy and wiping occasional dribbles of oil and vinegar off my chin with a paper napkin. About halfway through, I had taken enough of the edge off my hunger to give my friend my full attention, and I realized with a start that she looked awful.

Her eyes seemed bruised, the soft skin beneath them puffy from crying. The smile was forced, as was the chatter. It was overdone, even for Bitsy. She twirled the tall, frosty glass around in her hands, ice cubes rattling against the sides while she studied the flower pattern on the blue place mat with more attention than it deserved. Her sudden silence was a sure-fire clue that she had something on her mind.

I stuffed the last of the sandwich in my mouth, washed it down with tea, and reached for her hand.

"Bits, what is it? What's wrong?"

The tears came in a flood, cascading down her face. She made no attempt to wipe them away. I snatched tissues from the box on the counter and laid them in front of her, but she made no move to pick them up.

"Come on, tell me," I implored, moving around to the chair next to hers. I put an arm around her shoulder, and she collapsed against me. The sobs shook her entire body.

"Is it Cal again? What has he done?" I tightened my embrace and stroked her hair, the same way Lavinia used to comfort me when I was little. "I swear, if he hit you again, I'll take the Judge's .22 and shoot the bastard myself."

I felt the barely perceptible shake of her head against my shoulder.

Well, she'd deny it anyway, even if he had, I thought. I would never understand how a woman could stay with a man who beat her. Never.

I continued patting and crooning meaningless reassurances until soft hiccups and snuffles signaled the end of the storm. Bitsy sat up and offered me a watery smile, then reached for the wad of tissues on the table. She scrubbed at her face and blew her nose.

"I'm okay now, Bay, honey. Really."

"Sure?"

"Uh-huh." She took a sip of tea and rose to deposit the soggy tissues in the trash. "Got a cigarette?" she asked as she flopped back down at the table, and I returned to my chair across from her.

"A cigarette? Elizabeth Quintard Elliott, you haven't smoked since high school! And it always made you sick. You only did it to try to prove you were as cool as I was."

The real Bitsy smile was back on her gamin face. "It's a cigarette or a bourbon. Your choice."

I dug the pack out of my tote bag and shook two out. I leaned across to light it for her. She inhaled expertly and blew smoke toward the ceiling.

"You've been practicing," I accused, pushing the ashtray between us.

Her laugh was rueful. "What is it the kids say nowadays? Busted?"

We smoked in silence for awhile, Bitsy seeming to grow calmer with each puff.

That's why it's so hard to quit, I thought. *Sometimes there's just nothing so comforting.*

"Okay, girl, let's have it," I said at last.

Bitsy stubbed out the cigarette and gathered herself as if preparing for battle. "I think CJ is doin' drugs."

This was the last thing I'd expected her to blurt out, and I was momentarily stunned.

CJ? The star quarterback?

"That's crazy," I finally managed to splutter. "He's an athlete! He wouldn't do anything so stupid to his body."

Then names—famous ones—professional ballplayers in the headlines, flashed through my mind, and I realized what a thoroughly asinine statement that had been. It reminded me of Red the other day at the Judge's, ridiculing me for denying that teenagers could commit murder.

"That's what Big Cal said," Bitsy replied. "I tried to talk to him about it, and he just blew up. That's what we were really fightin' about last week, not just money like I told you. Sorry."

"That's okay. I knew you weren't telling me the whole story. You always were a lousy liar." I walked to the refrigerator and poured us out some more tea. "Want to sit out on the deck?"

The sun was behind the trees now, and the breeze would be kicking in from the ocean.

"Sure."

We carried our glasses and the cigarettes and stretched out on two chaises. The air was heavy with the smell of pine and salt, the light slanting through the oaks dappling the weathered wood of the railing.

"So what makes you think CJ is using?" I asked quietly. The very thought of that perfect young body riddled with drugs made me shudder.

"I think Mally knows. That was the first I really forced myself to look at it. But I think I'd been suspectin' something for quite a while without havin' the nerve to put a name to it."

"Mally told you?"

"Not exactly. She'd never rat out her brother. But she's been leaving pamphlets—you know, the kind of thing they pass out at school?—lyin' around where I'll be sure to see them. How to spot the signs, where to get help. That sort of thing."

Bitsy reached for the cigarettes and lit this one herself.

"So what are the signs?" For all the media blitz about teenagers and drugs, I realized I was woefully ignorant of the specifics. It was totally outside my experience.

"Well, to back up a little, I think he may have started out with steroids. You remember how scrawny he was goin' into high school?"

"Yeah, I guess I do. He was always built more like you than Cal, though, except for the height."

"I've been doing some readin', and I see now that it wasn't natural the way he just bulked up so fast. The summer between his freshman and sophomore years, he suddenly filled right out, got muscles, put on weight. I thought it was because he and Isaiah were workin' out all the time, lifting weights and all."

Isaiah Smalls! Please, God, I thought, *don't let him be involved in this, too.* It would flat out kill Lavinia and his parents.

"Anyway," Bitsy continued, "he developed skin problems later on that year, too. That's another sign. I assumed it was just the typical teenage thing, although neither Cal or I ever had a problem with acne."

That was true enough. Bitsy's flawless complexion had been the envy of every girl in high school.

"But steroids aren't that bad, are they? I mean, it's not like crack or heroin."

Bitsy picked a fallen twig up off the deck and began to strip the bark from it. "I think he's graduated up to some of those other things. Marijuana, for one. On the rare occasions when he lets me close enough to actually hug him, I can smell it. Sort of sweet and cloyin', isn't that how it smells?"

Leave it to my best friend to assume that I would be an expert on the aroma of a joint. Not that I hadn't tried it once or twice in college, but she didn't know that for sure. Actually, I hadn't been all that impressed with the whole thing. Being high meant being out of control.

"Yes, that's a pretty accurate description," I admitted. "But is that all you have to go on? I mean, don't you think you might be jumping to conclusions a little here?"

"Why else would Mally be leavin' all those drug brochures around? And CJ's grades did drop at the end of last year. He used to be a solid 'B' student."

"What does Cal think?"

"That I'm nuts. You know how he feels about CJ. He's been primin' our son to carry on the Elliott tradition at Clemson almost from the day he was born. If he thought for a minute it was true, he'd probably kill CJ and whoever he thought was supplying him. In fact, he said so the night he stormed out of the house."

"Have you asked Mally about it?"

"Oh, I couldn't do that! I couldn't put her in the position of havin' to betray her brother's confidence."

It was at times like these I was happy that Rob and I had decided against starting a family right away. We always meant to, one day, but the time just never seemed to be right.

"Look, Bits, do you want me to talk to Mally, see what she knows? It wouldn't be the same thing as telling you. It might be easier for me to persuade her that she was helping rather than squealing on him."

Bitsy rolled onto her side and regarded me expectantly. "What I'd really like you to do is talk to your friend, the psychologist. I think maybe she could help us. Do you think she might?"

"You mean Neddie ? What a good idea! She's a specialist on kids and drugs."

Nedra Halloran had been my college roommate for two years at Northwestern. We'd met in a computer class when she was still a business major. We were as different as Bitsy and I were, and again that somehow seemed to form the basis for a lasting friendship.

Neddie, Boston-Irish, with flaming red hair and sea-green eyes, had switched to psychology in our last year, right after her adored younger brother had died of a heroin overdose at the age of eighteen. She'd had to stay on and start nearly from scratch, but she was determined to do something with her life that could help to spare other families from the agony her own had suffered.

She had visited me on breaks and had fallen in love with the South. After completing her training, she'd made the move, setting up her practice in nearby Savannah. We kept in touch sporadically, but Neddie deserved a lot of the credit for getting me through this last year. Her sound, no-nonsense advice, offered only when I solicited it, had helped to keep me sane when the world around me seemed to have gone crazy.

"I thought maybe y'all could come to dinner, observe CJ in his natural habitat, so to speak. What do you think?"

"I still think you might be overreacting, but maybe Neddie could put your mind at rest. Want me to call her?"

"Do you think she'd do it? I mean, come to the house? Big Cal would never agree to take CJ to a psychologist. He doesn't hold with that kinda thing."

I nearly snorted out loud. I just bet Big Cal didn't want anything to do with a shrink. One of them might just figure out why *he* was so screwed up.

"I'm sure she will if I ask her to." I patted Bitsy's arm reassuringly and was rewarded with a dazzling grin.

"You're the best, Bay, honey, the absolute best." Bitsy glanced down at her watch and jumped to her feet. "Lord, look at the time! If I don't get on home, the kids will be tearin' the kitchen apart. I swear, those four can leave a place stripped of food faster 'n a swarm of locusts!"

I walked her out to the car, and we hugged.

"I'll call you and set up a time, shall I? Then you can check with your friend and see if it suits. I'll try to pick a night when Big Cal is visitin' one of the dealerships upstate." She slipped her sunglasses on and squeezed my hand. "That way I won't have to hire an off-duty policeman to keep you and my husband from murderin' each other."

"Good plan," I acknowledged as she backed the Mustang around and sped out of the driveway. I watched her take the turn too fast and kick up gravel from the side of the road. Her spirits had apparently been restored. Bitsy in a good humor was literally hell on wheels.

My indulgent smile faded as I turned and trudged back up the steps. Another complication in a week that was already threatening to swamp me. Just what I needed.

I picked up the phone and dialed the sheriff's office.

By the time Red called me back, late that night, so many things had happened in between, I'd almost forgotten why I wanted to talk to him.

I had spent so much of the day on the telephone the receiver had seemingly become an extension of my arm. None of the news had been good . . .

Dr. Winter's call, not long after Bitsy left, had started the flood of bad tidings. Miss Addie could not be awakened, and he feared she had slipped into a coma. He was surprised, because the bump on her head had been minor, and she'd seemed to be making good progress.

"I can be there in ten minutes," I'd told him, my heart sinking into my shoes. I'd grown attached to Miss Addie in the last few days. The thought that she might die was almost more than I could bear.

Dr. Winter forestalled me. He was moving her into intensive care, and no visitors would be allowed until she was stabilized. Apparently my legal status as next of kin didn't cut any ice with the good doctor. He promised to keep me informed.

I retreated back onto the deck, a portable phone and Miss Addie's address book in hand. Edwina, the invalid sister in Natchez, was upset, but unable to travel. She told me she was nearly paralyzed by arthritis. Her children and grandchildren were scattered over California, Nevada, and Montana. She didn't feel she could impose on any of them to make such a long trip when there was really nothing anyone could do right now.

"Adelaide is fortunate to have such good friends as you and your father," Edwina drawled.

I hung up, frustrated and more than a little angry at the cavalier manner in which she'd passed her sister's welfare over into the hands of virtual strangers.

Daphne was having one of her "bad" days, or so the sympathetic director of the nursing home outside Atlanta informed me. There was no point in my talking to her, since she didn't even know who *she* was at the moment.

"Late-stage Alzheimer's, you know." The woman spoke in a whisper, as if naming the dread disease might somehow provoke it into claiming the minds of still more of her elderly residents.

I left it to her to break the news, should a period of relative lucidity overtake Miss Addie's sister.

I had no idea how to go about finding Win, the disinherited scoundrel who had fled for parts unknown more that twenty years ago. Who even knew if he was still alive?

I sat for awhile, staring out at nothing, as shadows overtook the deck. On impulse, I stuffed the cigarettes in my pocket and trotted barefoot down the steps that gave onto the path to the beach. The sun was setting over the mainland, and streaks of mauve and orange spread through high, wispy clouds, diffusing the splendor from shore to horizon. I wandered along in the surf, kicking up little sprays of water. It was not yet high tide and there was plenty of beach left between ocean and dune.

I encountered a jogger, headphones firmly in place. The wire disappeared into the pocket of her shorts where the Walkman bounced against her leg with every stride. She nodded as we passed, the look of grim determination never leaving her face. An overweight couple, their matching neon-yellow T-shirts a bright splash against the darkening sky, bicycled by me. Tourists from the nearby Westin Hotel, I guessed, anxious to wring every last second of enjoyment from their limited vacation days. I hoped their red faces were a result of too much sun and not from the unaccustomed effort of pedaling beach bikes through loose sand.

I walked on toward the narrow spit of land that jutted out into the water. Beyond it, a long sand bank rose, barely visible now in the mid-tide shift. Farther out, I could just discern the outline of Bay Point off the tip of St. Helena Island. Presqu'isle lay at the other end. It was hard to believe that this narrow strip of water was all that separated me from my childhood home. It would take an hour to drive it going by land.

I sat below the dune and smoked, marveling as the faint, pinkish glow was overtaken by the deepening purple twilight. The sweep and grandeur of the ocean had its usual calming effect. I rose and strolled back toward the house.

I would never be able to live far from the water again.

The portable phone was ringing as I climbed the stairs. My soggy pantslegs clung to my ankles as I sprinted up the steps and grabbed it up before the machine could kick on.

"Hello?" I gasped, collapsing onto the chaise. My feet were caked with sand, and I had left powdery footprints all along the deck.

"Bay, honey, you okay? You sound out of breath."

My father's voice was soft and low, his usual bluff heartiness missing.

"I was down at the beach. I had to run to get the phone. What's up? You sound kind of done-in yourself."

"Oh, I'm fine, sweetheart, don't you worry. Just a little tired, is all. Vinnie was just here. Left a few minutes ago. She asked me to call you."

"I knew she'd never be able to trust Dolores to look after you. She probably had visions of your being force-fed tacos and burritos and refried beans."

"No, no. Nothin' like that. In fact the two of them seemed to get on pretty good. Spent more 'n half an hour gabbin' in the kitchen when Vinnie first got here."

The Judge sounded more than tired. He seemed weighed down by a weariness that would take more than a good night's sleep to cure. At that moment I decided to hold off telling him about Miss Addie's relapse. He had enough on his plate already.

"How is Lavinia holding up?"

"She's fine, just fine. Listen, Bay, they've released Derek's body to the family. The funeral is tomorrow, ten o'clock, at the AME church outside Bluffton. You know the one, don't you? On 278?"

"Yes, I know it. It's got that little fenced-in cemetery right next to it."

So this was the cause of his gravity. He would be feeling Lavinia's distress, sharing it.

"Aren't they going to have a viewing?"

"Under the circumstances, they thought it best not to. There's been enough publicity already. It will be a small, private ceremony. Family only. Vinnie just wants to get it behind them, let them get on with their lives."

I thought about Thaddeus and Colletta. And Isaiah. They, too, would undoubtedly like to see closure on what must be extremely painful for them all.

The silence lengthened, my father and I both wrapped in our own thoughts.

"I would like to attend the service, Bay." His voice, firm and strong again, startled me. "Vinnie has invited us, and I want you to take me."

This was another shock, to add to the many I'd had already today. My father rarely left the house. He never appeared in public.

"Are you sure?"

"Of course I'm sure. Do you think I'd let Vinnie go through an ordeal like this alone?"

"She's not alone. She has her family."

"*We* are her family, too," he bellowed, all trace of melancholy gone. "I'll expect you here by nine."

The slam of the receiver was loud in the damp night stillness.

Damn it all, I thought, reaching shakily for a cigarette, *why am I always the bad guy? I'm thirty-eight years old, and I haven't been able to please him my entire damned life. Why the hell do I keep on trying?*

I set the phone on the deck beside me and lay back in the chaise. Dew was beginning to settle as the air cooled, and the moisture had seeped into the cushions. I watched the stars wink on through the haze of the smoke I blew up toward the sky.

A soft, plaintive *meow* drifted up from the ground below me, and I called softly to Mr. Bones. He bounded up the steps and leaped eagerly onto my stomach. He was purring loudly even before he had settled himself. I stroked his night-damp fur and gave myself up to the pain.

I had struggled for almost a year to overcome the belief that life had cheated me, to rise above the despondency that had settled like a pall over my spirit after Rob was killed. I had denied myself the luxury of surrendering to the deep, wrenching grief. I had known instinctively that, given free rein, it would have crushed me.

Instead I had tried to heed the "Baynards are made of sterner stuff" crap my mother used to preach at me. I had sucked it up and gone on as best I could.

So that night, with the cat making soothing, kneading motions against my chest, I allowed myself to wallow in all the self-pity I had so long denied.

It felt good.

It didn't solve anything, but it felt good.

If Geoff Anderson hadn't picked that moment to call, things might have gone differently. He wanted to let me know he wouldn't be back until later the next day, business having held him up longer than he'd anticipated.

I was confused, unsure what to say, how to act, and it came through loud and clear.

Geoff was hurt, bewildered by my lack of response to his warmth, his expressions of love. I didn't blame him. I'd certainly led him to expect more from me than the curt, one-word replies he was receiving.

But he didn't get the message. He pressed. "What's wrong, Bay? What have I done?"

"Nothing."

"What do you mean, nothing? Something's bugging you. Tell me."

"I'm just tired."

"It's more than that. Is it your friend in the hospital? Or are you having second thoughts about last night?"

Damn him! I blushed, remembering that smug little speech I'd made to myself outside Geoff's bedroom door. The one about consigning Rob to a special place in my heart and getting on with my life. What a handy little piece of self-deception that had been!

"Bay? Are you? Having second thoughts?"

"No. Maybe. I don't know."

By the time we hung up, Geoff's hurt had blossomed into anger. I knew I could expect to find him pounding on my door as soon as he got back onto the island.

I disengaged the cat's claws from my cotton sweater and dragged myself inside. I needed food and sleep, in that order . . .

So I was scrounging in the cupboards when Red's call came in, bringing the disastrous day full circle. At first I let the machine answer and would have ignored him altogether, if my brother-in-law hadn't sounded so concerned. Next thing I knew, *he* would be over here, demanding explanations.

So I picked up the phone and made him wish he hadn't been so insistent. Red got the full brunt of my anger, guilt, and frustration. It wasn't fair, but, hey—that's what families are for. He took it well.

"Let's talk tomorrow, after you've had a chance to calm down a little, okay?"

Red spoke in that perfectly reasonable tone that made me want to strangle him.

I replaced the receiver for the final time that night without mentioning Miss Addie. There seemed no point now that she was comatose. Then I went back to foraging. I settled on two slices of toast piled with chunky peanut butter and a banana whose peel was more black than yellow.

Too keyed up to go to bed, I flipped on the television and stretched out on the couch. I fell asleep with the Braves trailing the Padres, four to one in the bottom of the sixth.

CHAPTER
FOURTEEN

It was too perfect a day to be dealing with death.

A cool front had lowered the humidity and the temperature to the mid-seventies, making it feel more like April than late July. Fat, cottony clouds, wandering aimlessly in a delft-blue sky, provided welcome patches of shade in the stark, treeless cemetery.

I stood beside the Judge's wheelchair, one hand resting on the rubber-tipped handle, as much for reassurance as for balance. The heels of my navy blue pumps were sinking into the soft, sandy soil.

Ours were the only white faces in the group gathered loosely around the splendid oak coffin. Draped in lavish sprays of lilies, roses, and carnations, it rested on a plain wood bier next to the yawning hole in the ground. Not for the first time in my life, I shuddered at the barbarism of funeral customs.

The gaunt, graying Reverend Gregory Jackson read the service. His voice rose and fell in a sing-song cadence that gave the clichéd words an unusual beauty. A soft chorus of murmured *amen*s could be heard now and then in the background. Many of the well-dressed women, eyes closed, faces uplifted, swayed from side to side, as if to the strains of an unearthly music only they could hear.

I looked across the tarp-covered mound of dirt next to the grave at the three women who huddled together at the foot of the coffin. Lavinia Smalls stood ramrod straight, her dry-eyed gaze fastened on the empty field beyond the church. One arm encircled the heaving shoulder of her sister, Mavis, whose son was about to be consigned to the ground. Chloe, the other half-sister, sobbed uncontrollably on Mavis's right, her brown face mottled by grief.

They were a strange contrast, these three products of the same mother and obviously different fathers.

Behind them and off to one side, the rest of the Smalls family stood tall and proud. Thaddeus looked strikingly handsome in a dark gray suit that lent him a dignity his postal worker's uniform could never achieve. He and Colletta flanked their only child, their stance at once protective and defiant. Their posture dared anyone to cast a glance of suspicion on the son whose head was bowed in respectful silence.

A mourning dove was cooing somewhere off to my left, a soft, measured refrain that seemed a fitting accompaniment to the close of the service. Reverend Jackson scooped up a handful of loose dirt and solemnly offered it to Mavis as the coffin was lowered into the grave. With a trembling hand, she sprinkled it over the rich gloss of the polished oak. As the mourners began to disperse, most pausing to offer a word of comfort to the weeping Mavis, someone began to hum the melody of an old, cherished hymn. Others picked it up, and soon the sad, sweet strains filled the tiny cemetery, rising unfettered in the clear air.

Around a surprisingly large lump in my throat, I found myself joining in, the words rising unbidden from some long-dormant corner of my memory:

. . . ye who are weary come home.
Earnestly, tenderly Jesus is calling,
Calling, O Sinner, come home.

The Judge added his clear baritone, and I wanted the peace I felt at that moment to go on forever.

When the song ended, my father and I smiled wistfully at each other, shared memory heavy between us. If only my mother's religious fervor had had room for such sweetness, such spontaneity, maybe . . .

Lavinia approached us, and the spell was broken.

"Thank you," she said simply, her gratitude encompassing us both. "Will you join us at Mavis's?"

"I think not," my father replied. "We'll just pay our respects here and get on back to the house. That'll be best, don't you reckon?"

"Of course. Whatever you think best." She took my hand and patted it gently. "It meant a lot to us that you were here today. Both of you."

Lavinia turned away and led us up to the small knot of family gathered around Mavis. The Judge shook her hand solemnly and offered his formal condolences. I added my own, and she thanked us for the flowers.

I helped the Judge maneuver his chair across the rough gravel parking lot and onto the ramp that would lift him into the van. *Got to give the old buzzard credit*, I thought, hitching up the straight skirt of my navy blue dress and climbing into the driver's seat. He had sat tall through the whole service, his infirmity displayed to a group of almost total strangers. Maybe there was hope for him yet.

"You look pretty handsome today, Your Honor," I remarked as I backed the big van around and headed down the drive. I hadn't seen him in a suit and starched shirt since I couldn't remember when.

My father snorted, a self-deprecatory little grunt, closed his eyes, and settled back in his chair.

"Okay, fine," I said.

I fiddled with the unfamiliar air conditioning controls, got the vents adjusted, and pulled out onto the highway toward Beaufort. The tune of the hymn kept running through my head, and I found myself humming it softly, trying to hold onto the serenity the music had brought me. It lasted until I pulled around a slow-moving green Bronco in the right-hand lane and glanced idly over at the driver.

Red Tanner, in civilian clothes and his own car, looked sheepishly back at me and waved. The stern, ebony face of Matt Gibson, chief death investigator for the Sheriff's Department, regarded me sternly from the passenger seat. His nod of recognition was curt and something less than cordial, although we'd known each other since grade school.

So you were staking out the funeral, I thought, accelerating past them and nearly cutting Red off as I whipped back into the inside lane.

The bastards! Why couldn't they leave Lavinia and her family in peace, at least on this one day?

"And just when I was beginning to like you again, Tanner," I mumbled as I reached for my cigarettes and stabbed in the lighter, "you have to go acting like a cop."

The Judge studied me for a second, one bushy white eyebrow raised, then settled back into his nap.

Dolores, no doubt in honor of the solemnity of the occasion, had set lunch out on the long mahogany table in the dining room. The second-best china—the Royal Doulton with the deep blue border—reflected the glow of the crystal chandelier, lighted in an effort to dispel the gloom of the dark paneled walls. Waterford goblets and highly polished heavy silver sparkled against the white damask cloth.

That'll teach them to underestimate Dolores, I thought as I walked around the elegantly proportioned room, idly touching these treasures that had been so important to my mother. Neither she nor Lavinia would have been able to find a single flaw in the perfection of the table. Even the flowers, picked that morning from the garden Lavinia maintained along with all her other duties, were artfully arranged in a low Chinese vase.

"It looks wonderful," I told a hovering Dolores.

"*Gracias, Señora.* Your mother, she had many beautiful things."

"Yes, she did."

I was about to ask why there were three places set when a timer *dinged* in the kitchen, and Dolores scuttled off. I was pretty certain I knew who our guest was going to be, and it was not going to make for a companionable meal.

What I really wanted to do was get out of these clothes, throw on a ratty T-shirt and rattier shorts, and flop myself on the beach for about three days. No phones, no problems—mine or anyone else's. Just me and the ocean and the sun.

But I couldn't let all of Dolores's efforts go to waste. Besides, I needed to be where the hospital could reach me. I had called this morning, before leaving home, but there had been no change in Miss Addie's condition.

The doorbell chimed, and I went to let Red in.

We eyed each other warily. I left him to close the door himself, and he followed me silently into the front parlor. This was one of my favorite rooms, small and elegantly decorated with claw-footed Empire furniture and pale yellow walls.

"Drink?" I offered as Red moved across the straw-colored carpet. He stopped in front of a glass-fronted highboy and studied my mother's collection of antique salts. "Oops, sorry," I sneered, sounding anything but, "I forgot. You're still on duty."

Red turned slowly to face me. "You know, it amazes me that my brother never beat you."

I could tell by the tilt of one corner of his generous mouth that he was joking, but it was a subject I couldn't take lightly. I'd applied too many ice packs to too many of Bitsy's bruises to find domestic violence amusing.

"If you're trying to piss me off more than I already am, you're making a damned good start."

"Profanity is the refuge of a limited vocabulary," my father announced from the hall. This doorway was too narrow to allow the wheelchair through. It had been my mother's room, anyway. The Judge had rarely entered it even when he could walk.

"Samuel Pepys. Or Ben Johnson. One or the other of them," I said as I pushed his chair toward the dining room. Red trailed along behind.

"Neither," the Judge tossed over his shoulder.

I settled him at the head of the table and walked around to the place on his right. Red, his face still crinkled in amusement, held the chair for me.

"Christopher Marlowe. John Donne." I fired names at him as I unfolded the damask napkin and draped it across my lap.

"Not even close."

"Okay, you win. I'm stumped. Who said it?"

The Judge lifted the cover on a silver chafing dish, releasing a pungent steam redolent of garlic, wine, and seafood. He smiled in triumph.

"My mama."

"Granny Simpson? That's cheating! She's not in Bartlett's."

"No, but she was a very wise and wonderful woman. You'd do well to heed her advice."

My only memories of my grandmother were of painfully twisted, arthritic fingers, a deeply lined face, and a soft, breathless voice that never failed to soothe. But I had been spellbound by all the stories about her. She had been a Southern lady in the truest sense of both those words. Even my mother hadn't argued with that.

We helped ourselves to the perfectly prepared filet of sole that fell apart in tender chunks at the slightest touch of the fork. Fluffy rice laced with baby peas and pearl onions was accompanied by crisp, green snap beans, blanched just enough to bring out their fresh-picked sweetness.

We spoke of inconsequential things, our concentration reserved for appreciation of the meal. By the time Red, the last to finish, finally leaned back in his chair, the atmosphere had mellowed considerably. I poured coffee for the men from a tall, antique pot.

"I can't believe you still do that." My father stirred cream into his cup and pointed at my plate.

A small row of peas lay off to one side of the otherwise empty dish. They were arranged in a neat semicircle, the green half-moon precisely symmetrical and evenly spaced.

"You know I hate the damned things, but Dolores keeps trying to slip them by me."

"Bay is the only person I've ever known," my father said, turning to Red, "who could eat a helping of vegetable soup and leave a pile of peas in the bottom of the bowl."

"A truly talented woman," my brother-in-law replied with a grin. "I've always said so."

I rose and began clearing the table, ignoring their little jokes at my expense. Dolores was just removing a bubbling peach pie out of the oven as I stacked the dishes on the counter.

"That was a fabulous meal, *amiga*. Thank you."

The flush of her olive skin might have been from the heat of the kitchen, but I suspected it was more from my calling her my friend. We had long ago passed out of the stage of employer and servant, so far as I was concerned. But it made Dolores uncomfortable, for some inexplicable reason, and she preferred to maintain a certain formality in our relationship.

"Will I serve the dessert now, *Señora*? There is also the iced cream. It is the peach, too. Your favorite, no?"

"My favorite, yes," I answered, pulling out the racks of the dishwasher.

"No, no, *Señora!* You must see to the guest. I will do."

She shooed me out of the kitchen, and I followed the smell of cigar smoke down the hall to the Judge's room.

". . . so it keeps coming back to Isaiah Smalls and the Elliott kid," I heard Red say as I walked into the blue haze. I slipped off my shoes and curled up on my favorite window seat. Red passed me an ashtray as I lit a cigarette.

"Why?" I asked, adding my own stream of smoke to the cloud hanging close to the ceiling. Even the combined efforts of the air conditioning and an oak ceiling fan whirling at full speed couldn't clear the air.

Red opened a window in self-defense, then looked at the Judge as if for permission to speak.

"What?" I demanded, suppressed anger rising again in my chest. "I have as much right as he does to know what's going on."

Again the two men exchanged glances, Red looking as uncomfortable as he had the day he came hunting for Lavinia.

Was that really less than a week ago? I asked myself incredulously. It seemed as if enough had happened in the past few days to fill at least a couple of months.

I rose and replaced the ashtray on the Judge's desk. I picked up a round glass paperweight and tossed it back and forth between my hands

"Well? So what's the big secret? Don't make me charm it out of you. I'm really not up to it."

My attempt to lighten the mood fell flat. The heavy silence lengthened, and I could hear the measured beats of the grandfather clock down the hall.

Red ran a hand through his thick, brown hair and mumbled, "You're not gonna like it."

"I don't like being kept out of the loop, either, so it's a toss-up. Come on, give."

"We've been investigating Geoffrey Anderson as a possible suspect in the murder of Derek Johnson."

The words came out in a rush. Red actually flinched as if he were afraid I was going to pitch the paperweight at him.

"And before you start beratin' poor Redmond as six kinds of a fool, sit down and listen to what he has to say."

The Judge's defense of Red shocked me into silence. I couldn't figure out whose side he was on anymore. I walked across the room and resettled myself on the window seat.

"I'm listening."

"Well, as I was tellin' the Judge, we turned up some very interesting information that made us want to take a closer look at Anderson. You know about this development deal he's got going?"

I nodded and shook a cigarette out of the pack.

"What isn't common knowledge is that there was a glitch—a big one. One of the sellers of a vital piece of property backed out. The whole thing was about to go down the tubes."

"Is that supposed to be a news flash? Geoff told me that the first night we went out. I know all about it." I didn't even try to keep the smugness out of my voice.

Red looked startled. "Why didn't you say something?"

"Why should I?" I countered, looking at my father His face was flushed, and his eyes slid quickly away from mine. What the hell was his game? Surely he had known about this, too. Why else send Miss Addie to me for help? I was thoroughly confused.

This would have been the perfect opportunity to demand an explanation from him about the extent of his involvement with Grayton's Race and with Geoff. But it was a private matter, between him and me. Red might be family, in the loose construction of that concept, but he wasn't blood.

"Anyway," I went on, turning back to Red, "it's a moot point. The deal's going through as planned."

"Sure it is," Red snapped, the color rising in his face, "because the troublemaker conveniently died. Pretty damned coincidental, don't you think?"

"Right. And the CIA killed Kennedy, and the underground militia planted the bomb in Oklahoma City, and the Navy accidentally shot down TWA 800. Any of your pet conspiracy theories I've missed?"

Red and I were on our feet now, shouting at each other across a yard of highly polished heart pine floor.

"And Geoff told me about *that*, too. Sorry to disappoint you, but I'm not 'shocked' by your less than startling revelations," I yelled.

"Did he also happen to mention that this conveniently dead problem was named Derek Johnson? Or didn't your pillow talk get that far?"

"You son-of-a—"

"That's enough! Both of you!"

The Judge's stern command was like a dash of cold water. I

retreated back to my refuge under the window. Red took a deep breath, expelled it, and collapsed into the leather wing chair next to the fireplace.

I was too shocked to speak.

Derek Johnson had been the heirs property holdout? Why hadn't Geoff told me that? He knew about my concern for Adelaide Boyce Hammond's investment, my involvement with Isaiah Smalls and CJ Elliott.

I'd told him. Hadn't I?

I tried to reconstruct our conversations—on the river after dinner, in my kitchen at three in the morning, on our outing to Geoff's homesite. And afterwards. In his bed.

I'd *meant* to tell him, but had I?

I dropped my head and studied my hands, clenched tightly in my lap. A deep flush rose from my throat to stain my cheeks. My mind couldn't recall everything we'd said, but my body remembered all too well. The electric touch of his hands on my flesh . . . the reawakening of the desire I'd thought dead along with my husband.

"Look, Bay . . ." Red's voice, pitched low and steady, was still a shock in the strained silence that had followed our shouting. "Look," he began again, "I'm sorry. I didn't mean to blurt it out like that."

I raised my head and met his eyes. "No, *I'm* sorry," I said, swallowing my shame. "You and I don't seem to bring out the best in each other lately, do we?"

He winced at that, and I could have bitten my tongue.

"Tell her the rest of it, Redmond," the Judge commanded from across the room. That presence that had quelled even the most rambunctious of attorneys still emanated from my father, despite his useless hand and withered legs.

Red looked apprehensive, his eyes darting between the Judge and me.

"Go ahead. Let's get it over with." I was tired of fighting. I just wanted to escape to the sanctuary of my beach house and shut out the whole damned world again.

"Well, we talked with Anderson. Matt Gibson and I. Asked him about his whereabouts on the night in question. And—bottom line—he had an alibi. A good one. We checked it out. So, he's clear. End of story."

I should have been relieved, but somehow I wasn't. I had a feeling I hadn't heard it all yet.

"And we've got a couple of other angles we're looking at. Mrs. Johnson says Derek was hanging out with a pretty rough crowd lately. Some of his friends have had a few minor scrapes with the law. But so far, I'm afraid Isaiah is still at the top of Gibson's hit parade."

I shook my head as Red Tanner rose and approached me. "I'll never believe that, Red. Not unless he confesses."

"I know. It's okay."

He seemed about to say something more, thought better of it, and turned to the Judge. "Thanks for lunch, Your Honor. I'll be in touch."

"Aren't you staying for dessert?" I asked as Dolores appeared in the doorway.

"No, thanks. My *official* shift starts at three. Got to get home and change."

He seemed very anxious to make his getaway. "Great meal," he said to Dolores who smiled her thanks. With a wave, he was gone.

My father and I demolished the slices of warm peach pie and smooth mounds of ice cream in silence. When Dolores had reclaimed the empty plates and left us with frosted glasses of lemonade, I broke the stillness.

"What was it that Red didn't want to tell me?" I asked.

The sharp lift of the Judge's chin confirmed my suspicions: there was more to come.

"You've been hurt so much already," he murmured, so low I almost missed it.

I knew he would get to it in his own way, so I lit a cigarette and waited.

"It's about Geoffrey Anderson's alibi," he said at last, looking directly at me. "He was in Miami. With his wife."

For a moment I didn't get it.

"You mean his *ex*-wife," I said stupidly. "He has two of them, you know."

The Judge shook his head sadly.

"No, sweetheart. He has *one* ex-wife. And one current one. I'm afraid your Geoff is still very much a married man."

CHAPTER
FIFTEEN

The brand-new courthouse, squatting behind the Law Enforcement Center and adjacent to the jail, baked unshaded in the afternoon sun. A triangular pediment rose over the wide double doors. Fake columns flanked the shallow steps that led up from a circular, brick-paved courtyard. It was an attempt to imitate the classic Georgian architecture that typified older halls of justice, the kind that dominated village greens in so many Southern county seats. The effort fell flat. It looked exactly like what it was: a cheap imitation of the original, set down in a barren landscape, a functional building without grace or beauty.

I had come straight from the Judge's. All I really wanted was to go home and forget about this entire day. But I needed information, and this was the place to get it.

I trotted briskly up the steps, anxious to escape the merciless heat. Inside, a uniformed officer dropped my bag onto a conveyor belt that rolled it through an x-ray scanner. I stepped through the arched metal detector and retrieved it on the other side.

Not exactly a scene out of *To Kill a Mockingbird*, I thought as I skirted the curved, balustraded staircase that led to the three courtrooms on the second floor. It was split into two sweeping sections, another abortive attempt at antebellum splendor. I located the county tax assessor's office, handed over my request, and was told to come back in about half an hour.

I plunked two quarters into the soda machine and carried my Diet Coke out onto the relative shade under the front overhang. I wanted a cigarette and some solitude. Neither was permitted inside the bustling courthouse.

The Judge's revelation had hit me like a blow to the stomach.

Geoff was still married.

He had held my hand, looked me straight in the eye, and lied through his teeth. And I had bought it. He had even aroused my sympathy—intentionally, I was now convinced—with his tale of alienation from his sons because of his divorces from their mothers.

Divorces. *Plural.*

There was no way I had misunderstood *that.*

So the next logical question was, what else had he lied about?

That was what I was here to find out. My frustrated attempts at computer hacking had gotten sidetracked by my infatuation with the object of the search. I checked my watch. In a few minutes I would know who the owners of record of Grayton's Race were, how much they had paid, and, possibly, how deeply in debt they were. And to whom.

Sergeant Red Tanner and Matt Gibson seemed to think there was motive for murder somewhere in the Grayton's Race deal. I wasn't buying it. My concern was for Adelaide Boyce Hammond, still comatose in the intensive care unit, and for the viability of her investment. Unless something drastic happened to make me change my mind, I was going to recommend that she sell out as quickly as she could, even if it meant taking a loss.

I'd tell Big Cal Elliott the same thing, if in fact, as I suspected, he too was an investor.

My father, whose pitying glances after his disclosure about Geoff had sent me bolting out of the house, would hear my advice, too. Whether or not he chose to take it was out of my hands. Though he had so far sidestepped my attempts to pin him down, I was certain he had another agenda that he was keeping to himself. It would only be revealed when he was damned good and ready to share it.

I downed the last of the soda, now sickeningly warm in the near ninety-degree heat. The day, which had begun with such cool promise, had turned into another mid-summer scorcher. The breeze had dropped, and the temperature soared. I deposited the empty can in an overflowing trash container and submitted to the security check once again before making my way back to the tax office.

I pushed through the heavy door to confront the pudgy, white-clad form of Hadley Bolles leaning proprietarily against the counter. He clutched several pages of computer printouts in his sausage-like fingers.

"Well, Bay, darlin', we meet again. I don't see you for months, and then—wham! We run into each other three times in one week. It must be fate, it surely must."

I ignored him and addressed the matronly woman behind the counter. "Do you have my information ready? It's been half an hour."

Her kindly, lined face colored up, from the end of her pointed chin to the roots of her gray-brown hair. She cast a quick, fearful glance at Hadley.

I didn't need to ask. I ripped the papers out of his hand, flipped them back into order, and found my handwritten request paperclipped neatly on the front.

"You really are a snake, Hadley," I snapped, folding the sheaf of printouts and stuffing them into my bag. "You've got all the moral rectitude of a pit viper."

"Now, now, little girl, don't get your back up. Nothing secret about those ol' documents. Information in the public domain, ain't that right, Doris?"

The county employee ducked her head and scurried back to her desk.

"Besides, you don't wanna go makin' slanderous comparisons like that in front of witnesses. That wouldn't be smart, darlin'," he sneered, "not smart at all."

"You're right, Hadley," I replied, one hand on the door. "The snake might sue me for defamation of character."

I probably hadn't left him speechless. Hadley so rarely was. But I was out the door and down the hallway before he could summon up a suitably scathing comeback.

The smarmy bastard, I fumed as I gunned the LeBaron into evening rush hour traffic and crawled my way back toward the island. Now everyone in the county would know about my interest in the particulars of Grayton's Race.

Well, so what? It wasn't as if *I* had anything to hide. Geoff and I were definitely through, although he didn't know it yet. So if my snooping around pissed him off, too bad. The sooner my involvement in this whole mess was history, the better.

I crossed over the Broad River bridge, pausing in my internal monologue long enough to admire the incredible beauty of sun, sky, and water reflecting back on each other in a dazzling shimmer of light.

Why couldn't people just leave well enough alone? It wasn't as if we *needed* any more houses or golf courses. Maybe the protesters were right. Maybe I'd take Geoff's tongue-in-cheek advice and join them at the barricades. After I'd extricated my family and friends from any financial involvement, of course.

I tapped my horn lightly and waved as I sped by the afternoon shift of picketers. Three of them sat on the hoods of their pickup trucks with "SAVE OUR RIVER" placards resting on their shoulders.

Almost an hour later, I rolled onto the bridge over the Intracoastal Waterway and exhaled slowly in relief. I was nearly home. Lavinia would be back with the Judge tonight, Dolores free to return to her family.

Tomorrow things could start getting back to normal for all of us.

I roundly cursed whoever had invented the answering machine, and myself for buying one. For the first half hour after I walked into the house, I ignored the little red light. It blinked accusingly—four times in rapid succession, then a pause, then the sequence repeated itself.

I stripped down to my pink lace underwear and added my dress and stockings to the pile already on the floor. I thought back to this morning, when, of course, I had overslept. I had awakened to the cheerful chatter of Katie Couric coming from the TV I had left on all night long. It had been a race to get myself showered, shampooed, dressed and out the door in time to make my father's deadline of nine A.M. The clothes I had slept in had fallen where they lay as I flung them off on my mad dash to the bathroom.

Laundry tomorrow, I decided as I dropped my frothy lace bra onto the heap.

I hated wearing a bra, and I avoided it whenever decency allowed. No matter how wide or soft the straps, they seemed to cut into the tender flesh around the grafted skin on my left shoulder.

I clasped my hands together high over my head and went

through a series of stretches designed to work out the kinks I had acquired from sleeping on the sofa last night. I followed that up by dashing cold water over my arms, neck, and breasts, and toweling myself briskly dry.

I scrubbed my face clean of the minimal makeup I had put on that morning. My eyes looked tired, I thought, as I met my own gaze in the mirror, and I had been spending too much time indoors. The rosy glow had faded from my cheeks. I brushed my hair into a ponytail on the top of my head and secured it with an elastic band.

In Rob's old C of C T-shirt and my grungiest cutoff jeans, I felt ready to face the machine. I lit a cigarette and punched the button.

The first two calls were from Geoff. His anger of the night before had reverted back to pained confusion.

Why was I acting like this? What had gone wrong? He felt sure we could work it out if only I would talk to him. He was certain I was there, screening calls, and refusing to pick up. He cursed the business that would keep him in Miami for at least two more days.

Yeah right, buster, I thought, stabbing the cigarette out viciously. *Is that what they're calling it these days? Business?*

He ended both messages with protestations of love.

I was hard pressed not to pick the damn machine up and fling it across the room. It was a relief when his honeyed, hypocritical voice was replaced by the bright babble of Bitsy Elliott.

"Bay, honey, are you there? Pick up if you are. It's me." A pause, during which I could hear the click of a lighter and the soft rush of exhaled smoke. "Okay, I guess you're not. You probably went to the Johnson boy's funeral. CJ wanted to go, but his daddy and I told him it wasn't a good idea. Besides, it was just for family, right? Anyway, how about this Friday night for dinner? Big Cal will be in Greenville from Thursday 'til Sunday. Some problem up there with the bookkeeper. Anyway, if you could get Dr. Halloran to come, she could stay over with you and y'all could have a good long visit over the weekend. Course, we could do it Saturday, but the older kids are gonna scream bloody murder if they have to stay home on a Saturday night! Anyway, let me know. Love ya! Bye!"

I smiled despite my annoyance at myself for having forgotten to call Neddie. You couldn't help but smile at Bitsy's nonstop chatter.

The last message was another from Geoff. He would definitely be back on Friday, probably late. He would come straight over from the airport. He had things he needed to tell me. We had to talk.

We'll see about that, Mr. Geoffrey Snake-in-the-Grass Anderson, I thought childishly.

If everything worked out right, I wouldn't be here Friday evening. And if I came back from Bitsy's to find him lying in wait for me, I'd have an ally. Neddie Halloran had an Irish temper to match her frizzy red hair. Geoff wouldn't stand a chance.

I left messages on both Neddie's office and home machines, asking her to call me the next day. I had a nagging feeling there was something else I was supposed to do, but I couldn't remember what it was. I rummaged through the clutter of the junk drawer with its matchbooks, shoelaces, pencil stubs, and old grocery receipts and finally came up with a small, spiral-bound notebook with three pages left in it.

Since premature senility seemed to be overtaking me at a rapid rate, I was going to have to start writing things down. I set the pad next to the phone, found a pencil end that was still long enough to get my fingers around, and wrote, "Neddie at Bitsy's— Fri" followed by "time" and a question mark.

It wasn't much of a list. But the way things had been going lately, I would probably be adding to it soon.

My stomach growled, and I surveyed the pristine kitchen. I knew from last night's foray into the cupboards that I would find little to eat behind their gleaming, light oak doors. Thank God Dolores would be back tomorrow.

I lifted the receiver and dialed two numbers I knew by heart: the guard gate, to leave a pass, and the pizza delivery place that could find their way to my house blindfolded. A medium mushroom and pepperoni would be here in twenty minutes.

I slid on my reading glasses and spread the papers from the tax office out on the kitchen table. I grabbed a legal pad from the office and my favorite Waterford pen from my bag.

By the time the doorbell announced the arrival of my dinner, I

was already deep into the tangled web of corporations and holding companies that masked the real names of Geoff's associates—
and alarm bells were going off in my head.

I awoke the next morning to a cacophony of birdsong and the
tart smell of the ocean. I squinted at the bedside clock through
bright sunshine pouring through the open French doors. I
couldn't tell if the first numeral on the digital face was an eight or
a nine, only that it was round.

I rolled over and thought about going back to sleep. Then the
memory of last night's discoveries—or lack of them, actually—
wormed its way into my consciousness, and I decided I'd better
get up.

I stretched out my sleep-cramped muscles and concluded that
I also needed some exercise. My body had become used to a daily
routine of tennis or golf, and it was starting to rebel. And besides,
it looked like too glorious a morning to spend it all indoors.

I brushed my teeth, tied up my hair, and selected a dark tur-
quoise bathing suit from among the several I'd had made after the
explosion. One-piece, cut daringly low in the front, the back was
solid material that covered almost all my scars. Only the slightest
hint of the skin graft could be seen at the top of my shoulder. I
slathered it with SPF 30 sun screen, threw on a T-shirt and sandals and headed for the kitchen.

Dolores was humming softly to herself as she brought order
out of the mess I'd left last night. I'd meant to clean it up before
she got there, but exhaustion had won out.

"*Buenos dias, Señora*," she chirped, stuffing the greasy pizza box
into the trash.

"Good morning, Dolores. I'm really sorry about all this."

She smiled and shrugged. "*Es nada.*"

"And don't worry about the bedroom," I added, remembering
the mound of discarded clothes on the floor. "I'll get the laundry
together later."

I drank a quick cup of tea, waved off Dolores's offer of breakfast, and walked briskly toward the ocean. The beach was deserted except for a couple of locals and their dogs. I peeled off
the T-shirt and plunged into the surf.

I'm not a strong swimmer, but I've got stamina, despite the smoking. As I stroked back and forth in the warm salt water, I again resolved to give up the habit. *How*, I wasn't sure, but I'd do it. Soon.

Back at the house, refreshed and more relaxed than I'd been in days, I found a note from Dolores on the kitchen table.

Stor was all it said.

When I entered my room, I found the bed neatly made and the pile of dirty clothes gone from the floor. She'd taken the laundry, too.

I emerged from the shower determined to get my act back together and stop letting other people pick up after me. As I pulled on white shorts and a hot pink cotton golf shirt, I spied the day's *Island Packet* on the chest at the foot of the bed. On top of it was a folded piece of plain white paper.

I recognized it immediately. It was the photocopy of the letter I had found in Miss Addie's apartment and stuffed hurriedly into my slacks. I had forgotten all about it. Dolores must have come across it when she gathered the laundry and went through the pockets.

I sat down on the bed, reached for my cigarettes, and opened the letter.

As I had suspected, it was from Miss Addie. J. Lawton Merriweather was apparently her attorney, although I thought I remembered that her family had used a big firm in Charleston. It had been written last Thursday, the day Miss Addie called me and began the whole weird chain of events that had disrupted my quiet, reclusive life.

The letter confirmed that Law was to meet her at The Cedars last Saturday morning to effect the changes they had discussed earlier. She also wished to consult him on the possible liquidation of some assets. Adelaide Boyce Hammond expressed her appreciation for his coming to her, since she had been unable to drive for some years.

Miss Addie must have real clout, I thought as I refolded the letter and carried it into the office. Anyone who could get a lawyer to make a house call—and on a Saturday morning in the middle of the summer—must have pushed some serious buttons. I tucked the paper under the desk pad, unsure of exactly what it meant, but certain Miss Addie would want me to keep it.

I spent the rest of the morning on the phone.

My first call was to Columbia. My hands shook a little as I punched in the once-familiar number.

It had taken them a long time after the bombing to appoint a replacement for Rob. The Special Investigations unit of the State Attorney General's office had been his baby, conceived, staffed, and administered pretty much by my husband himself. His background as a lawyer with the Justice Department had given him contacts in Washington that made him uniquely qualified for the job.

Belinda St. John, a tall, willowy black woman of Haitian descent, had been his hand-picked assistant. Her stunning good looks often caused those around her to underestimate her keen, incisive mind. But for a scheduling snafu that had forced her to be in court that day, Belinda would have been on the plane with Rob.

When she had been passed over for his job in favor of the inexperienced college pal of a prominent political hack, Belinda St. John had threatened to take her sharp wits and voluminous knowledge into private practice. Instead she had accepted the newly-created post of Special Counsel to the Governor. I had seen her smooth, high cheek-boned face in the background of many news conferences and photo ops, always just behind the handsome, boyish figure of our state's Chief Executive.

Belinda wouldn't have the information I needed, but she could get it for me. Discreetly.

I'd had some time to think about the "coincidence" of Hadley Bolles showing up at the tax office at precisely the right time to intercept my request for the owners of record of the Grayton's Race tract. I didn't believe in coincidences. Someone had alerted him, and that made me very nervous. I decided the fewer people who were aware of my continued interest, the better.

The conversation with Belinda St. John was strained, punctuated by uncomfortable silences. After she had inquired into the progress of my recovery and I had asked after the well-being of her two children, we seemed at a loss for something to say. So I got quickly down to the reason for my call: I needed the names of the stockholders and incorporators of the various corporations and holding companies that were listed on the tax records as the owners of Grayton's Race.

"You can get that from the Secretary of State's office," Belinda told me, her voice full of unasked questions. "It's all public record."

"I know. It's just that I don't want to make a formal request, have a record of it anywhere. It's a long story, and I'll give it to you if you want. But right now I'm just operating on hunches and suspicions. I don't really have anything concrete to go on."

"Sounds like the old days," she said, a catch in her voice. A lot of the tension between us dissipated.

"Yeah, you're right. I even tried hacking into the computer system, but I'm afraid I've lost my touch."

"I didn't hear that."

"Gotcha."

"Bay, is this something the SI unit should be advised about?" Her tone had turned serious. "The guys Rob and I used to investigate play for keeps. You of all people should know that. This doesn't have anything to do with one of his old cases, does it?"

"No, no. It's strictly a local thing, Bel. Just doing a favor for some old friends."

"No one's called me 'Bel' since Rob was killed. God, I'd like to nail those bastards!"

When I didn't reply, she backed off. "Sorry. Bad memories. I'm sure you don't need to be reminded."

"Why haven't they? Nailed them, I mean." I tried hard to keep the quaver out of my voice. "How can they just let it go, all those deaths?"

"Politics, honey. In this town, it's always politics." Then her tone turned to steel. "But don't think we've forgotten. There are a lot of us here who will never forget. The game's not over."

Belinda would be out of town on a junket with the Governor for the next few days, she said, but she'd give my request to her aide, Dennis Morgan. He was absolutely trustworthy, she assured me, and could be relied upon to operate with complete discretion. I gave her my fax number, and she said I should have the information in the next couple of days. I thanked her, and we hung up with mutual promises to stay in touch that neither of us believed we'd keep. Our connection had been severed with Rob's death.

Dolores returned with the groceries, and I helped her unload the car and restock the larder. I chided her for dealing with the laundry, but she shrugged it off.

"You have many things on your mind, *Señora,* many troubles. I do small thing to help is all."

Impulsively I hugged this little woman who only came up to my shoulder. She wriggled away in embarrassment and chased me out of the kitchen. Now that there was food in the house, lunch was her first order of business.

I gathered up my notes and the phone and moved my base of operations out onto the shade of the deck.

I spoke to the intensive care nurse's station, and they managed to track down Dr. Winter. He was a little more optimistic than he'd been the day before. He was exploring the possibility that Miss Addie had had a reaction to one of her medications. He had changed the entire course of her drug therapy. He assured me that my friend was in no immediate danger, although she was still unconscious. One of the many knots in my stomach relaxed a little at the news. He still didn't want her to have visitors, so there was little I could do but wait. Dr. Winter promised to call me the minute there was any change.

I left a message for Law Merriweather to call me when he got back to the office. I didn't think he'd tell me anything about his discussions with Miss Addie—privilege and all that—but I at least wanted to inform him about her condition. As her attorney, he had a right—and a need—to know.

I bullied Dolores into sitting down at the kitchen table and sharing the huge mound of pasta with clam sauce she'd whipped up for me. She caught me up on the news of her family. She was very proud of her three kids, all of whom spoke perfect English and did well in school. Then she launched into a catalogue of the wonders of Presqu'isle. Dolores had been extremely impressed with the beauty of my mother's antiques and with the splendor of the house itself.

I tried to match her enthusiasm, but the place held no charm for me. Growing up there had been like living in a museum, everything untouchable and off limits. Had there been love, it might have been bearable. As it was . . .

I sent a protesting Dolores off for a well-deserved free

afternoon and cleaned up the kitchen myself. I was wiping down
the green marble counters, happy to be doing something useful,
when Neddie returned my calls.

"Hey there, Tanner, how the hell are ya?" she greeted me in
her booming voice. "Long time, no hear."

Despite her many years in the South, Dr. Nedra Halloran had
kept her broad New England accent. That last word had come
out "heah-uh."

"Hey, Neddie. I'm okay. How's the wonderful world of mental
medicine?"

"The kids are great. I swear, though, most of the parents could
use a brain transplant. They oughta make you get a permit to get
knocked up. It's tougher to get a driver's license than it is to drag
some poor, unsuspecting kid kicking and screaming into the
world."

It was a familiar, recurring theme. Neddie believed that bad
kids were generally made, not born. While I wasn't a whole-
hearted subscriber to her theory, she had a lot of experience to
back it up.

"Good thing you and I skipped the motherhood thing," I said.
"Imagine what kind of screwed up offspring *we* might have
produced."

"Speak for yourself, Tanner. I would have made a fabulous
mother. Too bad my ovaries had other plans."

Neddie's inability to have children had contributed to the
breakup of her short-lived marriage to a popular Savannah news-
caster. But in typical Neddie fashion, she had faced the disappointment and moved on.

"So, what's up?" she asked. "You really doing okay?"

"Yeah, I'm fine. Well, not really *fine*, but all right. Listen, I've
got a proposition for you."

"If he's tall, rich, and Catholic—and not absolutely repulsive
looking—I'm available."

"Try to control yourself, Nedra. Aren't there any guys left in
Savannah?"

"Not many single, straight ones. At least none that are looking
for a strictly carnal relationship with a slightly overweight, shanty-
Irish redheaded shrink."

"With a resume like that, they should be beating down your

door. Listen," I said, dropping the banter, "remember my friend, Bitsy?"

"That disgustingly petite little thing with the gorgeous blond hair and no butt? Of course I remember her. I hate her."

"She's got problems, Neddie, and I think you could help."

I detailed Bitsy's concerns about CJ, her belief that he was exhibiting the signs of drug abuse, and her inability to get any support from her husband. I had Neddie's attention now, and I could hear her scribbling notes while we talked. All business now, she asked a couple of probing questions I didn't have the answers to.

"So the old man won't let her bring the kid in for evaluation, huh? The classic ostrich syndrome—if I don't know about it, I don't have to deal with it. Boy, parents like that really piss me off."

"So how about it? Want to spend a couple of glorious, fun-filled days at this fabulous beach resort without cost or obligation? Say yes, Neddie. I'd really love to see you."

"Sure. On one condition."

"What's that?"

"You don't cook. Nothing. Not even an egg. I'm in the kitchen, or we eat out."

"You're so good for my ego, Halloran. No wonder you're such a successful psychologist."

"Hey, I usually get ninety bucks an hour for this routine. You want charm, it costs extra."

As usual after a conversation with my irreverent ex-roomie, I hung up laughing. Neddie's last patient on Friday was at two o'clock, so she should be here sometime before five. I called Bitsy and set dinner for seven. I told her to save her gratitude until we heard what Neddie had to say.

I figured that was enough work for one day, so I called the club to see if I could scare up a tennis match. Brad, the young pro, told me to come by about four. If no one was looking for an opponent, he'd play me himself.

As I stripped off my clothes and stepped into my tennis whites, I realized that I hadn't thought about Geoff Anderson all day.

Things were definitely looking up.

CHAPTER SIXTEEN

Neddie and I had just enough time for a quick swim on Friday afternoon before we had to dress for dinner at the Elliotts. My friend turned heads all up and down the beach when she peeled off her white mesh cover-up to reveal a scandalously skimpy, emerald green bikini.

"My God, Halloran, why did you bother? I mean, why not just go naked?" I asked as a couple of gawking college guys nearly ran their bikes into the ocean.

"You don't like it?"

Neddie surveyed herself critically, turning to look over one shoulder at the thin strip of fabric covering barely a third of her rounded bottom. She had a lush figure, full-breasted, with long legs and generous hips. With her shoulder-length, frizzy hair blowing in the slight breeze off the water, she reminded me of Bette Midler in *Beaches*.

"Of course I like it. It is quintessentially you. I'm just insanely jealous of your body, that's all."

"Yeah, right. There's not an ounce of flab on you. And that gorgeous tan! I look like a fat, white slug that just crawled out from under some rock."

Neddie has that creamy, softly freckled skin that frequently blesses Irish redheads.

"Come on, Halloran, quit bitching. Let's get in the water before someone jumps your bones right here in front of all the tourists."

"Promises, promises."

Back at the house, we dressed casually, Neddie in white slacks and a shimmering silk blouse in her favorite green. I chose ivory colored linen trousers and a soft peach sweater. Neddie tied a brightly patterned scarf over her wild tangle of hair as we climbed into the convertible.

"I can put the top up if you want," I offered as we pulled out of the driveway.

"No, this is great. I love the feel of the wind. It's just that this mop will look even more like I just stuck my finger in a light socket if I don't tie it down."

Traffic was light, the locals already home from work, and the tourists nursing their sunburns before heading out to dinner.

"Anything else I should know about this bunch before we charge into battle?" Neddie asked as we eased over the speed-bump at the entrance to Spanish Wells. It was one of the few areas of exclusive homes on the island with no security gate.

"No, I think you're pretty much up to speed. I really haven't spent that much time with the kids, at least not since they've gotten older."

I turned into the long drive and parked in front of Bitsy's massive, Spanish-style home. Its red tile roof gleamed in the rays of the waning sun, towering live oaks casting long shadows across the smooth adobe walls.

"Wow, this is kind of out of character for Hilton Head, isn't it?" Neddie marveled. "Looks like it belongs in California."

"Big Cal's choice. He thinks it has 'class'. Bitsy would have been happy with something smaller and more regional, architec-turally; but, as usual, she didn't have much to say about it."

"Not your favorite guy, is he?" Neddie commented as we mounted the steps and rang the bell.

"Look up 'pond scum' in the dictionary, and you'll find his picture." The door opened, and we were engulfed in the warmth of Bitsy's welcome.

After the obligatory tour of the house, during which Neddie made the appropriate *oohs* and *aahs*, we sat down to a Lowcountry feast of oysters, crab, shrimp, and corn with new potatoes and homemade rolls. Unlike me, Bitsy is a whiz in the kitchen and had done all the cooking herself.

The four kids, scrubbed and shining, were well-behaved and surprisingly good company. Neddie, her easy rapport with them evident from the start, drew them into the conversation. Even Brady, the youngest, his slight stammer more endearing than an-noying, had us laughing at his convoluted tales of life in the third grade.

I kept stealing glances at CJ whose muscular frame occupied his father's place at the head of the table. He alone seemed ill at ease, responding to Neddie's gently probing questions with monosyllabic answers. Not until she got onto football—an area she was surprisingly knowledgeable about—did any animation light his somber, almost sullen, expression.

"Yeah, the Panthers are awesome, aren't they? They could have a shot at the Super Bowl this year."

"You think so? I'd bet Dallas will have something to say about that. Or the Forty-Niners."

Mally, who, at fifteen, was almost a carbon copy of her mother at that age, nattered away about school, friends, boys, and getting her driver's permit. She had helped Bitsy serve and clear and was now placing thin wedges of dark pecan pie in front of each of us.

"If this is homemade, I'm going to have to arm wrestle you for the recipe," Neddie said around a mouthful of the sweet, rich dessert.

"Actually, Mally made it." Bitsy beamed with pride.

"I'd be happy to copy off the recipe for you, Dr. Halloran. It's my Grandmomma Quintard's." She lowered her voice conspiratorially. "It's got bourbon in it."

"Just a dash," Bitsy hastened to add, glancing at me.

The two youngest kids, Brady and Margaret, wolfed down the pie and asked to be excused. They distributed exuberant hugs all around the table before scampering off toward the family room.

"They want to watch *Jurassic Park*," Bitsy explained, smiling fondly at the retreating backs of her children.

"Yeah, for about the hundred and fiftieth time." The sarcasm brought the scowl back to CJ's face. "Can I be excused, too? I got things I gotta do." He rocked back on two legs of the heavy oak chair and stared at his mother.

"No!" Bitsy cast a panicky look at Neddie, who made an almost imperceptible stop motion with her hand, as if to say, *Cool it. Go easy.*

"I'd rather you stayed," Bitsy said more calmly, "just for a while longer, okay?"

The front two legs of CJ's chair landed with a *thump* that sounded unnaturally loud in the strained silence.

"Why don't you go bring in the coffee," Bitsy suggested to her glowering son, "and some tea for your Aunt Bay. Mally will help you."

"I don't need any help." CJ flung his balled up napkin on the table and stalked off to the kitchen.

Bitsy shrugged an apology.

Neddie smiled and shook her head. "Don't worry about it. I've seen much worse."

"CJ can be such a creep," Mally offered from the wisdom of her fifteen years. "Honestly. Boys!"

By ten o'clock it was obvious that CJ was not going to participate in any more attempts at conversation, so we rose to take our leave. Mally, on the other hand, had chattered almost nonstop, asking Neddie pointed questions about her work and seeming absorbed by the answers. She had left the table only long enough to refill the coffee pot.

"How about lunch tomorrow?" I asked Bitsy as the five of us stood alongside my car in the soft, humid darkness. We'd had no opportunity to talk alone, and I knew she'd be anxious to hear Neddie's preliminary diagnosis.

"What a great idea." Neddie had picked up on my train of thought. "Doesn't your club do a brunch on weekends?"

"Yes, and it's wonderful. Twelve-thirty okay with you, Bits?"

I hoped Bitsy could read my eyes, that she was getting the message. "Uh, sure. Yes. That sounds good," she said.

"Oh, can I come, too, Aunt Bay? Please?"

Mally's rudeness was so out of character I was momentarily at a loss.

"Mally!" her mother snapped, obviously embarrassed.

"Oh, please, Mom? Can I?"

"You don't want to spend your Saturday hanging out with a bunch of old ladies," I said. "You'll be bored to tears."

"Don't you have Ashley and Jennifer coming over tomorrow to swim in the pool? Besides," her mother added as Mally opened her mouth to protest, "I need you to look after Brady and Margaret for me."

"Mo—om." It was the lament of every thwarted teenager.

"Next time, okay, honey?" Neddie held out her hand. "Nice to have met you, Mally. And don't forget about that pecan pie recipe, okay?"

Mally reluctantly shook hands with Nedra and gave me a brief hug before flouncing back into the house.

Neddie was thanking Bitsy for the wonderful meal when CJ mumbled, " 'Night, Aunt Bay," and engulfed me in an unexpected bear hug. With his lips just inches from my ear he whispered, "I need to talk to you. Can I come over? Tomorrow morning?"

"Sure," I murmured, completely taken aback. "Sure."

"What are you two whisperin' about over there?" Bitsy sounded edgy and suspicious.

"I was just apologizing for being such a dud tonight." CJ lied with a practiced ease that made me nervous. "Too much football practice, I guess. It really wears me out."

He turned the full force of his considerable charm on Nedra. "It was nice to meet you, Dr. Halloran. I hope you'll come back real soon. I promise to be better company next time."

"I'll look forward to it."

As we rolled down the driveway, I turned back to wave. CJ had draped his arm across his mother's shoulder, and hers was wrapped around his waist.

"Well," I asked while Neddie retied the scarf around her hair, "what do you think?"

We turned onto the parkway and picked up speed.

"What did he really say to you just now?"

I cocked an eyebrow at her, and she smiled knowingly.

"Honey, I've been lied to by my patients in every conceivable way known to man. You think I can't spot bullshit when I hear it?"

"He's coming over tomorrow morning. He wants to talk to me."

"Good."

"What do you mean 'good' ? I don't know how to deal with someone with a drug problem. He should be talking to you."

"It's not him."

"What do you mean, it's not him? What the hell are you talking about?"

"It's not him. With the drug problem."

I had to stop for the light at Mathews Drive, and I turned to face Neddie.

"What exactly are you saying?"

Neddie shrugged and looked me squarely in the eye.
"It's the girl. It's Mally."

We were still arguing about it at midnight as we got ready for bed.

"I don't get it, Tanner," Neddie mumbled around a mouthful of toothpaste.

I sprawled on the bed in the guest room trying unsuccessfully to blow smoke rings. I heard her rinse and spit, then the light clicked off in the adjoining bath. Neddie, whose oversized T-shirt was even rattier than mine, flopped down beside me.

"Give me one of those," she said, pointing at the cigarette.

Reluctantly, I tossed her the pack. "God, I'm corrupting everyone around me. First Bitsy, now you."

"Don't flatter yourself, girl. I can navigate the road to hell very nicely on my own, thank you."

"What don't you get?" I asked as she lay down on her back and blew a perfect circle on her first try.

"You, that's what."

"Why?"

"Well, you drag me up here to find out if one of your friend's kids is on the stuff. I confirm your worst fears, and then you argue with me. Who's the expert here, anyway?"

"I know, I know. It was just such a shock to hear you say it was Mally. I still can't believe it."

Neddie stubbed out the cigarette and rolled over onto her stomach. "Look, kid, it doesn't give me any joy to be right, you know? But she's definitely on uppers of some kind. I think CJ knows it, too. That's why he was so hostile."

"What am I supposed to say to him tomorrow? I mean, I don't want to make things worse."

"Just play it by ear. Listen closely, hear him out. Most of all, don't make judgments. He's feeling very protective of his little sister. He could be a big help in getting her into therapy voluntarily."

"Make judgments? *Moi?*" I asked in mock surprise.

"Yeah, you." Neddie flung the comforter back and jerked the pillow out from under my head. "Now get out of here, will you, and let me get some sleep?"

I clambered off the bed and paused in the doorway when she called my name.

"What were you so nervous about when we drove back in tonight? You looked as if you expected someone to jump out of the bushes and grab you."

I *had* been surprised—and more than a little relieved—not to find Geoff Anderson waiting in the driveway. I hadn't been aware that it showed. But then Neddie was trained to see below the surface of the faces we all put on for each other. Trying to fool her was pointless.

"There was that possibility," I admitted.

Neddie was instantly alert. "Are you in some kind of danger?"

"No, it's nothing like that. Just someone I didn't particularly want to deal with tonight."

"Would this by any chance be a male someone?"

"Goodnight, Nedra." I flipped off the overhead light.

"Okay, but don't think you're gonna worm your way out of telling me. Tomorrow I expect to hear the whole sordid story, including the intimate and prurient details."

"You're a sick, perverted woman, Halloran."

"I know. That's why you love me. G'night."

I closed the door and walked across the hall into the office. Sometime between the time we went out for our swim and the time we got back from the Elliotts, Belinda St. John's assistant had come through. Several pages of printing lay in a neat stack at the base of the fax machine.

I was surprised, because the fax had been acting up the last time I'd used it, spewing paper out onto the floor. Since I am extremely mechanically challenged, I'd made no attempt to find the problem. It must have fixed itself in that mysterious way that machines sometimes do, I decided as I stood and glanced down the list of names.

Nothing leaped right out at me, but one or two were vaguely familiar. As I'd suspected, some of the incorporators were themselves corporations and partnerships. Dennis Morgan was good. He'd anticipated my needs and done additional research so that every entry was cross-referenced to the individuals involved, where possible.

In a handwritten cover sheet, he said that some of the businesses were out-of-state, mostly from Florida. He had some friends in the statehouse there, he wrote, and I should let him know if I wanted those stockholder names, too.

I decided it could all wait until tomorrow. My head was already stuffed with enough things to worry about.

" 'Sufficient unto the day is the evil thereof'," I muttered as I crawled in between the freshly laundered sheets.

Old St. Matthew sure had that right, I thought as I drifted off.

CHAPTER
SEVENTEEN

The sound of Nedra Halloran's deep, husky laugh drifted in through the open French doors. A second voice, obviously male, responded. I finished dressing quickly, embarrassed that CJ Elliott had apparently arrived while I was in the shower.

I stepped out onto the deck and followed the hum of conversation around the corner to the screened-in area off the great room. Neddie and CJ were sprawled in my deep-cushioned wicker chairs, empty coffee mugs dangling from their hands. Egg-smeared plates and forks lay on the round table. Toast crumbs peppered the bright yellow tablecloth.

"Hey, she rises!" Neddie greeted me with a grin and hooked her foot under another chair, pulling it up to the table. "Want some breakfast?"

"No, thanks. You know I never eat before noon if I can help it. Sorry I overslept, CJ," I said to my honorary nephew.

"Hey, no problem, Aunt Bay. I got here awful early. I just hung around in the driveway until Dr. Halloran came out for the paper and found me."

"Sure I can't fix you something?" Neddie asked again. "Toast or a bagel?"

"You should have one of the Doc's omelets. They're awesome." CJ poured himself more coffee.

"I made tea for you. It should still be hot. Wanna grab the pot for me, CJ?"

"Sure," he said, leaping from his chair.

"Looks like you've made another conquest," I remarked under my breath as CJ bounded up the steps to the kitchen.

"He's a real good kid," Neddie replied, "but he certainly has something on his mind. I'm gonna disappear in a minute and leave you two alone."

She correctly read the apprehension on my face. "Don't worry.

Just listen. That's all you need to do right now."

"Okay, if you say so."

CJ slid the screen open with his foot and set the teapot and a clean mug down on the table in front of me.

"Well, I'm off to the beach," Neddie announced. I could see through the mesh of her cover-up that she wore a more modest, one-piece suit today. "Catch you guys later."

"See ya, Doc." CJ's eyes followed her as she trotted down the stairs and disappeared among the trees.

I busied myself stirring sweetener into my tea and lighting a cigarette. CJ studied the generic seaside prints on the back wall, the collection of shells and dried sand dollars on the end table, even the woven rush mats on the floor.

He looked everywhere except at me.

"So. What's on your mind?" I prodded him.

CJ gulped a mouthful of coffee and countered my question with one of his own. "Why did you and the Doc come over last night? My mother set it up, didn't she?"

"She invited us, yes," I hedged.

"She thinks I'm doin' drugs, doesn't she." He delivered it as a statement of fact in a wry, almost patronizing voice.

I wasn't sure how much I was supposed to contribute, so I waited for CJ to continue. When he didn't, I said quietly, "She has expressed some concern about you."

"Damn it! How could she think I'd be so stupid? I'm an athlete. I wouldn't put that crap in my body!"

It was almost a word-for-word rendition of what I had said to Bitsy a couple of days ago. Up until last night, I would have been overjoyed at CJ's convincing denial. As it was, I already knew that he was not the problem. I took Neddie's advice and kept silent.

"Well, as usual, she's got it all screwed up," he scoffed.

"Should she be more concerned about your sister?"

His head snapped up at that. "Who said anything about Mally? Who told you it was her?" He paused, then nodded knowingly. "The Doc, right?"

I poured more tea and gave CJ an opportunity to digest this information. "Aunt Bay," he said at last, "you have to promise that you won't tell anyone about any of this, okay?"

"If Mally has a drug abuse problem, your parents have a right to know. They have to get her some kind of help."

He looked at me oddly, as if I weren't getting it. "I know that. It's already taken care of. I talked to Mally last night, after you guys left. She really liked Dr. Halloran. She said she'll go into treatment if Mom and Dad will let her go to the Doc. We're going to talk to them tomorrow when Dad gets back."

CJ's casual dismissal of his sister's drug problem rankled me more than a little. He didn't seem to notice.

"That's good. See that you follow through. This is not something to be taken lightly. Neddie—Dr. Halloran—is the best. I know she'll be able to help Mally." I lit another cigarette and relaxed back into the chair. "And don't worry. None of what we've said here will leave this room."

"Thanks, but that's not why I really came over. I wanted to talk to you about Zay."

"Who's Zay?"

"You know, Isaiah. That's what all the guys call him."

"Oh, right."

"Anyway, it's about me and Zay. And Derek. And you promise you won't tell anyone about it, right?"

For a moment I was too shocked to answer.

Derek? This was about Derek Johnson?

I had no idea what he was going to say, but I wouldn't lie to him. This was too important.

"I can't promise that, CJ. If you know something about Derek's murder, you have to tell the police. Come on, you know that as well as I do," I snapped as he jumped up and began pacing. "Just sit down and tell me. We'll decide together who else has to get involved. I promise I won't do anything without checking with you first. Deal?"

"Okay," he conceded after a short pause. "But, see, Zay told me not to say anything, and I gave him my word. But the cops want to talk to me again, on Monday. That guy Gibson called yesterday. And I'm afraid Zay is still a suspect, and I don't know what to do."

CJ looked close to panic, and I wanted to put my arms around him, offer comfort. Instead, I let him fight his own battle for control. When he had it back, he jumped right in.

"See, Derek was a dealer. Everyone at school knew you could

get just about anything you wanted from him. Uppers, downers, crack, dust. Even heroin and coke, if you had the money."

My God, I thought, stunned. *Poor Lavinia. And Mavis.*

I shook my head in disbelief. "Was he supplying your sister?"

CJ nodded. "She's not hooked real bad, you know? Just pills, and she knows she has to get off them. She'll be okay."

"Why the hell didn't anyone turn him in? Why didn't you?"

"He was Zay's cousin, sort of. Besides, nobody narcs, not if you want to keep your friends."

It was a perverted code of teenage ethics that I would never understand. "Go on," I urged him.

"Well, that day at football practice—you know, the day Derek . . . died?"

I nodded.

"Derek was hangin' around, like he did sometimes. He got steroids and growth hormone for some of the guys on the team, stuff to build up muscles. But lately he'd been offering free samples of the 'good' stuff—crack and like that. Trying to get kids hooked. And Zay told him to take a hike, to leave the guys alone."

"And that's what the fight was about," I interrupted. There it was. The answer to the question that had been nibbling at my subconscious was staring me right in the face.

You're an idiot, Tanner, I berated myself silently. It was so obvious. In all the discussions of the day of Derek's death, I had never once asked what the big argument with Isaiah had been about.

"Yeah," CJ said, jerking me back, "Zay hates that drug shit. He told Derek if he came around practice again—or around Mally— he'd kill him. Derek laughed at him, made some crack about Zay bein' a pussy. Then they started throwing punches."

"So what happened next?"

"Well, Zay said we had to teach Derek a lesson. Make sure he got the message. Derek's got that little fishing shack on the river, you know? On that land his granddaddy left him and his momma? He hangs out there a lot."

The heirs property. So Red had been right about that, too.

A lot of things were beginning to make sense.

"So you and Isaiah went looking for him?"

CJ hung his head. "Yeah," he muttered. "We told our folks we were going camping, and we pitched a tent down river from the shack. After it got dark, we headed up that way. Zay had . . ." CJ faltered and looked away.

"What? What did he have?" I demanded.

"A baseball bat."

"Oh, God!"

'Blunt trauma to the back of the head' I could hear Red saying. 'He was dead before he went into the water.'

"We were just gonna threaten Derek, honest. He's . . . he was a lot bigger 'n Zay. We were just trying to even things up a little."

Two against one was more than even, I thought, but kept it to myself.

"So what happened when you found him?"

"We didn't, that's just it. He wasn't there. We waited, but he never showed up. We went back to camp, ate some sandwiches, and went to sleep."

"And that's it?"

The boy squirmed and bit at his right thumbnail.

"Come on, CJ. You've gone this far. Let's have the rest of it."

"I woke up about two o'clock. Zay wasn't in his sleeping bag. And the bat was gone. So I got worried and started down the path to the shack, and Zay and I nearly ran smack into each other. He looked real scared and told me to shut up and get back to the tent."

The words were pouring out. CJ had wrestled alone with this dilemma for more than a week. I couldn't have stopped him now if I'd wanted to.

"When we got back, Zay said he went off on his own because he didn't want to get me in any trouble. But when he got close to the shack, he heard voices, loud, like people arguing. He waited behind a tree. There was a boat tied up at the old dock, and two guys were yellin' at Derek."

"Could Isaiah see who they were?"

"No. Just that there were two of 'em—white guys—and they were big. A lot bigger 'n Derek. Zay turned to sneak away, and he must've made some kind of noise, because one of the guys yelled, 'Who's there?' and started walking toward where Zay was hiding. The guy had a gun. Some kind of automatic rifle, Zay said, like maybe an Uzi or somethin'. He could see it in the light from the lanterns in the shack."

I was on the edge of my chair. "What did he do? How did he get away?"

"He just crawled back into the brush and hid. They didn't look real hard. Probably figured it was a raccoon or a deer. Anyway, Zay finally made it back to the path, and that's when we ran into each other." CJ sat back, exhausted. "Could I have a Coke or something, Aunt Bay? My throat's really dry."

"Sure, honey." The childish endearment slipped out before I could stop myself.

I walked up the steps to the kitchen, torn between keeping my promise to CJ and grabbing up the phone and getting Bitsy over here on the double.

Honor won out. I carried glasses of ice and two cans of soda back onto the deck.

"Sorry, all I've got is diet."

"That's okay. Thanks."

I listened to the rest of CJ's incredible tale in stunned silence.

The boys had stayed awake the rest of the night, trying to decide what to do. They didn't want to start up the car for fear of advertising their presence to whoever was threatening Derek. At first light, they crept back up the trail. The boat was gone, and Derek was nowhere around. But lying along the bank, not far from the dock, they found Isaiah's baseball bat. He'd dropped it in the woods when he'd fled the night before.

"And it had stuff all over it. Blood and hair and . . . stuff."

Derek Johnson's brains, I thought, and shuddered.

"And Derek's place was trashed, like there'd been a big fight. So we figured somebody had gotten hurt, maybe even killed. And it was Zay's bat. His name was scratched in the handle. So if it was Derek that was dead, they'd be sure to think Zay did it. Because of the fight at school."

"What did you do with the bat?" If the police had found it, Red would have told me.

"We buried it in the woods and went back to camp and waited for someone to come."

Leaving your prints all over, and screwing up any other evidence that might have been on it, I thought bitterly.

"Why didn't you just get the hell out of there?" I asked.

"We figured it would look bad if we ran. We'd told our parents we'd be gone a couple of days, and it'd seem funny if we came back early. Besides, on TV the cops can always find clues to prove you were somewhere even if you think you've cleaned everything up. Or someone could have seen us turn off the highway. So we just decided to stay put for another day, and, if they came, we'd just play dumb and stick to it."

I had to admit there was a certain convoluted logic in their thinking. What a load these two kids had been carrying around! But there was still a question I needed to ask, and I wasn't sure I wanted to hear the answer.

"You never actually saw these two men at Derek's dock, right? You only know what Isaiah told you about them."

CJ jumped to his feet, his fists balled at his sides. "You think Zay's lying? You think he killed Derek and made that other stuff up?"

"I'm just trying to make sure I have it all straight," I lied. Because that was exactly the scenario that had leaped into my mind, much as I tried to suppress it. For the first time since Red Tanner first suggested that Isaiah Smalls might be involved in his cousin's murder, doubt was gnawing at my belief in the boy's innocence.

"So what should I do, Aunt Bay?"

CJ's earnest young face looked trustingly down at me. I felt a sudden surge of that maternal instinct that must kick in when an animal's offspring are threatened. Even though he wasn't my kid, I wanted to give him money, ship him out of the country, whisk him far away from this awful mess.

I couldn't do that, and I knew it.

So did he.

"I think you already know what you have to do, CJ," I said softly. "You just wanted me to confirm it, right?"

After a long pause during which we stared silently at each other, CJ Elliott nodded.

"Good boy. I'll help you talk to your parents and your lawyer. Who is it, by the way?"

"Mr. Merriweather. From Beaufort."

Well, that's handy, I thought. At least it wasn't some stranger who might question my right to get involved. Law would understand my loyalty to both families.

"And then we'll contact Mander Brown. That's Isaiah's attorney. I'll also run this by my father and Isaiah's grandmother. We can trust them."

"Isaiah's gonna think I narced on him."

"He probably will, at first, but it has to be done. You could be in real trouble, CJ. Didn't you ever hear of an accessory-after-the-fact to murder? You two were crazy to lie to the police. Anyway, once we're all on the same page, we'll go to the sheriff. Together."

"That won't be necessary."

The disembodied voice sent me rocketing to my feet. Then the tall, wiry frame of my brother-in-law made its way slowly up the back steps and onto the deck. The sun glinted off the brass nameplate pinned to the pocket of Red Tanner's beige uniform.

CJ shot me a panicky look that quickly hardened into one of betrayal.

"Sorry. I didn't plan it this way." Red looked at me and shrugged.

"You son-of-a-bitch! How much of that did you hear?"

"Enough," he said softly.

CHAPTER
EIGHTEEN

"CJ, sit down and don't say another word."

"No way. I'm outta here." He grabbed his car keys off the table.

"I'm afraid I can't let you do that, son."

Red Tanner had his thumbs hooked into the belt of his sharply-creased trousers. All traces of my shy, bumbling brother-in-law were gone. He looked every inch the tough, implacable law officer I often forgot he was.

"I'm not your son. And you can't make me stay if I don't want to."

"CJ, sit down!" I yelled. "Shut up and let me handle this!"

His teenage bravado was an act. A closer look revealed a frightened kid on the verge of tears. He dropped into the chair and stared at his feet.

"I'm calling your lawyer and your mother. And you don't have to talk to him," I said, gesturing at Red. "Don't answer any questions, got it?"

"Bay, why don't you stay out of this? You know he's going to have to talk to me, sooner or later."

"Probably. But it's only going to be with his attorney present. And his parents. Or did you forget he's still a juvenile?"

I turned and dashed into the house, grabbed the portable phone, and was back on the deck in less than a minute. No one spoke as I punched in Bitsy's number.

"Bits? It's Bay. Listen, we've got a problem here."

I gave her a quick synopsis of the situation, leaving out the details of her son's startling revelations about the night of the murder.

"Get hold of Law Merriweather, and the two of you get over . . . Hold on." I covered the mouthpiece with my hand. "Are you arresting him?" I snapped at Red.

"He's gonna have to come in for questioning."

"Damn it, answer me straight. Are you taking him in now?"

"I can wait for his mother and his lawyer. There's no rush. I'm not trying to railroad the kid."

I gave him a look that said what I thought of his assurances. "Bitsy? Come over here. Both of you. What? No, I won't let him say anything more. Okay. Right. Hurry."

I hit the OFF button and immediately dialed again. With trembling hands I lit a cigarette. Red reached for the coffee pot, picked up my empty tea mug, and poured himself a cup. His eyes traveled back and forth between CJ and me as if he expected one of us to bolt.

In the fifteen years we'd known each other, I had never been so angry at him.

"Lavinia, let me talk to the Judge. It's urgent."

I repeated the story I'd told CJ's mother while my father listened intently.

"No, he didn't Mirandize him. I've been present the whole time," I replied to his first question. "No, he doesn't have a warrant, either. He was just sneaking around my house, eavesdropping on a private conversation." I glared at Red who met my stare unflinchingly. "Okay. I'll keep you posted."

I dropped the phone onto the table. "Everything's under control, CJ. The cavalry's on the way."

The boy jangled his keys in his hand. His right leg had started to jump in jerky little spasms that betrayed his fear.

"Stay put, okay? We'll be right back."

I jerked my head toward the deck, and Red followed me out. I walked a few feet down the porch, out of earshot of CJ. Red positioned himself so that the boy was in his line of sight.

"What the hell are you doing here, Tanner? How did you know the kid was going to spill his guts to me? Of all the underhanded, sneaky . . ."

Trying to keep my voice low and explode with anger at the same time was making me shake with frustration.

"Calm down, Bay. It was an accident, I swear to God. I just dropped over to talk to you. I heard voices, so I walked around back. When I caught the gist of the conversation, I had no choice but to listen. I'm a cop, damn it, and we're talking about murder here. Can't you get that through your head?"

"I know exactly what we're talking about—a sixteen-year-old

kid who's scared out of his mind. He came to me for help, and thanks to you, I've betrayed him."

"Bay . . ." Red laid his hand on my shoulder, and I slapped it away.

"No. I don't want your apologies. Maybe you didn't plan this, I don't know. But the damage is done anyway, isn't it?"

He didn't have an answer for that.

We stood silently for several moments.

"You know, this might not be a bad thing, my takin' him into custody. If the kid's story is true—and I'm not saying I'm buying it all—then he and his buddy could be in danger. If one of them actually saw the real killers."

I hadn't thought about that. He could be right. Although CJ said that Isaiah hadn't seen the two men clearly, he might remember enough.

"Hey, what's up?" Neddie's voice from the path below startled us both. "Something wrong?"

As she trotted up the stairs, CJ jumped to his feet. "Hey, Doc!" he called. "Doctor Halloran!"

Neddie paused, one foot on the top step. "Bay? What's going on? I saw the sheriff's car in the driveway. What's he doing here?"

She glared at Red, and I realized that, though I had spoken often of Rob's brother, the cop, he and Neddie had never actually met.

The doorbell saved me from awkward introductions and explanations.

Within fifteen minutes, the house had emptied. At Bitsy's urging, Neddie accompanied the group to the sheriff's office. Her statement that Neddie was CJ's therapist wasn't strictly true, but Red was beyond arguing. They'd sort it all out down there.

I had been pointedly requested to stay out of it by everyone involved.

It wasn't until I called to report in that the Judge revealed what Red had apparently come to tell me: early that morning Isaiah Smalls had been formally charged with the first-degree murder of Derek Johnson. They would seek to try him as an adult.

And CJ and I had just unwittingly handed them all the ammunition they would need to make it stick.

• • •

I spent the rest of the morning pacing and chain-smoking. The Judge had assured me they couldn't use anything CJ had said against him since he hadn't been advised of his rights. Red couldn't testify to it either. Hearsay.

It sounded right, but I was still afraid. I kicked myself for not paying better attention in the few law courses I'd taken before changing majors. Regardless, I was pretty sure they could—and would—use what CJ had revealed to pry the truth out of Isaiah Smalls.

Since Dolores didn't come on weekends unless I had something special going on, I cleaned up the kitchen, made the beds, and ran the vacuum cleaner over an already spotless carpet. It was something to do.

I resisted the urge to call Red's office and find out what was going on. My father had advised me to stay out of it and, for once, I intended to take his advice.

To keep my mind from running around in fruitless circles, I flopped myself down at the desk and studied the list Dennis Morgan had faxed to me the day before. The same two names that had caught my eye in my first cursory glance last night, again set off bells in my memory: Southland Real Estate Investment and Meridian Partners Group.

Both were among the several Florida companies whose stockholders Morgan had been unable to provide me. I accessed my word processing program, and composed a letter asking him to check it out at his earliest opportunity. I faxed it to the private number Belinda St. John had given me.

Then I went to the kitchen, wolfed down a bagel to pacify my rumbling stomach, and settled myself in a shady corner of the deck.

Back in our college days, Neddie Halloran had taught me the benefits of meditation. I'd never really been able to "empty" my mind completely, but I had learned to quiet it. I had used the technique to help me through some of my more painful rehabilitation after the explosion.

I closed my eyes, rested my hands, palms up, loosely on my thighs, and breathed slowly. I focused on pushing out of my consciousness all the conflicts and anxieties that had beset my life in the past week. I concentrated instead on the constancy of my own steady breathing, felt the ebb and flow of the blood through my veins as my heart sent it out and back . . . out and back. The sweet songs of a dozen different birds faded into the background until there was only the peace and solitude of a tranquil mind and the measured rhythms of my own body . . .

When I came back, almost twenty minutes later according to my watch, I felt calm and refreshed. A lot of the confusion that had muddied my thinking had been blown away, leaving a clear, sharp certainty that I would find the pieces I needed to complete the puzzle.

And I now knew why the two names on the list of the Grayton's Race incorporators had seemed so familiar. I had held the solution in my hands just a few days ago and had failed to recognize it.

I strode purposefully into the bedroom closet and pried up the false floorboard that concealed the safe.

When Red Tanner dropped off Neddie Halloran, shortly after four that afternoon, he sent her in as point man to see if I had calmed down enough to talk to him. She found me in the office amid a clutter of computer discs, cigarette butts, and several pages of yellow legal paper filled with scribbled notes and numbers.

"What happened?" I demanded when she appeared in the doorway. "How are the kids?"

"I need a drink." She turned and headed for the kitchen, calling back over her shoulder, "And don't give me any grief about it either, Tanner. I'm not in the mood."

Neddie made straight for the cupboard over the refrigerator and rummaged through the bottles I hadn't touched since the last time Rob and I had entertained. She selected a half-empty fifth of tequila and busied herself with limes, ice, and salt. Glass in hand, she sat down at the kitchen table and motioned me to join her.

"That was a cheap shot, Neddie," I said as she sipped gratefully at the clear liquid. "I've never tried to impose my hangups on you or anyone else."

"Yeah, you're right. Sorry. It's just that you always look so damned disapproving when anyone drinks around you. Your face gets all puckery—like you just ate a pickle."

She demonstrated, and I had to laugh. "I couldn't possibly look that bad. Besides, my faces are more a reaction to watching you gulp that stuff than to anything else. How can you stand it? It smells like bad cough medicine."

"Red wants to talk to you," she said, changing the subject abruptly.

It hadn't taken the two of them long to get on a first-name basis, I thought angrily, then stopped, surprised at myself. Where had that come from?

"Tough," I said, touching the flame of my lighter to a cigarette. "Talking to my brother-in-law can be hazardous to your health, or hadn't you noticed?"

"Seems like a nice enough guy to me." Neddie regarded me over the rim of her glass. "And there's no use beating a man up for doing his job. He feels bad enough as it is, without you dumping any more guilt on him."

"Is this free advice, Dr. Halloran, or is the meter running?"

Neddie downed the last of her drink. "I'm going to ignore that last crack, Tanner, because I know from experience how your mouth can get away from your brain."

We stared at each other for a long minute. I wasn't sure which one of us started to smile first, but we were both grinning when Neddie got up from the table and came around to give my shoulder a quick squeeze.

"Okay, we're even," I said.

"No, I think I'm one up, but I won't argue with you." Neddie moved toward the hallway. When she turned, her face was once again sober.

"Isaiah Smalls is still in jail. They can't have a bail hearing until Monday, or so Mr. Merriweather said. They questioned CJ for about an hour, but he was pretty cool. He only answered when his lawyer told him to and didn't volunteer any information. I said the kid was under tremendous stress—which is true—and that keeping him any longer could be injurious to his emotional well-being. Which is also true. He's riding a fine line between doing what he knows is right and maybe helping put his best friend on death row. A lot tougher people have cracked under a lot less pressure."

"So they let CJ go?" I asked.

"Yes. His father showed up right at the end of everything. He may be a loudmouthed s.o.b., but he gets results. We were out of there about five minutes after he started throwing his weight around."

"Big Cal doesn't make all those campaign contributions for nothing."

"Whatever he does, it works. His kid's at home. The other boy's lawyer—the one with the strange name—is going to interview CJ at the house tonight. Get his version of the story."

"Mander Brown."

"Yeah, that's the one. So anyway, that's where it stands. Except that I'm so confused I don't know which end's up. Somebody needs to explain this whole thing to me. All I've gotten so far are bits and pieces."

"I know. We really pitched you under the bus, didn't we? Thanks, Neddie. Not just for what you did for CJ and his family. But for being there for me every time I need you."

Neddie waved my gratitude away. "You'll pay. Starting tonight. I want a very large, very rare steak and a bottle of excellent wine which I intend to drink entirely by myself. Your treat."

"You're on. I've got so much to tell you. I think a lot of things about this mess may be coming together. I want to run it all by you, see what you think."

"You mean there's more to this Derek Johnson thing than meets the eye?"

I nodded. "Lots."

"Anything that could get these kids off the hook?"

"Maybe," I said, "if they're telling the truth. Their story's so fantastic, I'm inclined to believe them. It's almost too bizarre for them to have invented it. And there are some other connections I don't think even the cops are aware of. I just need to work it all out, make sure of my facts. We'll talk after dinner."

"Boy, you sure do lead an exciting life for a reclusive widow-lady. I should hang out with you more often." Neddie began to unbutton her blouse. "Now get out there and make nice with that handsome brother-in-law of yours. He's waiting in the cruiser. I'm going to have a swim, a shower, and nap, in that order. Okay?"

"Enjoy," I said. I rose and tucked my cigarettes and lighter into the pocket of my shorts and went to get some answers from Sergeant Redmond Tanner.

CHAPTER
NINETEEN

I let Neddie pick the restaurant. She opted for a local favorite that specialized in both beef and seafood. Tucked away in a small marina on Broad Creek, its wide windows overlooked the salt marshes glowing golden-red in the setting sun.

Neddie poured the last of the Cabernet into her long-stemmed wine glass and leaned back in her chair. "I'm not sure I'm following any of this, Bay. Some of your conclusions seem to be based on pretty flimsy evidence."

"I know there are still holes in it. That's why I need to do some more digging into Rob's files when we get home. But those two names—Southland Real Estate and Meridian Partners—came up in one of his investigations, I'm sure of it. That's why they sounded familiar to me. And with what Red told me this afternoon, it's all starting to hang together."

"But what's the connection with what's been going on here? The murder of the Johnson kid and this land deal business? And your friend, Miss Hammond? I still don't get it."

"Keep it down, Neddie." Her voice had risen steadily with each glass of wine. "Let's not announce it to the whole world yet, okay?"

"Sorry." Neddie covered her mouth with her hand and looked guiltily around.

The restaurant, off the beaten trail but still jammed with tourists at the height of the season, had filled steadily while we ate our leisurely meal. Seven o'clock reservations had been a good idea. Now, just before nine, there wasn't an empty table in the place. Even the long bar, adjacent to the smoking section where we sat, was crowded with people waiting to be seated.

"Look, let me run through it again," I began. "First . . ."

The tall, tan body of our college-age waiter materialized at my elbow. He wore a bright blue Hawaiian print shirt and white shorts. He was a good-looking kid, clean shaven and muscular. He and Neddie had been flirting lightly all night long.

"What else can I get for you ladies? Another bottle of wine? How about a peek at the dessert menu?"

"Nothing for me, thanks. Neddie?"

"I'll have a Bailey's, on the rocks. And bring my friend here some hot tea. Constant Comment, if you have it." She winked at the boy, then whispered loudly, "It's okay. She's the designated teetotaler."

He laughed dutifully and moved away.

I lit a cigarette and stared out into the deepening twilight.

"You have to learn to lighten up a little, Tanner. Everyone who takes a drink isn't on the slippery slope to alcoholism." Neddie's voice had lost its bantering tone. She was deadly serious now.

"I'm aware of that. But what is that old expression? Something like, 'Blood will out' ? I've got enough proof right here of my addictive tendencies, don't I?"

I stubbed out the half-smoked cigarette as the waiter reappeared with my tea and Neddie's liqueur.

"Sure I can't interest you ladies in some dessert? The New York cheesecake looks really good tonight."

"No, thanks. Just the check please." I reached for my bag.

"That's already been taken care of."

"What do you mean? By whom?"

The young man gestured toward the bar. "By that gentleman over there. The tall one with the silver hair. Blue shirt, navy pants. See him?"

I turned and looked in the direction he was pointing. Geoff Anderson leaned back on his barstool and touched one finger to his forehead in a mock salute.

"That won't be necessary," I snapped, ignoring Geoff's tentative smile. I pulled out my wallet and slapped my gold card on the table.

"Sorry, ma'am. Like I said, it's already taken care of. You ladies have a nice evening." The waiter moved off before I could mount an argument.

"Damn him!" I spluttered, shoving my credit card back in my wallet. "Come on, let's get out of here."

"What's the rush? Let me finish my drink. And what are you so ticked off about, anyway? I can't remember the last time a handsome stranger picked up my tab. Probably never, now that I think about it."

I pushed back my chair and slung my bag over my shoulder. "Are you coming?"

Neddie folded her napkin and placed it deliberately on the table. "He's not a stranger, is he? This wouldn't by any chance be the mysterious 'someone' you wanted to avoid last night, would it?"

I stood and dug the car keys out of my bag.

"Okay, you win." Neddie rose and followed me toward the exit. "But I want an explanation, and I want it soon. You're acting pretty weird here, even for you."

I ignored her as I took the long way around, avoiding the bar. My precautions were pointless. As we crossed the crowded parking lot, I could see Geoff Anderson slouching nonchalantly against the side of my car.

"Bay, I want to talk to you."

"Get out of my way, Geoff."

I edged around him toward the driver's side, but he moved to block my path.

"No. Look, this is making me crazy. You have to tell me what's the matter. Everything was so great Sunday. *We* were great. And now you won't even take my calls. What's happened? What have I done?"

"Oh, quit playing the wounded lover, Geoff. That routine's getting old. Now get out of the way, or I'm going to call the cops."

"Who, the ever-present Sergeant Tanner? He'd love that, wouldn't he? Riding to the aid of the damsel in distress. He's the cause of all this, isn't he? He's finally succeeded in turning you against me."

Geoff's face twisted into an ugly sneer, his voice low and nasty. It was a side of him I hadn't seen before, not even when we were kids. Red had been right about one thing. I didn't know this man at all. Maybe I never had.

"How's the wife?"

My words dropped into the charged stillness like rocks into a pond. The bluster went out of Geoff Anderson like air out of a slashed tire.

"Who told you? Never mind, I can guess," he said resignedly. He moved away from the car and closed the door gently as I slid behind the wheel. The slam of the door on the other side made me jump in surprise.

I had totally forgotten about Neddie, an unexpectedly silent witness to this humiliating scene.

As I cranked the engine, Geoff leaned over, his breath warm on my face.

"It's not what it looks like, Bay. There are reasons, ones I couldn't tell you about before. If I lied about some things, it was because I had to. But I never lied about my feelings for you. And they haven't changed. If you ever want to hear my side, you know where to find me."

I stared straight ahead as Geoff gently kissed the side of my face, then walked away. A minute later, I heard the guttural roar of the Jaguar as he sped off into the night.

"You okay?" Neddie touched my shoulder as I dropped my head onto my hands. I had the steering wheel locked in a death grip. "What in the hell was that all about?"

"I've really made a mess of it this time," I whispered.

"Want to talk about it?"

"Yeah, I do. But not here, all right?"

"Sure. But let me drive. You just relax and get yourself back together."

"Are you sure you're okay to drive?"

"You mean am I sober enough? I won't even dignify that with an answer. Move over."

We switched places. I lay back against the headrest and watched the stars overhead stream by.

"I had a crush on him when I was a kid," I began. "I must have told you about him when we were roommates."

"I seem to recall your mentioning something about it. Military, wasn't he?"

"The Citadel."

"That explains it then."

"What?"

"The arrogance. Subtle, but apparent. Your father has it, too."

I smiled into the darkness. "They prefer to call it 'confidence'."

"Right."

I told Neddie the story of our accidental reunion a week ago, our mutual instant attraction. How Geoff seemed able to overcome my reluctance and indecision with a look or a touch.

How I had gone willingly to his bed only three days after our first meeting.

"Lust at first sight," Neddie said wryly.

I squirmed uncomfortably and didn't reply.

"Nothing wrong with that," she added as we turned into the plantation. "And besides, it's not as if you picked up some stranger in a bar. This was someone you had a history with. Look," she went on, "you and Rob had a damned near perfect marriage. I always envied you that. It's a rare thing these days . . . And then he died."

We pulled into the driveway, and Neddie shut off the car. She made no move to get out, turning instead to look at me slumped down in the seat.

"After you recovered from your injuries, you hid out here. No dates, no involvement, no men, period. You even avoided your father. Just as you're feeling ready to get back into the world, *wham*! Along comes a man you had feelings for a long time ago, someone you always thought of as unattainable. And he wants *you*! You, the scrawny little nuisance he never had time for. How am I doin' so far?"

"Let's go for a walk on the beach."

I got the flashlight out of the glove box. We left our shoes in the driveway, and I led the way down the path.

We wandered a while in silence, the *sshsshing* of the ocean our only accompaniment.

"So you slept with him. Big deal. Quit beating yourself up about it. You were lonely, vulnerable, and celibate for too damn long. You didn't know he was married. When you found out, you ended it."

I kicked up water with my bare feet as we waded through the shallows.

"You did end it? I mean, that's what tonight's little scene was all about, right?"

"Yes, it's over. I just hadn't gotten around to telling him yet." Neddie laughed. "So I gathered."

She couldn't see my answering smile in the darkness. I was beginning to feel better.

"You did the right thing, honey. You made a mistake—a totally understandable one. Forgive yourself, learn from it, and move
on. But most importantly, don't let this sour you. Now that
you've gotten out into the world again, don't go crawling back
into that hole you dug for yourself."

"You're pretty damn good at this, you know?"

"That's why I get the big bucks. Come one, let's head back. I
promised the Elliotts I'd call and see how it went with CJ and the
other kid's lawyer."

We turned around and retraced our steps. As we approached
the house, movement on the deck made me stiffen. Then the
plaintive *meow* of Mr. Bones drifted down, and my shoulders
slumped in relief.

We mounted the steps, and Neddie scooped up the purring
cat. "Oh, you're a lover, aren't you, you mangy old thing?"

The cat rubbed his head under her chin.

"What are you so jumpy about?" Neddie asked, her attention
still focused on the cat.

"I'm not sure," I answered, flopping down on the chaise. "It's
just a feeling, like something's . . . I don't know, not quite right.
Out of place, like I'm looking at something and not really seeing
it. It started the night I came home late from the hospital, the
night Miss Addie got hurt."

I folded my hands behind my head and tried to put my vague
unease into words.

"There were lights on the beach that night. They were moving
away from the path, now that I think about it. Fast. As if someone were running. And then there's the fax pages."

"Fax pages?"

"Yes. They were in a neat pile. Before that, the machine was
spitting them out onto the floor. And how did Geoff know where
to find us tonight?"

"Are you saying you think someone's been in the house?
Geoff? Why?" She set the cat back on the deck and perched on
the edge of the chaise. "Are you sure you're not getting just a little
paranoid here?"

"I don't know, maybe. But Geoff is involved in this land
business up to his eyeballs, and he's lied to me at every turn. He's

certainly proved he can't be trusted. I wrote the number of the restaurant on the pad by the phone when I called to make the reservation. He could have seen it there and followed us."

"I think you're reaching. All this digging into Rob's files is bringing back bad memories, old fears. You're transferring. It's almost classic."

"Thank you, Mrs. Freud. So how do you explain Geoff's showing up where we were eating? There are hundreds of restaurants on the island. Are you telling me it was a coincidence?"

"They do happen, you know." Neddie rose and stretched. The cat immediately jumped up and began winding himself around her legs. "You got anything to feed this little hobo?"

She reached down to scratch him behind his ears.

"Lower cupboard to the right of the stove. Dolores always gets a few cans of catfood when she shops."

Neddie picked up the cat and started toward the door.

"So you think I'm getting all spooked over nothing?" I called, and she turned around to face me.

"I always believe in listening to your own instincts, so I'm not dismissing your fear out of hand. Why don't you wait a couple of days, see how you feel? If you still think it's not just a reaction to all the turmoil of the last week, then call a locksmith. Get the locks changed, install an alarm. That's the sensible approach, don't you think?"

Neddie and Mr. Bones disappeared into the house. Through the screen I could hear the cat's loud mewing accompanied by the whir of the electric can opener. I sat for awhile and let the tranquility of the night wash over me.

I was relieved to have the confrontation with Geoff behind me. It was good it had happened the way it did, spontaneously and without warning. With no time to prepare or rehearse what I wanted to say, the break had been much cleaner, much easier than I'd feared.

I would probably never be sure exactly what my feelings for Geoff might have been. I knew it was all mixed up with my grief for Rob, my self-imposed isolation, and a fond remembrance of a childhood crush. What if he really were single, if he hadn't lied? Would I ever have come to care for him as he claimed he did for me? Or was it simply as Neddie had observed, lust and nothing more?

I decided to be thankful I had found out the truth before I became so emotionally entangled that the pain of it would have been worse than it already was.

But to be fair, I owed Geoff something, too. He had shown me that it was possible for me to give of myself, to be open to the possibility of finding love again. I'd made a bad choice, but in doing so I'd been reminded that I still needed trust and honesty in a relationship for it to have any hope of succeeding.

Forgive yourself, learn from it, and move on.

Neddie's words wrapped themselves around me in a soft blanket of comfort.

When I walked into the house, she was sitting cross-legged on the kitchen floor stroking an obviously contented Mr. Bones. The whole room smelled like tuna fish.

"You talk to Bitsy?" I asked. I got the iced tea pitcher from the refrigerator and poured myself a glass.

"The line was busy. I'll try again in a few minutes. You want to finish what you started telling me over dinner? About how this is all coming together?"

"No, not yet. You were right. I have some big holes to fill in. If you don't mind, I think I'll go work on my research some more. I have a couple of ideas I want to check out on the Internet."

"No problem. I'm going to put on a CD and get through a couple of articles I brought along. I never seem to find time to keep up with the literature when I'm at home. Then I think I'll hit the sack. It's been a busy day."

"Great. See you in the morning then. And make sure you put the cat out, okay? I don't want fleas all over the house."

"She's a hard woman, isn't she, Bonesy?"

The cat pricked up his ears, then went back to grooming his paws.

It took me only a few minutes to lose myself again in the intriguing paper trail that was the Grayton's Race development. What had first alerted me to the possibility that things might not be strictly on the up-and-up was the list of owners I'd gotten from the tax office. Every one of them had been a corporation. No individuals had been listed. When the shareholders of these companies turned out to be other corporations, I knew I was onto something. This was a classic method of concealing the real money men behind a project, especially if the disclosure of their identities would somehow adversely affect the deal. Such as, if the investors were convicted felons. Or had known ties to organized crime.

This was what Rob and I had encountered time and again in his investigations into drug trafficking in the state of South Carolina. He had brought down more than one of these "paper" organizations through persistent digging of the kind I was engaged in now.

Money laundering was the "white collar" end of the drug trade, but a vital one, nonetheless. Cut off the money and you cut off the supply. Rob had never gotten to the roots of this diseased tree, but he'd managed to hack off quite a few branches. He had been getting closer, though, and he was certain it was only a matter of time before he had enough proof to nail the big boys.

So was I. In fact, I was convinced he'd died for it.

None of the individuals' names that Belinda St. John's assistant had turned up had meant anything to me. They were likely just fronts, small-fry attorneys in big law offices or cousins of the wives of the real investors. This, too, was typical of a shady operation. It always drove Rob crazy because these "red herrings" were so hard to track down. That was what had made me remember another recurring name on the documents Dennis Morgan had faxed to me.

It was a law firm out of Palm Beach, Florida, and they had prepared most of the articles of incorporation for the bogus companies, even the South Carolina ones: Winningham, Masur, LeBrand, and Holt.

I logged onto the Internet and tried several websites before I hit on the right one. The Florida Bar Association had thoughtfully provided a listing of their member firms with officers, partners, and associates arranged in alphabetical order. I scrolled down the screen until the Winningham firm popped up. The roster of its staff attorneys followed the bios of its managing partners.

The first name on the list was Geoffrey Anderson.

CHAPTER
TWENTY

I don't know how long I sat chewing on the implications of my discovery.

At first, Geoff had told me he had been the initiator of the project; that he had found the land, put the deal together. Later, as we sat on the gentle rise where he planned to build his house, he had talked about feeling lucky to have been chosen to head up the development. He'd also claimed to have given up his law practice. So why was he still on the payroll of the firm whose name kept popping up on every legal document connected with Grayton's Race?

If I called him right now and demanded an explanation, I was certain he'd have a plausible story all ready to refute every one of my accusations. But since he'd already proved he could lie with conviction, confronting him would be pointless.

When Neddie stopped in the doorway on her way to bed, I decided to withhold this troubling new information until I was sure where it fit in. Instead, I asked her how the Elliotts were doing.

"Well, it's good news for CJ, bad news for his friend. Isaiah's attorney said that Isaiah has pretty much substantiated the story that CJ told you and that Red overheard. Which means that CJ's out of it as a suspect. And he can't testify to anything other than what he actually saw."

"Which also means that he can't be Isaiah's alibi, either."

"Right. They'll be taking Isaiah out to the river tomorrow so he can show them where he buried the baseball bat."

My thoughts went to Lavinia Smalls. I hoped her fierce pride and love for her family would see her through this terrible time.

"Oh, I almost forgot," Neddie went on. "Bitsy said to tell you that she and her husband will help with Isaiah's bail, if it's granted. She said you'd offered before, but they want to do it themselves. Sort of a gesture of their faith in their son's friend."

"I thought they were having money problems. At least that's what Bitsy led me to believe."

"Apparently not. Her husband said they'd be at the hearing Monday morning, ready to do whatever was needed. Maybe he's not as bad as you think he is."

"Trust me on this, Neddie. I've known the man for twenty years. There's something in this for him, even if it's only to bolster his image and get his name in the paper. Big Cal Elliott never does anything that isn't to his own personal or business advantage."

"You're probably right. As you say, you know him better than I do. Anyway, I'm off to bed. Don't stay up all night with that stuff, okay? I'm going for a swim first thing in the morning, and then we can do brunch. I want to head back to Savannah before the traffic gets too heavy."

I nodded absently, my mind struck with an idea I wasn't sure I wanted to explore.

"Bay?"

"Huh? Okay, sure. G'night," I mumbled.

"You're really out of it, girl. I put the cat out and locked up, so you quit worrying about whatever it is you're worrying about and get to bed, you hear?" she called and closed the bedroom door behind her.

Big Cal never does anything that isn't to his own personal advantage.

My own words kept ricocheting around inside my head. Why would Cal Elliott be willing to put up the bail for Isaiah Smalls? What would it gain him?

Nothing, I decided, at least nothing I could make sense of. I discounted altruism right up front. Besides, Isaiah had almost gotten CJ thrown in jail as an accessory. That couldn't have endeared him to Big Cal's heart.

What if he found out about Derek Johnson's being the holdout on the Grayton's Race project? If he had a lot of money tied up—money he couldn't afford to lose—would that be enough of a motive for murder? Maybe not. But what if he also knew that Derek was the one supplying his daughter with drugs? Mally didn't rank as high on Big Cal's list of priorities as CJ, but still . . .

I racked my memory trying to recall exactly when Bitsy said he'd disappeared. Hadn't she told me he wasn't there when the police came to tell her about CJ's arrest?

"This is crazy," I said out loud. Here I was, trying to construct a case against my best friend's husband. Granted I didn't like the guy, but could I really see him bashing some kid over the head with a baseball bat, then throwing his body in the river, knowing full well that Isaiah would be blamed?

No, I answered myself, I couldn't believe that.

Hiring somebody else to do it? Big Cal had a lot of connections. It wouldn't be hard for him to find out how to . . .

Enough! This is getting you nowhere. Leave it to the police.

I forced the whole wild scenario out of my mind and turned back to the computer.

I had been making a handwritten key to help me organize the dozens of discs Rob had compiled over the years of his investigations into drugs and organized crime in the state. For security reasons, none of them was labeled, and all were passworded. I knew Rob's favorite security codes, but not which one applied to which disc. It made for slow going.

But I was determined to keep at it. I had a theory. All I needed was one link between Southland Real Estate or Meridian Partners and the Palm Beach law firm that Geoff was apparently still affiliated with.

If Rob had turned up any evidence that Southland or Meridian was a front, I could blow the whole Grayton's Race project out of the water. I would expose it for what I was now sure it really was: a money-laundering scheme run by south Florida drug traffickers.

I wasn't yet sure where Derek Johnson's murder fit into the whole picture, but my instincts told me it might be connected.

Sergeant Red Tanner had confirmed CJ's claim that Derek was a pusher when I'd talked with him that afternoon. Red had checked the story out with the narcotics unit. He'd shown them the morgue photos, and they'd identified Derek as a small-time street dealer they knew only as "Boomer." No connection had been made with the dead boy until CJ had put it together for them.

"Boomer" had been suspected of being a member of a gang calling themselves the Sunshine Boys, a local distribution network for illegal drugs flowing in from Florida. It was an ongoing investigation, but the understaffed unit hadn't gathered enough hard evidence to make any arrests. Apparently, Derek kept a low profile, avoiding the periodic sweeps that netted the occasional user or his immediate supplier. Most were pled out, and the offenders back on the streets in a matter of months.

At any rate, the Sunshine Boys were considered small potatoes compared to the organizations targeted by Rob's SI unit and by the State Law Enforcement Division.

It was almost two o'clock when my eyes forced me to take a break. The tightly packed words on the computer screen were beginning to run together. I took off my glasses and leaned back in the chair.

In less than a minute, I was sound asleep.

Mr. Bones probably saved my life.

When the cat, claws extended, leaped onto my lap, I shot straight up out of the chair. Discs, papers, and an overflowing ashtray went flying in all directions.

"Jesus, Mary, and Joseph, cat!"

I had the presence of mind to keep my voice down, but I was sure the hammering of my heart was more than loud enough to wake Neddie. The poor cat, as startled as I, cowered under the desk.

"Come on, kitty, I'm sorry. It's okay. You can come out now," I coaxed.

I crawled around on my hands and knees picking up the computer discs and trying to scoop the cigarette butts back into the ashtray. Now that the initial shock had passed, I was beginning to see the humor.

"Come on, baby, I'm not going to hurt you. You scared me, too, you know. Come on, you have to go back outside."

I paused and sat back on my haunches. "And how the hell did you get *in*? Neddie said she put you out."

Suddenly the situation was no longer amusing.

My hand shook as I reached up and turned off the goose-necked lamp on the desk. The only illumination now came from the bright rectangle of the computer screen. I crouched on the floor and listened intently.

The soft hum of the air conditioner masked any sounds an intruder might have made. Besides, thick carpet would help muffle footsteps, and there were no creaking stairs or groaning floorboards to betray a stealthy misstep.

But someone was in the house. I knew it. Someone had opened a door, allowing the cat to streak in unnoticed. I could feel the ocean breeze drifting in through the open doorway of the office.

I cowered there in the dark, my brain frozen in fear. *Think!* I ordered myself.

There was only the modem line in this room—no phone. The closest one sat on my bedside table down the hall. I didn't have a gun, wouldn't have known how to use one if I had. But if someone meant me harm, why hadn't he struck while I was asleep in the chair? And what the hell did he want?

When I finally reached a decision, it seemed as if an hour had passed. In reality it couldn't have been more than a couple of minutes. Neddie had a cell phone in her purse. We'd use that to call the cops after we locked ourselves in the guestroom. It was a cowardly solution and might put Neddie at greater risk, but I couldn't help it. I needed the comfort of another human presence.

I rose up onto my hands and knees and crawled toward the doorway. My eyes had grown accustomed to the dark, and I risked a quick look up and down the hallway. No one lurked in the shadows, at least as far as I could tell. Neddie's door was slightly ajar. I crept cautiously across what seemed like an acre of carpet, eased the door open with my shoulder, and slipped inside. I scrambled quickly to my feet, pushed the door closed, and twisted home the lock.

My sense of relief was out of all proportion to the safety I had achieved. A determined thug could splinter the hollow door with a couple of well-placed kicks. I tip-toed across the room and tentatively approached the bed.

"Neddie!" I whispered urgently, "Neddie! Wake up!"

I knelt by the bed, my face inches from hers. I put my hand on her arm and shook it gently. Her eyes fluttered open.

"Wha-a-a-t . . ." she mumbled, and I clamped my hand over

her mouth.

"*Ssshh*! Someone's in the house!"

Neddie came instantly awake, her eyes darting around the room. When I was sure she recognized me, I took my hand away.

"The cat's inside, and there's a door open somewhere. I could feel the draft. Get your cell phone and call 911."

"What? What are you saying?"

"Get your cell phone!"

"I can't! It's in my bag. I left it in the living room by the sofa."

"Damn! Now what?" I couldn't think, couldn't focus on anything but my fear.

Neddie sat up and ran her hands over her face and through her tangled hair. "Wait a minute. Let's stay calm. Did you actually see anyone?"

"No! I didn't go exploring, damn it! But if you locked up, then someone had to break in, didn't they? I don't think it's probably a social visit at three A.M."

"Maybe they've taken whatever they came for and left."

"Then why is the door still open?"

"I don't know! Let me think."

I slid to the floor, my hands clasped tightly around my knees, while Neddie crawled quietly out of bed and pulled on a pair of sweatpants under her nightshirt.

The moon moved out from behind high, drifting clouds and bathed the room in a soft, eerie light.

"The window!" I hissed. "We'll go out the window, over to the neighbors and call the cops."

Neddie hesitated for a second, then reached down to help me to my feet. "Let's do it."

I slid open the wide window next to the bed and checked the ground below. With the garage built underneath, the house sat up high. The drop looked to be about twelve feet.

"Let me go first, then I can help you down."

I slung one leg over the sill.

"Bay, hold it." Neddie grabbed my arm and moved close to my ear. "Is this a good idea? I mean, maybe we should wait. We're not even sure there's anybody here."

"I'm sure. Come on. We can do this."

I got my other leg out, squirmed around until both my hands

gripped the ledge, then "walked" myself down the cedar siding. I let go and landed, knees bent, in a soft pile of pinestraw the landscapers replenished regularly.

Neddie poked her head out the window, and I gave her the thumbs up. Shorter than I, she had a longer fall, and I tried to cushion her landing as she dropped. We were both breathing heavily, more from fear than from exertion. Even so, I couldn't suppress a "we did it" grin. Neddie clapped me lightly on the shoulder.

It was then I heard the soft, metallic *clink* from the front of the house. We both froze. Then Neddie gestured frantically toward the back and turned in the direction of the path that led through the trees to the house next door. I grabbed her hand and shook my head.

Now that I was no longer trapped inside, fear was giving way to anger. Out here in the open, I felt less vulnerable. Someone had violated my sanctuary, not once, but several times if my instincts were correct.

I wanted to know who it was. And why.

Neddie plucked at my arm and tried to drag me toward the path. I turned and put my mouth close to her ear.

"You go. Call the cops. I'll stay here in case he tries to run for it. Go!"

I pushed her gently. She looked as if she wanted to argue with me. "Go!" I hissed again, and she disappeared around the corner of the house.

The pinestraw muffled my footsteps as I crept cautiously forward, my back pressed up against the side of the house. I inched toward the driveway, held my breath, and darted a quick look around the corner.

I might have missed him if it hadn't been for the soft glint of the moonlight off the tool he held in his gloved hand. Dressed entirely in black, his face was covered with a dark ski mask.

He was sliding out from underneath my car.

I jumped back, my heart thudding wildly.

A bomb! He was wiring my car with a bomb!

Nightmare memories of a rain of hot metal—and scorched flesh—flashed through my paralyzed brain. It took every ounce of self-control I had left not to run blindly down the path, away from this terrifying scene.

I should have realized there would be two of them. I never heard his accomplice creep up behind me, but some sixth sense made me turn just as the blow was delivered. It glanced off the side of my head. My injured shoulder took the worst of it.

With a cry of agony, I crumpled to the ground. Through a gray haze, I felt strong hands under my armpits, knew I was being dragged toward the driveway. My brain told my body to resist, but the messages weren't getting through.

The sharp blare of sirens, approaching fast, penetrated my half-conscious mind. My attacker dropped me, face down in the pinestraw, and sprinted away. I heard muttered curses, then two sets of footsteps receding in the direction of the beach.

I had just managed to struggle to my hands and knees when the night was shattered by a blast so loud it seemed to come from inside my head. I had barely a second for the smoke and flame to register on my numbed senses.

Then choking darkness enveloped me.

CHAPTER
TWENTY-ONE

The first person I saw when I opened my eyes was Rob.

At least, in those first confused moments after my return to consciousness, I was sure it was his well-loved face, furrowed with concern, hovering just a few inches above mine. Then a puff of breeze blew some of the lingering smoke away, and I realized it was only Red.

My throat closed with the bitter pain of remembrance, and I turned my head to hide the tears I couldn't control.

"It's all right, Bay. You're safe now."

Red smoothed my matted hair back off my forehead, touched the wetness on my cheeks. I let him think they were tears of relief.

Gradually, the sounds of the chaos around me penetrated the muted roar that still reverberated inside my head: the shouts of the firemen as they directed hoses toward the twisted wreckage that had been my car; the excited babble of my neighbors gathered at the end of the driveway, kept at bay by a uniformed officer.

Then a single voice, raised high in indignation, made my lips twitch in the beginnings of a smile.

"God damn it, let me through! I'll have your ass, buddy!"

Red looked up. "Hey, Mike," he called, "it's okay. Let her through."

Neddie Halloran shouldered her way past the deputy and was at my side in seconds.

"Oh, my God! Bay, are you all right? Is she all right?" Neddie grabbed the shirt of a blue-clad paramedic who had been hovering just out of my line of vision. For the first time I realized I was lying on a gurney.

"She appears to be, ma'am, from an initial examination." He gently pried Neddie's fingers from his pocket. "We need to get her transported, though. We'll know more once we get her to emergency."

"No!" I struggled to sit up before I realized I was strapped down. "Neddie!"

My friend turned and clutched the trembling hand I held out to her.

"Don't let them take me to the hospital! Please!"

"*Ssshh*, honey, take it easy." I watched her cast a helpless look at Red.

"Bay, don't be ridiculous." My brother-in-law moved around to the other side of the gurney. "You have to go to the hospital. You were unconscious. You could have a concussion. And it looks like you took a hell of a whack on that shoulder."

Some of the shock must have been wearing off. At the mention of my shoulder, I became aware of the deep, aching pain concentrated just below my neck on the left side. Tentatively I rotated the joint and winced. It was bad, but not nearly as bad as it had been after my first close encounter with a bomb.

"Is it broken or anything?" I asked the young paramedic who stood observing me from a short distance away.

"No, ma'am, doesn't appear to be. Especially since you have motion. But it really should be x-rayed, just to be sure."

"Then I'm not going to the hospital. Get me off this thing."

Red and the paramedic looked exasperated. I counted on Neddie to understand.

"They can't make me, can they?" I asked her. My red-rimmed eyes implored her to help me, to be on my side.

"No, they can't make you, honey. But I think you should. I really do think you should."

"You can take care of me, can't you? You're a doctor."

"For crissake, Bay, I'm a shrink, not an internist."

"I'll go in tomorrow—or later today," I amended as I realized that dawn had broken, the sky above me lightening with each passing minute. "I promise. I just want to go under my own power, in my own time. Neddie?"

The paramedic threw up his hands and walked away toward the ambulance. Neddie undid the straps that held me, and she and Red eased me into a sitting position. It was probably intentional that they faced me away from the smoking ruin in the driveway.

They couldn't do anything about the smell. The air was heavy with gasoline and oil fumes, and the unmistakable stench of burned rubber.

"How bad is the house?" I asked, afraid to look.

"The garage and the kitchen took the worst of it. Most of the windows on this side are gone, and there'll be some water damage. The firemen hosed it all down, just in case."

Red's recitation was blunt and emotionless. I knew he was angry at me for refusing to go to the hospital and shaken by my narrow escape. Just how close it had been made me shudder.

The paramedic, whose name tag proclaimed him to be Andy Petrocelli, approached and handed me a clipboard with some papers on it.

"We'll need you to sign these releases if you're really serious about not going to the hospital." He sounded aggrieved and just a little ticked off.

I took the pen he offered me and scratched my signature where he pointed.

"No offense, Andy, okay?" I asked as he turned to go. "I know you guys are the best. It's just a personal quirk."

"No offense taken, ma'am," he drawled. His smile made him look younger, more like the twenty-something he probably was. "You just make sure you get to a doctor and get checked over, hear?"

"You bet. Thanks for everything."

Andy Petrocelli touched his forehead in a little salute, then climbed into the ambulance. Red and Neddie supported me as I climbed off the gurney. The rescue squad collapsed the stretcher and loaded it into the back. Then the vehicle moved slowly down the drive. My gawking neighbors stepped aside long enough to let it pass, then reformed.

None of them knew me well enough to be genuinely concerned, I thought. It was just the ghoulish curiosity that affects us all in the face of a disaster.

"Well, now what?" Red's voice was tinged with exasperation and weariness. "Want me to run you over to the Judge's? You sure as hell can't stay here."

"I don't see why—" I began when we were interrupted by another sheriff's deputy.

"What is it, Woody?" Red asked.

"Sarge, we got a lotta press out here. Papers and TV. What

should I tell 'em?"

I turned to look toward the end of the driveway, and immediately the lights of several video-cams clicked on. I could hear shouts of "What happened?" and "What's the story?" coming from the crowd that seemed to be growing rather than diminishing. "Anybody dead?" was my personal favorite.

"Tell them this is a crime scene and to stay the hell out. Better get some tape up, by the way. I want this whole area sealed off. And post a man on the beach path so we don't get a lot of gawkers or reporters wandering up from there. I want everything secure when the detectives get here."

The patrolman hurried off to carry out his orders. Red watched him go for a minute, then turned abruptly back to me.

"And I suppose you were about to say you're staying here, right?"

"If my bedroom's still intact, yes. You got a problem with that?"

"Jesus! For someone who's supposed to be smart and savvy, you sure can come up with some stupid ideas. Of course I have a problem with that. Somebody just tried to blow you up! Has that even registered in that stubborn head of yours?"

"Could I sit down?" I asked meekly. My legs were getting wobbly, and I had a headache that threatened to explode out of my eyes.

Instantly Red's strong right arm was around my waist. He and Neddie practically carried me to his cruiser where I collapsed gratefully onto the front seat.

"I'm sorry, Bay. I didn't mean to yell at you. If you want to stay here, I'll post a couple of men. I'm sure the Captain will okay it. I'm off duty in a couple of hours, and I'll come and relieve them myself. Just let me check with the firemen and make sure it's safe to go in, okay?"

"Red . . ."

"You just rest here. I'll check it—"

"Red, shut up!"

He stopped then, his handsome face an agony of regret and confusion.

"It's okay, Red. I know you're just trying to protect me. Like you always do. And I'm an ungrateful bitch. Wait!" I commanded as he began to protest. "I know my staying makes it more difficult for you guys, and I'm sorry about that. But I can't run, not anymore."

I looked across at Neddie who had slid into the seat on the other side. Again, I counted on her to understand. "If I let them force me out, I might never have the courage to come back."

"She's right," Neddie said softly. "It has to be Bay's decision."

I raised my face to look anxiously up at Red. He smiled and laid a hand gently against my cheek.

"When could any of us Tanner men ever say no to you?"

He wheeled and strode off in search of the fire captain.

"You sure about this?" Neddie asked as I leaned back against the seat. "We could go to a hotel or bunk in with the Elliotts."

"We?" My eyes, gritty from the smoke and ash, were getting heavier by the minute. It was all I could do to stay awake.

"You don't think I'm leaving you alone, do you? I'll call my service and have them reschedule my appointments for the next couple of days."

"Neddie, I don't want you involved in this. I think you should go home. If anything happened to you—"

"Shut up, Tanner. If you're staying, I'm staying. You're stuck with me, so get used to it."

I squeezed her hand and managed a shaky smile. "Okay."

"Besides," she went on, her natural quirky humor never suppressed for long, "I intend to help you pick out your new car."

I dozed a little then, I think. When Red returned, he and Neddie escorted me, one on either side, up the outside steps, across the deck, and directly into my bedroom. Except for the lingering smell, the room was exactly as it had been when I'd changed for dinner the night before.

Neddie led me straight into the bathroom, turned the taps in the shower on full blast, and helped me peel off my filthy, tattered clothes.

"I think we'll just burn these," she said, wrinkling her nose as she dropped my slacks and sweater into the wastebasket. "Now don't come out of there until the hot water runs out." She steered me toward the tub. "I'll just leave the door open a little. Call me if you need help."

The steam rose around me in soothing clouds. I soaped myself three times before the water stopped running black. I let the stinging spray pound on my neck and back, working the deep soreness out of the spot where my assailant's blow had landed. By the time my hair was squeaking through my fingers, I felt a thousand percent better. But I was still bone-weary, anxious only to crawl into bed and sleep for a week. If the cops had questions, they'd have to wait. I didn't have that much to tell, anyway.

As I toweled myself dry and slipped into the nightgown Neddie had left for me on the vanity, the fear and the horror were almost gone. I would sleep, give my body a chance to heal. But I would no longer cower in the shadows as I had done for the past year. This time, I would fight back.

As I tucked the sheet up around me and slowly drifted off, my thoughts were not of fire and noise and death. If I dreamed at all, I knew it would not be of the dark pit of terror, but the hot, sweet light of revenge.

As it turned out, I slept without dreams, at least none I remembered. I rolled over onto my back and stretched, wincing a little at the tightness in my shoulder. I flexed my elbow, then the fingers of my left hand. Everything seemed to be working the way it was supposed to.

Gradually I became aware of activity at the front of the house: the *clang* of hammers on nail heads, the buzzing of an electric saw, and the voices of what sounded like a hell of a lot of people.

It was just after two in the afternoon, and harsh sunlight pushed around the edges of the closed drapes. I got up then and dressed in shorts and a T-shirt. I was just running a brush through the rat's nest of my hair when Neddie stuck her head around the door.

"Hey, you're up! How're you feeling?"

I pondered the question for a few seconds. "Surprisingly good," I said, and meant it. "What's all the racket out front?"

"Some guys are here boarding up the windows. It's gonna be a few days before they can get all the glass cut and replaced. And I called a locksmith. All the locks have been changed except for this one in the bedroom. They were waiting for you to wake up."

Neddie drew three sets of keys from her pocket and set them

on the nightstand. "Thought you might want these, too," she said and pitched a fresh pack of cigarettes at me. I caught them in mid-air with my left hand.

"Thanks."

"Well, you ready to meet your adoring public?"

"What does that mean?" I dug a book of matches out of the nightstand drawer, lit up, and inhaled gratefully. "I'm not talking to the press. Period. No exceptions."

"Oh, they're long gone. Red's boys wouldn't even let them on the property. 'Victim under doctor's care, all official statements to come from the press liaison officer at the department', etc., etc. Just like on TV."

"Then who wants to see me?"

"Only the rest of the immediate world. Let's see, there's your father, Lavinia, a black couple I believe are her son and daughter-in-law, and the entire Elliott clan. Red, of course, and a big black cop named Gleason or Gibson, or something like that. Plus the head of the arson squad of the fire department and a couple of 'suits' with very impressive-looking credentials from SLED. Oh, and our friend from the restaurant last night. Geoff, isn't it?"

"They're all here *now?*" I sank down on the bed, unsure of my ability to face such a mob.

"I can't be sure. I haven't taken attendance recently. Some have come and gone and come back. Dolores and Lavinia and I have been hopping trying to keep them all fed and watered."

"Sounds like you've been having a damned party!" I snapped.

"Well, it *has* been sort of like an Irish wake—without the corpse, of course."

I knew Neddie's gallows humor was meant to help me deal with the horror of last night, not minimize it. The wicked grin on her face brought a grudging smile to my own.

"You're something else, you know?"

"Want me to clear some of them out? I think the cops are gonna want first crack at you. I've already told them everything I know, which isn't much. Red says they've picked up a few clues, but they're counting on you to fill in a lot of the blanks."

"They're going to be disappointed. The one guy had a ski mask on. The other one was just a . . . presence, I guess. He hit me from behind, so I never got a look at him. Except . . . "

"What? What do you remember?"

I closed my eyes and let the nightmare images click through my mind like slides in a projector. "Nothing specific. Probably nothing at all, really. I just got the impression that he was big. I mean, really big. I'm five-foot-ten, and when he hit me, it came from above. I think that's what made me turn. I caught a flash of the—whatever it was—out of the corner of my eye on its way down."

The memory of how close it had been to being my head that took the full force of that blow made me shiver.

"And another thing. When he was dragging me. He didn't grunt or anything. Just hauled me along as if I weighed nothing at all."

"Be sure you tell all that to Red. You never know what could help."

I leaned back against the headboard, reluctant to move out of the sanctuary of my bedroom to face a crowd of people, no matter how well-meaning. I had hated being the center of attention from the time I was a kid, and nothing had changed. Neddie, curled on the end of the bed, regarded me with a professional eye.

"What are you thinking?" I asked.

"I guess I've been waiting for you to show some effects from nearly getting blown up last night. You're too damned calm. It's worrying me."

"Would you feel better if I went screaming around the house tearing at my hair?"

"It might be a more natural reaction than this 'hey, no problem' mode you seem to be in."

I lit another cigarette and watched the smoke drift upward toward the ceiling fan. "Neddie, this isn't an act. Believe me, I'm as surprised as you are. But you know what my overwhelming emotion is right now? It's anger. And determination. I'm going to find out who did this and make sure they pay. No more cringing and hiding. Does that make me crazy?"

"We don't use the term 'crazy', honey. At least not in public. I just want to be sure that you're not deluding yourself, putting up a good front. I don't want a delayed reaction to sneak up and smack you right between the eyes."

"I honestly don't think you need to worry." I stubbed out the cigarette and dug my sandals out from under the bed.

"Well, shall we do it?" Neddie moved toward the door.

"Wait a sec. Before I talk to the cops, what did you tell them about what's been going on? I mean, about my feeling that some-one had been in the house before last night?"

Neddie raised an eyebrow. "Why?"

"Just answer the question."

"Nothing. I didn't think it was my story to tell."

"Good. Okay, let's go." I ran my hands through my thick, dark brown hair. "Do I look all right?"

Neddie's head was cocked to one side. I knew she wanted to pursue the subject, but then thought better of it and pulled the door open. "A tad bit singed around the edges," she mocked, "but otherwise as homely as ever."

"Go to hell," I laughed.

They were clustered in little knots, organized by age, race, occupa-tion, and relationship to me. Or something loosely approximating that. Only Geoff Anderson, leaning on the rail of the deck and staring out at the ocean, stood alone.

A pariah to everyone, apparently.

I hesitated on the edge of the great room. Suddenly I was sixteen again and unsure of what was expected of me. It reminded me of the night of my first cotillion, floating self-consciously down the great oak staircase at Presqu'isle. My parents, Lavinia, and my date all waited at the foot of the steps, their faces turned expectantly up at me. I remembered three of those faces smiling in approval. Only my mother's had been pinched in apprehension as if she expected me to trip and fall and disgrace her once again.

It was a few seconds before anyone realized I was standing there. The *whir* as the Judge activated his wheelchair and rolled in my direction seemed to galvanize everyone else to action. Soon I was engulfed in the embraces of people who seemed genuinely to care about me, wrapped in the warmth of their concern.

I was touched more than I cared to admit.

Eight-year-old Brady Elliott saved me from the humiliation of bursting into tears.

"Hey, Aunt B-Bay," he stammered, yanking on the leg of my

shorts to get my attention, "can I ride in your new t-t-tank? Daddy said you n-needed one."

The general laughter broke the tension, and I could feel the whole room relax.

"Tell him to find me a good deal on one, kiddo, and I'll consider it," I said, tousling his short blond hair.

I caught Big Cal's eye, and he looked quickly away.

My neighbors must have scurried straight from the end of my driveway back to their own kitchens that morning. The table in the dining area sagged under the weight of casseroles, desserts, and assorted trays of meats and vegetables. The series of folding doors that allowed the kitchen to be closed off were shut. I wasn't ready to deal with that yet, but I could tell by the pained expression on Dolores's face as she bustled back and forth that it was bad.

The kitchen was much more her room than mine. I decided right then to let her redesign it to suit herself when it came time to get the repairs done. I had so few opportunities to repay her for her care of me. Perhaps this would be a gesture she would accept.

As people drifted off to replenish empty plates and glasses, I glanced out toward the deck. Geoff's soft blue eyes were boring into mine. I couldn't read his face. It seemed to have been wiped clean of all expression. When he realized I was looking at him, he held something up in his right hand. I couldn't tell what it was from that distance. He made an exaggerated motion of placing whatever it was on the wrought iron table.

He said something, then turned and disappeared down the outside steps. A few seconds later I heard the roar of the Jaguar receding down the road.

"What was that all about?" Bitsy's voice at my side made me jump. "What did he say?"

I shrugged and moved away. I'd wait until I was alone to find out what Geoff Anderson had left for me on the deck.

And I wasn't entirely certain my lip-reading had been accurate, but I'd thought he'd said, "I'm sorry."

CHAPTER
TWENTY-TWO

Except for my father and the "official" guests at this impromptu party, Dolores was the last to leave. For once I didn't have to force her to take the leftover food with her. I had no place to keep it.

I'd finally braved a look at the kitchen, and there wasn't much left of it. Part of the ceiling had fallen in, probably from the weight of the water that had been poured onto it. Although most of the mess had been cleared away and the windows secured with huge sheets of plywood, the room was definitely unusable. The only good news was that the structural integrity of the house seemed to be intact, although the garage underneath was pretty much gutted. The electricity, knocked out in the explosion, was back on, but it would be tomorrow before my phone service could be restored.

Having nothing more of substance to add to the statement she'd already given, Neddie had retreated to the guest room for a well-deserved rest. I sat in one corner of the off-white sofa, my legs tucked up under me, surveying the solemn faces of the men arrayed in a semicircle in front of me. It shouldn't have been an adversarial situation, but it felt like one.

My father confirmed my feeling the second Neddie had left the room. "What an incredibly stupid thing that was to do, Lydia," he growled around the cigar clamped tightly in his teeth.

I knew he was really angry. I was never "Lydia" except when he was seriously ticked off at me.

"What on earth possessed you to try to apprehend these people on your own?" he continued, shaking his head at my supposed recklessness. "What were you thinking of? That any child of mine could be so—"

"Mind if the accused gets a word in edgewise?" I snapped. "First, I didn't try to 'apprehend' anybody. I was just watching to make sure they didn't skip before the cops arrived. And secondly," I said, more reasonably than I felt, "I don't think these gentlemen are here to listen to you scold me as if I were some naughty four year-old, okay?"

He shut up then and busied himself with adding bourbon to the drink sitting next to him on the end table. I glanced at Red and saw his lips twitch before he got his face under control again.

"Okay, let's get this over with," I said firmly. "Who wants to go first? Or should I just tell it, and let you ask questions after?"

Red, Matt Gibson, and the two men from the State Law Enforcement Division avoided looking at each other. Silver and— for a moment I drew a blank on the other one's name. Neither was anyone I knew from the old days. Heywood, that was it. Silver and Heywood, in almost identical gray suits and red striped ties, conferred with their eyes, then Silver spoke.

"This is your case, gentlemen. We're just here to observe and to help in any way we can. However you guys want to play it."

Red pulled a mini tape recorder out of his breast pocket and set it on the coffee table. "This will save time," he said to me, pushing the RECORD button. "This way they can get your statement typed up, and you can just come in and sign it tomorrow. Any objections?"

I shook my head and lit a cigarette while Red identified himself, the date, time and those present. I was beginning to feel more like the suspect than the victim.

Matt Gibson, the death investigator, took over. "Why don't you just give it to us in your own words first. If anyone needs clarification we'll wait until after you've finished. Agreed?"

He looked at his fellow officers and got nods all around.

I'd had plenty of time to decide just how much I was going to reveal about the events of last night and my suspicions about what had led up to them. I tried to stick only to the facts, starting with the cat's jerking me awake and my realization that someone must be in the house. I took them through it step by step, ending with my impressions of the size of my attacker.

There was only one logical question left to be asked, at least from their perspective, and I wasn't prepared to answer it. They would want to know why. I intended to keep my thoughts about that to myself, at least for now.

"Do you have any idea why someone would try to kill you, Bay? And by this particular method?" Matt Gibson spoke quietly, his face grave as he waited for my reaction.

I'm a terrible liar. You can usually see it in my eyes, so I try not to look directly at people when I'm about to tell a whopper. I studied my hands as I spoke. "I don't know, Matt, unless it has some connection with what happened to Rob. Am I right in assuming they were pros?"

The law enforcement officers looked pointedly at each other. No one spoke. After a moment, Agent Heywood cleared his throat and extracted a notebook from his pocket.

"The device was wired to the ignition of your car. It would have detonated when you turned the key. It's a standard technique of the mob, among others. Forensics have been over what pieces we were able to recover." He consulted his notes and continued, "Apparently you interrupted the perp before he had a chance to finish, and it went off prematurely."

Silver jumped in. "Or, your coming on the scene like that may have caused them to alter their plans. This big guy you describe may have been trying to drag you to the car so they could be certain you were in it when the bomb exploded. Either way, you're damn lucky."

What Neddie had called my unnatural calm was beginning to fray a little around the edges. Somehow, hearing my close brush with death being discussed with such bland detachment, made it all the more horrifying. I could feel a nerve in the corner of my right eye begin to jump.

"But that still doesn't answer why," Matt Gibson persisted. "If it had anything to do with your husband or his work, why wait almost a year to do something about it? What could have spooked them into acting now?"

I felt the blood rush out of my head as the answer struck me like last night's blow. Of course! That had to be it!

Red, who knew me better than anyone there except my father, leaned forward in his chair. "What is it, Bay? You've remembered something."

"No, no, it's just . . ." I stammered. I fumbled for a cigarette and lowered my head to the flame of the lighter. I needed those few seconds to get myself under control. I had to think this out before I said anything more. When I looked up, five pairs of eyes—my father's included—were staring at me intently. I exhaled and ran a hand through my hair.

"It's just that . . . I'm really tired, I guess," I finished lamely.

The faces of Red and the Judge clearly said they weren't buying it, but both let me slide.

"Neddie said you'd picked up some clues," I said, hoping to shift the attention away from myself. "Anything I should know about?"

Red sat back in his chair, appearing to relax. His eyes never left my face.

"A partial tire track—probably from one of those ATV's—and a heel print. On the beach near the end of your path. We were able to get photos, but the tide came in and wiped them out before we could get casts. They won't be much help unless we get something to compare them with."

Heywood flipped his notebook closed and replaced it in his pocket. "We'll send the bomb fragments up to the FBI lab, see if they can get any signature from it."

"Signature?" I asked. "What's that?"

"The people who make these devices generally do it the same way every time," Agent Silver offered. "Use the same kind of tape and wire, construct them in the same configuration. If the feds have this particular pattern on file, we may get a hit. They have the fragments from the other . . . incident, the one involving Mr. Tanner. They'll certainly compare those two."

"I think my daughter should rest now, gentlemen." The Judge spoke for the first time since I had politely told him to butt out. "If she thinks of anything else that might assist you with your investigation, we'll be in touch with your office."

I was about to protest his highhanded interference when he quelled me with a look. I got the message and uncoiled myself from the sofa. I shook hands with the two SLED agents and thanked them for their help.

Matt Gibson covered my hand with both of his chocolate brown ones and nodded encouragingly. "We've got men, front and back. They'll be here 'round the clock until we nail these bastards. So you sleep easy, hear?"

"Thanks, Matt. I'll be fine."

Red walked with them out to their cars, but I knew he'd be back. He and my father had exchanged a few whispered words while I was saying my goodbyes. By the time I had cleared away the dirty glasses and stacked them in the sink of the half-bath that had become the makeshift kitchen, I heard the front screen door bang, and my brother-in-law was dropping a gym bag in the entryway.

"Before you start yelling, I'm sleeping on your couch tonight. Your father agrees; and, even if he didn't, I'd do it anyway. So save your breath."

"Good," I said, curling up in my corner again. "I was going to suggest it. I'll feel a lot better with you in the house."

He looked a little stunned at not getting an argument, but recovered quickly and crossed to resume his seat.

"Now, daughter," my father began, "let's hear what it was that Matt Gibson's question triggered. You remembered something. I could almost hear the light bulb click on in your head." He glanced over at Red. "Redmond is off duty, so you can speak freely. It won't go any farther."

There was no point equivocating with my father. My own stubbornness was a trait passed directly from his genes to mine. I would not be able to wiggle out from under his stern gaze with lame excuses of fatigue and confusion. But it had to be on my terms.

"Okay, you're right. I think I'm onto something. But before I lay it out for you, I have to get it straight in my own head. I need proof, and I'm close to having it. I'm not making any accusations or involving either of you until I'm certain. When I am, you'll both hear it. Immediately, I swear."

"This is crazy." Red jumped up and paced back and forth in front of the empty fireplace. "It's not your place to get proof, damn it! You're not the cops, *I* am. You tell me what you know, and we'll take it from there. Isn't almost getting killed twice enough for you? You want to go for three?"

"Want to keep it down a little in here?" Neddie appeared at the end of the hallway, her eyes heavy with sleep. "How's a girl supposed to rest with people shouting at the top of their lungs?"

"Sorry. But maybe you can talk some sense into this thick-headed friend of yours. I sure as hell can't."

Neddie mostly listened as the battle raged for another fifteen minutes. In the end, the Judge and Red had to admit defeat. I wasn't sharing my theories until I was damned good and ready.

"Don't worry about me, Judge. Red's here, and the other cops. I know what I'm doing," I reassured my father as I stood beside the open passenger window of his van. An off-duty patrolman had volunteered to drive him home.

"I hope so," he said, refusing to look at me.

I convinced Red and Neddie that I would be perfectly safe while they went out to pick up some dinner for us. It was still light outside, and there were three deputies stationed near the house. And I desperately needed to be alone. Reluctantly, they went.

I felt as if I had been cooped up inside for days. I stepped through the French doors and out onto the deck, breathing deeply of the salt-laden, pine-sweet air. A mockingbird squawked at me from the end of the railing.

I crossed to the table, reached down, and picked up a set of keys fastened to a business card. The logo was from the local luxury import car dealer, and the embossed name printed underneath was *Buck James, Sales Professional*.

I turned the card over. The block letters were neat and compact. Geoff had written, *If you don't like this one, Buck will give you the same deal on whatever you choose*. It was signed simply "G.A."

Oh, Geoff, I thought, clutching the keys tightly to my chest, *why can't you just let it go? Let me go?*

I walked slowly back into the house, making certain to lock the door behind me. I moved down the hallway toward the office. In all the excitement of last night and this afternoon, I had forgotten all about my notes and Rob's computer discs. It was past time I got them back in the safe.

I stood in the doorway for a full minute before it finally registered.

I didn't have to worry about putting anything away.

It was gone. All of it.

CHAPTER TWENTY-THREE

The breeze off the ocean was blessedly cool. It rattled in the fronds of the palmettos, whose long, sharp leaves clacking against each other sounded like fingernails tapping on a window. Had I been inside, it would probably have scared the hell out of me.

But, at three A.M., I had slipped out onto the deck and settled myself in a chaise lounge. I'd made my presence known to one of the deputies who'd nodded at me sympathetically, then continued his patrol.

Now, at somewhere around five-thirty, I watched the sky beginning to glow pink and gold with the first hint of dawn. Bluejays, cardinals, mockingbirds, and grackles began to call to one another from the moss-laden live oaks and towering pines. Soon the whole island would stretch itself awake.

And I still had no answers.

Who had stolen the disks? And why?

Those were the questions that had plagued my rest, kept me tossing in tangled sheets until I had given up and wandered outside. I knew I hadn't checked the office after the explosion. All I was sure of was that the disks were there when I crawled fearfully across the hallway into Neddie's room last night. That my assailant had taken them made the most sense, although the house had been crowded with people while I slept. In the confusion, anyone could have slipped into the office, shoved the disks into a bag, and walked unchallenged across the deck to deposit them in a trunk or a glove box for later disposal.

But who? And again, why? The clear, blue eyes of Geoffrey Anderson materialized before me in the hazy predawn stillness. He alone of my many visitors had an interest in stopping me from delving farther into the intricately constructed house of cards that was the Grayton's Race ownership. But could I picture him sneaking around, ransacking my house while I slept peacefully in the room next door? While my friends and family waited anxiously just a few feet away?

No, I decided, no more than I could buy Red's insinuations that Geoff might have been involved in Derek Johnson's murder, regardless of how fortuitous it had been for the viability of his project. He wasn't capable of it. Deceit? Definitely. Fraud, probably. But murder and robbery? I just couldn't see it.

No, the theft—and the attempt to silence my curiosity permanently—were the obvious motives for last night's bizarre chain of events.

And the likely suspects? That was easy. The men who had murdered my husband were the same ones who were involved in the construction project headed by Geoff Anderson. I knew it as surely as I knew the sun would come up this morning. So I was doubly dangerous to them. A bomb had worked before, and they'd walked away scot-free. So why not try it again? Killing me would be the proverbial two birds with one stone.

And how had they known I was a danger to them?

When Matt Gibson asked the question, "What spooked them?" I knew immediately what they had done.

Stanley Wojeckewski could have told me in a minute, not only what type of device, but how long it had been in place and probably the location of the terminal that was intercepting. My phone might even be tapped, too. Stanley was an electronics whiz, one of those nerdy computer guys that lived for a chance to dive into boards and chips. Rob had employed him to "sweep" our terminal and the phones once a week to prevent just such a thing as this from happening. I was convinced that, on one of their forays into my house, someone had wired my computer so that everything I brought up was "mirrored" onto another terminal. What I saw, they saw.

It was the only explanation that made any sense. No one else but Neddie was aware of the existence of the discs, or that I had been searching them for a connection between the Miami drug underworld and Grayton's Race. If the phone was indeed tapped, that had only been a bonus for them.

I could feel the warmth through the back of my shirt as the sun climbed over the horizon. I lit a cigarette and stretched out full-length on the chaise.

I could call Stanley, have him run a diagnostic on my computer, check out the phone, but it would have been pointless. Locking the old barn door after the horse had galloped away.

But without the discs, I had little hope of proving my theory about Grayton's Race. If I laid it all out for Red, he might buy it simply because it came from me. Without evidence, though— something other than my unsubstantiated recollections of a couple of names maybe glimpsed briefly over a year ago—he would be unable to take it any farther. Even if he could convince someone to investigate my claims, all it would accomplish would be to alert those I suspected that I had not given up. They could run to ground, cover their tracks. Even have another crack at me.

Which is probably what they're planning right now, thanks to your incredible carelessness, I berated myself. I shifted onto my side and drew up my knees.

Or maybe they weren't. Maybe getting their hands on the only evidence that could possibly link the drug cartel, the money-laundering scheme, and Grayton's Race was enough for them. Maybe they felt safe now.

"Men willingly believe what they wish", Julius Caesar had written a couple of millennia ago. Apparently the same held true for women.

And philosophizing was pretty pointless at this stage of the game. What I had to do was decide where to go next. Accompanied by Red Tanner's soft snores from the living room couch, I chased my options around in my head. In the end, there were really only two choices: pursue it with everything I had, or back off. There was no middle ground.

If I went forward with my efforts to discredit the development project and extricate my family and friends from their unwitting involvement with drug money, I would have to find an alternate source of information. Belinda St. John, Rob's former assistant, seemed the logical place to start.

But, as much as I wanted to believe her fierce insistence that Rob had not been forgotten by his colleagues, where was the proof? The investigation my husband had begun was as dead as he was. Nothing had been done, no progress made in the long months since his plane exploded. Not only was that probe going nowhere, there had apparently been no concerted effort to find

his murderers. The whole incident was an ugly stain on the reputation of the state and those charged with its administration. I
couldn't picture any branch of the government, unless it might be
SLED, stirring up the whole mess again.

So what did I expect Belinda to do? Her career and her
children's well-being were tied to her ability to keep the boys in
Columbia out of the headlines, except for the ones they wanted to
be in. How much rocking of the ship of state would she be
prepared to do on behalf of a man who'd been dead for almost a
year, and his widow who had been, at best, a marginal friend? Her
loyalties were no longer owed to Rob and the SI unit, her success
no longer tied to them.

Pursuing would also mean dealing with Geoff Anderson, the
one tangible link I had between the project here and the Miami
drug lords I was sure were behind it. How much could I count on
his professed feelings for me? Or were they, too, a sham, a cal-
culated attempt to get close to me, to find out how much I knew
or suspected? How deeply dented was the armor of my childhood
knight?

Backing off, on the other hand, would be the sensible thing to
do. I had built a good life for myself here, despite the continuing
pain of Rob's death. At thirty-eight, I was financially secure. I
could retire for good, if that's what I wanted to do. Even before
the first explosion, I had been gradually extricating myself from
the CPA practice I shared with two scions of old, moneyed families in Charleston. They would have no trouble finding someone
to buy me out.

I had friends—good ones. They had proven that yesterday.
Geoff Anderson had shown me that it was possible for me to
give of myself again, when the time—and the man—were right. If
they never were, well, I'd learn to deal with that, too.

But where did this option leave me? Back in the old, sheltered
existence, avoiding involvement, responsible to and for no one
but myself. I sure as hell didn't want to die. There had been times,
after Rob's murder, when I thought I did. Last night had proved
to me that my will to survive was alive and kicking. But wasn't the
safe, self-indulgent life I'd been leading a kind of death, too?

Besides, I owed something to the people who mattered to me.
For better or worse, I had become intimately involved in the lives

of Adelaide Boyce Hammond, CJ Elliott, and Isaiah Smalls, not to mention my father, Bitsy, Mally, even Neddie. How could I walk away from that? From them?

And, if I were being perfectly honest with myself, a part of me was savoring the chase. Despite the danger, I itched to pursue the bastards who had most likely killed my husband and then tried to murder me. I wanted their asses in the slammer, and I wanted to be the one who put them there.

By the time Red, wearing only a pair of sweatpants, stumbled blearily out onto the deck, I realized I had already made up my mind.

"What are you doin' out here?" Red mumbled as he stretched and wandered over to lean on the railing. "It's not even six yet."

"Pondering the meaning of life," I said airily, trying to make light of the real battle that had been raging inside my head in the last, dark hours before sunrise.

"Heavy." Red looked over his shoulder at me and grinned. "Is that what almost getting blown up does to you?"

I padded over to join him at the railing. We stood silently, each of us marveling at the soft, luminescent quality of the light as it spread slowly across the vast expanse of the ocean.

"I guess I should be an expert by now, huh?"

"Do me a favor and don't go getting any more experience, okay?"

When I didn't answer, his face lost its teasing brightness.

"Red, there are some things I have to do that you're not going to like. But you have to trust me not to put myself in any unnecessary danger. You can't protect me for the rest of my life. Sooner or later I was going to have to step out of the shadows and into the sunlight. I've just decided that today's the day."

Red knew that opposition would only harden my resolve, so he kept silent. I turned away from the mixture of fear and longing I read in his eyes.

"So, here's the deal. I'm gonna go roust Neddie out and then have a shower. I'll use the guest bath and you can use mine. And make it snappy. We're going out to breakfast, and I'm starving. And you know how cranky I get when I'm hungry."

Red watched me gather up my things from beside the chaise and turn toward the door. "Bay? What is this all about?" he asked as he moved swiftly across the boards and grasped both my upper arms. "What are you up to?"

"I'm back in the game, Tanner," I said, twisting gently out of his grip, "and anybody who doesn't want to play better get the hell out of my way."

We took two cars.

Red dropped us off at the visitor's lot where—luckily, as it turned out—Neddie had left her pearl gray Mercedes on Friday afternoon. We rendezvoused at an unpretentious little diner set back off the main highway. It usually escaped the notice of the tourists who tended to congregate at the more well-known franchise place across the road.

Seated at the counter on high barstools, we put away over-easy eggs and piles of redskin home fries hot off the grill. I mopped up the last of the eggs on my plate with a piece of whole-wheat toast and sat back.

"Boy, for someone who doesn't eat breakfast, you sure inhaled that." Neddie sipped coffee and shook her head at me.

Conversation had been minimal and mostly concerned with trivia. There was no privacy in Frank's, which was one reason I'd picked it. Red had been pushing me about my intentions ever since our little talk on the deck. I hadn't formulated any definite plan yet, just a couple of vague ideas about who I needed to talk to.

Red's disapproval was evident in the long crease down the middle of his forehead as he scowled at me over his coffee cup. "I'm scheduled for the four-to-midnight shift this week, but I'm going to try to switch. I'd rather be at your place and settled in before it gets dark," he said.

"You really don't have to. I don't think I'll have any more trouble."

With the disks gone, my attackers had to think I was no longer a threat to them. Without evidence I was just another hysterical female. Having failed once, they would probably be reluctant to draw attention to themselves with another attempt, at least for a while. I figured I had some breathing room, and I meant to take full advantage of it. By the time they thought about having another crack at me, I intended to have their butts nailed to the wall.

Besides, any normal woman would have gone screaming back into hiding, or left the state. I was counting on their assuming I was just such a normal woman.

Red wanted to argue, but hesitated to make a scene in the close confines of the narrow diner. When his beeper went off, he cursed and strode angrily out to the cruiser to call in. I paid the check and hustled Neddie out the door. We waved at Red as we pulled out into the thickening Monday morning traffic.

The car dealership was nestled back in the trees about halfway up the island. I'm generally a "Buy American" consumer, but I'm not fanatic about it. I had to admit the gleaming chrome and sleek, fluid bodies of the foreign cars arrayed at the front of the lot had me salivating just a little. I jiggled the keys Geoff Anderson had left on my deck and wondered what had given him the idea I would let him pick out a car for me. Still, I had to start somewhere. I needed the independence of my own wheels if I were to get my half-formulated plans off the ground.

Buck James turned out to be a pleasant surprise. Far from a slick, stereotypical young hustler, Buck was fiftyish, balding, and soft-spoken. If he knew the reason for my unexpected need for a new car, he didn't refer to it. He simply led us to the back of the lot, chatting genially about what a good guy his friend, Geoff, was, and how he hoped I'd approve of his choice.

When I spotted the little two-seater convertible tucked in among the trees, it was love at first sight. A soft, pale aqua, the color reminded me of the ocean on a sunny day. I checked the sticker and gulped a little; but, when Buck named the price he had agreed on with Geoff, I knew I had to have it. I glanced at Neddie who was grinning as widely as I.

"If you don't buy it, I'm going to," she said, running her hand over the creamy top and matching leather interior.

Buck called a lot boy to wash it up and put on the temporary plate while he escorted Neddie and me into the dealership to take care of the paperwork. I wrote a check out of my investment account, and, in less than half an hour, I was on my way.

Neddie had agreed to go back to the house and await the arrival of the phone company. I instructed her to have them replace all the phones, even the undamaged ones. She looked a little askance at my request, but I didn't explain. The less Neddie knew about my suspicions, the better it would be for her. I also asked her to oversee Dolores's meeting with the contractor who was coming to give us an estimate on restoring the kitchen.

So, with the top down and my hair streaming out behind me, it was just past ten when I whipped into the parking lot of the hospital and began my quest for answers where the questions had all begun: with Adelaide Boyce Hammond.

Judy McKay, the nurse who had been on duty the night Miss Addie was brought in, looked up from behind the desk as I stepped off the elevator. Her face registered shock, then softened into sympathy as I walked up to her.

"My God, Mrs. Tanner, are you all right? I couldn't believe it when I read in the *Packet* about the explosion."

She wanted to ask me about what I had done to earn myself a murder attempt by a mad bomber, but was too well brought up to voice the question.

"At least I have some good news for you," she said, removing her glasses. "Your friend woke up yesterday, and she appears to be fine. We've moved her back into her old room. Dr. Winter tried to call you yesterday, but your phone was out of order. I guess . . ."

She stopped guiltily and let the thought trail off. We both knew why my telephones were inoperative.

"That's great," I said. It was the best possible news, far more than I'd hoped for. "Can I see her?"

"Sure. If you hurry, you might catch the doctor. He just went in a few minutes ago."

"Thanks." I moved off down the hallway. I could feel Judy McKay's eyes following me speculatively. I guessed I would have to get used to that. The survivor of an attempted professional hit was bound to arouse people's curiosity.

Dr. Winter, leaning over the bed, blocked my view as I entered the room. He straightened at my approach and greeted me with a grin.

"Well, Miss Hammond, looks like you've got a visitor."

Miss Addie was thinner and paler than the last time I had

stood here. Her lacy pink bed jacket hung on her as if it were made for someone twice her size. But a hint of the old sparkle shone out of her faded eyes, and someone had brushed her hair into a soft, white halo.

"Welcome back," I said as I bent to brush her sunken cheek with my lips. Tears welled up and threatened to spill over before I got myself under control.

"Thank you, dear." Her voice was creaky with disuse.

"How is she?" I turned to Dr. Winter who gave me an almost imperceptible nod of his head.

"Oh, we just need to fatten her up a little, and then we'll chase her out of here and make room for someone who's really sick. How about it, Miss Hammond?"

"Whatever you say, Doctor, but I don't seem to have much appetite."

"I've given the kitchen orders to whip you up some goodies that'll be irresistible, gooey things guaranteed to pile on the calories. Starting with lunch today."

Miss Addie nodded. She was trying hard to keep her eyes open.

"You go ahead and rest now," he went on in his hearty bedside voice. "I'll look in on you again this afternoon. A word, Mrs. Tanner?" Dr. Winter took my arm, and we stepped into the hallway.

"Is she really all right?" I asked as soon as we were out of earshot. "She looks so . . . shrunken."

"It was touch and go for awhile, but, yes, she'll recover. It was a strange reaction, one I've never encountered with that particular painkiller before."

My mind shot back to the pushy nurse with no name tag who had administered the pills to Miss Addie the day she lapsed into a coma. All my suspicions about her "accident" came screaming back into my mind. Was this another result of her sending me poking into the Grayton's Race project? Had Miss Addie, too, been the victim of an abortive attempt on her life?

"Are you sure it was the right drug? Could she have been given the wrong medication by mistake?"

Or by design? I couldn't bring myself to say it out loud.

I related the events of last Monday morning. Even before I

finished, Dr. Winter was shaking his head.

"No, no. The woman you're describing is Edie Benson. I know her well. She frequently forgets her name badge. She's been written up about it several times. No, we did a tox screen as a matter of course. Miss Hammond just happened to be allergic to this particular drug. Because of her age, her reaction was intensified."

His pager beeped. "I'm needed in Emergency. Miss Hammond is going to require some special care until she's completely back on her feet," he said, edging away from me.

"Don't worry. I'll take care of whatever she needs."
"Good. We'll keep her a few more days. That'll give you time to get something set up."

"Thank you, Doctor," I called as he turned and hurried off.

When I walked back into the room, Miss Addie was awake and looking much more alert. "There you are, Lydia. I hoped you hadn't left for good. I'm sorry about nodding off like that. I just seem to need these little catnaps. I'm feeling quite refreshed now."

"No problem. Whatever it takes to help you get better." I pulled up the bedside chair and sat down. "Up to a few questions? Just say so if you're not."

"Heavens, yes, child. I've been itching with curiosity about what you've been up to." Her eyes were dancing, and a little color had returned to her cheeks.

"Well, I went over to your condo last Monday right after you fell asleep."

She waved aside my apology for lifting her keys and pass from her handbag. "I was going to give them to you anyway, dear."

I told her about my encounter with Ariadne Dixon and the suave Mr. Romero, and about my feeling that they had lied about what they were doing in her apartment.

"Do you think it could be one of them who pushed you?"

"Gracious, I really don't know. I never saw anyone, you see. But I think whoever it was must have been hiding in the bathroom. I had my back to it when I felt the hands."

Miss Addie shivered then, a tiny *frisson* of remembered fear that made me want to kick myself for reminding her.

"You mentioned gardenias the other day. At least I think that's what you said."

"Did I? How odd! I've always hated gardenias."

"Did you smell them that night?"

"I really can't remember. It all seems so long ago now."

"Did you ever notice the fragrance before? On Dixon or Romero?"

"I don't think so, dear. I've had them both to tea a few times, and they seemed quite pleasant. I really can't believe either of them would do anything so . . . well, *uncivilized*. And what reason could they possibly have?"

I didn't have an answer for that.

We talked for a few more minutes, but nothing else revealed itself as bearing on the identity or motive of Miss Addie's attacker. Try as I might, I couldn't get hold of any connection between this assault and all the other strange occurrences of the past two weeks. Maybe it had just been a sneak thief, surprised in the act by Miss Addie's unexpected return. Maybe I should just call Red, turn it all over to the cops.

Adelaide Boyce Hammond's eyes were beginning to droop when I reached into my bag for my keys, and my fingers brushed up against a much-creased paper. It was the copy of the letter I had found in Miss Addie's handbag. Shoved underneath my desk pad, it had been overlooked by whoever had rifled my office. I'd retrieved it last night and stuffed it in my tote.

"Miss Addie," I ventured, and her eyes snapped open. "One more question. What did you meet with Law Merriweather about?"

I unfolded the letter and held it out to her. She glanced briefly at it, then turned away, her face flushed.

"What is it?" I pressed. "It might be important."

"Well, dear, I talked to Lawton about a number of things. The powers of attorney, for one. I hope you didn't mind about that." I shook my head. "Then, there was my will, and I wanted his advice about . . . Oh, dear. I'm afraid the Judge will be quite upset with me."

My ears pricked up at the mention of my father. "Why would the Judge be upset with you?"

"Well, dear, it's not that I didn't have faith in him. Or in you. And after your call that Saturday, to let me know that everything was fine with Grayton's Race, I did feel rather foolish."

"I don't understand."

"You see, I asked Lawton to look into selling some of my things. Mother's and Father's things, actually, that I'd inherited. Maybe one or two paintings or some of the porcelain." Her voice had sunk to an embarrassed whisper. "In case I needed the money."

I did my best to reassure her that neither the Judge nor I had taken offense. She was nodding off again as I tucked the blanket around her and tiptoed out the door.

I was no closer to finding the answers to my questions, but the conversation had served one useful purpose. It had reminded me that it was my father who had actually set the wheels in motion; first, by convincing Miss Addie and others to invest in Grayton's Race, but, more inexplicably, by urging her to contact *me* about her fears of losing her money.

Why had he done that? I would have been blissfully ignorant of the whole sordid mess if he had just kept his mouth shut. For some reason, he'd wanted me involved. Now he wanted me out. And he had yet to explain his own entanglement with Hadley Bolles and with Geoff Anderson.

Time for some answers. If I had to tie him down until he leveled with me this time, that's exactly what I'd do.

Spirits somewhat restored, I hopped in my new Z3 and turned her loose in the direction of Beaufort.

CHAPTER
TWENTY-FOUR

If all the picketers had been gone from in front of Grayton's Race, everything might have turned out a lot differently. But, as I made the turn toward Beaufort, I spotted a lone pickup truck still parked at the entrance to the property. On impulse, I pulled in behind it.

The lanky young man who climbed down out of the cab to greet me was quite a surprise. Far from the stained T-shirts, ripped bluejeans, and baseball caps of the others I had encountered, he was dressed in well-pressed khaki slacks, a crisp blue denim shirt, and Bass loafers. He looked to be in his early twenties. He reminded me more of a college student from some impressive eastern university than an eco-freak.

"Hi," he said as I approached the truck. "Something I can help you with?"

His smile was open, his brown eyes under thick blond hair, direct and non-threatening. I had a tough time picturing this guy dropping bloody squirrel carcasses into the backseats of open Jaguars or demolishing golf carts with a sledgehammer.

"Are you associated with CARE?" I asked, stopping a few feet from his open door.

"Founder, president, and chief cook and bottle washer. Nathan Spellman. My friends call me Nat."

I took the offered hand. His grip was firm, but not crushing.

"Bay Tanner. I wonder if I could ask you a few questions?"

"You from the press? Not that that's a problem," he added quickly, "but you're a little late. I could have used some publicity a few weeks ago."

I shook my head. "Sorry. Just a concerned citizen, I guess you'd say."

"Concerned citizens are always welcome, too. What can I do for you?"

"Well, I wanted to know about the group—your aims, your philosophy. How you recruit new members, things like that."

"You interested in joining? A little late for that, too, but I've got some literature here." He reached into the front seat of the truck and extracted a computer-generated flyer from a thick stack bound by a rubber band. While obviously homemade, the artwork and layout were surprisingly professional.

"Thanks, I'll look this over. But could you give me a short rundown of what you're all about?"

"Sure. See, I've been working on my master's thesis on ecosystem management. This was part of my research. I picked this area because it has such a dichotomy—rapid development in a relatively fragile natural environment. You from around here?"

"Born and raised," I said.

"So you know all about Hilton Head."

"As a matter of fact, I live there. But I always thought they'd done a pretty good job of keeping the sprawl under control."

"Oh, they have," he rushed to assure me, "don't get me wrong. I was going to use them as an example of how you can have the best of both worlds. Planned development that's also compatible with the environment. At least in the beginning."

I smiled to let him know I had taken no offense on behalf of my adopted island home.

"But this," he went on, his hand sweeping a wide arc toward the entrance to Grayton's Race, "and all the stuff springing up on the 278 corridor, that's another story. It's all happening too fast. Not enough studies have been done to determine what the long-term effects are likely to be. This is old-growth forest in here, some really spectacular trees. And you've seen the river, of course. Incredibly clean and unpolluted."

This was all fascinating, but not the kind of information I'd been hoping to get. Part of my half-formed theory rested on a connection between the incidents at Grayton's Race and Derek Johnson's sudden refusal to sign off on his property. I tried to steer Nat back toward my real area of interest.

"So how did you get all the guys I saw out here to join up? Are they researchers, too?"

A flash of suspicion darkened his wide-set brown eyes. "Are you a cop?"

"Me? No, of course not. Why?"

"Well, we've had some trouble with some of our . . . members. Vandalism, that kind of stuff. I never condoned any of it. In fact, I threatened to turn them in when I heard about it. I thought maybe you were undercover or something. See, a lot of the guys that jumped on the bandwagon are locals. Hunters, fishermen, like that. It took me a while to realize they had their own agenda."

Nat Spellman did something then that completely won me over. He blushed. "I'm a city boy, you see. Baltimore. This was my first experience with . . ."

"Rednecks," I supplied, and he laughed.

"Yeah. But that's all over with. As you can see, they've disappeared now that they got what they were after."

"What's that?"

"The head of the project—a guy named Anderson—met with some of them last weekend. At his office over there in the welcome center. They worked out a deal where part of the land will be set aside as a sort of game preserve where they can hunt and fish. He even promised to build them a gun club, with a target range and everything. So they've gone away happy. And me—I'm just going away, period. I was just getting ready to pack it in when you drove up."

"You've accomplished what you wanted to then?" I asked.

Though his words were upbeat, his face told me otherwise. "Enough, I guess. At least I'll be able to start writing my thesis when I get back to Maryland. And it's been a great learning experience. I just wish I could have made more of a difference. Looks like the development will be going through as planned."

"Hold on a sec," I said, turning back toward my car. I grabbed my checkbook out of my bag and hastily scribbled out a check. "Here." I handed it to him. "A donation for the cause."

His mouth dropped open when he looked at the amount. "Gosh, Ms. Tanner, I'm not sure I can accept this."

"Sure you can." I held out my hand. "It was nice to meet you, Nat Spellman. Good luck with your paper, and keep the faith, okay?"

"Thank you. Thanks a lot." He folded the check and stuck it in his shirt pocket.

I sat in the car and lit a cigarette while the earnest young grad student started up his truck and pulled out onto the highway. He waved as he passed me, heading north.

Sometimes I actually have hope for the next generation.

And his casual remark about a meeting in Geoff's office had been worth twice what I had given him. I backed the Z3 slowly along the shoulder of the road, then turned into the driveway of the Grayton's Race welcome center.

The modular building was larger than it appeared from the highway, about the size of a double-wide trailer. It sported a fresh coat of white paint, although here and there a faint shadow of the graffiti I'd seen in the snapshots Geoff had shown me still bled through.

There was no sign of the Jaguar. An older Pontiac Grand Am was the only car in the graveled lot. I parked and got out before I could change my mind. I had no real idea what I was going to say—or even what I thought I might accomplish here. But sometimes the best plan is no plan. I walked up three wooden steps and pushed open the door.

The air inside was frigid, which was probably why the red-haired receptionist was huddled inside a bulky cardigan sweater. She looked up and quickly closed the magazine she'd been reading. Deftly she slid it into the center desk drawer and gave me a practiced smile.

"Hey, there," she chirped, "welcome to Grayton's Race. What can I do for ya?"

It was the kind of drawl I probably would have retained if I hadn't spent a lot of my college years surrounded by flat, Midwestern twangs.

"I'd like to see Mr. Anderson, please."

"Oh, gosh, I'm sorry, he's not in. Could I help you with somethin'?"

She was so young and eager, I almost felt bad about scamming her. I made a show of checking my watch.

"I was supposed to meet him here at noon," I lied, "to take a tour of the property. Do you expect him back soon?"

"You had an appointment? Oh, lord, he didn't say anythin' to me." She reached for a leather-bound datebook and flipped pages. "I don't see anythin' here. Let me check the desk calendar in his office."

The receptionist swiveled out of her chair and started down a narrow hallway toward a closed door at the back. I stepped around a large laminated map of the project with the golf courses, streets, and lots marked out in bright colors, and followed right behind her. She looked startled when she glanced up from the desk to see me standing in the doorway.

"He doesn't have it written on his calendar, either. What did you say your name was?"

I hadn't, nor had I given any thought to needing a fake one, until she asked.

"Smythe," I improvised, and spelled it. "Mrs. Marian Smythe."

It was a little better than *Mary Smith*, but not much.

"Hi, I'm Tiffani. With an 'i'."

I could have guessed that.

"Gosh, I'm really sorry, Mrs. Smythe," she chattered on. "It's not like Mr. Anderson to forget an appointment. I could try to reach him on his car phone, but he was goin' to a couple of meetings today, and I'm not really sure where he is."

"Perhaps he'll be back soon. Why don't I just wait a while?" I crossed into the room and settled in one of the club chairs facing the desk. I gave "Tiffani-with-an-i" my most reassuring smile.

"Oh, gosh, I don't know, Mrs. Smythe. Mr. Anderson's real particular about his office. I'm not even supposed to be in here when he's gone. He usually keeps it locked. He must've been in a rush this morning."

The desk was standard office issue, the chairs comfortable, but inexpensive. The white-framed prints of familiar beach scenes were churned out by the thousands. They decorated every wall in every waiting room in the Lowcountry. The only things that could make this room worth locking were the three four-drawer filing cabinets ranged against the far wall. Heavy and gray, they sat beneath two small windows set high in the fake oak paneling.

This was precisely what I'd been hoping for. If Geoff had records pertaining to the project, this was where they'd be. The cabinets had locks, but they weren't pushed in. If I could get little blonde Tiffani out of there for five or ten minutes, I could at least see if they contained anything worth my while.

We were at an impasse, though, as Geoff's receptionist and I smiled woodenly across the desk at each other.

"I wonder if I might have a glass of water?" It was a tired ploy, but I was counting on innate Southern manners to win out over suspicion and job security. "Or maybe some coffee?"

I'd noticed a small kitchen on the opposite end of the building, an empty pot sitting in the bottom of a coffee maker on the counter.

"Well, sure, I'd be glad to. Would you like to wait out front?" Tiffani asked hopefully.

"Oh, I'm just fine right here, thanks. The sun feels so good."

I pointed toward the windows and gave her my best everything-will-be-just-fine face. With a shrug of defeat, she walked past me and down the hall.

When I heard the water start to run, I jumped up and yanked open the top drawer of the first cabinet. It appeared to hold paid invoices, arranged alphabetically. With a quick glance over my shoulder, I tried the next two. Nothing looked promising. I stooped and slid open the bottom drawer. The folders here were unmarked. The first one held what seemed to be legal documents. Before I had a chance to check any of them out, I heard the clack of Tiffani's high-heeled pumps on the uncarpeted hallway.

When she stepped into the room, I was leaning casually against the file cabinet, apparently admiring one of the bland pictures.

"Here we go," she announced in her cheerful little voice.

"Thanks so much." I took the offered mug from her and pretended to sip.

"I'm getting ready to go to lunch in a few minutes," Tiffani said apologetically, "and I have to lock up Mr. Anderson's office. But you're welcome to wait in the reception area if you like."

"Oh, no, that's okay, dear. I've decided I'll just get on out of your way. I'll call Mr. Anderson and set up another appointment. You've been so kind. Bye-bye now."

I pushed the mug into her hand and fairly trotted out the door. The wheels of the Z threw up a little gravel in my haste to get out of there.

Out on the highway, I took a deep breath to calm my racing heart. I pulled into the first commercial driveway I came to. With trembling fingers I lit a cigarette, then reached into my bag for the document I had pilfered. It was a copy of the Articles of Incorporation, the same ones I had received over the fax from Belinda St. John's assistant. It wasn't exactly news, but it was like finding a gold doubloon on the floor of the ocean. Where there was one, there were probably more.

Who knew what treasure that bottom drawer might hold? I was convinced it was my best chance for the evidence I needed. But how to get at it? I needed a really good scheme this time.

But first I had to settle things with my father. With that behind me, I could concentrate on just exactly how I was going to get my hands on the papers in that cabinet.

CHAPTER
TWENTY-FIVE

Lavinia insisted on fixing me lunch even though she and the Judge had just finished. My father had retired to his recliner for his customary afternoon nap, so I sat at the kitchen table while she reheated the pork and stuffing and brewed fresh tea.

Living up north, I had gotten away from the old Southern tradition of taking the heaviest meal of the day at noon. The custom dated back to the plantation era when work in the fields began at daybreak. It had made more sense for the cooking ovens to be fired up in the morning before the heat of the sultry afternoons descended.

Lavinia moved about the kitchen with a brisk economy of motion acquired over decades of preparing meals in this room for me and my parents. No clatter of pans or clank of dishes disturbed the companionable silence we had shared countless times before. Ever since I had gotten old enough to sit on my own at the worn oak table, I had loved to watch her. She moved as gracefully now as she had when I was too young to appreciate such things.

Lavinia put the casserole dish in the oven to warm, poured us both iced tea, and joined me at the table. It wasn't until her deep brown eyes looked directly into mine that I remembered what had taken place this morning in the courthouse just a few miles away.

"What happened at the hearing? Did Isaiah get bail?" I asked.

Her face told me that she knew I had forgotten. I felt the blush of shame at my thoughtlessness creep up my throat.

"It's all right, Bay. You've had your own troubles to tend to. Yes, he's home now, the Lord be praised. Mr. Brown said bail wasn't as high as it could have been, probably because so many folks came and spoke for him."

Lavinia brushed a hand across her eyes. I had never seen her look so weary.

"Your father even sent a letter to the court, vouching for Isaiah's character. Mr. Elliott put up the money. And he's going to pay for the lawyers, too. Lawton Merriweather will be working with Mander Brown when the trial starts."

"When do they think that'll be?" I asked, wondering again about Big Cal's motives.

Lavinia's worn fingers picked nervously at the fringed edges of the placemat. Her skin was almost the same color as the pale oak of the table. "At least a couple of months, so they say."

My father was still asleep when I finished what I could of the heavy lunch. When Lavinia refused my offer to help clean up, I wandered out the back door and settled into a rocking chair on the verandah. The Sound was unruffled by the light breeze that rattled the palmettos. Here and there its smooth surface was dotted with floating pelicans, their ungainly brown bodies rocking gently in the slight swells kicked up by passing pleasure boats. The air was alive with birdsong, and, in the sporadic silences, the sharp *tap-tap* of a woodpecker high in a loblolly pine sounded unnaturally loud.

This was the true beauty of Presqu'isle, I thought, not the polished tables and proud antiques. This part of my home I could love, and always had.

I kicked off my shoes and pushed the chair into motion. In the drowsy peace of the summer afternoon, I rocked and smoked and thought. It wasn't quite meditation, but it served the purpose. By the time I heard Lavinia stirring about the kitchen, squeezing fruit, no doubt, for my father's bourbon and lemonade, I felt calm and in control. It wasn't to last.

When I strolled back into the house, Lavinia looked as if she wanted to say something to me, then, with a shrug, changed her mind. I took the tray from her and carried it into the study.

If my father was surprised to see me, he didn't show it. I set the drinks on the low table next to his wheelchair, retrieved a cigar from the dresser drawer, and again held the crystal desk lighter for him as he performed the ritual. I settled myself in a corner of the sofa with my bare feet tucked up under me.

"You want to talk about the project, about Grayton's Race," the Judge began abruptly. "You're right. It's time."

My father's clear gray eyes regarded me steadily as he blew

smoke toward the ceiling. If he'd hoped to throw me off balance by taking the initiative, he'd miscalculated. I'd seen him in action from the bar as well as from the bench from the time I was in grade school. I'd spent many summer afternoons tucked quietly into a corner of the old courthouse, watching in rapt fascination as my father mesmerized with the sheer power of his voice, manipulated with clever argument, intimidated with a frosty stare.

Oh, yes, I knew all his tactics.

"Whatever you think," I said in the same reasonable tone.

I held his eyes, and slowly a smile began to twitch at the corners of his mouth.

"Damn, you should have stayed in law school, daughter. You've got the touch. With your looks and your brains, you could have stood this ol' county on its ear."

"Irrelevant, Your Honor."

My father took a sip of bourbon and settled back in his chair. The smile faded. "About six months ago, Hadley Bolles came to me with a proposition."

"I knew that fat weasel was involved in this somehow."

My father ignored me and went on. "He represented a group of investors who wanted to get in on the development boom goin' on around here. Before the environmentalists and the pre-servationists got their way with the county council and the legislature and shut it all down. Hadley seemed to think it was only a matter of time before those groups got together and began litigating. Even if they eventually lost, they could tie things up in court for years. In the meantime, there was money to be made—serious money—if his clients could get up and runnin' before all this hit the fan."

I lit a cigarette and leaned forward. "What did he want from you?"

"My name. And my influence, little as it is anymore."

I heard the wistful longing in his voice, a lament for the days when a word from Judge Talbot Simpson could sway any nego-tiation, make or break any deal.

"To what purpose?" I asked.

"Hadley's clients were outsiders, from out of state, actually. They figured the backing of a few prominent, local citizens would be helpful in greasing the wheels, getting approvals, permits, and so on. There's a lot of sentiment around here about the Race, you know. A lot of old-timers remember it in its glory years."

I thought about Adelaide Boyce Hammond and her teary nostalgia for the parties and cotillions of her youth. It wouldn't have been difficult to convince her and others that they were contributing to the preservation of local history while turning a nice profit in the process.

"How does Geoff fit into the picture?"

"Pretty much the same way. His father, Carter Anderson, was one of the most respected attorneys in this town, and you know Millicent's family were among the original settlers. She never tired of reminding your mother about that."

I shook my head at the remembered intensity of their competition, the constant jockeying for prominence among the DAR and Daughters of the Confederacy members. Millicent Bowdoin Anderson had my mother beat by a generation and never let her forget it.

"Plus he was affiliated with the Florida firm that represented the investors," my father continued. "Hadley figured he was a gift from the gods, and persuaded them to put him in charge of the project."

"So you knew all about Geoff before I ever accepted that date with him."

"Not everything," he said and refilled his glass.

And suddenly I wondered how accidental my meeting with Geoff on the verandah of the Fig Tree had really been. Hadley had been there, too. Coincidence? He'd been meeting with someone, I remembered now, the stranger in the white suit with the large diamond glittering against his olive skin. Was *he* the Miami connection?

But why would any of them have been interested in me then? It didn't make any sense. I had only become involved, and in the most peripheral manner, the day before. In fact, I had been in Beaufort only because of the questioning of Isaiah Smalls about the murder of Derek Johnson. Unless . . .

"Tell me about Derek Johnson," I said.

"What about him?" The calm, steady voice now shook a little, and my father looked everywhere except at me.

"Did you know he was the holdout on the heirs property?

That his backing out endangered the entire project?"

"What are you implying?"

"I'm not implying anything. I'm trying to get at the truth here. Isn't that what you always taught me to do? I've had a gut feeling all along that Derek's murder was somehow connected to Grayton's Race. Tell me I'm wrong."

His silence was my answer. It lengthened as he continued to avoid my eyes.

Finally, he said, "I can't prove anything."

"But you have your suspicions, haven't you? My God, Father, what have you gotten yourself involved in?"

The Judge activated his wheelchair and steered himself up the ramp and out onto the verandah. The screen door banged shut behind him.

I lit another cigarette and smoked it down to the filter before I followed him out into the blistering heat. What little breeze there was failed to move the wet, heavy air. I pushed a rocking chair up next to where he sat staring out at the placid Sound.

"Okay," I began, "you don't have to say anything, just listen. If I'm way off base, just shake your head."

"No, Bay. I want you out of this now. Drop it. Stop your meddling."

"Don't be ridiculous," I snapped. "You know I can't do that. I won't. You may be able to sit by and let Lavinia's grandson take the fall for a murder you know he didn't commit, but I sure as hell can't."

He whirled his chair around to face me then, his mouth a grim line of deep anger. "How dare you! You honestly think I would let that happen? The boy will never be convicted. Never! In fact, I fully expect the charges to be dropped. Law Merriweather will see to that. The state has a very weak case. All the evidence is circumstantial."

"Even the baseball bat with Derek's brains all over it?" I asked, and he flinched. "You're amazing, you know that? You and your cronies? You think you own the whole damn county, don't you? 'The boy will never be convicted.' You say it with such smug authority. From your lips to God's ear, huh? Well, what if he is? What if the sheriff decides not to play ball? What if a jury of just regular folks decides to ship him off to death row and let them stick a needle in his arm?"

"You don't know what you're talking about, daughter." He dismissed my concern with a wave of his hand. "Now just do as I say. It was a mistake to involve you in the first place. I'm ordering you to stay out of my business."

"Too late, Your Honor. You should have thought of that before you sicced Miss Addie onto me. What did you think I'd do, hold her hand and make soothing noises about everything being just fine, then crawl back into my hole and disappear again?"

The Judge turned his chair back around and gazed out over the sloping lawn down to the water. I had been dismissed.

"Well, as usual, Father, you've underestimated me. I have it pretty well figured out now, except for one thing. What could Hadley Bolles possibly have on you to force you into pimping for a bunch of drug dealers and covering up a murder?"

The broad shoulders that had carried me, literally and figuratively, all my life, slumped as all the defiance and anger went out of him. The blazing orator had vanished, leaving a helpless, crippled old man hunched in a wheelchair.

For a long time my question hung unanswered in the humid afternoon air. Then my father raised his weary face to mine and smiled, a sad, bittersweet look that made my heart turn over.

"I've never underestimated you, Lydia Baynard Simpson. Never."

"You're not going to tell me, are you?"

He shook his head sadly. "No, I'm not."

"But why? I can help, Father, I want to. We can fight this. You can't just sit by and let that bastard get away with blackmailing you! We can—"

"Hush, child, hush. You don't know what you're saying. There are others involved here . . . people who can be hurt, damaged. People who can no longer defend themselves."

"I don't—" I began when the real meaning of his words hit me. *People who can no longer defend themselves.* "It's about Mother, isn't it? Hadley has something on my mother."

I clambered out of the rocker and knelt in front of his wheelchair.

"But for God's sake, Father, she's dead! What can he possibly reveal that could hurt her now?" I took his good hand in mine and forced him to look at me.

"Leave it, Bay," he whispered, "please. I'll handle this in my own way. It's not your burden to carry."

The deep, long-suppressed fury found a crack in my defenses and erupted.

"Not my burden?" I shouted, jumping to my feet. "Not *my* burden? The woman has been a stone around my neck my entire goddamn life!"

I watched the pain flicker across his eyes, but I couldn't stop now. Nothing mattered but my need to spew it all out—the anger, the hurt, the humiliation of a lifetime of silence.

"What secret could she possibly have that would be worth sacrificing your honor for? My mother was a lush! Miss Emmaline Tattnall Baynard of Presqu'isle, DAR, Daughter of the Confederacy, socialite, philanthropist, and pillar of the Episcopal Church was a drunk! Did she think everyone didn't know it? Do *you?*"

I laughed, a harsh, choking sound and slapped my hand on the railing. "God, that would be almost funny if it weren't so pathetic. My third grade classmates knew she was a drunk. They used to call me 'Bay Rum' and snicker, did you know that? No, you probably didn't," I answered for him. "You were too busy making excuses for her. 'Mother's not feeling well.' 'Mother has a headache, go play outside.' 'Mother didn't mean to slap you so hard.' "

I could feel my mocking words slice into him, but I couldn't seem to stop myself. Maybe it all needed to be said, finally, for both of us.

"She hated me and despised you." I cut off my father's attempt to interrupt. "Oh, yes, don't deny it. I used to hear her shouting at you in the middle of the night. How she'd married beneath her—*everyone* said so—and that's why she had to bear the shame of a *common* child without one redeeming social grace. 'An unfortunate accident' she used to call me, didn't she? Well didn't she?" I screamed.

"That's enough, Bay! Leave him alone."

Lavinia stood in the doorway at the top of the ramp. Her words were sharp, but her face held only a deep sadness.

I didn't know how long she'd been there. I prayed she hadn't heard anything about my father's passive complicity in the railroading of her grandson. I didn't think he could survive without Lavinia's respect.

"How can you defend her?" I asked, my anger ebbing under her calm gaze. "She treated you like an indentured servant. You of all people saw what she was capable of."

Lavinia stepped onto the porch, a light cotton throw draped over her arm. She approached the wheelchair and spread the blanket gently across my father's useless legs. He raised his face to her, and their eyes locked. The look that passed between them took my breath away.

And in that moment, I knew.

As I watched, stunned by the enormity of the realization, her pale brown fingers reached out to brush his spotted white hand in a gesture of tender reassurance. Then, without a word or a glance at me, she turned and walked back into the house. The door closed softly behind her.

I stood for a long time staring after her, this woman who had sheltered and protected me as best she could. There was a lot I didn't understand. Perhaps I never would.

I turned back to find my father gazing searchingly up into my face. I couldn't meet his eyes, couldn't let him see the knowledge of his long-held secret reflected in my own. I dropped into the rocking chair, my entire body trembling with the aftermath of spent emotion.

"Bay, I want you to listen to me now. Please." His voice held a strange mixture of determination and defeat. "You must leave this alone. I want you to go away, take a trip somewhere. These are dangerous men. You must prove to them that they've succeeded in scaring you off. I swear no harm will come to Isaiah."

He reached out with his good hand and clasped my arm. "I've been a selfish, arrogant old fool, and you almost had to pay the price for it. I couldn't live if anything happened to you, Bay." His voice cracked, and his fingers tightened around my wrist. "Promise me you'll go. Promise me."

I wanted to throw myself at his feet then and lay my head in his lap. To let him stroke my hair and tell me everything would all right. But we had too much history between us, too many years of crouching behind our protective walls. In building a barrier against the pain of my mother's rejection, I realized that I had shut him out, too.

I couldn't change that now, but I could give him some measure of peace. I covered his wrinkled hand with my own. "Okay, Daddy, I'll go. Whatever you want."

I rose and left him there. I let myself quietly out of the house and down the sixteen steps. I stood for a moment, the splendor of the antebellum mansion shimmering proudly through the haze of my unshed tears.

Maybe I will live here again someday, I thought as I drew a deep, shuddering breath and pulled slowly away from Presqu'isle.

Then, eyes straight ahead, I forced myself to concentrate on adding the finishing touches to my plan for tonight. I had a lot to do, and time was running out.

CHAPTER
TWENTY-SIX

It took a lot longer than I expected to get everything down. Because I didn't want to risk using the computer, I wrote it out longhand on a yellow legal pad. When I was finished, I used the fax machine to make copies. The original I would lock in the floor safe. I put the other two sets in big manila envelopes and addressed one to Belinda St. John at the Statehouse. I'd mail it on my way out. On the other I printed Red Tanner's name in big block letters and left it propped up against my computer screen.

Mr. Bones, my feline security system, rose from his place on the floor and rubbed his head up against my legs as I pushed back my chair from the desk. I figured he had earned permanent resident status for his work on my behalf last Saturday night.

Persuading Neddie to leave had been less difficult than I'd anticipated. Without divulging the specifics of our conversation, I eventually convinced her that I was taking my father's advice and going on a trip. I even went through the charade of packing a couple of bags.

I was aided by the fact that, with the phones now restored, her service had finally gotten through to her with a message that one of her teenaged patients had been hospitalized. A drug overdose, she told me, shaking her head sadly. She really should go.

We threw together a salad and shared an early dinner before she tossed her bags in the Mercedes and turned to hug me tightly.

"I feel funny about leaving you here alone. Are you sure you'll be okay?" she asked, concern wrinkling her face.

"I'll be fine. I have a nine o'clock flight to Miami, then direct to St. Thomas," I lied.

"How long do you expect to be gone?"

"I don't know, a month probably. I might as well stay away until all the mess in cleared up with the kitchen. Dolores says it'll take that long for the remodelers to finish up."

"Well, have a wonderful time, and try not to worry. I'll call and check up on the Judge from time to time."

"Thanks for everything, Neddie," I said. "I couldn't have gotten through this without you."

"Hey, that's what friends are for, kiddo. Any time you need company climbing out your windows, I'm your girl." She settled herself behind the wheel and reached for my hand. "Be careful now, you hear?"

"God, Halloran," I laughed, "that was almost a *drawl.* We'll make a Southern belle out of you yet."

"Not in this lifetime. See ya." She backed the car around and headed out. About halfway down the driveway, she stuck her head out the window and shouted, "Thanks for everything, Tanner. It was a blast!"

I picked up a pine cone and threw it at her retreating taillights. I could hear her hoot of laughter as she moved out into the road.

After she left, I emptied my suitcases, then made a show of loading them into the tiny trunk, just in case Red decided to check up on me. I'd spun him the same tale about leaving town, and I was pretty sure he'd bought it. At least he made appropriate noises about being glad I'd finally come to my senses. He agreed to reduce the armed patrol around my house to one man, starting tonight.

The most difficult part was calling Geoff Anderson. I reached him at home just after Neddie left. He sounded relieved to hear from me.

Geoff asked after my health ("I'm fine), the house ("It's not as bad as it could have been"), and my new car ("It's perfect. I love it.").

The amenities completed, an awkward silence settled over us. I lit a cigarette, inhaled deeply, and plunged in.

"Geoff, I've been thinking about what you said, in the parking lot the other night. About there being reasons for what you told me? Or rather, what you *didn't* tell me."

"I never meant to lie to you, Bay, you have to believe that. It's just—"

"I understand that, Geoff." I didn't want him to start explaining. That wasn't part of the plan. "I'm ready to listen now. But I think we should do it face to face, don't you?"

"I can be there in no time at all."

"No! I mean, I have another idea."

I gave him my well rehearsed lie about leaving the country, to get away for awhile and recover. He, too, thought it an excellent idea.

"I'm leaving tonight, an eleven o'clock flight out of Savannah. I was wondering if you could meet me there, earlier. For dinner."

"Why don't I just drive you in myself? That way you won't have to worry about your car."

It was the one flaw in my scenario that I'd had to think really hard about. Of course, his suggestion made the most sense, but it certainly wasn't what I wanted. It defeated my whole purpose.

"No, thanks. I'm having a security system installed on the Zeemer while I'm gone, and I've already arranged for the shop to pick up the car from the airport lot."

It sounded feeble, even to me, but Geoff was apparently so eager to justify his string of lies to me that he accepted it without question. We arranged to meet at the Delta ticket counter at eight-thirty. I told him I might be a little late, what with packing and all, and he promised to wait for me.

He didn't have the nerve to tell me he loved me, but he tried hard to put meaning into his voice as we said goodbye.

So, if the gods smiled, that should keep Geoffrey Anderson far away from the welcome center during my covert rifling of his office files. When I failed to show up, he'd probably go back to Hilton Head or call my father in St. Helena. Either way, he would have no reason to look for me at Grayton's Race.

I spent the next hour practicing unlocking doors with a credit card. When Red had taught his brother and me, several years ago, it had been more of a parlor trick than anything else. We'd only done it for real once, when Rob and I had locked ourselves out of the apartment in Charleston. The ease with which we'd gained entry using Rob's American Express card convinced us to install deadbolts the next day.

Deadbolts hadn't stopped the creeps who had broken into my house here, I thought ruefully, but then they undoubtedly had a lot more experience at it than I.

As near as I could remember, there were no special locks on the welcome center, nor on Geoff's office door. I sent up a silent prayer to the patron saint of breakers and enterers, whoever he might be, that I hadn't missed spotting a padlock—or an alarm system.

The last thing I had done was to sit down at the desk and record my version of the events of the past two weeks and my interpretation of how they fit together. There was no reason to believe that I wouldn't be there to relate them in person. I should be in and out of Geoff's office in less than an hour, and everyone who might possibly come looking for me believed me to be safely on my way out of the country.

Still, I had nearly died twice in the last twelve months, and Rob . . . I reopened the envelope to Red and hastily scribbled instructions for Miss Addie's care once she was released from the hospital, adding a power of attorney that would enable him to access whatever funds he might need.

Nothing is going to go wrong, I told myself. I was merely taking the old computer mantra to heart: Backup, backup, backup.

At eight o'clock, I emerged from the bedroom, as confident as I could be for a total novice at this cloak-and-dagger stuff that I had covered all the bases. I was dressed in loose black slacks, a matching sweater, and low-heeled pumps. It was the closest I could come to a cat burglar outfit without arousing the suspicions of my solitary sentry.

I found him standing by my car when I trotted down the front steps with my oversized tote bag slung across my shoulders.

"You have a safe trip, ma'am," he said, touching his cap. "We'll look after things here."

"Thank you, deputy," I replied, sliding behind the wheel.

I pulled out onto the roadway and never looked back.

I had planned on arriving at the welcome center around nine, about the time it got fully dark. It was 8:58 by the digital clock on the dashboard as I eased past the Grayton's Race sign and coasted into the driveway of the nursery just down the road.

I cut the lights and coasted on around the building to the loading area in the back. I got out of the car and slipped off my pumps, replacing them with a pair of black Nikes I'd carried in my bag. I also extracted my dark Braves' baseball cap and stuffed my hair up under it. I took my Platinum Visa card from my wallet, tucked the keys and a mini-flashlight in my pocket, and locked my tote bag in the trunk.

I set off in the direction of Grayton's Race, following the road but keeping well back in the trees. There was very little traffic on this Monday night, but I stopped and turned my face away whenever approaching lights signaled an oncoming vehicle.

It took me a little over ten minutes to reach the drive. I skirted around its sharp bend and stopped dead.

The fence! I had forgotten about the damned fence!

The gate, seven or eight feet high at least, rose in front of me. It was secured with a huge padlock. The fence itself stretched away on both sides and disappeared into the trees.

I moved back into the brush and sat down in a pile of soft pine needles, my back against the scratchy bark of a gum tree.

How could I have been so stupid? How could I have missed the fence this morning? I had driven through the gate twice, and its presence had never even registered on my feeble brain. Besides which, Geoff had *told* me about it the night we . . . were together at his apartment.

Think! I ordered myself. *Calm down and think!*

What had he told me? Did the fence encircle the entire property?

No, of course not. That would be impossible, given the vastness of the place. Geoff had implied that its purpose was to keep out vehicles rather than people. So, all I had to do was follow it to the end, round the corner, and I was in.

But then another part of that conversation popped into my head. A security force! Geoff had hired private security to patrol the grounds!

I half-stood then, ready to bolt back to my car and get the hell out of there. This had been a harebrained scheme from the start. I had no business playing James Bond. I was totally out of my depth here. I took one step away from the tree and stopped.

If I turned tail and ran now, what would happen to my father? To Lavinia? The original point of this exercise had been to find proof of the drug connection. Once I had that safely tucked away, I could force Geoff Anderson and his pals to return the cash the Judge and his friends had unwittingly contributed to their little money-laundering scheme. If I could manage to come up with something that would help get Isaiah Smalls off the hook, that would be an added bonus.

Now, however, the stakes had been raised considerably. The only way to stop Hadley Bolles from continuing to blackmail my father was to get the proof of his criminal involvement in this whole scam and negotiate a trade: my information for his. It would probably keep the slimy bastard out of jail, but it just might be enough to keep him from trying anything like this again.

I sat back down, dying for a cigarette, but I had left them in the car. Besides, it would be the height of stupidity to provide the light that could lead a security patrol right to me.

I took a few deep breaths and willed my heart to slow down. I pushed the button to illuminate my watch face. 9:21. Time was indeed running out.

Nat Spellman, the founder of CARE, had told me that Geoff had reached an agreement with the destructive wing of the organization. So, no more vandalism, no need for security. It made sense, but could I count on that? I decided to wait and see if anyone made an appearance. Even if they were on foot, there would be no need for stealth. They were the good guys. I should be able to hear them coming long before they could spot me.

By nine-forty, my nerves were stretched to the breaking point. Only the rustle of night creatures and the occasional *whoosh* of a passing car had disturbed the silence. I rose, dusted off the seat of my pants, and followed the fence into the woods.

I had gone about thirty yards when the chain link I had been brushing with my fingers to keep me on line ended abruptly. I eased through the tightly-packed trees and reversed my course. I didn't hesitate when I came once again to the driveway. I walked swiftly across the open space and up to the building. A stranded motorist looking for a phone was my new cover story, and I would stick to it come hell or high water.

Maybe there is a patron saint of burglars, I thought, as I mounted the three wooden steps. A light fixture flanked the door on the left-hand side, but the bulb was burned out. And there was no deadbolt.

Moonlight glinting off the silver propane tank gave me just enough illumination. I dropped the card once, but it took me less than three minutes to pop the lock. The door creaking closed behind me sounded like a woman's scream in the heavy stillness. I shivered and clicked on the flashlight. Shielding it with my hand, I followed its feeble glow down the hallway to Geoff's office. That door was locked, too, but my confidence was running high. I got it on the first try.

I crossed immediately to the windows and closed the half-open blinds tightly. I risked a quick peek around the edge at the parking lot outside. All remained quiet.

The filing cabinet was unlocked. I opened the bottom drawer and sat cross-legged on the floor. I trained the flashlight on the first folder and began digging.

It was indeed a gold mine. Southland Real Estate Development. Meridian Partners Group. The familiar names leaped out at me. Correspondence, financial statements. I nearly shouted with the joy of it.

I removed off the baseball cap and tossed it on the floor beside me. I kept the documents in order as I carried each pile out to the big copier in the outer office. It was a beauty, with all the latest bells and whistles, cranking out copies as fast as I could feed in the originals. I kept glancing at my watch, conscious of the time I had wasted crouching in the woods in fear. No sense pressing my luck. I'd just copy everything the files contained and sort through them when I was safely away from Grayton's Race.

I did take care when I put the documents back, keeping everything in order so no one would know they had been compromised. I didn't want to spook them into running.

I had just shoved the last batch of copies into a big manila envelope I'd pilfered from Tiffani's desk when the overhead light snapped on, and Geoff Anderson walked into his office.

"I think you're going to miss your flight," he said.

CHAPTER
TWENTY-SEVEN

For one terrifying moment, I thought my heart had stopped. I couldn't seem to draw enough air into my lungs. My whole body trembled as I stood frozen in the glare, my eyes riveted on Geoff Anderson leaning casually against the door frame. His arms were folded across his chest, one leg crossed over the other. His wide shoulders filled the doorway. Even if I could force my legs to move, there was nowhere to run.

Slowly I placed the envelope of photocopies I'd been clutching to my chest onto the desk. With my right foot I gently eased the bottom drawer closed. My eyes never left his face.

I took a deep breath and leaned against the wall, mimicking his stance. "What tipped you off?" I asked in as calm a voice as I could manage.

"You didn't really expect me to buy that 'come back, all is forgiven' routine, did you? So out of character. I knew I'd lost you the minute you found out I was still married. Nice try, but you're not that good an actress."

Geoff strolled across the cheap brown carpet and perched himself on the corner of his desk. He was still between me and the door.

"You were pretty good, though," I answered, eyeing the distance between myself and possible freedom. "That was a very convincing performance. I was sure you'd be cooling your heels at the airport about now. So how did you figure out I'd be here?"

Geoff smiled and shook his head. "Mistake number two. If you're going to try and case a joint, you ought to wear a disguise. You're a very memorable woman, *Mrs. Smythe.*"

So Tiffani-with-an-i hadn't been the empty-headed little twit I'd taken her for.

"Plus," he went on, apparently relishing his role of knowledgeable expert, "if you're going to let someone you don't entirely trust pick out a new car for you, it might be a good idea to check it over before you drive it off the lot."

"You bugged my car," I said. Why hadn't I thought of that possibility before?

Geoff reached into the left pocket of his tan linen blazer and removed a small, rectangular box, about the size of a Walkman. "Cutting-edge electronics. It's really amazing what they can do these days," he said.

The tension of this cat-and-mouse game had made my legs begin to wobble. I edged around in front of Geoff and collapsed into the same chair I'd occupied just a few hours before.

"You wouldn't happen to have a cigarette, would you?" I asked.

"Those things are gonna kill you one of these days. Tiffani probably has some in her desk. Hold on."

He backed out of the office. I glanced longingly at the two windows flanking the filing cabinets. I would need a stool to reach them, and they were both so small I wasn't sure I could squeeze through even if I could get up there. Besides, Geoff could be back in here in three strides the second he heard me move.

"Sorry, they're not menthol," he said at my elbow.

Damn! The man moves like a cat, I thought as my heart settled back into some semblance of its normal rhythm.

My fingers shook only a little as I fumbled a cigarette out of the pack. Geoff struck a match and leaned over to light it for me. I was ashamed at how much better I felt when that first blast of nicotine hit my bloodstream.

Much calmer now than I had any right to feel, I exhaled and leaned back in the chair, resuming my pose of nonchalance.

"So what happens now?"

"That's entirely up to you. They're going to succeed in killing you, you know, unless you back off and somehow convince them you're no longer a threat."

His matter-of-fact delivery chilled me.

"Who's 'they'?"

"Come off it, Bay. Don't play dumb with me, please." He gestured toward the envelope of documents spilling out onto the top of the desk. "That was only for confirmation, right? You'd already found the evidence you needed."

How much did he know, and how much was guesswork? Maybe I could still bluff my way out of this.

"It's true I had some suspicions, but that's all. Nothing concrete. Once you stole the discs from my office, I had nothing. If you destroy the records you have here, all my proof will be gone."

I thought fleetingly of the envelope I had dropped in the mail box on my way off the island tonight. If I didn't manage to survive this, would Belinda St. John have enough to act on? Would she have the courage to do it?

Geoff shook his head as if at an obtuse child and straightened his jacket. For the first time I noticed the bulge in his other pocket. Another electronic device, or a weapon?

"They've been one step ahead of you all the way along the line. For a smart woman, you sure have been slow to catch on," he said.

That stung. "Catch on to what?" I snapped. I knew it was pointless to bait him, but maybe if I could keep him talking, some brilliant plan to extricate myself from this nightmare would pop into my head. "That you wired up my computer, tapped my phone? I figured that out the day after the explosion. It was the only way you could have known about my digging into the records. Did you enjoy creeping around my house in the dark? Get off on that, did you?"

"You really are an amateur. You don't actually think I do that kind of thing myself, do you? I'm an attorney, Bay, and a damned good one. That's what I do."

"And that's how you sleep at night?" I yelled, control finally deserting me. "How you live with yourself? You're just the middleman, hands squeaky clean, right? You think just because your finger isn't on the button, you're not responsible? Can you really be that delusional?"

That one hit home. Geoff tensed, the muscles tightening along his jaw. He rose then and began to pace, his steps taking him farther away from the door. I bent my head to light another cigarette and measured my chances of escape. I had him rattled now. Maybe I could use it to my advantage.

"What happened to you, Geoff?" I asked. "How did you ever get mixed up with people like this? Drug dealers, mobsters, murderers! How many people have you had killed?"

"You're not listening to me, Bay!" He whirled angrily, one finger stabbing the air, punctuating his shouted words. "I don't break into people's houses! I don't have people killed!"

"What about Derek Johnson, your holdout on the land deal? Are you telling me he just conveniently died?" Without realizing it, I had parroted Red's accusations, flung at me in anger in the Judge's study, what now seemed like a lifetime ago.

"Johnson? Was that his name? I had no control over that. The stupid kid thought he could hustle the system, thought he could hold out for more money. I hear he even threatened to blow the whistle on the drug operation he'd been running on the river. He signed his own death warrant the minute he put the squeeze on."

My hand trembled as I reached to stub out my cigarette in the round, metal ashtray on Geoff's desk. *My God*, I thought, *who is this man?* Where had he gone, the boy I'd idolized, standing tall and proud in his cadet's uniform?

"And I suppose you didn't try to have Miss Addie killed. Or me either, for that matter." As long as Geoff was willing to talk, I might as well get all the information I could. If somehow I managed to get out of this, I'd need all the ammunition against them I could gather.

"Of course not," Geoff said, his voice rife with scorn that I could think such a thing. "You can't seriously believe I had anything to do with that bungled attempt on your car, can you? I told them it wasn't necessary. I told them I had the situation under control."

His casual dismissal of my near brush with death stunned me. Could he really be that callous?

"What about Miss Addie? Were they trying to silence her, too?"

"The Hammond woman? You're saying someone tried to kill her?" I almost believed his perplexity was genuine. "I have no idea what you're talking about," he said.

"She was attacked in her apartment at the Cedars. She's one of your investors in Grayton's Race."

The one that got me into this mess, I thought.

"Why would they do that? I know they have some contacts there, a couple they use from time to time. Foreigners, I think.

But they're strictly smalltime players, nothing to do with the project. I hear they've got their own little scam going, something to do with ripping off valuable works of art and replacing them with cheap copies." Geoff ran his hands over his sleek, silver hair and came to perch on the edge of the desk once more. "What's the point of all this, Bay? You're not going to believe me anyway, are you? You're determined to think the worst. Besides," he added, checking his watch, "we're running out of time."

His hand slid toward his coat pocket, and my body tensed.

"Geoff, wait!" I cried. "Please! One more question."

His hand moved back to the desk, and I let my breath out slowly.

Stall! I told myself. *Keep him talking.* What other choice did I have?

"I've already said more than I should. You see how much I've come to trust you."

His open smile, strangely soft, indulgent, transformed his face. For a moment, the man who had awakened my body, nearly captured my heart, gazed fondly at me as if our talk of murder and larceny had never taken place. Was he so out of touch with reality that he believed I could overlook everything he'd revealed?

"How did you ever get involved in all this? What happened to you? What went wrong?" I didn't have to feign the sincerity in my voice. "Make me understand," I said softly.

"So you can do what? Save me? Turn me from my life of crime? Oh, Bay, you really are wonderfully naive."

I had to force myself not to shrink away when he reached out to cup my cheek in his hand. The look he turned on me then was bittersweet, a hint of the boy I used to know shining out from jaded eyes.

"You really want an answer? Let's just say that when I set up practice in Miami with my two buddies from Yale, we weren't too choosy about who we took on as clients. One morning we woke up to find out we'd become attorneys to the kind of people you just don't walk away from."

"Did you try?"

"Truthfully? No. After a while you get used to living well."

"But why go to Miami in the first place? You could have come home—"

"Back here? And done what? Gone into business with my father? The thought of it makes me shudder. You know what this town is like. It never changes. Everyone's still living in the last century, upholding their sacred traditions, pining for the glory days of 'The Cause.' Here I'd be forever known as Carter and Millicent Anderson's 'boy', forced to endure the same people, the same parties at the same clubs, year after dreary year. God, I'd rather be dead! You can understand that, can't you? You refused to live the life the Judge had laid out for you. You got out, too."

That Geoff could find our two life choices comparable finally convinced me that I was not dealing with a rational man. I needed him angry again, pacing, if I were to have any chance of making a break. Despite all his talk about my fate being in my own hands, I didn't believe him for a second.

"And this—what you have now—this is better?" I didn't have to force the disgust into my voice. "Look at yourself, Geoff. You're a drug dealer, even if you don't hang out on the corner and slip the bag into someone's hand. Your Saville Row suits and hand-stitched loafers only make you better dressed than the Derek Johnsons of the world, not any less despicable."

His reaction surprised me. "You've been watching too many gangster movies, Bay. It's a business, just like General Motors or IBM, one that's made me a very wealthy and powerful man. I can live with that."

Geoff stood then, and slipped his hand into the right-hand pocket of his blazer. My heart jumped in terror. But he withdrew, not a weapon, but a slim, blue passport. He tossed it into my lap. With shaking fingers, I opened the cover.

Mine.

"Where did you—?"

"That's not important. What matters is that you're getting out of the country. Now. Tonight."

"You mean you're not going to—?"

"Shoot you? I told you, Bay, I don't kill people. But others aren't so fastidious. You're booked on the last flight out to Atlanta, connecting to Barbados. You can buy whatever you need when you get there. Money doesn't seem to be a problem for you either, does it?" he added snidely. "From there, I want you to lose yourself. There's lots of little islands nobody's ever heard of. Find one and disappear."

"Disappear? But what about—"

"The Judge? Your precious brother-in-law? They all think you're on the run anyway, don't they? Hopefully you were more convincing with them than you were with me."

"Why are you doing this, Geoff?" Could he really be willing to let me go, let me just walk away?

He went on as if I'd never spoken.

"Of course, I'll have to cover my own ass, give them a good story. They aren't going to be happy that I let you escape. But I'll manage. They need me. I can convince them you're no longer a threat."

He had lost his mind. That had to be it. Or else it was a trap. Maybe they wanted me far away, out of contact with my family and friends, where a convenient accident could go unchallenged by anyone who cared about me. My mind raced. Could I trust him? Would I have a better chance out in the open? At the airport? Or would someone be watching, shadowing me, until I was isolated enough to make the job easier?

"After everything you've told me, you're willing to let me go? I have to know why, Geoff. I have to understand."

"Because I love you." He smiled and reached for my hand. "And after a while, when all this has blown over and the project is well under way, I'll find you. I have contacts in the islands, people I can trust. When you've had time to think it over, I feel sure you'll come to your senses, come to realize that we belong together. We always have."

I ripped my hand away and jumped to my feet. "You're insane!" I screamed, mindless of the consequences. "Do you seriously believe I could ever love a man who trades in misery and death? That I could ever bear to have you touch me again? You and your mobster friends killed my husband, you miserable bastard! You killed Rob!"

Geoff grabbed my wrist and twisted hard, forcing me back down into the chair. "Rob!" he spat at me. "I'm sick of him, do you hear me? Sick of listening to your endless whining, your constant worshipping at the feet of the almighty Rob!"

The vehemence of his attack took my breath away.

"What did he ever do for you? What? He pushed and pried

into things that were none of his business and got himself blown away for it. He left you alone and vulnerable. Look at everything that's happened to you! It's all his fault, all of it. *He* put you in this position. And who's here to get you out of it? Who's the only one that can save you? Me! Not your precious Rob. Me! He didn't deserve you. You're lucky he's dead!"

My scream of rage caught him completely by surprise, giving me the few extra seconds I needed. I threw all my weight at his shoulder, sending him toppling to the floor. I snatched the envelope off the desk and flew past him, slamming the door behind me.

The first bullets thudded into the wall just over my head. I ducked, skidding around the corner as a fusillade from the automatic weapon shredded the cheap plywood and shattered the windows around me. My fingers were scrabbling frantically for the doorknob when a giant *whoosh* seemed to suck all the air out of the building, and the propane storage tank exploded in a huge rush of flame.

The percussion knocked me to the floor. I sprawled there, stunned and breathless, while debris bounced off the building. I heard a loud ripping sound and managed to struggle to my feet just as the roof over Geoff's office collapsed in a shower of sparks. Clouds of heavy, black smoke rolled toward me. I flung open the door and threw myself down the steps, missing the last one and landing hard on my shoulder. I rolled away from the building, stopping only when I encountered the blessed coolness of dew-damp grass.

I lay there coughing, trying to draw oxygen into my lungs, when I heard his shouts.

"Bay! Help me! I'm trapped!"

Without conscious thought, I stumbled back toward the steps. Flaming tree limbs popped and snapped, crashing down around me as I ran. Smoke pouring through the open door made visibility impossible. I stepped back then, terrified of re-entering the raging blaze. Geoff's cries, hoarse and choking, were barely audible now above the crackling of the flames.

I pulled my sweater up over my face and charged into the

burning building.

I tried desperately to remember everything I'd ever heard about surviving in a fire. I fell to my knees and crawled toward the sound of his voice. The floor felt hot and sticky, the heat already beginning to melt the carpet. I yanked the sleeves of the sweater down over my hands. I collided with the receptionist's desk as I rounded the corner.

"Geoff!" I screamed. "The door's blocked!"

A beam, one end already glowing, lay jammed against the twisted door. I would never be able to move it! Sparks dropped from the ceiling, and I beat at my hair and clothes. A window exploded, showering my head with shards of glass. I felt a warm rivulet of blood trickle down into my eyes.

I forced myself forward and threw all my weight against the beam. It moved a fraction, and a flicker of hope leaped within me. Again I attacked the obstruction, wedging my good shoulder under it, and again I managed to shift it slightly before it fell back into place. Frantically I searched for something to use as a lever, but my hands encountered only useless, smoldering debris.

I was coughing continuously now, my lungs bursting with the need for air.

Flames were breaking through the floor behind me when I realized it was no use.

"Geoff!" I cried. "I can't do it! I'm going for help!"

I dragged myself across the burning carpet and threw myself once more out into the cool night. I could hear sirens wailing in the distance as I scrambled to my feet.

Through eyes nearly blinded by smoke and blood, I looked back at the inferno. Through the shimmering heat-haze I saw Geoff's blackened hands clawing desperately at the high, narrow window. I will hear his screams until I die.

The first fire engine was just blasting through the chain-link fence when the entire building erupted in a wall of flame and disappeared from sight.

CHAPTER
TWENTY-EIGHT

Two weeks later, on a sultry August morning, one year to the day from Rob's murder, I sat across the desk from Hadley Bolles, prepared to play the most important poker game of my life.

The cards I held, tucked neatly into the soft leather briefcase resting at my feet, were copies of the documents I'd duplicated and rescued from the welcome center at Grayton's Race. What kind of hand Hadley was holding was what I'd come to find out.

Once again I was dressed for battle. The sleeves of my white Armani suit failed to cover the matching gauze bandages that wound around both my hands. They were healing well, most of the burns only the first- or second-degree variety. Thank God the skirt was long enough to hide similar dressings on my knees.

I had barged in unannounced, hoping to catch the Pig Man off guard. Wearing his usual wrinkled shirt, plaid suspenders, and red bow tie, Hadley had barely acknowledged me as I walked into his office and seated myself, uninvited, in the spartan visitor's chair in front of his desk. He was studying a brief, the pale blue cover clutched in his pudgy hands. It might have been my imagination that the tissue-thin papers quavered just a little.

An antiquated air conditioner labored in the window that looked out onto Bay Street, but did little to dispel the layer of heat that blanketed the room. Without thinking, I reached to lift my mass of hair up off my neck, forgetting that most of it was gone, shorn off in the emergency room the night of the fire. The cut on my head had been ugly and deep, requiring seven stitches to close it. Having only a few inches of soft curls framing my face would take some getting used to.

I shifted in my seat, uncomfortable at not being able to cross my legs. My wounds were beginning to itch, and I resisted the temptation to dig at them. Hadley glanced up, I assumed to check if I were still there. If he thought he could wait me out, he had sadly miscalculated.

My eyes roved over the framed artwork on his wall, several quite good pencil sketches of local plantation houses along with a couple of oils in heavy gilt frames. The pictures sent my mind back to the day, just over a week ago, when Miss Addie and I had stood arm in arm in the shade of a towering live oak and watched three sheriff's deputies lead Ariadne Dixon and her Latin lover away in handcuffs.

Armed with the sketchy information I'd gotten from Geoff Anderson, Red had launched an investigation into the pair that netted surprising results. Dixon and Romero, who turned out to be husband and wife, were wanted by the authorities in sever ' states. They had run their scam of substituting clever fakes for the genuine artworks of elderly residents in upscale retirement homes from California to Florida. Ironically, it had been Miss Addie's meeting with Law Merriweather to discuss disposing of some of her treasures that had triggered their panic. They had been attempting to *replace* the original pieces when her unexpected return had surprised them. A professional appraisal would have blown their entire operation sky-high.

I smiled, remembering how eager each had been to blame the other for Miss Addie's injuries. I hoped it turned out to be the haughty Ariadne who took the fall for that. At any rate, where she was going, there would be no Saks or Ferragamo. I wondered how she'd look in penitentiary orange, and who would do her nails.

Adelaide Boyce Hammond was recovering nicely, the cast due to be removed from her wrist in a few days. Though she tried to hide it, I knew she still fretted about her investment. Her cause, as well as that of the other locals sucked into the Grayton's Race debacle, was one of the primary reasons I was here.

My own safety was the other.

"Hadley, put that damned thing down," I finally said. "Quit stalling and find me an ashtray."

Lighting a cigarette had become a major operation with my hands wrapped like a prizefighter's, but I'd managed to work out a pretty good system.

"I'd prefer it if y'all didn't smoke in here." Hadley looked earnestly into my eyes, and I laughed.

"Get off it, Hadley," I said, exhaling smoke toward the ceiling. "This whole place reeks of cigars."

He jerked open a drawer and slapped a cheap plastic ashtray onto the desk.

"Thanks."

"Well, missy, to what do I owe the pleasure?" He folded his dimpled hands in front of him, his thick thumbs working against each other in a gesture that betrayed his nervousness.

Good, I thought, *keep him off balance. He must have some inkling of why I'm here.*

"I want to negotiate a trade." I reached down and picked up the briefcase, settling it onto my lap.

"That presumes you have somethin' I'm interested in acquirin', which I very seriously doubt." His smirk didn't carry quite the confidence it normally did.

"Oh, I think you'll be interested in what I have to offer," I said. I pulled out a handful of the photocopies and spread them, fan-like, in my hand. "Your name is mentioned very prominently in this little bundle, and not exactly in a flattering light, I might add. I can't imagine what the bar association might make of them, let alone some of your stodgier clients."

His pudgy fingers itched to snatch the papers out of my hand, but for once he exercised restraint.

"I don't know what you're talkin' about, darlin', but I fear you have been seriously misinformed. If those papers refer to the few little legal matters I handled in regards to the Grayton's Race project, why I can't imagine what would make you think anyone would care a fig about 'em one way or the other."

The smarmy smile was back on his face, but his eyes gave him away. I hadn't seen fear reflected in them too many times, but I knew enough about the emotion to recognize it when I saw it. I stubbed out my cigarette and laid my bandaged left hand flat on the desk where he couldn't fail to get the message it implied.

Everyone in the county had read about the fire and Geoff Anderson's death. Only I knew the extent of the revelations that had preceded it. Or the exact contents of the documents I now waved under his nose.

"Look, Hadley, let's cut the crap, okay? Here's the deal, and it's not open for discussion. The Grayton's Race project is dead as of today. Not one bulldozer rolls onto that property, not one tree gets cut. And every one of the locals you forced my father to entice into investing gets their money back, with interest."

"Who the hell do you think—"

"Be quiet! I'm not finished. Then, you're going to retire. I've heard you bought yourself a nice little place down in the Keys. Go fishing. Enjoy the rest of your life."

"Is that all?" The bravado rang false, and he knew it as well as I did.

"No. You'll also bury whatever it is you think you have on the Judge. Not one whisper, not even a hint, or all bets are off."

"I could ruin the high-and-mighty Judge Talbot Simpson like that." He snapped his sausage-like fingers and tried to stare me down.

"You could try," I said, holding his eyes steadily. "But who do you think they'd believe in the long run? One of the most respected men this town has ever known, caught, perhaps, in a little indiscretion? Or the man tied to organized crime who blackmailed his friends into lending their names to drug dealing, money laundering, and murder?" I shook the papers at him for emphasis. "What's it going to be?"

The acrid smell of his sweat-stained shirt mingled with old cigar smoke and fear. But you had to give him credit. He didn't go down easily.

"What do I get out of it? Always supposin', that is, there's one grain of truth in anything you've been goin' on about."

I straightened the papers and shoved them back in my briefcase. "You get to live, Hadley, to a ripe old age probably, if you can convince your pals that all this wasn't your fault. And you get to do it in relative comfort, instead of rotting in some federal prison until you're old enough to need someone to wipe the drool off your chin." I paused, calling on every ounce of self-control I possessed not to blink. "So, do we have a deal?"

I held my breath. Even now, it could go either way. If he called my bluff, I would have to fold. I'd played every card I had.

"You'll leave the papers with me, of course." He held out his hand, and I nearly fainted with relief. I rose from the chair, willing my knees not to wobble as I headed for the door.

"I don't think so, Hadley. The originals and two other sets are already in safe places. As long as you keep your end of the bargain, that's where they'll stay. But if I hear one word of gossip about my father and Lavinia, or Miss Addie and the others aren't cashing their checks within thirty days, the documents will be in the hands of every newspaper in the state, not to mention the Attorney General and the FBI. And one more thing." I turned, my hand on the doorknob. "Tell your associates the same thing goes if I should meet with any unfortunate accidents. You tell them to leave me and my family alone, and they'll have nothing to fear from me."

"We're just supposed to trust you?" he shouted, his round face mottled in anger.

"Yes, you are. Contrary to your life experience, Hadley, there are actually people in this world who keep their word. I'm one of them. So long as you play straight with me, you have nothing to worry about. Have a nice day."

I marched through the door, head high, and trotted down the steps out into the blazing sunshine of Bay Street. I threw the briefcase into the front seat of the Zeemer and slid behind the wheel. I revved the powerful engine and laid a little rubber as I whipped out into a break in the traffic, just on the off chance that the Pig Man was watching from his window on the second floor. Two blocks down, I turned into the parking lot along the waterfront. I threw the gearshift into park and let my head fall forward onto the leather-covered steering wheel.

And for the next ten minutes I wept with the sheer relief of having pulled off the biggest con of my life.

Later that same afternoon I sat rocking on the back verandah, staring out over the water, when I heard the screen door swing open, followed by the soft *whir* of the Judge's wheelchair as it rolled up the ramp. He maneuvered himself in beside me and joined in my contemplation of the Sound.

These long silences had become commonplace during my recuperation at Presqu'isle. Until my house was restored and the kitchen once again useable, I had given Dolores a paid vacation and moved in here. Lavinia plied me with favorite foods from my childhood and refused to meet my eyes. About the only genuine contact we'd enjoyed had been our exuberant high-fives on the Saturday morning we turned to the sports page and learned that the previous night's football game had been won in the last few seconds on a forty-yard touchdown pass from CJ Elliott to Isaiah Smalls.

I reached out for the cigarettes lying beside me on a low table, but the Judge was there before me. He shook one out of the pack, placed it between my bandaged fingers, and struck the disposable lighter. I smiled at him over the flame.

"You'd think I'd had enough of fire, one way and another, wouldn't you?"

"You'd think," my father said, looking back out to the water.

A great blue heron rose suddenly on silent wings, startled into flight from the shallows where he had been fishing daintily on long, spindly legs.

I'd been torn, almost from the moment the rescue squad had hustled me into the ambulance, about how much to reveal of the awful events of that tragic night. No one asked why I'd been so insistent about returning to my car to retrieve my bag, or why I refused to let anyone take it from me, even in the emergency room. Once the envelope I had managed to stuff into the back of my slacks was safely in my purse, I didn't let it out of my possession.

I had to tell them about Geoff, of course, even though I knew there was no hope that he had survived. When the fire had finally been extinguished, they'd found his charred body curled in a fetal position beneath the narrow windows.

I was hailed as a heroine for my valiant rescue attempt, though I tried my best to downplay it. Even now, I couldn't explain why I had risked my life to save the man who had been trying to kill me. Maybe I never would.

If anyone ever figured out that it was Geoff's wild gunfire that had triggered the explosion, I never heard of it. Why we were there in the first place never came up.

In the end, I decided to keep my own counsel, giving Red and the Judge just enough bits of the truth so that they could help right the many wrongs Geoff Anderson had caused. No one but me would ever know the whole story.

"Talked to Law Merriweather this morning, while you were

out," my father said, and I turned to look at him. "The solicitor has decided he doesn't have much of a case against Isaiah. They found other prints on the baseball bat, unidentified ones, and a lot of smudges that might have come from someone wearing gloves, laid over top of the boy's. They've decided to drop the charges, pending further investigation. They'll hold an open indictment against person or persons unknown."

I breathed a deep sigh of relief. The last of the lives nearly destroyed by the madness of the past few weeks had been salvaged. I smiled and touched his arm. "That's good news," I said. "Lavinia will be relieved."

"Yes, I'm sure she will. So where did you go this morning, all decked out in your battle armor?" he asked, the twinkle back in his soft, gray eyes.

"Business," I said, and he laughed.

Then he turned his chair to face me, and his smile faded. "It's been one hell of a year for you, daughter. I hope the next one is a little kinder."

"Thank you, Daddy. Me, too."

He nodded once, then rolled down the ramp into the house.

I pulled up a wicker stool, propped my feet on it, and gazed out over the railing toward the Sound. The heron had returned to the shore. His long, pointed beak dug into the mud as he picked his way gracefully through the tufted grass. The shimmering haze of the late afternoon light, reflecting off the water, mesmerized me, held me, as if in a trance. Birdsong and the rustle of a light breeze high up in the branches faded. And in the depths of that sweet silence I felt the hard knot of grief and fear dissolve within me.

The heron rose then, in silent majesty, his great, gray wings barely ruffling the air. I watched until he disappeared, into the sun.

ABOUT THE AUTHOR

Kathryn R. Wall wrote her first story at the age of six, then decided to take a few decades off. She grew up in a small town in northeastern Ohio and attended college both there and in Pennsylvania. For twenty-five years she practiced her profession as an accountant in both public and private practice. In 1994, she and her husband, Norman, settled on Hilton Head Island.

Wall has been a mentor in the local schools and has served on the boards of Literacy Volunteers of the Lowcountry, Mystery Writers of America, and Sisters in Crime. She is also a founding member of the Island Writers Network on Hilton Head.

Wall is the author of the Bay Tanner mysteries:
IN FOR A PENNY
AND NOT A PENNY MORE
PERDITION HOUSE
JUDAS ISLAND
RESURRECTION ROAD
BISHOP'S REACH
SANCTUARY HILL
THE MERCY OAK
COVENANT HALL
CANAAN'S GATE
JERICHO CAY
ST. JOHN'S FOLLY
LIKE A BAD PENNY (short story)
JORDAN POINT

All the novels are set on Hilton Head Island and in the surrounding South Carolina Lowcountry.

visit Kathryn online at: www.kathrynwall.com

CPSIA information can be obtained
at www.ICGtesting.com
Printed in the USA
JSHW012140210922
30775JS00001B/4